IN SPITE OF ALL

A Novel

By Edna Lyall

CHAPTER I.

Many loved Truth, and lavished life's best oil

Amid the dusk of books to find her.

But these our brothers fought for her,

At life's dear peril wrought for her,

So loved her that they died for her,

Tasting the raptured fleetness Of her divine completeness:

Their higher instinct knew

Those love her best who to themselves are true,

And what they dare to dream of dare to do.

They followed her and found her Where all may hope to find—

Not in the ashes of the burnt-out mind,

But beautiful with danger's sweetness round her,

Where faith made whole with deed

Breathes its awakening breath

Into the lifeless creed;

They saw her plumed and mailed,

With sweet, stem face unveiled,

And all-repaying eyes look proud on them in death.

—Lowell.

There had been a heavy fall of snow in Hereford during the night, but the south walk in Dr. Harford's garden had been swept, and the still, frosty air and mid-day sunshine made the place as pleasant a playground as could be wished. The merry voices of a boy and girl had rung for the last half-hour in the pleasance, and the joys of snowballing were far too keen to allow the little couple to notice even for a moment the beauty of the wintry scene, with the rime-covered trees and bushes bordering the river, and in the background the cathedral, its massive tower surmounted in those seventeenth century days by a lofty spire covered with lead which glittered in the bright sunshine.

Presently the two playmates grew tired of snowballing and retired to a little arbour, commonly called the sun-trap, for here on the coldest days warmth could generally be found. There was a lull in the merry sounds, but it was only the calm which precedes a storm, for before long came a vehement expostulation, "Gabriel! Gabriel! let me have it. I will have it."

"Not till you have promised," was the teasing retort, and from the arbour there sprang out a small boy, with the most winsome and mischievous face, his hazel eyes sparkling with elfish mirth, while he held high above his head a wooden puppet, as dear to its small owner as the loveliest of modern dolls.

The bereft mother refused to enter into the game; it might be sport to him, but it was death to her.

"I won't promise!" she said, angrily. "Give me my babe."

"No," said Gabriel, laughing. "I can't have you chopping and changing. You said yesterday you would, and now you have changed your mind. Come, promise, Hilary, and I'll give you the puppet."

"Never!" said Hilary, furiously.

With a teasing laugh he tossed the puppet high in the air, intending to catch it as it fell; but, Hilary, frantic at this treatment of her Bartholomew babe, charged him with fury like a little goat, and the next minute both children were rolling in the snow..

By the time they had picked themselves up the whole situation had changed, for, much to their astonishment, a huge mastiff came bounding through the garden and, seizing the puppet on the path, began to worry it.

For a minute both paused, the girl aghast, the boy with knitted brows. It was well enough to tease his small playmate now and then, but he had not reckoned on this four-footed intruder. A sob from Hilary made him fly to the rescue.

"Leave go, you brute!" he shouted, trying in vain to drag back the mastiff by his collar.

This was clearly hopeless. He pulled and tugged with all his might, but the dog unconcernedly chewed the doll.

"Oh, my babe—my poor babe!" wailed Hilary.

Whereupon Gabriel, pricked at heart, made a valiant snatch at the puppet, got it firmly by the head and succeeded in wrenching it from the very jaws of death.

"There!" he said, flinging it towards the little girl in triumph; but the triumph was short-lived, for it was now the turn of the dog, who, defrauded thus unceremoniously of his toy, seized angrily on the arm of the knight-errant.

A scream of genuine terror from Hilary brought Dr. Harford rushing from the house, and in his wake followed a grave, stately gentleman whom the little girl at once recognised as Sir Robert Harley, of Brampton Bryan. Apparently the mastiff belonged to him, for at his stern summons it came to heel obediently, while Dr. Harford began to examine his son's arm.

"How did you anger him, child?" he asked, deftly unfastening Gabriel's dripping sleeve.

"It was my fault, sir," replied the boy, trying bravely to stiffen his lip. "I threw up the puppet, and then the dog worried it."

"I trust Nero has not hurt him much," said Sir Robert, concerned to see the wound on the small, shapely arm.

"Oh, we'll soon set it right," said Dr. Harford, leading the child to the house; "but with dog-bites you should never take half-measures. I must put a hot iron to it, so screw up your courage, laddie, and think how brave Cranmer thrust his hand into the flames."

Gabriel's heart sickened at the prospect before him, but he held up his head and stepped out more briskly, while Hilary crept after him with tearful eyes.

"You will excuse me, Sir Robert, if I see to this matter at once," said the doctor, "for delays are dangerous. I ran forth in such haste on hearing little Hilary Unett's scream that I have not yet even asked whether you will not lie here this night."

"Nay, I am to be the guest of Sir Richard Hopton at Canon Frome," said Sir Robert, seating himself by the fire in the doctor's study and watching his host's rapid movements as he prepared to dress the child's wound.

"I did but come to bear to you and to Doctor Wright the news of Sir John Eliot's death."

"What! Is he indeed gone?" said Dr. Harford, sorrow clouding his fine, thoughtful face.

"Here is a letter I received last night from London," said Sir Robert. "An you will I will read it."

"Sir John Eliot, one of the Members for Cornwall in the last Parliament, died this 27th day of November, after nigh upon four years' imprisonment in the Tower, for refusing to answer for his conduct in Parliament anywhere but in Parliament itself, this being, he maintained, one of the inalienable rights of the English people, without which a just liberty would be impossible. Having incurred the displeasure of His Majesty on this account, and for his fearless unveiling of divers other Court abuses and irregularities, the King refused to release him, and, indeed, for the last year did keep him close prisoner in a dark, cold and wretchedly uncomfortable room, denying him, even at his physician's request, air and exercise, and forbidding him to see any save his sons. His health was thus undermined, and a fortnight since, when he did petition for a temporary release to recover from his sickness, the request was refused by His Majesty, and now that he lies dead the King will not grant his sons' petition to carry the body for burial to Port Eliot, but orders that Sir John shall be buried in the church within the walls of the Tower. This harshness hath greatly angered all who knew the late Member for Cornwall, and, knowing him, could but admire his integrity, his courage and his patriotic devotion."

"A brave man—a truly great man," said Dr. Harford. "Sir John Eliot is the martyr who by his blood will safeguard our Parliamentary rights."

As he spoke he took the hot iron from the fire and drew Gabriel gently towards him.

"Now, my son," he said, in the voice which by its tender but firm cheerfulness had nerved many a sufferer, "what a joy it will be to your father if you follow in that great man's steps. Nothing could daunt Sir John; cost what it might he was ever true."

The boy being of a highly-strung, nervous temperament turned deathly white, but never flinched as the hot iron seared his flesh; only a stifled moan escaped him, and Hilary through her tears saw the strangest look of triumph in his dilated eyes—a look that made her heart throb with love and admiration. In a few minutes more the arm was carefully bandaged, the two gentlemen continuing meantime their grave talk.

"I will send word to Frank Unett that you are here, sir," said Dr. Harford, "for he, too, is one that deplores the present illegal rule without a Parliament; he will mourn Sir John's death."

"We call it a death," said Sir Robert, "but he has been as surely murdered by the rigours of imprisonment as though he had been stabbed in the Tower. Well," with a sigh, "the day of reckoning cannot long be delayed."

"There, laddie," said the doctor, drawing the sleeve gently over the bandage, "you have borne it like an Englishman; now run off into the fresh air and forget your troubles."

With respectful salutes to their elders the children returned to the garden; Hilary, with her pretty eyes still tender and subdued, slipped her arm caressingly round her playmate's neck. "I'm sorry, Gabriel," she said, in a tremulous voice, "and all the time I didn't really mean it. I will be your little wife."

Gabriel turned and kissed her soft, rosy cheek with great frankness and warmth. "If you will," he said, "I'll promise not to worry your puppets any more. I don't know how it is," he continued reflectively, "but there's something that makes a boy feel to a puppet like a dog does to a cat—he must worry it."

"There was the one you roasted last Lammastide," said Hilary, sadly.

"But you know it did make a glorious bonfire, and you enjoyed that part of it," said Gabriel, with mirth in his eyes.

"But I wanted the puppet back again afterwards."

"Well, well, I must try to remember you like the wretches. And you must really remember your promise, and not chop and change any more!"

"What does chop mean?"

"Go up and down like the sea; don't you know how old Nat the sailor says the sea was a bit choppy?"

"I won't be like the sea," said Hilary, her lovely little face flushing and her eyes shining. "I give you my real true promise to be your wife."

Gabriel did not repeat the kiss, for at that moment there flashed into his mind a fresh idea.

"Hilary," he exclaimed, "let us build a snow monument to Sir John Eliot; he shall lie in effigy like Bishop Swinfield in the cathedral."

"But your arm?"

"I can work with the right one," he replied, cheerfully, and the two were soon as happy as could be fashioning their recumbent snow man.

Later on Dr. Harford, passing down the south walk arm-inarm with Hilary's father, and still discussing the sad news brought by Sir Robert Harley, drew his friend's attention to the busy little pair.

"They make excellent playmates," said Frank Unett. "What would I not give for the hope of living to see my little maid grow up! But it will not be; Sir John Eliot's malady will carry me off long ere that."

Dr. Harford knew only too well that his companion spoke the truth, but he answered cheerfully, "You cannot look forward to long life, but with care you will be spared to us for some years, I trust."

"I should not dread leaving my wife and child behind were not the times so dark," said the invalid. "'Tis true my father-in-law is a learned and worthy man, but his views are not mine. Do what you can for them, Bridstock, they will need staunch friends."

"Sir, sir," said Gabriel, running towards them, "pray do come and see the monument we have made to Sir John Eliot."

The two gentlemen praised the work.

"And what do you know of Sir John?" said Mr. Unett, with a smile.

"I know how brave he was," said Gabriel, "and that he died to save us from being made slaves."

"He heard Sir Robert reading the news-letter," said Dr. Harford, putting his hand tenderly on Gabriel's head. "Somehow a child always contrives to go straight to the mark and grasp the essential point of a tale."

"Out of the mouths of babes and sucklings," murmured Frank Unett, glancing from the eager-faced children to the snow effigy—the only monument brave John Eliot was like to have in the land for which he died. "But what's amiss with your arm, lad?"

"Sir Robert's dog bit it, but my father has cured it again," said Gabriel, sturdily.

"It was my fault, father," said Hilary; "we were quarrelling."

"Eh? What was the disputed point? You two are for ever arguing."

"Yet their greatest punishment is to be apart," said Dr. Harford, with his genial laugh.

"I said I wouldn't be Gabriel's wife," said Hilary, hanging her head. "But we've made it up again, and I have given him my promise."

"Oh, you have, have you?" said her father, laughing; "and without so much as a 'by your leave' to me? Well, I could wish you no better lot. He will make a rare good husband, an I am not much mistaken."

"Come, Frank, you ought not to stand still this cold day," said the doctor; "'tis time you were in the house again." They moved on, the invalid still smiling over his daughter's words.

"The little minx!" he continued. "How innocently she said it. I should be heartily glad should their childish notion be carried out later on."

"Stranger things have happened, Frank," said the doctor, with a smile; "and I should be glad to have pretty Hilary for a daughter-in-law."

"I wonder what she will grow up?" said the invalid. "Well," with a sigh, "I shall not be here to see."

"Look, here comes that bustling housekeeper of yours," said the doctor, not sorry to turn the conversation. "Well, Mrs. Durdle, are you come to upbraid the physician for keeping your master out of doors?"

A stout, buxom, cheery-looking woman came hurrying towards them through the wicket-gate which led into the adjoining garden.

"Why, no, sir," she said, breathlessly, "though if I may make bold to say so, I think master would be a deal better by the hearth than out in the sun this December day; but the Christmas puddings, sir, are ready for stirring, and I was coming to bid the children take their turn, or they will have no luck at all next year."

"Heathen superstition, Mrs. Durdle," said the doctor, with a smile. "But make not overmuch of the bite Gabriel hath received, for in this case, truly, least said soonest mended. Tell him no tales about those that die of a dog-bite." The housekeeper promised and went in search of the children.

"Not but what I know many a tale," she reflected. "And, Lord! what a terrible thing it would be if the doctor should lose his son that way. They would bury the little lad in the cathedral, doubtless, for the Harfords, they come of a great family, as old as any in the county. I should go myself to help lay him out—that servant of theirs is a feckless wench. Oh, gracious me! Why, they're already making his tomb!" and in amaze she looked at the two children, who were putting the last touches to their snow monument.

"Lor' bless my heart, dearies!" exclaimed Mrs. Durdle, "what do you make that corpse-like thing for? Why couldn't you keep to an honest Jack Frost with a pipe in his mouth?"

"Why, Durdle, 'tis Sir John Eliot, the Parliament man. We're making his monument."

"Well, what can put such an idea into the child's head as to make a monument to a Parliament man? We're not going to have no more Parliaments they tell me, and a good job, too. Done without them these many years well enough, says I. Come in now, my dearies. Come and stir the Christmas puddings—here's nigh upon a week past since 'Stir-up Sunday.'"

The children were always glad of an excuse to visit the kitchen, where Durdle, a cheerful, chatty soul, ever gave them a hearty welcome. They wanted no second bidding, and were soon perched on the table with the huge pudding-crock between them and two strong wooden spoons.

"Wish, Hilary; it's no good stirring unless you wish," said Gabriel, swinging his legs, while he meditated what gift to ask of fortune.

"I wish for a beautiful new puppet at Christmas," said Hilary, without the smallest hesitation.

A flush rose to Gabriel's forehead; he felt pricked at heart, and was on the point of assuring her that he himself would make that wish true. But the old loathing of puppets died hard. He remained prudently silent.

Next came Mrs. Durdle herself with a wish about her valentine in the coming year, which the children thought profoundly uninteresting. What could a widow of thirty have to do with valentines, indeed?

"And now, Master Gabriel, for your wish," said Durdle, as the boy still hesitated.

"Yes, Gabriel, yours—be quick!" adjured Hilary.

He grasped the spoon and stirred the pudding vigorously, with an odd, far-away look on his intent face.

"Well," asked his companions, "what did you wish?"

"Oh, that," said Gabriel, colouring as he slipped down from the table—"that's my secret."

And neither Durdle's cajoling nor Hilary's earnest entreaties could make him say another word about the matter.

Before long, moreover, Hilary was summoned to her mother's room, and Gabriel ran home through the garden, pausing for one last look at the snow monument by the south walk.

"I wish to be like you," he whispered to the effigy of Sir John Eliot; "I wish to give my life for the country's freedom." Then, without a thought of what his wish might involve, he ran cheerfully home along the frosty paths singing a snatch of the old Bosbury carol:

"Oh! praise the Lord with one accord,

All you that present be;

For Christ, God's Son, has brought pardon

All for to make us free."

CHAPTER II.

From all vain pomps and shows,

From the pride that overflows.

And the false conceits of men,

From all the narrow rules

And subtleties of schools,

And the craft of tongue and pen;

Bewildered in its search,

Bewildered with the cry

"Lo, here! lo, there, the Church!"

Poor, sad Humanity

Through all the dust and heat

Turns back with bleeding feet,

By the weary road it came,

Unto the simple thought,

By the great Master taught,

And that remaineth still:

Not he that repeateth the name,

But he that doeth the will!

—Longfellow.

Frank Unett had spoken truly—it was impossible that he should live to see his child grow up; yet he made a hard fight with death, and, thanks to the tender nursing of his wife and the rare skill of his friend, Dr. Bridstock Harford, lived for some time after that December day when Hilary's future had been spoken of.

It always seemed to Gabriel that their childhood ended at his funeral, for then it was that they learnt of the separation in store for them. Hilary was to go with her mother for a long visit to some of her father's kinsfolk, and by the time she returned his own schooldays would have begun, Dr. Harford having decided to send him to Gloucester with Sir Robert Harley's son Ned, a boy some eighteen months his junior.

Very sorrowfully did the playmates take leave of each other, and Gabriel moped about sadly, understanding for the first time what it meant to be an only child.

It was on one of the days when he was missing his playfellow most that Hereford was thrown into a state of unwonted excitement by a visitation from Archbishop Laud. Gabriel found great relief and satisfaction in the crowded streets and the gala aspect of the city with its flags and decorations. But he was disappointed to find that the Archbishop himself was a little hard-featured, cold-eyed man in whom he could feel no interest at all.

"There was nothing to see but clothes," he said afterwards to his father. "Except for them his Grace was just a common little man, much like Dickon, the tailor, in Eign street."

Dr. Harford laughed. "I do not think his Grace is a large man either in body or mind," he said. "But there is no doubt he is a good man, Gabriel."

"You do not, then, hold with Sir Robert Harley," said his wife, "that the Archbishop would fain hand England over to the Pope."

"No, no, Elizabeth; Sir Robert is ever haunted by that terror. 'Tis a view held, indeed, by many, and doubtless the Archbishop's innovations and unwise ceremonies give colour to the charge. Also he deals out harder measure to the sectaries than to the Papists. But though I loathe his ear-croppings and nose slittings, I don't believe him to be a traitor to Protestantism," said the doctor. "On the contrary, I know of a gentleman of this county whom he dissuaded from becoming a Papist."

It chanced the next morning that Dr. Harford had to visit a patient in the direction of Brampton Bryan, and the day being very fine he told Gabriel that he would take him as his companion, and that afterwards he should see his future schoolfellow. There were few treats the boy enjoyed more than a ride with his father, for Dr. Harford was a great naturalist, and there were countless things to interest him in the Herefordshire lanes—details that Gabriel would never have observed at all if left to himself. They had not gone far along Bridge street that morning, however, when a messenger came running across the road with a paper, which he thrust into the doctor's hand.

"I am loth to be the bearer of this, sir, but a man must do the work of his office," he said, apologetically.

The doctor reined in his horse to read the paper, and Gabriel, glancing up at him from his sturdy little pony "Joyce," saw a look of intense annoyance upon his face.

"When am I to come?" he asked.

"At once, sir, if you please," said the messenger, respectfully. "'Tis very much against the will of every Hereford man, you may be sure, sir, but we have no choice in the matter."

"Well, I will go without delay; 'tis at the Archdeacon's court, I suppose?"

The messenger replied in the affirmative, and the doctor touched up his horse and went off at such a brisk pace that Joyce's short legs had some difficulty in keeping abreast of his roan mare. Arrived at his destination, he dismounted and threw the reins to his groom.

"I shall not be long, Gabriel," he said, looking round at his son as he entered the building.

A vague uneasiness filled the lad's mind. What was the matter, and why was Simon the groom speedily surrounded by a small crowd of eager questioners? Among them he could see old Nat the sailor, his wrinkled face bearing a look of indignation which he had never before seen there.

"Nat," he called, "pray come and speak with me. What does it all mean?"

"Why, master," said the old man, "it means that Archbishop Laud has summoned the best man in all Hereford because, forsooth, he does not bow his head to order in the church."

"Oh! Nat, you don't think they'll cut off his ears, do you?" said the boy in an agony, remembering in a flash all the gruesome and, alas! true tales he had heard of such practices.

"I don't know, master, but Simon here thinks it's a matter of paying a fine. I'm going into the court to see for myself."

In a trice Gabriel had dismounted. "Take me with you, Nat—please do," he said. He was small for his years, and doubted whether the officials would let him pass alone, but his confidence in the old sailor was unbounded, and Nat made no objection, but led the boy into the Archdeacon's court, where on the very last bench they found a spare place.

However small, however ill-furnished, there is generally something impressive about a court. To-day, moreover, all the diocesan officials were removed from their customary places, while raised above the ordinary mortals Archbishop Laud sat in a great chair of state. In the next tier were seated his vicar-general and various subordinate officials; while to the left side, at a lower level, stood Dr. Bridstock Harford. The doctor, who had married extremely early in his medical student days, was now not very much over thirty, a vigorous, intellectual-looking man, with one of those strong, quiet faces which inspire confidence. As Nat and Gabriel entered he had been asked what he had to say in defence, and Gabriel's heart pounded in his breast as he listened to the calm, courteous reply.

"Your Grace," said the doctor, "it is true that I have never practised any bowings or genuflexions, and for these reasons: First, nothing in Holy Writ seems to warrant it, the oft-quoted verse, 'At the Name shall every knee bow,' being, as all Greek students are well aware, truly the assertion that in the name of Christ all shall pray or worship. In another Scripture I read that God doth in no wise care that a man should bow his head like a bulrush; and in yet another that 'God hath made men upright, but they have sought out many inventions.' But, your Grace, what chiefly moves me to shun these formal bowings is the belief that in all matters of religion there should be a deep reserve betwixt the soul and God. Surely a reverence that is both sincere and profound seeks rather to express itself by inward and spiritual adoration than by any muscular movements, or ceremonies that are visible to others and which may become as like as not either Pharisaical or merely automaton-like. Christ spoke of a worship that should be in spirit and in truth, but gave us only two ceremonies, and those the simplest conceivable. For these reasons I object to complying with the order."

The harsh voice of the Archbishop broke the silence which followed. It was utterly impossible for him to understand any side of a question but his own, and his fatal lack of sympathetic insight blinded him to the noble nature of the man he was dealing with.

"Your arguings, sir," he remarked, "are what I should have expected from one of the teachers of science, falsely so called. Well was it written, 'Knowledge puffeth up.' How intractable, how lacking in humility is your nature I call on all here to witness."

The doctor's colour rose a little. He seemed about to reply, but thought better of it and held his peace. From the back of the court, however, came angry murmurs, for few men were more popular in Hereford. The people did not trouble at all about his views, but almost all of them knew what he was in times of sickness or distress. Nat, the sailor, swore beneath his breath in a soft monotone which seemed to relieve him, and Gabriel, with eyes like two live coals, slipped quietly through the crowd and made his way to his father's side, craving to be as near him as possible.

"Will you solemnly undertake never again to offend in this matter?" was the next question.

"Your Grace," replied the doctor, "I can undertake nothing of the sort, but do claim my right to stand fast in the liberty wherewith Christ hath set us free, and not to be entangled again in the yoke of bondage."

"Then every time you do not bow at the sacred Name be well assured that you will be fined," was the sharp retort, and sentence of the Court with the amount of fine was duly pronounced.

Gabriel breathed more freely. It was not a question of earcropping; but his heart burned with wrath at the way in which the Archbishop rebuked his father, and drawing nearer to him, he caught his hand in his and kissed it with a devotion and reverence that touched more than one spectator.

"Your own son teaches you that outward ceremonies are not valueless," said the Archbishop.

"Your Grace," said Dr. Harford, looking up with an unusual light in his quiet eyes, "should I value my little son's demonstration if there were compulsion in it—if it were a ceremony performed at fixed moments? And would it be worth aught to me if he were fined so many shillings for omitting it? Pardon my outspokenness, but your Grace, though a learned man, knows naught of fatherhood."

"Remove this prating Puritan and let the next case be called," said the Archbishop, harshly.

And as Dr. Harford and Gabriel moved away, the court rang with the clerk's stentorian voice shouting, "Mary Boswood, on a charge of refusing to wear a white veil when returning thanks after childbirth."

As they passed down the gangway they met the unlucky matron with flushed face and tearful eyes making her way to the place they had quitted, and deeming it a very hard thing that she, who had been a virtuous wedded wife for years, should be dragged into court for refusing to wear, as she expressed it, "a thing as like as two peas to the white sheet in which bad women did penance."

Gabriel gave a gasp of relief when once more they breathed the fresh outer air. He ran to Joyce and patted her neck and fondled her soft ears before mounting. Then in silence the father and son rode away together, not speaking at all until they had left the city and had had a good gallop over the broad strip of grass that bordered the road to Brampton Bryan.

"That has refreshed you, lad," said the doctor, glancing at the grave face beside him, "and yet you look as though you had something on your mind."

"Father," said Gabriel, vehemently, "I hate Archbishop Laud with my whole heart! Yet you said he was a good man!"

"Indeed I believe him to be a very good man, but he hath more zeal than discretion, and forgets that 'the end of the commandment is charity out of a pure heart.' Dr. Laud will one day find that he is making a great mistake. He is trying with all his might to make folks better by outward observances, by making clean the cup and the platter; that is to put the cart before the horse. You must first make them pure within, or you will but breed up a generation of ceremonious hypocrites and Pharisees."

"It is because of the discourteous way he spoke to you, sir, that I hate him," said Gabriel, fiercely.

"Nay, hate him not; I fared much better than I should have done had I been a parson. They tell me that twenty clergy have been deprived of their livings, only for this refusal to bow. As for the Archbishop's discourtesy, which makes him so much disliked by the gentry of the land, that is not altogether his fault, perhaps, for he had neither good birth nor good breeding. He said that 'Knowledge puffeth up,' and I was much minded to quote him the rest of the verse—'but love buildeth up.' Depend on it, my son, 'tis that love alone which can save our unhappy country in these difficult times."

"Will they still be difficult when I am a man?" asked Gabriel.

"I fear they will," said the doctor, gravely. "Therefore remember that you hate no man, howsoever his sayings and doings may offend you. Have your own faith, but see that you force it not on others, as is too much the custom; for Dr. Laud is wrong—compulsion never yet helped the good cause. What would you think of a physician who thought all men's ailments were to be treated alike? Men's souls are as different as their bodies, and their minds are cast in many moulds. The wise servant of Christ knows this, and seeks not to browbeat all men till they conform to one method. Never forget, lad, that your meat may be another man's poison. There is only one infallible remedy, and as the proverb hath it, 'Amor vincit omnia!'"

By this time they had reached the house of the first patient, and Gabriel was sent on with the groom to the neighbouring inn to order their noontide meal. When this had been discussed, and he had listened to the cheerful talk between his father and the landlord on the prospects of the crops, he had altogether forgotten Dr. Laud and his harsh words, and thought the world once more a pleasant place.

There was much, too, to divert his mind when they reached Brampton Bryan Castle. He quickly fraternised with Ned, the eldest son, and quite lost his heart to sweet-faced Lady Brilliana, Sir Robert's wife. She had travelled much, and had lived for many years in Holland, so that her talk was infinitely more easy as well as more interesting than that of any other lady he had met. Moreover, while Sir Robert was of the somewhat hard and narrow Puritan school, she was surely the gentlest Puritan dame that ever breathed, and seemed full of kindness to all, whatever their views. He began on that day, as they wandered about the castle, a friendship with Ned which was to last all through his life, and his pity for his father was great when, on returning from the most delightful scramble about the battlements, they found Sir Robert Harley still discoursing on the vestments—and what he indignantly called the 'altar-ducking'—which Archbishop Laud had ordered in Hereford Cathedral.

He was destined to hear much more of the Archbishop when, his schooldays ended, he was sent, at the age of fifteen, to Oxford with Ned Harley. They were entered at Magdalene Hall, at that time an especially Puritan college, and here his distrust of Dr. Laud and his ways increased not a little. For he rebelled with all his might against the Archbishop's notion of driving and coercing men into the ways he deemed best for them. Dr. Laud might, as his father always maintained, be a good man, but he was good after a fashion which stirred up all the combative elements in Gabriel's nature.

Meanwhile Hilary Unett was being educated after a very different fashion. On her return from visiting her Unett kinsfolk she scarcely stirred from home, and her interests were entirely bound up in the quiet cathedral town. It chanced that after two or three rapid changes at the Palace her grandfather, Bishop Coke, had been translated from Bristol to the see of Hereford. He was a good and kind-hearted man, with a great reputation for learning; but now that Mr. Unett was dead, and Gabriel only in Hereford at rare intervals, it naturally followed that every influence round the girl was ecclesiastical. She therefore almost inevitably fell into the way of looking at all questions from the palace point of view.

Now and then, as he watched her, Dr. Harford would recall her father's words on the day they had heard of Eliot's death; but as he thought how the paths of the boy and girl were already beginning to diverge, that dream of a future union looked less and less probable.

He sighed as in imagination he looked down the vista of the coming years, plainly foreseeing that stormy times were in store for the nation, and that grave troubles and divisions awaited every household in the land. But he was not a man of many words, and he kept his musings to himself.

CHAPTER III.

This is the time when bit by bit

The days begin to lengthen sweet,

And every minute gained is joy,

And love stirs in the heart of a boy.

This is the time the sun, of late

Content to lie abed till eight,

Lifts up betimes his sleepy head,

And love stirs in the heart of a maid.

—Katherine Tynan Hinkson.

It was in the spring of 1640, just when King Charles had dissolved the Short Parliament, after its three weeks' existence, that Hilary made a discovery. She possessed a voice, a voice which, after a few lessons from the Cathedral organist, proved to be a source of real pleasure to herself and others. This event meant much more to her than the fact that England had again relapsed into the woeful plight of the last eleven years, and was once more without a Parliament. At every spare minute she was practising her guitar, or singing scales and songs, and thus it very naturally fell about that Gabriel, returning from Oxford that summer, was greeted, as he hastened along the south walk to the little gate which made the boundary between the two gardens, by a song "more tuneable than lark to shepherd's ear." Stealing quietly forward, he could catch the words, which were set to the pathetic air of "Bara Fostus' Dream";

Come, sweet love, let sorrow cease,

Banish frowns, leave off dissension,

Love's wars make the sweetest peace,

Hearts uniting by contention.

Sunshine follows after rain,

Sorrows ceasing, this is pleasing,

All proves fair again,

After sorrow soon comes joy;

Try me, prove me, trust me, love me,

This will cure annoy.

The voice was a mezzo-soprano, with that strange gift of individual charm, without which far finer voices fail to please. It seemed to witch the very heart of the listener, and Gabriel, determined as he was not to disturb the song, was all on fire to see the singer.

As she played the interlude on the guitar at the end of the first verse he stole over the grass, and, climbing up the old filbert tree, swung himself noiselessly on to the wall, and looked down eagerly through the leafy branches. Not far off, at the opposite end of a grassy glade, sat Hilary, her soft brown curls, held back by a snood of pink ribbon, but falling nevertheless about her comely face as she bent over the guitar. She wore a pale grey gown with dainty trimmings of pink, and the delicate colouring of her sweet womanly face made one think of apple-blossom.

Gabriel's heart throbbed fast. Was this the child he had once teased? The companion he had sometimes wished a boy to share his rougher sports? The playmate he had quarrelled with so often, and kissed with careless kindliness when the dispute had ended? How had he ever dared to do it all? Then again the song thrilled him

Winter hides his frosty face,

Blushing now to be more viewed:

Spring return'd with pleasant grace,

Flora's treasures are renewed;

Lambs rejoice to see the spring,

Skipping, leaping, sporting, playing,

Birds for joy do sing.

So let the spring of joy renew,

Laughing, colling, kissing, playing,

And give love his due.

Gabriel's longing to see the singer's downcast eyes almost overcame him but he waited while once more the bird-like voice rang through the quiet garden—

Then, sweet love, disperse this cloud,

That obscures this scornful coying;

When each creature sings aloud,

Filling hearts with over-joying.

As every bird doth choose her mate,

Gently billing, she is willing

Her true love to take.

With such words let us contend

(Laughing, colling, kissing, playing),

So our strife shall end.

Gabriel swung himself down by the filbert tree, brushed the dust from his dark green doublet, set his broad-brimmed hat at the correct angle with unusual care, and made his way through the gate as though he had never climbed a tree or lounged upon a wall in his life.

Who would have dreamed that to walk down that familiar glade to greet Hilary, would ever have caused his throat to grow dry and his breath to come in so strange a fashion, for all the world as though he were running a race! At last she looked up, and with a glad cry rose to welcome him; the guitar slipped unheeded on to the grass, and both her hands caught his, while her dark grey eyes smiled in a way that fairly dazzled the youth, who had but just realised that he was her lover.

"So you have come from Oxford at last," she cried. "How long it is since we met!" He stooped to kiss her hand.

"Surely it was in some other life!" he said, with a strange feeling that suddenly all things had become new.

She laughed gaily as they sat down side by side. "Here, at any rate, is the same old stone bench where you and I used to learn our lessons," she said. "And yonder is the stump to which you tied my puppet the day you played at Smithfield martyrs."

"What a little brute I was."

"You were a rare hand at teasing; but I'll never forget it to you that you rescued my Bartholomew babe from the power of the dog. How the wretch bit your arm!"

"I am much indebted to him," said Gabriel, smiling, "and would not for the world lose that honourable scar. Nothing would please me more than to suffer again in your service."

His face was aglow, and Hilary, with a little stirring of the heart, turned from him and plucked a rose from the great bush of sweet-briar growing near the bench.

There was a minute's silence, broken by the snapping of one of her guitar strings. She took a fresh string from the case, and was about to put it on, when she found the guitar quietly taken from her.

"Let me do that," said Gabriel, pleadingly; and Hilary, with a novel sense of pleasure in being helped, allowed him to have his way, glancing now and again at his intent face, which was the same, yet not the the same, she had known all her life.

Truth to tell, Gabriel was no lover of books; he had not at all the look of the pallid student, and had burnt no midnight oil at Oxford. But the University life had changed him from boy to man, his chest was a good two inches broader from rowing; he had an air of health and vigour, and the clearly-cut features, which were of the Roman type, had kept their refinement, but had lost the stamp of physical delicacy they had once borne.

"How well I remember Nero's onslaught that day," said Hilary. "It was the day we heard of Sir John Eliot's death in the Tower."

"Did you hear that Mr. Valentine and Mr. Strode, who were imprisoned at the same time as Sir John Eliot, were released last January? They had been in gaol nigh upon eleven years," said Gabriel; and as he looked up from the guitar, Hilary saw an indignant gleam in his hazel eyes which startled her.

"Now you look as you used to look when we quarrelled," she said, smiling. "By the bye, what did we quarrel about the day the dog bit you? I have quite forgot."

"We wrangled over something in the sun-trap," said Gabriel, his eyes growing tender once more. "What was it?"

Laughingly they both turned their minds back to the days when they had been children together, and presently, in a flash, the whole scene came back to them. Once again Hilary saw her father's look of amusement as she gave her childish explanation of the dispute, "I said I wouldn't be Gabriel's wife, but we have made it up again, and I have given him my promise."

The colour surged up into her face as for an instant she met Gabriel's eyes, for in their liquid depths she could read love and eager hope, and withal just a touch of the mirthful expression which she knew so well of old. She knew that he, too, had heard that voice from the past.

Dropping the briar rose and hastily taking the guitar, she began to tune the string he had just fixed. The sound awoke Gabriel to the consciousness that they were not alone in the world, that the garden was no Garden of Eden, and that lovemaking was not so simple as in the days of their childhood. He remembered Mrs. Unett and Bishop Coke, who would assuredly have much to say as soon as this Midsummer's dream had formed itself into words. "Sing to me," he said, when the string at length was in tune. "So far I have but heard Bara Fostus from the other side of the wall—a sweet air, but somewhat melancholy."

Hilary racked her brain for a song which was not a love song, but failed to find anything better than "Phyllis on the New-Mown Hay," which she sang with a spirit so gay and debonnair, and a voice so exquisitely fresh, that Gabriel's passion was increased ten-fold. Like the lover in the song, he bid fair to be a most "faithful Damon," and Hilary knew it, and wondered how it had come to pass that but an hour before they had been well content to think of each other merely as old friends and playfellows.

They were deep in conversation when, looking up, Hilary saw her grandfather slowly pacing down the garden. The Palace was not far from Mrs. Unett's house, and the old man loved to escape from the state and ceremony that surrounded him, and to enjoy the quiet of his daughter's home. Gabriel, who had been much away from Hereford, had only met the Bishop occasionally. But when at Oxford he had heard complaints of the tyranny, the mischief-making and the political intrigues of bishops in general, he had always looked on their own Bishop as a remarkable exception to the general rule. Glancing now at the stately old man, whose scholarly face bore a striking resemblance to that of his brother, Sir John Coke, the recently-dismissed Secretary of State, he knew that he was confronting the arbiter of his fate, and noted with relief the kindly look in the Bishop's eyes as he caught sight of them.

"So, Mr. Harford, you are returned to us once more," said the old man, giving him a courteous greeting. "I heard my granddaughter's voice, but did not know of your arrival."

"The plague is increasing at Oxford, my lord," said Gabriel; "and it was thought best that we should not remain there. I returned to Brampton Bryan with Ned Harley."

The name of Harley brought a shadow over the Bishop's face, for Sir Robert's Puritanism met with little favour in the county. He reflected with some uneasiness that Gabriel Harford was of the same persuasion, in all probability, and not altogether a good companion for Hilary.

"Sing to us, child," he said, glancing at his granddaughter and Hilary, who had noted his change of expression, began his favourite air

"Hark, hark, the lark at heaven's gate sings!"

The song soon lulled the old Bishop into tranquility; he had taken out his ivory tablets with the intention of making some such entry as this: "Mem: to warn my daughter not to countenance any matrimonial proposal in respect of G. H. and Hilary." For was it not well known that Dr. Harford had spoken strongly against the war in Scotland—"the Bishops' war," now in progress—and who could tell what difficulties might arise in the future? But somehow, as the song proceeded, he slid into a state of dreamy content, and noted instead on the tablets a fresh idea for his treatise on the Epistle to the Colossians, which was suggested in part by the music and in part by the faces of Gabriel and Hilary. He looked benevolently across at the two young people, his mind hovering betwixt heaven and earth and the grievous divisions of his day all forgot.

Thus it chanced that through the halcyon days of that wonderful summer, Gabriel wooed Hilary in peace until, one morning, early in September, he found the present not sufficient for him, but must needs try to ensure the future, and hear from her own lips the promise that would set him at rest.

They had been out riding with the doctor, but had found the day hot, and, leaving the horses with the groom, had wandered across a bit of wild country bordering the road, to find rest and shelter in a little wood. Great beech trees made a solemn shade over the russet carpet of last year's leaves, and here and there the sunbeams slanting through the branches turned the russet to gold and threw a silvery sheen over the brake fern growing around. The robins sang cheerfully overhead, and now and then a squirrel would dance from branch to branch scampering the faster as it caught sight of the two intruders resting in the shade beneath.

The very quiet of the place made Gabriel think involuntarily of the strange contrast to be found in "towered cities" amid "the busy hum of men." Surely never again would he find so sweet a paradise in which to speak his love. The audacity of his childhood filled him now with amaze. What would he not have given for the easy flow of words which had then been at his command?

"This is perfection," said Hilary, taking off her hat and fanning herself leisurely with a great fern.

"There is one thing wanting," said Gabriel.

"You are exacting," said Hilary, with a little rippling laugh. "What more can heart desire?"

"A bliss that would last," said Gabriel, his voice trembling.

"Ah! but that is asking too much," she answered, musingly. "Nothing lasts."

"Nothing but love," he said, in a tone that made her lift her eyes to his, and speedily drop them.

The colour rushed to her face, but her confusion seemed to cheer him.

"Hilary," he exclaimed, "do you not know that I love you? You who first wakened love in me—who first made me truly live—surely you must know? I love you with all my being; only be mine—be mine."

"I am your friend," she faltered—"have ever been your friend."

"Friendship is not enough," he said, eagerly; "that was for childish days, but now—now—it is death to me to be without you. I am yours, body and soul. Give me hope, Hilary; give me hope!"

She raised her head and looked into his eager, hazel eyes, reading there the utter devotion of a first genuine passion, "I give you my heart," she said in a voice so soft that the words seemed more breathed than spoken, and the robin which had been the sole spectator of this love scene ventured a little nearer, even as she spoke, only taking flight when Gabriel caught her in his arms for what seemed the first kiss he had ever given her, so strangely did it differ from the careless salute of their childhood.

The robin sang overhead now, and sang so blithely that even the happy lovers gave heed to the song.

"'Tis the sweetest I ever heard," said Hilary. "Or is it that all things seem more beautiful because of love?"

"That must be it. Hitherto we have but dreamed; now we are awake, and this is the joy that lasts."

So they lived through that exquisite dawn of love, and their bliss knew no alloy until the ruthless groom strode into the wood.

"I ha' tethered the horses to the gibbet, sir," he said to Gabriel, "and ha' come to tell ye that the doctor is in sight."

The lovers started to their feet. Suddenly to see Simon's uncomprehending face; suddenly to hear the ill-omened word "gibbet," roused them roughly enough from their paradise. They hurriedly left the little wood, not once even looking back, for was not Simon tramping heavily behind them, driving them forth into the thorns and thistles of the world just as effectually as if he had been the angel with the flaming sword!

CHAPTER IV.

He cannot lie a perfect man

Not being tried and tutored in the world.

Two Gentlemen of Verona.

In the seventeenth century marriages, as a rule, were arranged in a very formal fashion by parents or guardians; then, after letters relating to money matters had passed on both sides, the young people were encouraged to meet. But the lifelong intimacy between Gabriel and Hilary had set ordinary customs aside, and before Mrs. Unett had in the least awakened to the idea that the old friendship had changed and developed, the morning in the wood had altered the whole course of her daughter's life.

In the Palace at Hereford it chanced strangely enough that on that very day another matrimonial project was being discussed, for late in the previous evening Dr. William Coke, of Bromyard, one of Hilary's uncles, had unexpectedly arrived to see the Bishop, bringing with him a formal letter of proposal for the hand of his niece from one Mr. Geers, of Garnons, a rich squire who had long been his friend. At the precise moment when Gabriel was confessing his love in the uninterrupted quiet of the coppice, and Simon the groom shrewdly guessing as he waited at the gibbet that "young maister was lommaking in the ripple," a grave discussion was going on in the Bishop's study.

"You see, daughter," said the old man, persuasively, "this proposal deserves consideration. Mr. Geers is a worthy man, and the settlement he would make is altogether satisfactory."

"Yet he is over old for Hilary," sighed the mother. "He would wish to wed without delay, and how can I spare my child?"

"She would still be in the county," said her brother cheerily; "however, I don't wish to plead for the gentleman, I am but his ambassador, not his advocate."

Mrs. Unett looked with relief at the speaker. The parson had always been her favourite brother. He had appreciated her husband and had shared to a certain extent in his views, which had not been the case with any other member of the Coke family. Then, too, he was so kindly, so genial; he had such a keen enjoyment of life and contrived to make his antiquarian pursuits so extremely amusing to other people. Unlike some hobby-riders, he was never a bore, and to see his good-natured face beam with satisfaction when he discovered a treasure for his collection was a thing to remember. His rare visits to Hereford never failed to delight both Hilary and her mother.

"Tell me what you advise, brother," said Mrs. Unett.

The parson laughed.

"You could not appeal to a worse man," he said. "I am an indifferent good judge of old oak, and know something of fossils, but of love matters I am as ignorant as a child of seven. It seems that worthy Mr. Geers wants a wife, he is not blessed as I am with the love of antiquities, and he finds his country mansion wondrous dull. If Hilary pines for a husband, why, then, I should advise you to let the gentleman woo her."

"I am very sure she is in no haste to wed," said Mrs. Unett, "she is not yet eighteen, and would be loth to leave her home."

"My dear, 'tis a good offer, and should not lightly be disregarded," said the Bishop. "In many ways it would be well that Hilary should be established, and her future happiness secured."

"Is that so easily done?" said Dr. Coke, with a quizzical smile. "Future happiness comes not with broad lands and a full purse. Perchance pretty Hilary would find the great mansion dull; or, again, she might, like a dame I once met, confess that the estate was all that could be wished, and that for the man—why, he was but a passing evil, and came of a short-lived family."

Mrs. Unett smiled at his droll voice as he quoted the philosophical wife.

"Hilary is not made after that pattern," she said. "Truth to tell, the maid has a will of her own, and is a trifle fastidious."

"My dear," said the Bishop, "she is a good, obedient maid, and if we show her that this arrangement is for her good, I make no doubt she will accept Mr. Geers' suit."

Dr. Coke smiled at his sister's dubious expression.

"Are we so sure it is for her good?" he said. "Let the little maid see her suitor and judge for herself. But I must not stay talking any longer of marrying and giving in marriage, for I am to visit Sir Richard Hopton at Canon Frome on my way home. Do you entrust me with a message to the owner of Garnons? He comes to stay with me to-morrow."

"Thank him for his courtesy, and say that we shall gladly receive him as a guest next week, if it suits his convenience," said the Bishop. "The two had best meet as you suggest, and we shall see what time will bring forth."

He returned to his treatise on the Colossians, and William Coke ordered his horse, kissed his sister, and, noticing her wistful expression, racked his kindly brain for some word that would cheer her.

"I am a doited old bachelor," he said, smoothing back his grizzled hair and adjusting his wide felt hat. "But I somehow fancy Hilary will be in no haste to leave her mother for this worthy gentleman."

Mrs. Unett sighed. Her voice had a mournful tone in it as she replied, "It is, after all, the way of the world, and what mothers must expect."

He moved towards the door, but suddenly returned to her side with a broad smile on his ruddy face, and a world of fun in his twinkling eyes.

"Make yourself easy," he said, "I don't think she will accept him. I am the man's ambassador, but there is one trifle I had forgot—I honestly admit that he squints."

He rode off laughing to himself, and gave little more thought to the matter, for, as he had very truly remarked, love affairs were not at all in his line, and some interesting relics at Canon Frome drove both Hilary and her suitor from his mind.

The poor Bishop, however, was not long allowed to dwell on the spiritual characteristics of the men of Colosse; for in the late afternoon Dr. Harford craved an audience of him, and after due apologies for Gabriel's impetuous love-making, told Hilary's grandfather of Mr. Unett's words in the past, and begged his consent to the union of the two old playmates.

The Bishop was dismayed at the proposal, and ruefully remembered that the dangers of constant intercourse had struck him when Gabriel returned from Oxford, but that a sudden idea as to the position of "Tychicus, a beloved brother and faithful minister," had driven out the prudent reflection. His treatise had prospered wonderfully that summer, but meanwhile his granddaughter had been free to see as much as she pleased of the physician's son.

"To be frank with you, sir," he said, "I have other plans for Hilary, and am at this moment in treaty with Mr. Geers of Garnons. But even if she declines his suit, I am fain to confess that a marriage with your son is not what I should wish for her."

"My lord, it was her father's wish," said Dr. Harford.

"Ay, but times have changed since the death of my son-inlaw. We do not think alike, either in religion or in politics, sir; and I should hesitate to give my grandchild in marriage to one likely to oppose me in matters both of Church and State."

"The lad is scarce eighteen," said Dr. Harford, "and is as yet a mere observer of current events. He hath, I am well assured, nought but respect and affection for you, my lord, and his whole heart is set on wedding Hilary. Other proposals may be in a worldly way more desirable, but the children have loved each other, if I mistake not, all their lives, and 'tis ill meddling with hearts."

"The matter shall be referred to my daughter," said the Bishop, rising. "Personally, I have nothing against your son; on the contrary, I think him full of promise. But he is over young to marry, and there are many objections to a long betrothal."

Dr. Harford could only withdraw, and the Bishop, chafing a little at having to spend his time on these mundane matters, went to his daughter's house to tell her what had passed.

Mrs. Unett had, however, already heard Hilary's version of the story, and the thought of giving her daughter to Gabriel was so much more congenial to her than any notion of entertaining Mr. Geer's proposal, that the Bishop found an opponent where he had looked for an ally. After a prolonged discussion, Mrs. Unett—never well able to resist the opinion of a man—sent for her daughter by way of support, and Hilary, who, after telling her mother of the events of the morning, had gone to her own chamber to dream it all over again, came down to the withdrawing room in no small trepidation.

"Child," said the Bishop, "I have had a proposal for your hand."

"Yes, my lord," she said, curtseying as she approached him.

"Sit down, my dear, and let me tell you of the gentleman."

Hilary's eyes widened. Was Gabriel a gentleman she needed telling about? She could have laughed at the notion had not good manners obliged her to wait dutifully for the next remark.

"His estate is very large, and is in this county; although some years your senior, he is still only in middle life, and will, I am assured, make you an excellent husband."

"Mother!" gasped Hilary, in dismay. "What does it mean?"

"Your grandfather refers to an offer from Mr. Geers, of Garnons, which he received before that of Mr. Harford. I think, my dear, you must at least see the gentleman next week when he stays at the Palace."

"Certainly," said the Bishop, with decision. "And I must tell you, Hilary, that his offer is not to be lightly refused. I cannot approve of any betrothal between you and Gabriel Harford, though very naturally some idle thoughts of love may have arisen from your being so much together."

Hilary's breath came fast. There was a choking feeling in her throat, nothing but pride kept her from tears—pride and a determination that, cost what it might, she would never yield.

"My lord," she said, quietly; "I will certainly see Mr. Geers if it is your wish, but do not lead him to think that I shall accept his offer—that were impossible."

"I very much wish you to accept the offer, but of course, I will not compel you, my child," said the Bishop. "As to this other offer, however, I altogether disapprove of the notion, and I beg that you will discontinue all intercourse with Gabriel Harford."

"My lord, he is the man my father wished me to marry," said Hilary. "Does that count for nothing? He is the man to whom I have given my heart, does that weigh nought with you?"

There was a break in her voice, and a quivering of her lip as she spoke. The Bishop took her hand caressingly.

"Child, you are young—you are young," he said, tenderly. "'Tis an easy matter to let the heart go to the first handsome face and the first flattering tongue that appeals to you.

Believe me you have not yet seen enough of the world to judge. Gabriel Harford has a winsome way with him, but he is as yet wholly unformed, you cannot tell what he will grow into."

"I love him—and can afford to trust the future," said the girl, confidently.

The old Bishop shook his head sadly; nevertheless, the depth and reality of Hilary's love had touched his heart.

"Let us leave it in this way," he said. "See no more of the young man while he remains in Hereford. Give Mr. Geers a fair and unprejudiced hearing, and let us see what time will bring forth." He rose to take leave of them, pausing at the door to counsel Mrs. Unett to send a letter without delay to Dr. Harford, acquainting him with their decision.

"It is better so, my child," said the mother, when once more the two were by themselves. "Your grandfather is no doubt right. Gabriel is very young, and you cannot tell what manner of man he will be. I must write to his father. To do that does not rob you of all hope, it merely means that we must have good proof of Gabriel's constancy before making promises as to the future."

"We can wait," said Hilary, firmly. But then she remembered the rapture of the morning, and the confident tone of Gabriel's voice, as he said: "This is the joy that lasts."

Alas! How soon had their day been over-clouded! She turned aside to the window and looked out at the cathedral through a mist of tears, hearing the scratching of her mother's pen with a dull heartache. Presently down in the street below she saw a very carefully-dressed, spruce little lady, with grey curls and a benevolent face. It was kind-hearted Mrs. Joyce Jefferies, speaking to a little bare-footed lad and making him happy with a penny. In taking out her purse she dropped her handkerchief, and Hilary, running swiftly out of the room, threw open the front door and hastened to restore the handkerchief to its owner, The old maiden lady thanked her, but noticed the sad look in her eyes. "What is amiss, child?" she asked, stroking the girl's cheek. "I met you riding this morning with a very different face."

"Nothing lasts!" said Hilary, with tears in her voice.

"Yes, one thing," said Mrs. Joyce Jefferies, a light dawning in her kind eyes. "There is an old poem in which you will find a truer saying, 'All goeth but Godde's will.'" The gentle little lady walked on, but although she said nothing, she was able to make a shrewd guess that her god-son, Gabriel Harford, was in some way the cause of Hilary's trouble, and on reaching her house in Widemarsh street, she penned him a note inviting him to dine with her one day in the next week.

Hilary did not return to the withdrawing-room for fully half-an-hour, and then found that her mother was only just folding the formal letter, which had been hard to write. "May I enclose this to Gabriel, ma'am?" said the girl, putting a tiny sealed packet on the table.

"I do not think your grandfather would approve of a correspondence between you," said Mrs. Unett, hesitating.

"'Tis not a letter—I will show it to you, if you wish, mother."

The mother looked up into the dark eyes, saw the traces of tears, and forgot the Bishop's prudent objections.

"I will send it, child," she said, kissing her tenderly. "Do not think that I have forgot my own young days. And bear not so sad a face, Hilary, for I have great confidence in Gabriel, and would spare you to him in the future, more willingly than to any other man."

Hilary's face lighted up at these comfortable words. Surely time would prove to everyone's satisfaction that they were indeed well suited to each other.

To fill up the hours of waiting Gabriel had gone out fishing, and when the light failed he lay on the bank of the river watching the dark trees as they stood out russet, grey and purple against the mellow evening sky, their heavy summer foliage hardly moving, so still was the air. All the world seemed beautiful, and he was far too happy to have any doubts. What could stand in his way when Hilary herself had owned her love? Not all the bishops in England could really interfere between them! And over and over in his mind there rang her softly spoken words, "I give you my heart."

By this time surely his father's visit to the palace would be well over, and the consent won? He sprang to his feet, shouldered his rod, and, with a glance at the fish he had caught, closed the basket, resolving to carry it to old Durdle, the housekeeper, for Mrs. Unett's breakfast.

As he walked through the fields he whistled, "Phyllis on the New Mown Hay," for sheer light-heartedness, and had some difficulty in pacing gravely through the streets when he reached the city. Old Nat, the sailor, meeting him in High Town, noticed his blithe face.

"Good e'en to you, sir," he said, "you're looking piert and heartful. Have ye had good luck?"

"Ay!" he replied, "it has been a lucky day with me. Look!" and he opened the basket. "You must have one of these fellows for your supper."

With a cheery "Good night!" he passed on, leaving the old sailor divided between admiration of the trout and its donor.

"Takes after his father, he does," muttered the old man, "an open hand and a good heart. But it'll go hard with him in times like these, for he's independent, and none too fond of knocking under to great folk."

Twilight reigned in the house when Gabriel closed the front door behind him, but a streak of lamp-light came from the region of the study-door, and on entering the room he found his father and mother gravely discussing an open letter. Something in their faces struck a chill to his heart.

"Did you see the Bishop, sir?" he asked, eagerly.

"Sit down, lad," said the doctor, pointing to a chair by the table which his patients were wont to occupy while he interviewed them. "Yes, I saw him; our talk was not satisfactory. Still, I would not have you lose heart altogether."

The reaction from the morning was too great, however. Gabriel turned deathly white; he could not frame his lips to the question he longed, yet dreaded to put. The pain carried him back curiously to a former scene in that very room, when in an agony of nervous anticipation he had waited for the hot iron to be put on his mangled arm, and again he seemed to hear the words: "Nothing could daunt Sir John Eliot; cost what it might, he was ever true!" With an effort he pulled himself together.

"May I hear, sir, what actually passed?" he said.

And the doctor hastened to tell him all, then placed Mrs. Unett's letter in his hands.

It was a kind, incoherent, weak letter, but Gabriel saw with relief that the writer did not at all favour the suit of Mr. Geers of Garnons. His mother, however, quickly dispelled what little consolation he had gained. There had never been much love lost between the two ladies.

"Never mind, my son," she said. "In my opinion, you are very well out of the whole affair. Hilary is an only daughter, and has been spoilt and indulged by an over-fond parent, till she thinks everything must give way to her whims. Depend upon it, she would have been ill to live with."

"I will wed none other," said Gabriel, passionately, and, finding the discussion intolerable, he rose to go.

The doctor put a little packet into his hand. "It is for you," he said. "Courage, lad! After all, the Bishop can but enforce a certain time of waiting on you if you are true to each other."

The words carried some comfort with them, and hope rose again in his heart as he strode hurriedly through the garden to the south walk, where he eagerly opened the packet directed to him in Hilary's somewhat laboured handwriting. The moon had just risen, and by its soft light he saw a curl of dark hair tied with a narrow ribbon, on which some letters were traced. With no little difficulty he made out the motto, "All goeth but Godde's will."

The message brought him fresh courage. It seemed to put everything in a true light. After all, what were differences of opinion on religious matters when words such as these could be their mutual comfort? He had never troubled to think whether they differed or not. The mere fact that the Bishop was one of the Laudian prelates, and that his father objected to the tendency to revert to Mediævalism in the English Church, could not surely affect the question of his marriage with Hilary? It was sheer nonsense to think that such a thing could part them when they were united already by love, and by trust in the Divine will, which could not fail. So, although he was sore-hearted and downcast, he was far from hopeless, and after a while was ready to throw himself with ardour into his father's plans for his future.

CHAPTER V.

Let my voice swell out through the great abyss

To the azure dome above,

With a chord of faith in the harp of bliss:

Thank God for love!

Let my voice thrill out beneath and above

The whole world through,

O my love and life, O my life and love,

Thank God for you!

—James Thomson.

It seemed so doubtful whether Oxford was doing Gabriel much good, and the unhealthiness of the place was so great just then, that Dr. Harford decided to send his son to London and to enter him as a student at one of the Inns of Court. Sir Robert Harley had arranged to do the same with his eldest son, and as the two were friends, Gabriel was greatly pleased with the notion, and began to look forward to his new life. He discussed his prospects with Mrs. Joyce Jefferies a few days later when he dined with her at her pretty house in Widemarsh Street, but having known him all his life, she quickly detected the sadness that lurked beneath all his cheerful talk.

"Eliza," she said, turning to her god-daughter, Miss Acton, who lived with her, "will you take this biscuit out to Tray, he has been barking and whining the last half-hour."

"And what does Hilary Unett say to your leaving the University ere taking your degree?" she said to Gabriel when they were alone.

"She knows naught about it," he replied, colouring. "We are no longer allowed to meet. The Bishop does not approve of our love."

"Ah! that accounts for the change I noticed in her," said the little lady. "I grieve for you both. But you are young; matters may right themselves in a year or two."

They had reached the dessert stage, and Mrs. Joyce Jefferies had just put a bunch of grapes on her godson's plate, when she was startled by a loud knock at the door. Miss Acton, returning from her mission to the low-spirited dog in the garden, met the visitor in the entrance-hall, and with heightened colour ushered him into the dining-room.

"Godmother, here is Mr. Geers," she said, her pretty eyes bright with pleasure.

Now Mrs. Joyce Jefferies, having the kindest of hearts, loved nothing better than to set the course of true love running in safe and smooth channels. It had long been her desire to see Mr. Geers and Eliza Acton wedded. Unfortunately, Mr. Geers at present showed no signs of making any proposal for Miss Acton's hand, and since the godmother was no matchmaker, she dared not even hint at what she so greatly wished.

"This is my godson, Mr. Gabriel Harford," she said, having received the visitor with a warm welcome. "Gabriel, you have not, I think, met my cousin, Mr. Geers, of Carnons."

Gabriel bowed, but his whole face seemed to stiffen, much to the astonishment of his godmother.

Mr. Geers would take nothing but a cup of sack, having already dined. He was a most quaint-looking person, but spite of the wandering eye which Dr. Coke had mentioned, there was something not unpleasing in his good-natured, shrewd expression and in his wide mouth, about which there lurked a kind of satirical smile.

"I have come to you, cousin," he said, "to be cheered and heartened before going through a great ordeal. The fact is, I am going a-wooing."

"Indeed," said Mrs. Joyce Jefferies, feeling perplexed.

"I have only once glimpsed the fair lady, and have not yet been introduced to her. The ceremony is to take place this afternoon at three o' the clock, and I have a sinking feeling here already." He placed his hand on his heart. Then taking out a watch from a shagreen case that hung at his fob, "There are yet two hours, and I pray you to hearten me up."

The hostess laughed cheerfully, but all the time her kinsman had been speaking she had observed with discomfort the pallor of her goddaughter's face, and the extraordinary way in which Gabriel was swallowing the grapes she had put on his plate—certainly a most terrible fit of indigestion must be the result.

"We will do our best to hearten you, but could do so better did we know the fair lady's name," she said.

"Her name," said Mr. Geers, with a humorous gleam in the well-regulated eye and profound gravity in the squinting one, "her name is the worst part of the whole affair. They christened her 'Hilary,' which is a name that may be borne by man as well as woman. Now I desire a very womanly woman, no masculine she, and Hilary smacks somewhat of lawyers and their terms. But the surname is still worse, for that would lead one to believe that the lady means to die single and hath no intention of going in double harness. I confess that the name of Mistress Hilary Unett discourages me mightily."

Mrs. Joyce Jefferies, feeling convinced that in another minute Gabriel would choke, bethought her of a plan which would relieve them all.

"You amuse me greatly," she said, with a well-feigned laugh. "I must have a confidential talk with you. Let us send off these young people and enjoy a tête-à-tête. Eliza, my dear, take Mr. Harford to see my throstle in the twiggen cage; I see he has finished his fruit."

The two accepted the suggestion with alacrity, Mr. Geers watching them thoughtfully as they left the room.

"What's amiss with that young man?" he said, "is he in love with pretty Eliza?"

"Oh! my dear Francis, do you really imagine Eliza would think twice of a lad younger than herself?" said Mrs. Joyce, marvelling at the dense stupidity of men. "But you are right in one way; the lad is in love, and, as ill-luck will have it, with the very same lady you are going to court."

"What! with Mistress Hilary Unett? Great heavens! and I made merry over her name in his presence. Now tell me all about it, cousin, for hang it! the lady won't look at a plainfaced man like me if that young spark has spoken to her."

"Dear Cousin Francis, we all know that you would make the very kindest of husbands, but as you wish me to speak the bare truth I do not think Hilary Unett will accept your suit unless her grandfather forces her to do so."

"She likes this handsome godson of yours?"

"Well, it is not for me to say yes or no to that question; but they have been playmates ever since they could walk, and next-door neighbours. You can judge for yourself whether it is likely or not."

"I am greatly obliged to you for your sensible way of heartening me ere I go courting," said Mr. Geers, smiling broadly. "I am bound to go through with the matter, but if the lady is true to herself nought will come of it, and young Mr. Harford need not again come so near to choking himself with burning rage and gulped grapes."

The good-natured rival laughed till the tears ran down his sunburnt cheeks.

"But it was hard on the poor fellow," he said, after a while. "Clearly he knew all about my proposals, for his face grew flint-like as you told him my name. Give him a comforting hint when I am gone, or he may seek a grave in the Wye and afterwards haunt me, which would make Garnons a yet more unpleasant home."

"Garnons is over-lonely for you," said Mrs. Joyce. "Yet I cannot think that Hilary Unett is well fitted to be its mistress."

Perhaps Mr. Geers agreed with this shrewd remark when he had been introduced to the bishop's granddaughter. Her reception was so grave, her manner so distant, that, as he confessed afterwards, it would have been easier to woo an iceberg. Fortunately, his cousin's words had given him the clue to the girl's manner and bearing, and on the third day of his visit to the Palace he called at Mrs. Unett's house, and finding Hilary in the garden, resolved to speak out boldly, and make an end of this highly unsatisfactory courtship.

"Mistress Unett," he said, "the Bishop has been very good in allowing me to propose an alliance with you, but I can scarcely flatter myself that the idea is pleasing in your eyes. I am a plain-spoken man and will not try your patience with further compliments or professions of my high esteem and sincere admiration, but will ask you truthfully to tell me whether you think you could honour me with your hand?"

"Sir, you have done me great honour by the proposal," said Hilary, nervously. "But I should only wrong you did I consent to be your wife. You ask me to tell you the truth, and you have been so kindly a suitor that I will do exactly as you bid me. The truth, sir, is that my heart belongs to another."

Mr. Geers bowed. "You honour me by your confidence, madam," he said, gallantly. "I withdraw at once in favour of the lucky man who has won so great a treasure."

"Alas! he is not lucky at all," said Hilary, her eyes filling with tears. "They say he is over-young, and will not allow us to meet."

"For that, dear madam, there is a sure remedy. Have patience; we grow old only too fast in these harassing days."

And after that the good-natured suitor, with a pitying remembrance of Gabriel Harford's unhappy face, tried to do him a good turn with the Bishop, by showing how utterly hopeless it was to woo a maid whose heart had been given to another man since nursery days, and how extremely probable it was that the lady's health would suffer if she were too severely tried.

The words made no apparent impression on the Bishop, but they returned to him uncomfortably one Sunday morning in the cathedral, when his eye happened to rest for a minute on Hilary's face. It suddenly struck him that she had grown curiously pale and thin during the last fortnight, and glancing across at the place usually occupied by Gabriel Harford, he noticed that in him, also, there was a change; the lad looked much older, his sunburnt face had lost its boyish carelessness, his eyes seemed larger and more sad. Yet there was a curious vigour about him in spite of his trouble, and as he joined in the metrical Psalm something in his expression appealed to the Bishop. The cathedral rang with the sweet voices of the choristers as they sang to the tune of the old 137th, Sternhold and Hopkins' quaint version of King David's words:

"In trouble and adversity,

The Lord God hear thee still;

The majesty of Jacob's God

Defend thee from all ill.

And send thee from His holy place

His help in every need;

And so in Sion stablish thee

And make thee strong indeed.

"According to thy heart's desire

The Lord grant unto thee,

And all thy counsel and device

Full well perform may He.

The Lord will His anointed save,

I know well by His grace;

And send him help by His right hand

Out of His holy place."

It was Gabriel's last Sunday in Hereford. On Tuesday night he was to lie at Brampton Bryan; on the following day to set off, in company with Sir Robert Harley and his son for London. His heart was heavy as he wondered when he should again see Hilary, yet, although they were not allowed to meet, there was no small comfort in this glimpse of her at morning service, from which no one had the right to debar him; there was comfort, too, in the words they were singing together, and hope and confidence began to possess his heart, and to bring a look of strength to his face.

The Bishop noted it, and bethought him of what Mr. Geers had said. After all, was he perhaps giving these two unnecessary pain? Was it, indeed, useless to try to put an end to love which had grown with their growth and strengthened with their strength?

By the end of the service Gabriel had decided that to leave home without a word of farewell to Hilary was intolerable, and being too honourable to steal an interview without leave, he waited in the Bishop's cloisters hoping to see the prelate as he returned to the Palace, and to make his request. The sunshine blazed on the grass and daisies without, but the cloisters with their vaulted roof and exquisitely sculptured figures and foliage were cool and sheltered; Gabriel leant against one of the mullions of the great windows, glad to feel the fresh September air on his heated forehead. At length steps were heard, and looking up he saw the Bishop approaching, with his chaplain in attendance. Wishing the attendant anywhere else he stepped forward, and bowing low, said, "My lord, may I have a word with you?"

Gabriel's manner was good, and the worthy Bishop, taking the deference in the tone for awe of his office, though it was in truth merely reverence for his age and his learning, felt that he had misjudged Hilary's lover. Moreover, those who have just joined their prayers and praises see each other in a clearer atmosphere, raised somewhat above the fogs of prejudice and the murky smoke of differing opinions.

"You need not wait," said the Bishop, glancing at his chaplain.

"I am glad to see you, Mr. Harford, for I have just learnt from Mrs. Joyce Jefferies that you are about to leave Hereford."

"I am to be entered as a student at Lincoln's-inn, my lord, and I crave your leave to say farewell to Hilary."

The mere use of the Christian name at such a time reminded the Bishop of the closeness of the intimacy between the two. Although he himself had only lived four years in Hereford, Gabriel and Hilary had spent their lives in the place as near neighbours. It had been easy enough to discuss the betrothal as a mere matter of business with Dr. Harford, but it was hard to the kindly old man to resist the appeal of the lover himself.

"Merely to grant you a farewell would be a cruel kindness," he said, thoughtfully. "You are just leaving for a much wider and more varied life; mayhap you will in London find others that will please your fancy more than my granddaughter."

"My lord, if I cannot wed Hilary, I will wed no other," said Gabriel. "We Harfords do not lightly change."

Something in the confidence of his tone was so full of youth and inexperience that the Bishop felt a fatherly compassion taking possession of him.

"My lad," he said, quietly, "you think thus in all honesty, but you are going to live in one of the most wicked cities in the world. You know not how great are the temptations you will have to face."

"Yet if love be in truth akin to love Divine, it will 'defend us from all ill,'" said Gabriel, musingly; and to both of them it seemed that the music of the old Psalm echoed softly through the cloisters.

It was not very often that the Bishop turned from his theological studies to direct talk with one of Gabriel's stamp; he began now to think that, after all, poor Frank Unett's notion had been right, and that a Harford would make a good husband.

"Lad," he said, "believe me, I desire only what is best for you and my grandchild. If I were to consent to a betrothal now on the understanding that it is not publicly announced, would you on your part undertake to avoid Hereford for the next two years? Time would then test and try you both." Gabriel's face fairly shone.

"My lord," he said, breathlessly, "I will gladly bear any waiting if only we are permitted to be betrothed; and no one need be aware of it except my parents, and, if you will permit it, my godmother, Mrs. Joyce Jefferies."

The Bishop smiled. "Yes, let Mrs. Jefferies know, for, in truth, it was a few words she spoke to me that inclined me to listen to your appeal. Go now, and talk over matters with your father, and I will prepare Mrs. Unett and Hilary for your call." All this time Hilary had seen no member of the next-door household save little Bridstock, the brother born during Gabriel's school days, who had, of course, no notion of keeping aloof from her and knew nothing of their trouble. Her face grew radiant when the Bishop told her of his interview with Gabriel. Nevertheless, the call—a state visit, paid in company with his father—was a rather formidable affair for the lovers, who left most of the talking to their elders, but their spirits rose when Dr. Harford proposed a ride for the following day.

"I have to go over to Bosbury to see a patient," he said, "and if the day is fine I hope Mrs. Unett will entrust you to me."

That Hilary should often accompany Gabriel and his father had long been a custom, and the enforced home-keeping of the past fortnight had been hard to bear. The girl's face was radiant when once again she found herself riding with her lover through St. Owen's Gate and out into the lovely country beyond. The unexpected relief after those weary days of sorrow made it wholly impossible to trouble as to the future. To-morrow there would indeed be parting, but for this one day they were as happy and light-hearted as children, and with an added rapture which no child can feel. On they rode past hedges bright with briony berries and brambles, or veiled with feathery traveller's joy; past hopyards where the pickers were hard at work, their many-coloured raiment making patches of brightness in the long green avenues; past orchards where the trees were bending under their load of rosy or golden apples; while ever and anon would come glimpses of the Malvern hills with their exquisite colouring, not to be surpassed in richness by any other hills in existence. At length the pretty village of Bosbury was reached, and Dr. Harford pointed out to Hilary the old house of the Harfords in which some of the happiest days of his childhood had been spent—a fine gabled mansion with heavily mullioned windows. It had passed now into other hands, and the doctor never willingly entered it, being a man who disliked seeing his sacred places under new conditions.

"I have to see old Mr. Wall, the vicar," he said to his son, "and as my visit is likely to be a long one we will bait the horses at the Bell, and you may show Hilary the monuments if she is disposed to look at them."

Hilary did not much mind what she looked at so long as Gabriel was her cicerone, and the lovers, dismounting at the gate, walked through the churchyard.

"What a strange tower it is standing quite separate from the church," said Hilary. "Why was it built in that fashion?"

Gabriel glanced up at the solid brown old tower with its mantling ivy.

"No one precisely knows, but some say it was that it might be used as a place of refuge," he replied.

They entered the south porch and found the door open and the fresh air blowing through the beautiful church; from the lovely little chantry chapel at the end of the south aisle came a flood of golden sunshine mellowing the white pillars, while the wonderful dark oak chancel screen, which was the special feature of the place, lifted its rare fan tracery and rich carving in sombre contrast. There was something in the quiet of this country church and in its beauty which appealed strongly to Hilary, while to Gabriel, also, though he was much less responsive to mere loveliness, the place had a homelike feeling, so often had he been there with his father, and so vividly had Dr. Harford described to him his own childish days at Bosbury.

The Harford monuments in the style of the early Renascence were on either side of the sacrarium, and Gabriel, with a smile, pointed out to Hilary a mistake in one of the inscriptions, which stated that there lay Richard Harford, of the parish of Bosbury, Armiger, and Martha his wife.

"This lady in Elizabethan dress who rests beside my great uncle, is, in truth, his first wife, Katherine Purefoy; and Mrs. Martha does not rest here at all, but had two more husbands—to wit, Michael Hopton, of Canon Frome, and John Berrow, of Awre."

"I did not know you were connected with the Hoptons."

"Yes, in this fashion, besides by a close friendship betwixt my father and Sir Richard Hopton, and that again is cemented by their political views being of the same order."

"Have politics aught to do with friendship?"

"With friendship, yes, but with love nothing at all."

"That is well, for you and I, perchance, might not agree," said Hilary.

"We could always agree to differ, but in truth we neither of us as yet know enough of matters of State to have any opinions," he replied.

"I don't quite understand your ancestry yet," said Hilary, laughing. "There is great-grandfather John, and here is great-uncle Richard, but where is the grandfather?"

"He was Henry Harford, of Warminster," said Gabriel. "But my father, being the son of his second wife, Madame Alice Harford, inherits none of the Harford property. Madame Harford still lives near London, and I am to visit her. They say she is a most formidable personage, and has never forgiven my father and mother for marrying when they were mere boy and girl. For my part I am glad they did, for it makes my father understand our case."

"Yes, he understands well, and has been most kind to us. Had it not been for him and for Mrs. Joyce Jefferies, we should have had sad hearts to-day."

They wandered back into the churchyard and sat down to rest on the steps of the old stone cross which for many generations had stood there. So quiet and peaceful was all around that it was hard to believe that the village street was within a stone's-throw, and the lovers, absorbed in their own happiness, did not hear the quiet footsteps of a man approaching them, did not dream that just as surely as time advanced with cares and sorrows in his train, so did this austere-looking figure come into their lives, bringing with him the shadow of a coming agony.

They both started when upon their love-making was cast the sudden shade of the new-comer's presence. Gabriel rose hurriedly, responding to the man's grave salute in some confusion.

"I understand that Dr. Harford is at the vicarage; can I leave with you, sir, a message for him?"

"Certainly; what name?" said Gabriel, looking at the questioner's sombre, deep-set eyes, in which there smouldered a strange fire. A look of resentment, indeed, darkened the whole face, which, though full of strength and purpose, was far from pleasing.

"My name is Peter Waghorn, and yonder to the east of the church, in the house with the tiled roof, my father, some years ago Vicar of Miltoncleve, lies at the point of death."

"I will tell Dr. Harford directly he leaves Mr. Wall," said Gabriel. Then with a thought of Hilary, "It is nought of an infectious kind, I suppose?"

Peter Waghorn smiled grimly.

"My father is dying of a disease that has been over-rife in the country since Dr. Laud got the upper hand. He was driven from his living in Devon and imprisoned by the Bishop of Exeter for speaking against Dr. Laud's preaching. They then sent him to the Court of High Commission, and he was deprived, degraded and fined."

"But for what offence?" asked Gabriel. "Merely for disapproving of the Archbishop's doings? The prisons would be full of the gentry and the most learned men of the day were all sent to gaol who disliked Dr. Laud."

"'Twas for preaching against decorations and images in the churches," said Peter Waghorn, a gleam of fierce wrath flashing across his face. "So little do the punishments of the Archbishop match the offence, that for this my father suffered the loss of all things, and for daring now and again to preach afterwards, he was sent to Bridewell, mercilessly flogged, and for a whole winter chained to a post with irons on his hands and feet in a dark dungeon. 'Twas the cruel cold and damp that ruined his health, for he had nought but a pad of straw to lie on, and was kept on bread and water."

"Truly they may well say that the oppressions and cruelties of the prelates are enough to drive a wise man mad," said Gabriel. "But surely he may yet be saved? My father has brought many back to health that other physicians despaired of."

"'Tis over-late," said Waghorn, bitterly; "he lies sick of a wasting fever, and his limbs are stiff and useless with rheumatism. Yet his end may perchance be eased by a skilled physician."

At that moment Dr. Harford came out from the vicarage, and Peter Waghorn, anxious to lose no more time, hastened forward to meet him. In close conversation they walked down the village street, and Gabriel returned to his place on the steps of the cross.

"How you do hate Archbishop Laud," said Hilary, with a gleam of amusement in her eyes as she looked at him. "For my part, if the older Waghorn is like the younger I think he can have been no great loss to the Church. Come, why vex yourself thus over the misfortunes of this poor vicar? I thought you had no great liking for parsons."

Her tone jarred on him. "I don't understand," he said, "how you can be so little moved by a tale like that. It makes one's blood boil; and 'tis not only parsons who suffer. Remember how Mr. Shirfield, a bencher of Lincoln's Inn, was treated by the Star Chamber."

"What was his crime?" asked Hilary.

"Merely that as Recorder of Salisbury he permitted the taking down of a blasphemous window in St. Edmund's Church—its removal had been agreed to by a vestry when six justices of the peace were present."

"But a window cannot be blasphemous," said Hilary, looking perplexed.

"Indeed it can," replied Gabriel. "Why, this one had seven pictures of God the Father in the form of a little old man in a blue and red coat, with a pouch by his side and an elbow chair. The people used to bow to this as they went in and out. Merely to speak of it sickens one."

Hilary still looked puzzled. She could not feel that it mattered much. "And what did Dr. Laud do to Mr. Shir-field?" she asked, anxious to understand why Gabriel's indignation was so hot.

"He stood up and moved the Court that the Recorder should be fined £1,000, removed from the Recordership and thrown into the Fleet Prison till the fine was paid. And still worse was the fate of my father's friend Gellibrand, Professor of Astronomy at Trinity College, Oxford, who, for encouraging the printing of an almanack in which the names of the martyrs from Foxe's book were mentioned and the black letter saints omitted, was literally hounded to death by Dr. Laud. My father was present at the trial in the Court of High Commission, and the Professor was acquitted by Archbishop Abbott and the whole Court except Dr. Laud, who was full of wrath at the acquittal, and urged that the Queen desired him to prosecute the author and to suppress the book. Then when the Court still persisted in acquitting the accused, Dr. Laud turned upon him in fury, saying that he ought to be punished for making a faction in the Court, and vowing that he would sit in his skirts, for he heard that he kept conventicles at Gresham College after his lectures. Afterwards a second prosecution in the High Commission was ordered, and this so affected the Professor's health and spirits that it brought a complaint on him, of which he afterwards died."

"Oh," said Hilary, with a little impatient sigh, "let us have no more doleful tales; these things have nought to do with us. Let us enjoy this happy day while we can."

Gabriel's whole face changed at her appeal. The indignation gave place to love and tenderness, and a mirthful look came into his eyes; when, as if in response to her words, they heard the voices of some little village children singing,

"Then to the maypole let us away,

For it is now a holiday."

The ardent, generous spirit which made him quick to resent any sort of cruelty or oppression also gave him the power to be such a lover as might well content the most exacting of maidens, and there were probably no happier people in England that day than these two lovers as they sat under the shadow of Bosbury Cross.

Meanwhile in the tiled cottage to the east of the churchyard an old clergyman, in the last throes of a lingering and painful death, faintly gasped the words, "Lord, how long?"

The physician sorrowfully watched the havoc wrought by man-inflicted ill, from time to time speaking a word or two of comfort and good cheer, or gently raising the dying man into an easier posture. And at the foot of the bed, his face buried in his hands, knelt Peter Waghorn, his frame shaken with sobs, his heart consumed with hatred of Dr. Laud, and in his mind the psalmist's passionate cry, "Let there be none to extend mercy unto him! . .. Because that he remembered not to show mercy, but persecuted the poor and needy man, that he might even slay the broken in heart." A last faint gasping sigh made him raise his head. The physician was gently laying down the worn-out body and closing the sightless eyes.

From the open casement the wind wafted into the quiet room the glad sound of children's voices, and as the little people ran down the road the words and the clear high notes floated back to the lovers by the cross, and to the bereaved, sore-hearted man:

". . . let us away!

For it is now a holiday."

Dr. Harford noted the strange contrast within the room and without. He laid his hand kindly on Peter Waghorn's shoulder.

"Your father, too, keeps holiday," he said; "be comforted, he has entered into rest."

CHAPTER VI.

"England, it has been said, has been saved by its adventurers—that is to say, by the men who, careless whether their ways were like the ways of others,... have set their hearts on realising first in themselves and then in others, their ideal of that which is best and holiest. Such adventurers the noblest of the Puritans were. Many things existed not dreamed of in their theology, many things which they misconceived, or did not conceive at all; but they were brave and resolute, feeding their minds upon the Bread of Heaven, and determined within themselves to be servants of no man and of no human system."—S. R. Gardiner.

Gabriel quitted Hereford the next day, carrying with him the lock of dark hair and the ribbon with the motto as the outward and visible symbols of his betrothal, and deep in his heart the spiritual presence of the mingled love of two souls. These, together with the vigorous and sincere Christianity which had been the result chiefly of his father's, example and training, were the best equipments he could have had for his London life.

Yet, perhaps, had the Bishop of Hereford known how strangely trying the next two years were to be, he would not have imposed on his granddaughter's lover a test so excessively severe. Never had the country passed through such a grave crisis.

It was towards the end of September that Gabriel arrived with his companions at Sir Robert Harley's lodgings in Little Britain. Only a short time before, London had been given over to demonstrations of joy on hearing that the King's army had been utterly routed by the Scots, for the English, who had always detested the Bishops' War, felt that the cause of the invaders was the cause of the invaded, and were rejoiced to hear that Newcastle and the two northern provinces were in the hands of the Covenanters. Scotch and English alike were sternly resolved no longer to endure the intolerable misgovernment of Charles, and the people crowded to sign the petition to the King which complained of the grievances of the military charges, of ship-money, of the rapine caused by lawless troops, of the Archbishop's innovations, the unbearable growth of monopolies, and, above all, of the unlawful government without a Parliament.

The city seethed with exasperated discontent, and the very day after the travellers arrived they found themselves in the heart of the struggle. It was Sunday, and they had gone to morning service at one of the City churches, where all had seemed tranquil enough. But at the time of giving out notices the Bishop's Chancellor roused the congregation to fury by calling upon the churchwardens to take the oath to present offenders against the ecclesiastical law.

All the wrath which had been gathering through the long years of tyranny, all the hatred of Laud's unwise revival of obsolete lawrs and punishments seemed to concentrate itself in the shouts of "No oath! no oath!" which burst from the congregation. Gabriel was startled, but the next moment all his sympathies were with the people, for an apparitor stood up angrily haranguing the objectors and most foolishly dubbing them "A company of Puritan dogs." This was too much to be tamely endured; the people rose in wrath and hustled the apparitor, while the Sheriff, who had been called to restore order, had the good sense to do so by taking the obnoxious apparitor to gaol, the Chancellor making his escape in such haste that he left his hat behind him.

Gabriel, remembering how galling the prosecution of his own father had been, remembering, too, how Peter Waghorn's old father lay dead at Bosbury, a victim of the same overbearing régime, could not but rejoice in the people's triumph. The only marvel was that they had so long endured the intolerable tyranny—a tyranny which, during the last eleven years, had driven twenty thousand English Puritans to seek a new home in America.

Meanwhile the King had found himself between the devil and the deep sea; Strafford's infamous scheme of debasing the coinage had been checkmated by the firmness of the London merchants in the summer. It was impossible to raise money anymore after the illegal fashion of the past eleven years, and, hemmed in by his angry Scotch subjects in the north and his indignant English subjects in the south, Charles at length, in his speech to the great Council assembled in the hall of the Deanery at York, announced the issue of writs for a Parliament to meet on November the third.

Sir Robert Harley lost no time in establishing his son and Gabriel Harford in chambers at Lincoln's Inn, then returned once more to Brampton to be again elected one of the Members for Herefordshire.

It was the turn of the tide, and during October, before the Parliament met, the impatience of the people was no longer to be restrained. The High Commission Court, where so many cruel sentences had been passed, was invaded on the 22nd by an angry mob;

sentence was about to be pronounced on a separatist, but the proceedings were not allowed to be carried on, the angry populace seized the books, broke down the benches and flung the furniture out of doors. It was all in vain that Laud called on the Court of Star Chamber to punish these disturbers; his influence over the Court had been utterly swept away by the passion of an outraged people.

It was not until November that Gabriel rode down to the house at Notting-hill, where old Madam Harford lived, for on his arrival in London she had been taking the waters at Tunbridge. In some trepidation he drew rein before the doorway of a square red-brick mansion standing on the crest of the hill, and was ushered into a very pleasant room where the lady of the house sat, not at her spinning-wheel or her embroidery-frame, but at a well-contrived reading-desk, poring over a great folio.

There was no doubt that report had spoken rightly in terming old Madam Harford "a very formidable personage." Her greeting was kind, but curiously silent, and there followed a pause while she scrutinised her visitor very closely, as though to take his measure before committing herself.

"You have your father's features," she said at length, making room for her grandson on a carved oak settle beside her. "What news do you bring from Hereford?"

Gabriel was glad enough to talk on this subject, and they naturally spoke, too, of Bosbury, and of his ride there in September. Then the case of Peter Waghorn's father was mentioned.

"I remember the name in old times," said Madam Harford, her face lighting up. "There was a skilled carver in wood who lived nigh to the church, and he had a very clever son who went to college and took holy orders."

"That must be the very man," said Gabriel. "One of Dr. Laud's victims."

"The Archbishop will soon be called to his account," said Madam Harford, her shrewd, wrinkled face expressing no vindictiveness, but a quiet, strong conviction. "My Lord Strafford's high-handed and tyrannical doings have brought him very justly to a prison and, if I mistake not, Dr. Laud also will be impeached."

"Sir Robert Harley says that Mr. Pym has damning evidence against Lord Strafford which will startle all men at the trial," said Gabriel.

"Truly it must have been a strange scene in the House of Lords, when one so haughty and powerful as the Earl was called on to kneel while the order was read which sequestered him from his place in the House, and gave him into custody," said the old lady, musingly. "They tell me that the Lords hated his system of government even more than the Commons."

They were interrupted by the arrival of a visitor, the servant announcing Sir John Coke. Gabriel looked with great interest at the old white-haired man who entered, for was he not great uncle to Hilary?

"I bring you a startling piece of news, ma'am," said Sir John, sinking down into the elbow chair which Gabriel had placed for him. "We have fresh evidence of the great Popish plot, for to-day, when Mr. Heywood, a justice of the peace, was crossing Westminster Hall, a man rushed at him and tried, with a knife, to stab him to the heart. He was known to have a list of Papists marked out for removal from the neighbourhood of the Court and of the Houses."

Now, in the existence of this great Popish plot the whole country firmly believed, and the attempted assassination of Mr. Heywood was quite enough to rouse the people to anger and to something very like panic. Pym and Hampden, who two years later were fighting against the King, and Falkland and Capel, who afterwards fought for him, were at one on this point. The truth probably was that the great bulk of the English Papists were only anxious to live in peace, but for some time a small number of them had made the Queen's rooms at Whitehall a nest of intrigue. Sir John Coke had known this well enough when he had been Secretary of State, and Gabriel listened now with interest to what he was telling his old friend. It was, indeed, what he told all the world, and possibly his annoyance at having been dismissed from office on the score of his age, made him a little more ready to reveal what he knew to the Queen's discredit.

"Count Rossetti, the new Papal agent at Court," explained Sir John, "was full of fears last winter that the Short Parliament would demand his dismissal. The Queen therefore obtained a promise from the King that if objections were made he would say that her marriage-treaty secured her the right to hold correspondence with Rome. Now this, ma'am, was a lie; the marriage-treaty, as the King and Queen knew well enough, contained nothing of the sort. Never was there a sadder day for England than that which brought to her shores a French princess of the Popish religion to be the wife of a Protestant prince. All our worst troubles have come out of this luckless marriage. 'Tis very well known that the Queen hath begged the Pope to send men and to advance money to aid the King in governing the people against their wishes."

The old man's words lingered long in Gabriel's mind; he began to understand something of the gravity of the situation, and scarcely a week passed without bringing fresh evidence that the country was in the gravest peril.

It was inevitable that with all the ardour of youth he should side with the Parliament which was reforming bit by bit the evils of the past.

To stand in a crowded London street and to hear the shouts of joy as Burton was brought back from prison, to look on the haggard face so cruelly mutilated, and to know that this awful punishment had been incurred because the man had spoken and written against turning communion-tables into altars, against bowing to them, against crucifixes, and against putting down afternoon services on Sunday—this was indeed an object-lesson which would last a lifetime. While the wrath kindled by the piteous condition of Dr. Leighton, another of Laud's victims, who had been so barbarously treated in prison that when brought forth he could neither walk, see, nor hear, filled his heart with that intolerable resentment of cruelty and oppression which made many in those days feel no sacrifice to be too great if it did but stop such doings.

There has always been in Englishmen a vigorous and healthy hatred of clerical domination, and it was this which united men of widely differing views in their attack on Laud's system and on the new canons which Convocation had issued when it had continued sitting after the dissolution of the Short Parliament. These were now declared to be illegal, and on December 18 Archbishop Laud was impeached of high treason, and committed to custody by the House of Lords. Not a voice was raised on his behalf; so cordially was he detested that, in spite of his many virtues and his sincere love of the Church, men rightly felt that he was "the root and ground of all their miseries," and that his rigid, unsympathetic rule, his preferment of such men as Strafford and Windebank, and of many tyrannical Bishops—the hated Bishop Wren among them; above all, his merciless determination to crush Puritanism and to make Parliamentary government impossible, constituted grave dangers to the country. Was the entire teaching power of England to be left in such hands? Was Laud to have the training of all those to whom each Sunday the people were compelled to listen? The idea was not to be borne.

At Sir Robert Harley's rooms in Little Britain Gabriel naturally heard much of what was passing during those two eventful years. In May London was stirred into the wildest excitement by the discovery of the Army plot, and although the full details were not generally published, it was known to all that the scheme concocted by the Queen and her evil counsellors, and certainly in the knowledge of the King, had been to bring in French troops from the south, to which end the Queen was about to go to Portsmouth. Meanwhile the English army was to join with the Papists against London and Parliament, and the Irish army was to attack the Scots. Gabriel learnt from Sir Robert that the plot had been revealed by Goring, Governor of Portsmouth, and also by a merchant who had received news of the intended attack on the city and the Tower of London from an acquaintance at Paris.

The discovery of the King's intrigues and the absolute hatred of the Queen which now prevailed, robbed Strafford of his last hope of escape: Charles knew that to refuse to sign the Earl's death-warrant would be to expose his wife to the gravest peril; the choice was a most cruel strain upon him, and at length, worn out with agony of mind, he stifled his conscience, and to screen his wife, sacrificed his friend.

The next triumph of the Parliament was the abolition in July of the hated Star Chamber and the Court of High Commission. But, on the question of religion, signs of disunion in the Parliamentary ranks began to be evident. Bishops were then the nominees of the King, and those who wished to retain them were tending to become supporters of the independent authority of the monarch, while the opposite party, who feared to retain the bishops in the Church lest they should prove hostile to Parliamentary government, were gradually becoming, not without good reason, more and more distrustful of Charles.

All through this eventful time Gabriel had heard but little of Hilary. In each letter which he received from home she was allowed to send him some message; but it was an understood thing that the lovers should not correspond, and, somehow, ere long, the messages grew formal and unsatisfactory. More cheering than these occasional words from afar was the great kindness of the Bishop of Hereford, who often invited Gabriel to visit him at his London residence.

Truth to tell, politics were not in the Bishop's line; his thoughts were far more with his work on the Epistle to the Colossians than with his work in the House of Lords; and when one day late in December he invited Gabriel to dine with him, their talk never once turned on the topics which absorbed the rest of the nation.

Gabriel had now spent his second Christmas in London, and was eagerly looking forward to his return home in the following September. It was a keen delight to him to listen to Bishop Coke's description of his recent visit to Hereford, and the kindly old prelate spoke at some length about his granddaughter.

"She cheered us all with her sweet voice on Christmas night," he remarked as he rose from the table and led his guest into the library; "and better than all her other songs was a carol which she told me you had taught her as a child."

"That must have been the Bosbury carol which I learnt from my father," said Gabriel. And back into his mind there flashed a vision of the past—a snow-effigy of Sir John Eliot lying in the old garden, and a perception that had come to him that the words, "All for to make us free," were perhaps the best words that could be said of any man.

The Bishop at that moment caught sight of his manuscript, and, to Gabriel's disappointment, said no more about Hilary. "My commentary on the Colossians is complete," he remarked, turning over the leaves with a loving touch. "This afternoon I place it in the printer's hands."

Gabriel was saved a reply, for the door was opened, and the servant announced Lord Digby. Withdrawing a little into the oriel window, he watched the entrance of a fine-looking man, with eager eyes and impetuous manner. In his hand he carried a parchment roll, and Gabriel, knowing that he was generally considered to be the King's evil genius and most rash counsellor, wondered on what errand he could have come. A greater contrast than this young, hot-headed nobleman and the gentle, dreamy-eyed Bishop could not be conceived—they might have stood for ideal representatives of the worldly and the heavenly mind.

"I will not detain you a minute, my lord," said Digby, declining a chair. "I am in the greatest haste and only came to beg you to set your signature to this Protestation. They tell me you are but to-day returned from Hereford, and doubtless you have not heard what has passed. The mob at Westminster saw fit to shout 'No Bishops!' and the Archbishop of York, clutching at a 'prentice to silence him, was set upon by the crowd and hustled on his way to the House. Luckily Colonel Lunsford and some of his men drove back the dogs when they passed into Westminster Hall, and a free fight followed, when many of the rogues were wounded. 'Tis no longer safe for the Bishops to venture to the House—this parchment is a protest against such conduct, and I am sure you will gladly aid us by lending your name."

Gabriel wondered what intrigue lay beneath this apparently simple request. That the matter was of considerable importance in Digby's eyes he felt convinced, for his expression as he looked at the saintly old Bishop was at once anxious and wily.

"Do not trouble, my lord, to read the document through," urged Digby; "'tis a mere recital of the wrong under which the Bishops are suffering through this ill-conduct of the mob. I am sure you will agree that such an insult is not to be tamely endured."

"I see that Bishop Hall has signed," said the old prelate; "I have a deep respect for Bishop Hall."

And after a little more talk on Digby's part the Protestation was signed and the noble lord bowed himself out.

He had only just gone when the servant came to say that the Bishop's coach was waiting, and Gabriel hastened to make his farewell.

"Nay," said the Bishop, "I have yet much to tell you as to Hereford matters. If you will come with me we can speak of them as I drive down to the City."

The precious manuscript was to be conveyed to the printers, and Gabriel was much afraid that the Bishop would be too much occupied with it to talk of his granddaughter. However, in the course of the drive he heard many little details which the home letters had failed to give him, and as he parted with the kindly old man he felt more than ever drawn to him. His dismay was, therefore, all the greater when, happening to be with Ned Harley in Sir Robert's room late the next day, he heard that the Protestation which Bishop Coke had signed inadvertently was very far from being the simple matter that Digby had represented it to be.

"It seems," explained Sir Robert, "that Archbishop Williams took it to the King at Whitehall last night, that his Majesty without reading it handed it to Nicholas, who gave it to the Lord Keeper to place before the House of Lords. Doubtless his Majesty knew beforehand what it contained."

"What did it contain, sir?" asked Gabriel, curiously.

"It protested that all laws, orders, votes and so forth made in the absence of the Bishops were null and void. Clearly it was got up by my Lord Digby, who was in high ill-humour because a day or two since he had been worsted in his effort to obtain the assent of the Lords to a declaration that Parliament was no longer free. It would have suited him very well that this vote should be treated as null and void. The unfortunate Bishops will pay dearly for their protest."

"Why, sir, what has been done to them?" asked Gabriel, with some anxiety in his tone.

"The Lords at once acquainted the Lower House that the Protestation entrenched on the fundamental privileges and being of Parliament, and Mr. Pym told them that a scheme for seizing the Parliamentary leaders was on foot; he then moved that the Bishops who had signed the Protestation should be impeached of treason for having tried to subvert the very being of Parliament. I believe that they are all by now in the Tower."

Gabriel, having mixed of late with men of every shade of opinion, had learnt to hold his tongue. He said not a word as to having been present when Digby visited Bishop Coke. But the next day he hurried off to the Tower, where he found the Bishop of Hereford in sore distress.

"You well know that I had no treasonable intention in signing," said the old man. "I merely wished for order in Palace Yard, and that we might be able to go to and from our duties in Parliament unmolested. Well,'tis after all my own fault. I ought to have read the document through instead of yielding to my Lord Digby's haste. Truth to tell, my thoughts were more with my manuscript—and now what will become of it?"

"My lord, if you will trust me as a messenger, I would bear your wishes to the printers, who saw me of late with your lordship," said Gabriel.

And thus it came to pass that the proofs of the Commentary on the Colossians went to and from the Tower in the charge of Dr. Harford's son, and that the Bishop's tedious weeks of imprisonment were cheered by the work he loved.

It happened one day early in January that Gabriel, crossing Tower-green with the second batch of proofs, caught sight of no less a person than Archbishop Laud himself. He was standing in converse with a friend, and laughing very heartily over a caricature which the other held. Gabriel saw at a glance that it was a picture which represented Archbishop Williams as a decoy duck leading his eleven brethren into prison. On his return from Bishop Coke's room he saw that Dr. Laud had parted with his friend, and was pacing the green alone with bent head and an air of great dejection. Remembering the pomp of his entry into Hereford years ago, Gabriel could not help feeling great pity for the captive; what a contrast did he now present! Feeble, bent and sad, he seemed another being from the haughty overbearing prelate who had roused his wrath as a child by that harsh rebuke to his father. Even the bitter enmity between the two Archbishops which had scandalised people, was now a thing of the past, though, perhaps, there had been a little malice in Dr. Laud's laughter over the caricature representing Dr. Williams's mischance. The Archbishop had turned and was pacing slowly back again, when his leg suddenly gave way beneath him, and he fell to the ground. Gabriel ran forward and helped the old man to rise.

"I thank you, sir," said Laud, feebly, giving him a long look out of his inscrutable eyes. "They have taken all my attendants from me save one, and my strength is failing."

A warder approached them, and, again thanking Gabriel, the Archbishop bade the man take him back to his room in the Bloody Tower.

But, nevertheless, though it was impossible not to feel compassion for the forlorn plight of one who a short time before had enforced his will on the whole country, there rang in Gabriel's ears the words that had been spoken to him in Bos-bury churchyard, and he could not but think of the far worse plight of Waghorn's father in Bridewell, heavily ironed, and chained for months to a post in a foul, damp dungeon.

His thoughts were grave enough as he was rowed up the river that cold afternoon, and the recollection of the startling news he had heard on the previous day as to the King's impeachment of the Parliamentary leaders, and his illegal demand for their arrest, filled him with uneasiness; it seemed to him that they were all living on the brink of a volcano.

Bidding the boatman set him down at the Parliament stairs, he sprang ashore, and was just paying his fare, when he chanced to notice two gentlemen getting into the next boat. He recognised them at once as Hazlerigg and Holies; as he mounted the steps he had to stand aside to make room for two more gentlemen who seemed in haste to join them; the first was Mr. Pym, with his usual air of strength tempered with bonhomie, and close behind him came Mr. John Hampden, his fine genial face no longer cheerful as it was wont to be, but sad and stern, with the expression of one who is steadily confronting some grievous national danger.

Gabriel took off his hat and bowed low; he had met the Member for Buckinghamshire more than once at Sir Robert Harley's.

"This is a dark day for England, Mr. Harford," said Hampden, returning the young man's salute. "But God reigns—with His help we will take no step backward."

The boat was pushed off, and Gabriel saw that the four Members were being rowed in the direction of the city.

Hurrying up the steps, he walked towards the Houses of Parliament, and as he approached Westminster Hall, it was very clear that most unusual work was on hand. Fighting his way through the crowd he gained the doorway, gathering as he did so that the King was close by, coming, men said, to arrest the Parliamentary leaders. The notion seemed too wild to be believed; yet it was, alas! true.

Just as the clocks struck three the King's coach, surrounded by some three or four hundred armed men, drove up to Westminster Hall; the guard filed into the great building, while the King, alighting, wrapped his fur-lined cloak about him, for the bitter January wind blew gustily, as though it would have protested against his entrance. Gabriel was swept by the throng inside the Hall, but he could see well enough, and watched intently as the King strode rapidly through the armed ranks, towards the entrance which led to the House of Commons; here he turned and bade his retinue wait outside, then once more moved forward to enter that door which no English King had ever passed.

Apparently his command to the retinue to wait without only applied to a certain number, for Gabriel observed that some eighty of them flung off their cloaks and left them in the hall, then, with their sword arms free and provided also with pistols, they passed on into the lobby. Gabriel noticed that the first to pass in after the King was Captain David Hide, the husband of one of the Coningsbys of Herefordshire, a notorious scoundrel, with a savage and uncontrollable temper; he was one of the officers who had drawn their swords on the people a few days before, and was said to be the inventor of the opprobrious term of "Roundhead," which during the last week had come into vogue as applied to supporters of the Parliament.

Then followed a long time of waiting, which chafed the King's followers sorely.

"I warrant you," said one standing within earshot of Gabriel, and cocking his pistol as he spoke, "I am a good marksman, I will hit sure."

The lad's blood grew hot. What would happen when the King found the Members he sought absent? That he had contemplated using force if the House refused to give them up was evident. What would happen now?

As he mused a thrill of expectation passed through the waiting people; the King appeared in the doorway—his brow was dark, it was plain to all that he had been baffled, and the disgust of his retinue would have amused Gabriel had not his heart burnt within him at the thought of the grievous wrong that had been intended. He learnt afterwards that Mr. Strode, the fifth Member, had refused to quit the House, and had only been forcibly dragged out by a friend a moment before the entrance of the King.

For days after the whole of London rang with the angry cry, "Privileges of Parliament!" It was in vain that the King ordered Gurney, the Lord Mayor, to proclaim Lord Mandeville and the five Members of the House of Commons as traitors. Gurney, loyal man as he was, sturdily replied that the proclamation was against the law, and the King, thus hopelessly beaten, could only save the Queen from the consequences of her rash intrigues by hastily quitting Whitehall, and making preparations for her departure from England.

It was not until May that the imprisoned prelates were released, but when the King had consented to the Bishops' Exclusion Bill, and there was no longer anything to dread from their political interference, they were allowed to quit the Tower. Bishop Coke had indeed received a special permit to go to his wife during her illness, and early in June he returned to Hereford, never again to visit London.

Hilary, who not unnaturally laid the blame of her grandfather's imprisonment on the Parliamentary leaders, and hated them accordingly, was entranced to hear the Bishop's warm words of appreciation as to Gabriel Harford, nor did it once occur to her that her lover had learnt to look on almost every disputed subject from a point of view exactly opposite to her own.

CHAPTER VII.

"We sin against our dearest not because we do not love, but because we do not imagine."
—Ian Maclaren.

"And so Master Gabriel be at home again," said Mrs. Hurdle, glancing across the kitchen at Hilary one September morning as she made the pastry with deft hands. "Home again, and quite the man. I reckon his mother be thankful to you for bringing him to Hereford just now."

"What do you mean, Durdle?" said Hilary, colouring. "Of course he comes home to see his father and mother."

Durdle, with an expressive shake of the head, sprinkled flour on her board and took up her rolling pin.

"My dear, you don't throw dust in my eyes," she said, "being that I've known you both from cradle days. Depend upon it, if it wasn't for your pretty face, Master Gabriel would be off like my Lord Scudamore's sons and all the other gentry to fight for the King."

"Maybe he will yet go," said Hilary, with a vision of girding him for the fight like the maidens of olden time—a vision that was at once painful and inspiring. How bravely he would face the foe, how chivalrous he would be to the weak and defenceless!

She took a basket on her arm and strolled slowly down the garden to gather apricots for preserving; the housekeeper's words had turned her thoughts to the war, the topic that now engrossed all England. She had not greatly heeded the rumours which for many months had been current, but when it was known that the Queen had sold the Crown jewels to raise troops in Holland, and that the Parliament was putting the kingdom into a state of defence, then, indeed, the prospect of war began to kindle in her heart that fire of eager interest which the duller details of the long struggle between opposing principles had never been able to quicken. By the time the King had raised his standard at Nottingham, Hilary, like almost every other dweller in Herefordshire, had become a most devoted Royalist, and it never occurred to her that in other parts of England, people just as well bred, just as honest, were equally devoted to the Parliamentary cause.

Her basket was about half full when a merry voice greeted her.

"'Go tie me up yon dangling apricocks,' as said the gardener in Shakspere's play."

"Nay, I want them pulled down," said Hilary, laughing, as she glanced round into her lover's mirthful eyes. Gabriel, having made his conditions and received payment in kisses, worked with a will, and before long the tree was stripped. Then he called a truce, and induced her to rest for a while on the old stone bench under the briar bush.

It was now three days since his return, and they had been days of almost unmixed happiness. Their long waiting had been bravely borne, and each had matured during the time of absence; in Hilary, Gabriel saw more clearly than ever his ideal of all that was beautiful and good, while she was quick to note in him a manliness and a strength of character, the result of the life he had lived during the two years in London. How they laughed as they spoke of the troubles of the past, and recalled the wooing of Mr. Geers, and the kindly offices of Mrs. Joyce Jefferies.

"You would never believe how hard it has been for dear Mrs. Joyce to tell no one of our betrothal," said Hilary, gaily. "She had the greatest longing to tell Eliza Acton, and laugh with her over that memorable dinner when you were all so discomfited."

"The time for telling outsiders is close at hand," said Gabriel, blithely. "If only the Bishop were at the Palace the waiting would be over."

"Whitbourne suits him better in the summer, and in truth he needs more air after his imprisonment, and all his anxiety about my grandmother," replied Hilary. "You'll never know how grateful we were to you for what you did for him while he was in the Tower; he told me that no grandson could have been more attentive and thoughtful."

"It was little enough I could do," said Gabriel, "and everybody must love one like the Bishop."

"Do you know what Durdle said just now?—she has, you know, a very shrewd notion of the truth about us, though she has never been told in so many words—she protested that had you not wanted to come back here and see me you would have been riding off to offer your services to His Majesty."

Gabriel started, a strange look dawned in his eyes; the suggestion had evidently awakened a train of thought that was far from pleasant. Hilary fancied that he shrank from the idea of leaving her, and only loved him the better for it, even though that thought of fastening on his armour still allured her.

"Had you no longing to take part in this war?" she asked, watching his thoughtful face.

"Such a notion never occurred to me," he said. "My hope is that one great battle may be fought within the next few days, which will decide the vexed question once for all."

In this he only expressed the anticipation of most people.

"Yet somehow I should have expected you to want to have your share in fighting for the right," said Hilary.

He seemed about to speak but checked himself, and Hilary, with a puzzled consciousness that something she did not understand was troubling him, watched him anxiously.

"You are shivering!" she exclaimed the next minute. "What is amiss?"

But Gabriel did not easily put his deepest feelings into words; he could not explain to her at that moment what fighting for the right might mean for him, any more than years ago he could have told her of his childish wish to follow in Eliot's steps. The torture of the sudden perception that the cause he had learned to hold sacred would assuredly lose for him Hilary's sympathy and approval made him silently turn to her and clasp her in his arms with a passion far too deep for speech. Then, releasing her, he hastily rose, and picking up the basket of apricots, resumed with an effort his usual manner.

"Do you not want these carried to the still-room?" he asked. "Stoning is the next process, if I remember right."

"Why, to be sure," said Hilary, laughing. "Stoning with a good deal of eating intermixed. I think one in twenty used to be Durdle's allowance."

"Here she comes to set the limit," said Gabriel, with a smile. "She bustles about more briskly than ever; and look how her face beams!—something extraordinary must have happened."

"Miss Hilary, such news!" cried the housekeeper, her fat face wreathed in smiles. "Haste, my dear, and hear it all from the Bishop's secretary who is talking to the mistress at the front door. He is going to ride straight over to Whitbourne and tell his lordship."

"But what is it, Durdle? What has happened?"

"Why, thank God! the Roundheads have been beaten near Worcester—go and hear what Mr. Jenkinson is telling of the rout."

Hilary clapped her hands with delight.

"Good new's, indeed! come, Gabriel, let us hear all about it," and she ran into the house eagerly.

"Let me take the basket, sir," said Durdle, expecting Gabriel to follow her.

But he shook his head, and himself carried the fruit to the still-room, leaving the housekeeper to bustle after Hilary, all agog to hear the details of the fight.

The still-room was cool and shady; great bunches of lavender were hanging from the ceiling, and a tray full of dead rose petals spread to dry was on the window seat. He set the basket of apricots on the spotless deal table and began to pace to and fro in miserable agitation. All desire to know the details of this battle was held in check by the perception that the parting of the ways had come, and that from henceforth the sympathy between him and the woman he loved was gravely broken. Who could have thought that Hilary of all people would be so deeply stirred by any public news? She had never been roused to take interest in the wrongs and grievances under which England had so long groaned. How was it that the news of fighting should awake, not only her interest, but her keen partisanship?

It was with a pang that he saw her radiant face as she rejoined him. He had known her too long and too well to imagine that she was faultless, but her rapture now gave the first shock to his belief in her perfect womanliness.

"Why did you not come and hear for yourself?" she cried, gaily. "Prince Rupert has beaten the Roundheads at Powick Bridge, near Worcester. None of our men are killed, but fifty of theirs, and the rest have fled helter-skelter, like the cowardly traitors they are."

"Nay, an you gloat in that fashion over the slaughter of your own countrymen, I will not stay to listen," said Gabriel, his eyes flashing with anger.

Hilary had thrown aside her sun-bonnet, and was drawing a chair to the table that she might sit down and begin the stoning of the apricots. She paused, however, aghast at his look and tone. "I disown them for my countrymen," she said quickly; "they are traitors."

"If you knew more about them you would see that they desire only to save the country from ruin and to save the King from his evil counsellors," said Gabriel. "Do you think men like Mr. John Hampden and my Lord Brooke and Sir Robert Harley and the other leading Parliamentarians are to be dubbed traitors and overcrowed by a young German prince, who doth not in any way understand the liberties of England?"

Hilary faltered. "I don't know what you mean," she said. "To hear you speak, one would fancy you were a Roundhead yourself."

"It is scarce worthy of you to use the new term of reproach," he said. "You would think it unfair were I to term all in the King's army 'Malignants' or 'Cavaliers'; let us leave such spiteful party names to these who hate as well as differ. But you and I, though we may disagree, shall ever love, and therein lies a mighty difference."

Hilary sank down on to the chair. She had turned very pale, and the suffering in her face made Gabriel's heart ache. He drew nearer.

"My beloved, do not take it thus hardly. Here in Herefordshire you inevitably look on matters from a different point of view; but had you seen what I saw in London, did you but know of the abominable plots and intrigues hatched at Whitehall, you would, at any rate, understand why many Englishmen feel that, to defend our liberties, the King's evil counsellors must be defeated, cost what it may. Don't let these matters of State grieve you so sorely; our love, is surely proof against all such passing matters."

She had listened to him intently, nor could she altogether hide the love which shone in her dark-grey eyes as they met his. He bent over her, his arm stole round her protectingly; but the sense of his strength and protectiveness was exactly what she could not at that moment endure to realise. With an impetuous gesture and a look which wounded him to the quick, she freed herself from him, and, springing to her feet, confronted him with such pale anger in her face as he had never before seen.

"Don't touch me! You have deceived us!" she said. "Why did you not tell me before?"

"How was it possible when we were not allowed to write to each other?" said Gabriel. "And, indeed, had I been able to write I should scarce have thought you would take any interest in public affairs. The contest between King and people has been going on in reality for many years; why is it that you only care now that the bloodshed has begun?"

"You did deceive us," said Hilary, ignoring his question because she could not answer it. "You won my grandfather's favour and waited on him, while you in your heart sided with his enemies."

"You do but show your injustice by urging that against me," replied Gabriel, hotly. "I had no thought but to help one who had shown me kindness, and who had been most unfairly cosened into signing the Protestation when he knew not what it involved."

"And now I can understand your frequent visits to the Tower," she said, in the most bitter tone. "It was all part of your plan to deceive us—you even, I believe, tried to get into Archbishop's Laud's good graces, for he spoke of you to my grandfather."

At this, spite of himself, Gabriel burst out laughing.

"Do you really think that any gentleman could have seen the poor old Primate fall to the ground and not have offered to help him up?" he said. "Long before I went to London you knew that I hated his system; and if the Royal Army indeed prevails now, the Archbishop, with all his tyrannies, will be brought back, the Puritans will be driven from the land or left to languish in gaol, and Mr. John Hampden—the patriot who tried to save us from the curse of ship-money—will probably die on the scaffold with the other Parliamentary leaders. Now, perhaps, you understand why some of us feel that we must defend our country."

"Then you must choose betwixt what you call your country and me," said Hilary, drawing herself up proudly. "For I will never be betrothed to a man who is a rebel."

Gabriel breathed hard, his hands clenched and unclenched themselves like those of a man in mortal agony.

"And I," he said at length, throwing back his head, as though choking for want of air—"I, with God's help, will be true to the Great Charter which bids Englishmen resist any prince who seeks to rob them of their just privileges."

She dropped him a curtsey—not mockingly, but in grave farewell. Then, taking up her sun-bonnet, she turned to leave the room. But Gabriel strode forward and intercepted her, "Hilary!" he cried, passionately, "you cannot end all betwixt us like this."

"I both can and will," she said, with quiet coldness very little in accordance with her throbbing heart.

"It is impossible that matters of State can part those who love," he urged vehemently. "They are affairs of another sphere—what has our love to do with this hateful war?"

"It has this to do with it, that I will not love a man who is a rebel," said Hilary, proudly.

"'Tis the thrice-accursed fighting that hath so changed you," he said, despairingly. "You, who cannot bear to see a dog hurt, or a boy whipped for thieving, can glory over the fifty Englishmen killed at Powick Bridge!"

"Yes, for their rebellion is justly punished," she said, "and I punish yours in the only way open to me. Go, sir! I will look upon your face no more."

She drew back from the door and motioned to him imperiously to leave her.

Gabriel paused for a minute as though to gather his strength together. It was no time now to argue, to plead; words availed naught. The time for deeds had come, the call to be true to country and conscience. With a look of reproachful love that was to haunt her all her life long, he bowed low, and quitted the room in silence.

For a few minutes Hilary sat down calmly to her fruit-stoning: then all at once the pride that had upheld her gave way, and, burying her face in her hands, she sobbed as if her heart were broken.

CHAPTER VIII.

"Who like an April morn appears,

Sunshine and rain, hopes clouded o'er with fears,

Pleased and displeased by starts, in passion warm,

In reason weak."

—Churchill.

Now, whether it was due to the kitchen fire or to the war fever, it would be hard to say, but Mrs. Durdle on that cool September morning gasped with heat, and as she digested the news of the Powick fight and put her pastry into the oven, she hailed with relief any excuse for leaving her domain.

"I'll see how they young folk be getting on with the apricots," she said to herself, wiping her hot face and setting her cap straight. "There'll be more lommaking than stoning, an I'm not mistaken. And, Lord love 'em! they do make a fine, handsome couple, nobody can't deny it."

She had just bustled out into the passage when, to her astonishment, she saw Gabriel Harford closing the door of the still-room behind him, with a face which had suddenly lost all its boyishness. Haggard and pale, with wide eyes that seemed to see nothing of his surroundings, he strode by the housekeeper and passed rapidly down the garden path.

Mrs. Durdle stood quite still, staring after him.

"Lack-a-day!" she cried. "Now what should that bode? He passed me by and never so much as saw me—me that am of a pertly presence, and was never overlooked before in all my born days. Save us! But'tis clear as day they have had their first quarrel—that is, their first lovers' quarrel, for they was always at it like hammer and tongs as children, bless 'em, though their greatest punishment was to be apart."

The next question was—who should make the peace? They were now past the days of cuffing and scolding; indeed, Durdle fairly quaked at the thought of addressing either of them, and feeling that discretion was the better part of valour, she stole on tip-toe to the still-room door, and made careful and noiseless preparation to look through the keyhole. First, she hitched up her gown, then, supporting herself by the doorpost, she slowly lowered her massive form on to one knee and, crouching forward, applied a sharp, twinkling, little grey eye to the keyhole.

Alas! the apricots were pushed aside, and Hilary, with her face hidden, was sobbing in that silent, restrained fashion which always alarmed the housekeeper.

To get up from her crouching posture without making a sound was even harder than the descent had proved. However, Durdle valiantly gripped both doorposts, and with a tremendous effort heaved herself on to her feet, and tiptoed across the hall to the dining-room.

"Oh, ma'am! do pray come to Mistress Hilary," she exclaimed, addressing poor Mrs. Unett in the most startling fashion. "She is crying her heart out alone, and Mr. Gabriel he's gone off with a face the colour of a monument and eyes as big as egg-cups, and I am certain sure that they have had a desperate quarrel."

"Say nothing to anybody else, Durdle," said Mrs. Unett, hurriedly rising, and making her way with an anxious face to the still-room.

Hilary sprang to her feet as the door opened, and became engrossed in the withered rose petals on the window-sill.

"When shall we make the pot pourri, ma'am?" she said with averted face.

But Mrs. Unett was not to be deceived or repulsed. She put her arm about the girl, and gently turned the tear-stained face to her own, kissing her daughter without a word.

That was more than Hilary's pride could withstand, she sank down on her knees and clung to her mother, sobbing anew.

"It's all over," she said, piteously; "I have been quite—quite deceived. Oh, mother! he has sided with the Parliament."

"We might have expected it, after all," said Mrs. Unett; "for his father hath ever inclined to that side, yet I never thought—never dreamt that if it actually came to war he could be disloyal."

"Oh, he has some fine arguing about being faithful to the Great Charter," said Hilary, bitterly. "But I told him I would never love a rebel—and I bid him choose between me and the country."

"And he?" said Mrs. Unett.

"He chose the country, and I said I would see him no more," said Hilary, with a rush of tears.

Little by little Mrs. Unett gathered most of what had passed, and her kindly heart was rent with conflicting feelings. After all, Gabriel had spoken truly when he said their love could not really be touched by any matters of State; Hilary was too young to understand the full truth of that thought. And yet, in spite of all, how could the Bishop give her in marriage to one agreeing with those who had just turned the Bishops out of the House of Lords?

"If only I had some man to counsel me," thought poor Mrs. Unett. "But I can't consult Dr. Harford, and the Dean must not know of the betrothal. I must go to Whitbourne and get my father's advice—how is a lonely woman to judge in so difficult a matter?"

"Hilary," she said, in a tone of relief. "We will drive over this very day to Whitbourne and consult your grandfather. Dry your eyes, child; he will be sure to tell us what it is right to do."

Now Hilary was quite without her mother's tendency to consult a man in every difficulty, nevertheless she hailed with no small satisfaction this notion of going to Whitbourne, for Whitbourne was twenty-three miles from Hereford, and with every inch she felt that she would be stronger to harden her heart against Gabriel. Nothing would have induced her to confess this thought to anybody, but deep down in her own consciousness she was aware of a great dread. If she met Gabriel, and if again he were to give her that look of reproachful love she feared he might break down her power of resistance.

There was a certain comfort, moreover, in the hurried preparations for departure; they would inevitably stay for a few days, for a journey over the proverbially bad roads of Herefordshire was not by any to be taken in hand lightly or unadvisedly, but required a little breathing time in which fragile ladies of Mrs. Unett's constitution might recover from the severe shaking undergone.

By the time the coach was at the door Hilary had contrived to wash away all traces of her tears, and only a very careful observer would have noticed that her smile was forced, and that her laugh did not ring true.

Great rejoicings were going on in the city, and the cheers of the crowd excited her, until suddenly the shouting began to form itself into actual words, and a man who had been loyally drinking himself drunk in honour of the victory of Powick Bridge, hung on to the coach door, wildly waving his hat and bawling at the top of his voice, "God save King Charles, and hang up the Roundheads!"

Hilary, in deep disgust, promptly drew the leathern curtain across the window, but though she could thus shut out the hideous leering face of the pseudo-patriot, she could not banish his words, which persistently rang in her ears as the coach lumbered out through Byster's Gate and along the rough road to Whitbourne; nor could she shut out the mental picture which the words conjured up, the picture of Gabriel Harford with a rope about his neck.

"I wish I had not used the term 'Roundhead' this morning; 'tis only fit for such people as that drunken wretch in Bye-street," she thought. And, having once begun to see something amiss in her words, she continued the salutary, but depressing, occupation all through the drive, ending with the humiliating perception that she had defended the cause she believed to be right in the wrong way, and that although nothing would induce her to be betrothed to a rebel, she had certainly by her harshness done much to confirm him in his convictions.

It was quite dusk when they arrived at the Bishop's country residence, the evening air had grown cold, and the two ladies, stiff and weary with their drive, were glad to see the lights within the pretty gabled house, and the door flung wide to welcome them. The Bishop's surprise and pleasure at their unexpected arrival touched Hilary, who was always at her best when with her grandfather, and Mrs. Unett's explanation that she had come to talk over a family matter, having been made, the Bishop, possibly guessing from his grandchild's face what the "family matter" was, deferred the talk till the morning.

They supped quietly with Bishop Coke and his chaplain, and the name of Harford was never once mentioned, but the talk turned inevitably to the news of Powick Fight, until the Bishop, with a sigh, used the very same words which Gabriel had used in the morning as to hoping that all would be swiftly decided by one great battle. Then, rising from table, he led the way to the hall, where the household assembled for evening prayers, read by the chaplain, after which Hilary, in a much softened mood, was glad to go to bed.

She woke the next morning with an aching head and a sore heart, wondering whether every future awakening would be so full of misery and desolation.

"It shall not be!" she determined, vigorously; "I will not allow my life to be spoilt in that fashion." And springing out of bed she dressed rapidly, hurried through her prayers—because she found that on her knees tears were somehow apt to come into her eyes—and without waiting for food hastened out of the house.

The fresh morning air was a relief, and she hailed with joy the sight of a visitor riding up the approach. On nearer view she recognised him as Dr. Rogers, one of the Cathedral canons and rector of Stoke Edith.

"Why, Mistress Hilary!" he exclaimed, "I had not thought to find you here; you are a sight to cheer a downhearted man on a sad morn."

"But we had good news, sir, yesterday, of the victory," said Hilary. "They brought us the news at Hereford."

"Ay, my dear, but I come from Worcester with yet later news of defeat. My Lord Essex, who is in command of the rebel army, entered Worcester and has taken possession of the city. With my own eyes I saw his vile troops quartered in the cathedral; the knaves had no sort of reverence, and have stabled their horses in the cloisters. But there! I could not offend your ear by describing the scene. Would that I had the hanging of them! They should have but short shrift!"

The worthy canon was an ardent—even a bitter—Royalist, and his burning words added fuel to the fire already kindled in Hilary's heart. She listened eagerly to all he had to tell of the occupation of Worcester, and received passively and contentedly the exaggerated doctrine of the unquestioning obedience which was the sole duty of the subject, and the supreme, divinely-given authority which was the prerogative of the King—the King who, according to Dr. Rogers could do no wrong.

Few people are at their best in the early morning before breakfast, after any special fatigue on the previous day, and Hilary, who at another time might have been capable of seeing the weak points in Dr. Rogers's harangue, drank it in now without any misgivings, reflecting all the time what a bulwark it would make against that secret dread lest she should be conquered by Gabriel's love.

And so it came to pass, that whereas on the previous night she had been gentle-minded and sorrowing over her own shortcomings, when morning service time came and they all went by the little wicket-gate in the drive to the church close by, she was in a very different mood, and never prayed a single prayer, because the whole time she was picturing the scene in the cathedral described by Dr. Rogers.

"It is to vile men like this that Gabriel has allied himself," she thought, indignantly; "men without any reverence, men who have turned the Bishops out of the House of Lords, and who would fain abolish the Prayer-book! Nothing is sacred to them—not even a church!"

It never occurred to her that perhaps by her thoughts she was more grossly desecrating the building she deemed sacred than the troops of Lord Essex had desecrated the cathedral, which, of course, in Puritan eyes, was only a large building that could at once be used as a shelter from the cold, and which they considered no more sacred than the rest of the world to Him Whose throne is the heaven and Whose footstool is the earth.

Dr. Rogers remained to the noontide meal, and then rode on to other houses to impart his news. When he had gone the Bishop was closeted alone for some time with Mrs. Unett, and at length Hilary was summoned to the family conclave. She had no misgivings now, all the tenderness of the previous evening had vanished, and the kindly old Bishop was astonished at the change that had come over her.

"Child," he said, "I am much grieved to learn from your mother that Gabriel Harford hath ranged himself on the side of the Parliament. It is doubtless the effect of overmuch intercourse with Sir Robert Harley. Still matters of State, matters soon I trust to be satisfactorily settled, need not greatly affect your future happiness. God forbid that I should part you from one I know to be as clean-souled a man as you will ever meet. An you still love him I will not refuse to wed you in due time."

"But I do not still love him," said Hilary with decision, nettled, she scarce knew why, by her grandfather's tribute to Gabriel. A day or two ago her heart would have throbbed with delight to hear his praises; now the demon of pride had turned all to bitterness, and she was defiantly determined to stand to all that she had said to her lover during their dispute.

They discussed the affair for some little time, but Hilary was not to be moved, and the Bishop could not but admit that there might be difficulties in the future should the war prove longer than was expected.

He was scarcely quit of his granddaughter when to his discomfort Dr. Harford was announced; it appeared that, having learnt from Gabriel what had passed, the Doctor had called on Mrs. Unett, but hearing that she had gone to Whitbourne had deemed it best to approach the Bishop himself.

"My lord," he said, "Gabriel is in despair over the unlucky dispute of yesterday. I promised him to see if there was any hope that your granddaughter would reconsider the matter. The boy is hot-tempered and admits that he might have put his views before her more considerately. But the fact was they were both excited by the news of the defeat at Powick Bridge, and were betrayed into a dispute and quarrel which he bitterly regrets."

"It is true then that he has allied himself to the side of the Parliament?" asked the Bishop.

"Yes, quite true, my lord, but he will not admit that political matters have aught to do with a love already given, and I agree with him."

"I said as much to Hilary but now," said the Bishop. "The maid vows she will not love a rebel. You had better see her yourself, doctor. So much do I value your son's high character that I told her, spite of his views, I would gladly wed her to him. But Hilary is not easily led, nor will I attempt to coerce her. There she goes, walking towards the moat; do you, if you will, sir, follow her and plead your son's cause."

The doctor willingly obeyed, and the Bishop, with a sigh, took up an old fourteenth-century manuscript entitled "Sixteen Revelations of Divine Love," and tried to forget the sorrows and distracting cares of his times by reading words written hundreds of years before by Juliana, an anchorite of Norwich:—"And He will that our hearts be mightily raised above the deepness of the earth, and all vain sorrows, and enjoy in Him. This was a delectable sight, and a restful showing that is without end; and the beholding of this whiles we are here it is full pleasant to God and full great speed to us. And the soul that thus beholdeth, it maketh him like to Him that is beholden, and oned it in rest and in peace by His grace."

Meanwhile, Dr. Harford followed the graceful figure in the soft grey gown crossing the trim lawns which stretched down to the moat. In those days of hand-loom weaving, dresses were costly and lasted long. Hilary still wore the one she had been wearing on the day of Gabriel's return from Oxford when he had been "Shot through the ear with a love-song; the very pin of his heart cleft with the blind bow-boy's butt-shaft." But the morning was very cold, and she had put on a little short cape and hood of grey, lined with rose pink, in which she looked so ravishingly beautiful that the doctor felt a fresh pang of compassion for Gabriel's loss.

Her face clouded when on turning round she saw him approaching. He had always had a great influence over her, and, being in a perverse mood, she set herself to resist any appeal he might make, and tried naughtily to criticise his grave, strong face. The sudden brightness of his smile, however, which was so like Gabriel's, somewhat disconcerted her, and her greeting was less cold than she had intended.

"The Bishop told me to seek you here, Hilary," he said, gently. "I am come in a two-fold capacity—as Gabriel's father and as your father's friend. Have you forgotten how greatly he wished a union betwixt you two?"

"The war has changed all that," said Hilary. "He would not approve now, sir."

"I assure you that he foresaw troubled times," said Dr. Harford. "And knowing that in many points your grandfather did not hold with him, he begged me to do what I could to help you. 'Tis the memory of his words that brings me here today."

"Many desired reforms then who would not side now with the Parliament," said Hilary. "Doubtless he would have followed my Lord Falkland's example."

"I do not think he would; their natures were wholly different. But, child, it is of hearts, not of politics, I would speak. Do you quite realise what you are doing when you vow you will never again see the man who for so long has devotedly loved you?"

"It is he who has changed," said Hilary, fighting hard to keep the tears out of her eyes.

"It is true," said the Doctor, "that no young and unformed nature could possibly have lived in London through these perplexing years without growth and development. But as a lover, he is unchanged, absolutely constant, and broken-hearted at this untoward dispute. Is there no hope that you will reconsider what you said? He quite admits that he might have explained things more considerately yesterday, but you were both of you stirred by the news of the fighting."

Hilary stifled her inclination to yield; the very sound of the word "fighting" had called back her powers of resistance.

"And to-day when we have just heard how the rebel troops have defiled Worcester Cathedral you think to find me more amenable?" she exclaimed, indignantly. "Tell Gabriel, sir, that I am more than ever resolved to have nothing to do with those who side with the Parliament. He has given me up for what he calls the 'country' and, pray, tell him that I care only for the King."

In her sparkling eyes, in the hard look which dawned in the naturally sweet face, the doctor saw that his mission was hopeless. Very sadly he bade her farewell, convinced that further words would only strengthen her in her resolve; his keen, all-observant eyes seemed for a moment to look her through and through, then, with profound gravity, he turned and walked back to the house.

Hilary, with a heavy heart, sauntered aimlessly along beside the moat. She was not well pleased with herself, for as she grew cooler she perceived that her last words had not rung true, and if there was one thing she prided herself on, it was on a high standard of truth and honour. Was it absolutely the case that she cared only for the King? Was her loyal devotion to an unseen head of the State to eclipse every other claim? She pictured Gabriel's face as he received her curt, cold message, and her pride began to waver; slowly she re-crossed the lawns towards the house—should she not add some more kindly word? Was it not possible to be true to her notion of loyalty yet less harsh to the man who loved her?

Glancing up at the study window she saw the old whitehaired Bishop, and remembered how infinitely more thoughtful for Gabriel he had been. Yet no one could dare to call his loyalty in question. What was it that made him view the matter so differently?

Drawing nearer she saw that he was standing with clasped hands and closed eyes, his serene face showing plainly that he was in a region far above the petty divisions and difficulties of English life.

"He sees beyond the struggle and lives in another atmosphere," thought the girl, all her hardness melting as she looked at the saintly old face. Then, quickening her steps, she hastened on to overtake the doctor before he mounted, not pausing to think what words she should say, but with an eager desire to undo the effect of her needlessly cold message.

"Where is Dr. Harford?" she asked, encountering one of the servants.

"He would not stay for food, mistress," replied the man. "I saw him mount his horse but now."

With an impatient exclamation, Hilary ran through the hall and out into the drive; surely she should be in time to stop him, it could not be too late.

But the doctor, less calm inwardly than he had appeared to her, had set spurs to his steed and was already out of sight, though she could hear the sound of horse hoofs in the distance. They seemed to her fancy to beat out the words she had sent back to Gabriel, those words which were after all not wholly true. Choking back a sob, she tried to turn her thoughts to Dr. Roger's harangue on the Divine right of kings. It was but cold comfort.

CHAPTER IX.

"There is no time so miserable but a man may be true."

—Timon of Athens.

How Gabriel lived through the next few days he never clearly remembered. Afterwards it seemed to him as if he had been struggling up some huge mountain, crawling inch by inch with no very definite aim, but simply because he thought it would be the part of a coward to lie down and die. He rode with his father, he went fishing, he read Burton's "Protestation Protested," and tried to grasp the tolerant notion of a National Church surrounded by voluntary Churches which had occurred to Dr. Laud's victim during his long imprisonment. He read, too, Lord Brooke's "Discourse on Episcopacy," and got a further glimpse of that toleration which was as yet so little understood by either side in the great struggle. But, through all, the grievous wound in his heart made itself constantly felt, and the dreary emptiness of the world seemed to offer him no grain of comfort.

One night he remembered that the life, which seemed so unbearable as well as so useless, might at least be laid down for the country. Hilary had rejected him, but was not the Lord General at Worcester, and only too glad to accept any able-bodied man who would volunteer? It was well known that the Earl of Essex, Sir William Waller, Hampden, Cromwell—all the leading Parliamentarians, in fact—were profiting by the first repulse at Powick Bridge, and were straining every nerve to get soldiers of a spirit that would control such panic as had disorganised the men when they had unexpectedly encountered Prince Rupert.

Gabriel was alone in his father's study when this thought first came to him. The evening had closed in; his mother, weary with a long day's work, had retired early, and the doctor had been summoned to see a dying man in St. Owen's street.

It was characteristic of him that the very thought of temporising had never crossed his mind. He had not dreamed in London that public matters could possibly separate him from Hilary, but now that he had found how dearly he was to pay for his views, he was never even for a moment tempted to shrink back. The Harfords, as he had said, to the Bishop, did not change. Having once fairly studied the questions of the day, he would be true to the cause he adopted, cost what it might; and having once given his heart to a woman nothing could make him untrue to her.

On this Saturday evening, just a week after their unhappy dispute and parting, there came to him for the first time the sense of returning life. Of life, and even of a certain sweetness in life—for was it not his to lay down in a good cause? Soon, too, perhaps within a few days or weeks, it might all be over, and the pain which was making each hour a misery would be ended; his body would lie on some distant battlefield, and he would be free and at rest.

Stormy and wet as the night was he could not stay in the house, but wrapping his cloak about him strode down the garden and paced rapidly up and down the south walk. The place was haunted by memories of Hilary. How they had played and quarrelled and kissed and made it up again in the old times! How little they had dreamed in those happy, careless days what the joys and pangs of love really meant! And how very vague had been his childish notion of patriotism in the dusk of that December day when he had whispered to Sir John Eliot's snow effigy, the words, "I wish to be like you; I wish to give my life for the country's freedom!" Well, his chance had come. Here was the very opportunity he had ardently desired, but it had brought with it an agony that no child would have had the power to imagine.

At last a deluge of rain drove him into the little arbour and, impelled by some association of place, he drew forth the small leathern case which for the last two years he had always carried and looked at the dark glossy curl which Hilary had sent him. It was a rash thing to do, for the very touch of the soft hair broke down the stern self-control he had kept up through the week, while nature herself seemed to feel with him as the wild wind swayed the branches to and fro and the rain came down in torrents.

Lying there on the floor of the arbour he sobbed his heart out, tortured by the words of Hilary's last message—tortured more cruelly still by the memory of her relentless face as he had last seen it. At length a lull in the tempest began to influence him; he struggled to his feet again and looked out into the night. The rain had ceased for a few minutes; the cold, wet air revived him, and he stood watching the stormy sky and the bleak-looking moon which shone out now and again through rifts in the hurrying black clouds.

Cold and careless as the moon is of all the sorrow's she looks down on, no lover could ever resist the fascinations of her mysterious light. He thought he would look to-night for the last time at that grassy glade and at the old stone bench by the sweetbriar, where Hilary had been singing to her guitar on the day he first realised his love. Quietly opening the wicket-gate, he walked with sad steps over the soaking turf, wondering—as the young always must wonder—how it was possible that a joy such as theirs had been could have turned to such bitter anguish.

And then all at once the invincible hopefulness of youth came to his aid. It could not all be over! This love that he knew to be pure and true, was it possible that it should be wasted—cast away as a thing of little worth? To think that it could end would be to doubt God the Giver. In this world or the next they would yet be united.

He went to the bush of sweetbriar and gathered a spray, recalling as he did so the old folk-tale of the prince who at the right time had fought his way through the thorn hedge, and how the thorns had turned to roses, and the sleeping princess had been wakened at length by his kiss of love.

Perhaps Hilary's love was, after all, not dead, but only sleeping; perhaps his Princess Briar-rose would be wakened one day by a love which would fight its way to her, be the obstacles never so great.

At that moment screams coming distinctly from the direction of Mrs. Unett's house fell upon his ear. He knew well that Hilary and her mother were still at Whitbourne, and fearing that something must have gone amiss during their absence, he walked up to the door which led to the back premises, and knocked. At this, however, the screams only grew more piercing.

He called to Mrs. Durdle, asking what was the matter, and at last she was persuaded to open the door a few inches, and to peer cautiously out, her fat face almost the colour of the guttering tallow candle which she grasped in her capacious hand.

"Oh, Master Gabriel! I be glad to see you, we be that frightful!"

She used the Herefordshire phrase for being frightened, but Gabriel could hardly restrain a smile, for her terror had certainly not improved her looks.

"What has frightened you?" he asked, following her into the house. "And who in the world is making that noise?"

"Aw, sir, 'tis naught but Maria, she's always timbersome, and to-night there's good cause with the soldiers clamouring at Byster's Gate."

"What soldiers?" exclaimed Gabriel in astonishment. "I had heard naught."

"Parliament soldiers, sir," said Durdle, trembling. "Mick Thompson, my Valentine, he told me they've been standing outside these two hours, and he do think Price, the mayor, be going to let 'em in. Peace, you hussy!" she added, turning to shake the hysterical maid who had come out into the passage at the sound of a man's voice.

"Oh, sir! Oh, sir!" cried Maria, "don't let 'em kill us!"

"No, Master Gabriel, say a good word for me," said Durdle, imploringly. "For if I have called 'em Roundheads and traitors, 'tis the tongue which, as the Scripture says, is a deadly evil. You'll be witness, sir, that I always had a tongue that would be wagging; some are born that way, and others they be as mum as mice, but the quiet ones is often the most dangerous, being you don't know what to expect of 'em."

"Why, Durdle, do you take them for savages? They won't molest you," said Gabriel, with a smile.

"I'll never say another word agin the Parliament if only the soldiers will let me be and not come nigh the house," said Durdle. "But if they was to come here, and me left with naught but that screeching hussy for company, I should go stark mad with fright."

"I am joining the Parliamentary army myself," said Gabriel, "and my first piece of work shall be to guard this house, Durdle. And now let me out by the front door and bolt it after me; I must go across to Byster's Gate and see what has come to pass."

"Blessings on you, sir, for promising help to the defenceless," said Durdle, fervently. "I always did say there was a wonderful comfort in havin' a man to protect you."

Gabriel, not a little amused by the old housekeeper's confidence, hurried across the city to see what truth there was in her tale. The streets boasted no lamps, but there were lights in most of the windows, and a stir and bustle in the place which was certainly unusual at such an hour. Bye Street was thronged with people when at length he reached it, nor did anyone heed the heavy rain which once more came pouring down.

"Shame on the Mayor, say I," exclaimed a burly citizen.

"Nay, 'tis Alderman Lane that's the traitor," retorted another. "They do say he has persuaded the Mayor."

"What has chanced?" asked Gabriel.

"Why, sir, the Earl of Stamford is marching to besiege Hereford, and his advance guard has been parleying these two hours at the gate, standing knee-deep in the mud and mire."

"Here they come!" shouted a bystander. "Plague take the Mayor, he's letting in the cursed rebels."

And amid groans and jeers the men of the advance guard filed through Byster's Gate, so wet and weary that they were almost ready to drop.

Scanning them closely as they formed up within the gateway, preparing to stand on guard through the night, Gabriel caught sight of a well-known face, and hastened forward to greet Ned Harley.

"Welcome to Hereford!" he said, greeting him warmly.

"There are not many that will join with you there," said Ned laughing. "My father is with the main body; they will enter, no doubt, to-morrow morning, and will at least be spared standing to the mid-leg in dirty water, as we have been for the last two hours."

"You are half frozen," said Gabriel.

"Ay, and half-starved to boot," said Ned Harley. "Such foul weather never was! We have had naught but snow and rain since we started, and one of our soldiers died on the march so bitter was the cold."

Gabriel tried to picture Lady Brillianas dismay could she have seen her favourite son in his forlorn plight, for Ned, at the best of times, was far from strong. Meantime, the citizens, having had a good look at the soldiers, withdrew, bolting and barring their doors; and it was with much difficulty that fuel was procured for the great fires which the officers ordered to be kindled in the street. Gabriel was doing his best to help with these when he was joined by his father, and they worked with a will to get food for the weary men, retiring after midnight, and taking Ned Harley with them for the rest he sorely needed.

When his friend had been fed and warmed, and left to the blissful quiet of a great four-post bed in the guest chamber, Gabriel followed his father to the study. The doctor was smoking his short clay pipe beside the fire, and he looked with a certain expectancy at his son, whose change of expression was noteworthy.

"Sir," said Gabriel, "I crave your leave to join the Parliamentary Army. I had determined to ask it before the arrival of Lord Stamford's force, but this will make matters still easier and to-morrow Sir Robert Harley himself will be here."

The doctor's face was sad, and he sighed heavily.

"I am not surprised that you wish to serve," he said. "I will try not to grudge you to the good cause, my son. But God grant that this fratricidal war may be a brief one."

"Were it not a war in defence of our rightful liberties, I would never draw sword, sir," said Gabriel. "But since the discovery of the Army Plots I know you also hold that there was naught for the Parliament to do but in defence of the country's rights to seize on the Militia and prepare us to face foes from without and from within. The King makes specious promises 'on the word of a King,' but his word has been proved to be wholly untrustworthy. They say he is swayed by evil counsellors, and if so, let us fight to deliver both King and country from that curse. I for one would gladly enough die."

"Lad," said Dr. Harford, reading his thoughts, "you are sore-hearted and in great heaviness, but forget not that your life is a sacred trust; fight like a brave soldier, but give me your promise that you will not rashly plunge into peril for the sake of ending a pain which you should live to conquer."

Gabriel was silent, he leant his head on the carved wooden chimney-piece and looked down into the glowing embers.

"Remember," said Dr. Harford, "that thousands have to bear just what you are bearing, and that some weakly succumb or sink to lower levels, while others, like your hero, Sir John Eliot, make pain and harsh treatment and contumely so many stepping stones in their career."

"I see not how pain of this sort is to be conquered," said Gabriel, still watching the embers in which his fancy could picture Hilary's face.

"Live on bravely, and you will find that it will be conquered by life," said the doctor. "Remember the poet's saying:

'He life's war knows,

Whom all his passions follow as he goes.'

And may God Almighty spare you to me, my son."

With those words to hearten him Gabriel volunteered his services to Sir Robert Harley, who entered the city with the Earl of Stamford and Sir Richard Hopton on the Sunday morning, taking up his quarters in the Bishop's Palace. It was hard to enter the place associated so much with Hilary under these strange new conditions.

"I will write you a recommendation to Sir Philip Stapleton," said Sir Robert. "Hundreds of gentlemen have volunteered, and though you begin as many of them do in the ranks, you are certain to get promotion."

Gabriel thanked him, but as he stood waiting for the letter a sharp stab of pain went to his heart, for he caught sight of a painting of Hilary as a child, her eyes looking straight into his with that curious dignity, that "touch me if you dare!" expression which she had always been wont to assume when confronted by strangers.

On the following Tuesday he bade farewell to his father and mother, and in company with Edward Harley and the forlorn hope, left Hereford for Worcester, where the Earl of Essex with a military committee of twelve noblemen of the county was endeavouring to bring the neighbourhood into thorough subjection to the Parliament. Before long, as all realised, the two armies were bound to find that opportunity for a pitched battle which they both eagerly desired. And in the meanwhile Gabriel, amid the duties of drilling, and the work which fell to his share, fought out his own private battle in manly fashion, not forgetting his father's words as to the sacredness of life, yet not wholly without a lingering hope that the coming fight might end a life that had grown distasteful.

CHAPTER X.

"Some day the soft ideal that we wooed

Confronts us fiercely, foe-beset, pursued,

And cries reproachful, 'Was it, then, my praise,

And not myself was loved? Prove now thy truth;

I claim of thee the promise of thy youth;

Give me thy life, or cower in empty phrase,

The victim of thy genius, not its mate!'

Life may be given in many ways,

And loyalty to truth be sealed,

As bravely in the closet as the field,

So bountiful is fate;

But then to stand beside her,

When craven churls deride her,

To front a lie in arms and not to yield,

This shows, methinks, God's plan,

And measure of a stalwart man."

—Lowell.

It was on Wednesday, October 19, that the main body of Essex's army set out from Worcester, and after making slow progress, owing to the terrible state of the roads, they reached the little market town of Kineton between nine and ten o'clock on the Saturday evening. The people, who in those parts were favourable to the Parliament, received them with no little kindness, and Gabriel soon found himself in comfortable quarters in the house of a certain Manoah Mills, a saddler, whose wife, Tibbie, was eager to bestow the good supper she had provided on six of the soldiers she thought most in need of it.

The worthy couple stood in their doorway to make choice of their guests. "We will have naught but knowledgeable men," said Manoah, shaking his bald head shrewdly. "Good talkers that can tell us the news, and good men that can argue a point in theology."

"Nay," said Tibbie, "but I will have for one yon lad with the sad eyes, he's sore in need of mothering, by the look of, Pshaw! a mere boy, and not even an officer," protested Manoah.

But Tibbie had a will of her own, and while her husband brought in some shrewd and knowledgeable men to his taste, she beckoned to Gabriel. "Me and my husband can give you shelter for the night, sir, and a good supper, if you'll step in. 'Tis hard if those who are fighting for us can't get food and lodging on a cold night like this," she said.

Gabriel thanked her, and gladly sat down to the excellent supper of fried eggs and bacon, and rye bread which the good woman provided; but when the "knowledgeable men" passed from the events of the day to a warm argument on a difficult point in theology, he fell far below Manoah's standard, not being able to take any interest at all in the discussion, but growing more and more sleepy, till at length, when he had nodded violently in the middle of his host's eager remarks on election and fore-ordination, Tibbie kindly pointed to an old oak settle by the fire. Here he stretched himself in great content, and leaving the theologians to edify themselves with their favourite pastime, was soon lulled by their voices into dreamless sleep.

Sunday was to be a day of rest, and he woke with a relieved consciousness that there would be no more ploughing their way knee deep in mud through the country lanes. Tibbie provided them with an excellent breakfast, and was just expressing her admiration of the way in which they all prepared to attend morning service at the Church, when the bugle sounded "to arms," and like wild-fire the news ran through Kineton that the King was only two miles from them. Already the Royalist cavalry were forming on the top of Edgehill, a high hill overlooking the little market town, and Essex promptly drew out his forces in the open ground between, lining the hedges and enclosures which lay upon one side with musketeers.

Gabriel, in the Lord General's regiment under Sir Philip Stapleton, found himself on the right wing next to Lord Brooke's purple-coated troop, on the one side, and to Cromwell's troop on the other.

Then came the apparently interminable waiting which most severely tries those who have never before been under fire. The day was cold and windy, moreover, and much rain had fallen during the night; to wait hour after hour while the King's army massed itself on Edgehill was far from inspiring.

At length, about one o'clock, when it became apparent that Essex was too good a general to scale heights guarded by a far more numerous army, and intended to wait in the admirable position he had chosen, at some little distance from the foot of the hill, the Royalist forces were brought down into the plain, and somewhat before three o'clock the dull roar of the cannon began. Then the Royalists advanced to the charge, and the left wing of the Parliamentary army, thrown into utter confusion through the treachery of Sir Faithful Fortescue, who had previously arranged with Prince Rupert to change sides on the field, broke and fled before Rupert's fiery charge. Their panic, though partly checked by Denzil Holies, would certainly have ruined the hopes of the Parliamentary army had not Rupert been carried away by his usual impetuous zeal, and hotly pursued them as far as Kineton, where the sight of the valuable baggage waggons proved irresistible to him, and he and his troopers, totally ignoring the battle, lingered over the plunder till they were perforce driven back to the field by the advance of the Parliamentary rear-guard under Hampden and Grantham.

Meanwhile, Gabriel, who had had the good fortune to be in the admirably steadfast right wing, had passed through some strange experiences.

During the first exchange of cannon shots after those long hours of waiting, and before the first Royalist charge, a sickening imagination of what awaited them, for a minute half-paralysed him. He was grateful to a rugged-looking Scotsman beside him, who, understanding his sudden pallor, said: "Hoots, laddie, a' that will pass by; think that the Cause has muckle need o' just yer ain sel'."

And at that minute, glancing towards the next troop, Gabriel perceived Cromwell a little in advance of his men, not looking harassed, as he had often seen him in London on his way to the House of Commons, but with an indescribable light in his strong, noble face—the light of one inspired: while from the manly voices of his troopers there rang out the psalm which, for Gabriel, would be for ever associated with Hilary and the morning in the cathedral when both had been so full of heaviness.

In trouble and adversity

The Lord God hear thee still,

The majesty of Jacob's God

Defend thee from all ill.

What followed was more like some wild nightmare than like real waking existence; for awhile it seemed that the Parliamentary right wing was to be annihilated as the left had been, for beneath the splendid charge of Wilmot's men Fielding's regiment suffered grievously. By a rapid and clever movement Balfour and Stapleton slipped aside, that they might outflank the enemy, but Wilmot made precisely the same mistake made by Prince Rupert, and pursued the remnant of Fielding's men, failing utterly to reckon with the men led by Cromwell, Balfour and Stapleton, who with great skill hemmed in the Royalists and fought with a desperate courage that carried all before it.

Of how matters were going Gabriel had scarcely a thought; he could realise only his near surroundings. He saw his Scotch neighbour drop to the ground, killed instantly by a ghastly injury of the head, and he sickened at the sight, till the memory of the dead man's words came back to him. "The Cause has muckle need o' just yer ain sel'."

The next minute, with a horrible shriek, his horse reared wildly, and he found himself on the blood-stained turf. Struggling to his feet, still half-stunned by the shock, he snatched at the bridle of the dead Scot's horse, and, mounting it, pressed eagerly forward, fighting now with an ardour and an impassioned zeal which he had not before felt. The Royalists were making a strenuous resistance, but they could not stand against the splendid charge of the Parliamentary troops, who, utterly undaunted by the line of pikes, pushed on with a steadfastness that was destined to retrieve their fortunes.

For Gabriel, however, it was soon merely a matter of blocking the way with his body, his second horse fell a victim, and as he leapt to the ground a pikeman ran him clean through the thigh; then came a crash and a sudden darkness, after which for some time he knew no more.

When he slowly revived and became conscious of the confused din of battle he for a moment thought himself in hell; the most horrible and unearthly screams close by made him shudder, and the pain of his wound, of which till then he had only been dully aware, became intolerable agony, as his shrieking horse in its dying struggles plunged on to him.

"God!" he cried, in his torture, "let me die!"

His words were heard. At that moment a horseman close by sharply reined back his galloping steed, put a pistol to the head of the plunging horse and ended its death agony, then, swiftly dismounting, bent for a moment over Gabriel, with a look of ineffable pity as he dragged him into a less torturing position.

He was a short man, and to Gabriel's astonishment he wore the dress of a Royalist officer. Where had he before seen that broad-browed, kindly-eyed, yet decidedly plain face?

"Poor lad, I can do no more for you," said a quiet voice which could scarcely be heard in the uproar.

"My Lord Falkland!" cried Gabriel, in amazement. "You!"

And then before he could say a word of gratitude, the black cloud began to steal over him once more and his eyes closed.

Falkland thought him dead, and remounting, rode back to rejoin Wilmot and urge him to attempt a decisive charge, for, like so many, he clung to the hope that the war might be ended by one great battle. At the same moment Hampden was urging a similar request to Essex, but the Generals on either side refused to venture a further attempt, and the gathering twilight gave them some excuse. The King's standard-bearer, Sir Edward Verney, had been killed; the Royal Standard was taken; thousands of men lay dead or dying on the blood-stained plain, and the drawn battle of Edgehill was over.

Gabriel's swoon must have lasted long, for it was quite dark when he again came to himself, he was too weak from loss of blood to wish definitely to live, though still the dead Scotsman's words sounded in his ears and braced him to a certain extent, kept him, at any rate, from voluntarily letting go his precarious hold on life. Then a memory of Falkland's pitying face came back to him, and he tried to think how it could have been possible that the Secretary of State should be there just at that minute. Early in the afternoon he had seen him with Wilmot's men and had been surprised that one in his position should have exposed himself so needlessly. It must, he imagined, have been while returning with Wilmot from the pursuit of Fielding's routed troop that he had chanced to ride in his direction. He moved a little, longing to make out where he lay, and how the day had gone, but the frightful agony of the attempt quickly made him desist; he sank down with his head propped up a little on the dead body of the horse which Falkland had put out of its pain.

And now he could make out here and there fires at some little distance on his left, while two or three fires on the top of Edgehill led him to think that the Royalists had retired again up the heights, and that Essex's army intended to remain on the field throughout the night. Doubtless, in the morning, hostilities would be resumed.

The far away sound of a psalm raised him for a time above his pain; he prayed silently for the cause that had cost him so dear, and his thoughts wandered back to his home and to Hilary. How her face would have lighted up if he could have told her about Lord Falkland! Somehow, he could almost fancy the same pitying tone in her voice, had she come upon him in so terrible a plight. The thought gave him no little comfort.

But what was this horrible cold creeping over him? This icy chill which made the torture of his wound almost intolerable? Was this how death came when men were left to bleed on the battle-field? Was the death he had once so ardently desired coming to him now? All the youth within him rose up as if in protest. He longed, with an agony of longing, to live, and be once more physically strong.

Very quickly, however, the lifelong habit of direct and most simple communion with the Unseen came to his aid. And in answer to his cry he heard the comforting words, "The beloved of the Lord shall dwell in safety by Him." What did it matter whether life went on here or in some other world, since neither death, nor life, nor principalities, nor powers, could separate him from the love of God?

The sharp frost and the bitter, nipping cold of that autumn night killed some of the wounded, but saved many by the painful process of freezing their wounds and thus staunching the blood. When the age-long hours had been lived through, and the next day dawned, Gabriel was quite unable to move, even when he heard footsteps and voices close by, he was too dull and exhausted to call for aid; it was not until a young, vigorous-looking man, with a mass of wavy golden hair, stooped over him, that he raised himself to see whether he had fallen into the hands of friend or foe. The green coat and orange scarf told him in a moment that this was one of Colonel Hampden's men.

"What of the battle?" he asked, faintly.

"Neither side was wholly victorious, but in the main they say that we made the best fight, as our infantry and cavalry acted better together. But doubtless the finest charge of the day was Prince Rupert's."

The momentary light in Gabriel's face died out. The speaker broke off hurriedly and moistened the dry lips of the wounded man with water.

"You are badly hurt," he exclaimed. "We will get you carried to Kineton, where the surgeons will attend to you."

"Let me be!" said Gabriel, wearily. "The war has robbed me of all I value in life; for God's sake, let me die in peace."

"That will I not," said the other, firmly. "You are but worn out with suffering; remember that the country yet needs you."

He beckoned to two soldiers with a roughly extemporised litter, and then went on to look for others in need of help.

"Who is yon officer?" asked Gabriel, as the men set down the litter beside him.

"'Tis Cornet Joscelyn Heyworth," replied the soldier, and without any loss of time he lifted Gabriel with little care and less skill from the ground, a process fraught with such hideous pain that a cry was wrung from his lips.

Joscelyn Heyworth hastily rejoined them.

"Take your water bottle to yonder man by the carcase of the white horse," he said. "I will help to carry this gentleman to Kineton."

Gabriel gave him a grateful look, but he was past speaking, and could with difficulty strangle his groans through the long rough journey.

At last he saw the church and the welcome sight of the houses in the little market town. His bearers hesitated for a minute as to where to take him.

"Try the house of Manoah Mills, the saddler," he said, with an effort. Somehow the recollection of Tibbie's motherly face carried with it a world of comfort.

"Here, lad," said Joscelyn Heyworth, beckoning to a small boy who was playing hop scotch as unconcernedly as though there were no such things as wars and fightings amongst them, "guide us to the house of Manoah Mills and serve one who suffers that you may live in safety."

The boy looked with awe at the bloodstained soldier on the litter and leading the way up the street knocked at the door of a gabled house, then stood aside as Tibbie appeared, and pointed her to the little group in the road.

"Woe worth the day!" she cried, running out with a face of pity. "Why,'tis Mr. Gabriel Harford that was our guest."

"Can you tend him and give him a bed to lie on while I fetch the surgeon?" said Joscelyn Heyworth. "He's badly hurt, and hath lain out in the frost all night."

"Bring him in, sir," said Tibbie. "He shall have the best bed in the house. Lord ha' mercy on us! To think that one so young should lie at death's door."

"Don't tell him that," said Joscelyn Heyworth. "An he thinks he's lying at the door, he will be minded to step inside." Very gently he set down his comrade in the room that Tibbie showed him, and took it as a good omen that his words called up an amused look in the dark hazel eyes which mutely thanked him for his help.

He had great hopes that the battle would be resumed and a more decisive action promptly fought out, but in this he was doomed to be disappointed. The day was spent in burying the dead and attending to the wounded and then the Royalist forces withdrew, while the Parliamentary army rested that night at Kineton.

Joscelyn Heyworth, finding himself with free time on his hands, went to the saddler's house again. Tibbie reported well of the patient, who, having had his wound attended to by the surgeon, had spent the greater part of the day in sleep, but was now, as she expressed it, "Turning contrairy, just like a man, and thinking himself worse when in truth he was mending."

"I will take a turn at watching by him," said Joscelyn. "You have had a hard day's work."

"Well, sir," said Tibbie; "I'll not deny that I'd as lief have a night's rest. My man's with him now; I'll show you up."

She led the way to the room to which the wounded man had been carried, and as she opened the door the voice of Manoah was heard discoursing on his favourite topic of election and foreordination. Gabriel lay wearily listening, and even the submissive Tibbie was roused by his look of patient endurance.

"Man!" she exclaimed, putting her hand on her husband's shoulder, and gently shoving him from his chair, "I do believe you'd talk the hind leg off a donkey! Theology's not for sickrooms, Manoah; go and discourse with them that's not been wounded."

Manoah made no objection, for what was the pleasure of arguing if there was no one to take the opposite side? He had never been able to drag more than a reluctant "possibly" or "perchance" from Mr. Harford. And theology, as he had severely told him, knew nothing of such vague words, but was a matter of "yea, yea," and "nay, nay."

However, he was somewhat mollified by Gabriel's courteous thanks for his hospitality and great anxiety to give as little trouble as possible. And he never noticed the look of relief with which the patient heard Joscelyn Heyworth's proposal to remain on night duty.

It seemed to Gabriel a long time since he had had a comrade of his own age and standing to talk to, and that strong link of contemporary life, in itself did him good, while naturally he was drawn to one so frank and friendly as his rescuer. There was a strength, too, about Cornet Heyworth which appealed to him; young as he was he nevertheless had the look and bearing of a man who had suffered for his convictions.

"How long have you been saddled with the saddler?" he asked, taking Manoah's vacant chair.

"For an hour by the clock," said Gabriel, "and never wished more for the use of my legs, that I might flee from his long tongue."

Joscelyn laughed.

"Oh! you are mending," he said, cheerfully. "Last time I saw you, you were not wanting to run but to die."

"A man's not responsible for what he says in extremity," said Gabriel. "'Twas an award's wish, and I'm ashamed of it now that I can think clearly."

"A wish to be fought and conquered," said Joscelyn, musingly. "But one that comes to us all in moments of the greatest suffering."

Then, with a little hesitation, he told Gabriel that the war had robbed him also in cruel fashion, and in listening to what he was willing to tell of his story, the wounded man forgot his own troubles, and the two began a friendship that was to stand them in good stead.

"I owe my life to you," said Gabriel, gratefully. "To you, and strangely enough, to my Lord Falkland."

He told of the incident on the previous day and of his amazement that the Secretary of State should be there.

"In truth," said Joscelyn Heyworth, "I heard from no less a person than Colonel Hampden's cousin, Cromwell, that my Lord Falkland had ridden about the field more as one that wished to spare life than to take it, and he had heard from others that the Secretary of State intervened several times when the Royalists would have slain the fugitives, and urged that they should have quarter on throwing down their arms."

"But as Secretary he was not bound to fight at all," said Gabriel.

"No, but 'twas well known that he ever counsels the King to make peace and, like all peacemakers, he is misunderstood and miscalled a coward; therefore, no doubt, he loses no chance to give the lie to those that taunt him, by throwing himself fearlessly into an unnecessary peril. Never has man been in harder case, for he is disliked now by both parties, and very scurvily treated, they say, by the King, who doth not like his plain-speaking and his scrupulous truthfulness."

"Why did he ever desert the Parliamentary cause to which he was once true?" said Gabriel.

"Colonel Hampden, who hath a great regard for him, says that he distrusted Archbishop Laud's teaching and his narrow intolerance, but dreaded the narrowness of the extreme Puritans even worse. Being thus in a strait betwixt two parties he, to Colonel Hampden's great sorrow, cast in his lot with our opponents."

"May God keep us from all evil passion in our fighting and make us as merciful foes as Lord Falkland has proved," said Gabriel, sorely perplexed in his mind as he recalled the fiery spirit which had possessed him after he had seen the ghastly death-wound of his Scottish comrade. With what a strange, fierce joy he had hurled himself and his steed against the Royalist pikes, and with what burning heat the blood had coursed through his veins! Yet now the mere remembrance of the awful sights he had seen turned him positively faint.

Joscelyn Heyworth made him take some of Tibbie's strongest cordial.

"I am but an ill nurse," he said, "and have let you talk over much. Remember that the noblest men on both sides have tried their very utmost for years to settle matters peacefully; this is a last stand for freedom and truth against kingly despotism which, in the end, would leave England a prey to Rome, for the King is ruled by the Queen, and the Queen is ruled by her confessor."

Gabriel remembered the dead Scotsman's words, and they rang in his ear in very comforting fashion as at last he fell asleep.

His rescuer watched him thoughtfully. He had spoken of his home and his parents, clearly the war had not robbed him of them; it must, then, be some yet dearer tie that had been severed. And long before the morning dawned Joscelyn knew practically the whole story, for all through the night the feverish wanderings of the wounded man took the form of last interviews and broken-hearted partings with a maiden named "Hilary," who refused to remain betrothed to one she thought a rebel and a traitor.

CHAPTER XI.

Love doth unite and knit, both make and keep

Things one together, which were otherwise,

Or would be both diverse and distant.

—Christopher Harvey.

It was not until the latter part of October that Hilary and her mother returned to Hereford. The news of the occupation of the city by the Earl of Stamford had kept them longer at Whitbourne than had been expected; but the cold of the country did not suit Mrs. Unett, and both mother and daughter were glad to settle down once more in their own home.

Unfortunately, all the girl's gentle thoughts had been banished by hearing of the occupation of Hereford by the Parliament's army. She was once again a vehement little hater, and was revelling in the thought of the resolute way in which she would keep Gabriel at a distance, refusing even to notice him if they passed in the street.

As a matter of fact, the city looked exactly as usual on their return, not a shot had been fired, no harm had been done to the cathedral, and except for the discomfort of having soldiers in the place, few people had complaints to make. Even Durdle shocked her young mistress by the favourable way in which she spoke of the army.

"They do say there was some mischief done to Mrs. Joyce Jefferies' house," she admitted, "for she and Miss Acton they fled to Garnons in a panic. But had they stayed here all would have been well, for Mr. Gabriel Harford would have taken care of them as he did of us."

Hilary's face flamed, but she was too proud to question the housekeeper.

"He was down in the garden the night the soldiers was clamouring at Byster's Gate," resumed Durdle, after a pause, "and hearing Maria screaming, he came to the door to ask if aught was amiss, and no one could have been kinder like, nor did he ever let a soldier come nigh the house. And he came to bid me farewell on the fourth of October, when he went away to Worcester to join the army, and spoke that civil and pleasant just as though he'd been naught but a lad still."

Hilary's brain seemed to reel; she made a pretence of stooping to pick up a tortoiseshell cat which dozed by the kitchen fire.

"Bad puss, have you been eating blackbeetles, to grow so thin?" she exclaimed, stroking her pet with well-assumed indifference.

"What was that you were saying about Worcester, Durdle?"

The good-natured housekeeper gasped, her simple mind could not in the least understand the subtle workings of Hilary's more complex nature.

"Talk about pussy's bowels being injured by beetles," she said to herself, "'tis my belief the lassie has no bowels at all. Was ever such a heartless speech!"

"Well, Mistress, I was saying how Mr. Gabriel Harford had gone to join the Earl of Essex's army, along with his friend Mr. Edward Harley that was at Oxford with him."

"Oh, indeed," said Hilary, carrying her head high. "Dr. Rogers tells me the troopers stabled their horses in the nave and cloisters at Worcester. Send up Maria to fetch my cape and hood, Durdle; they got crushed in the coach, and had best be ironed."

Then humming a cheerful song, she quitted the kitchen and sauntered out into the garden, her heart throbbing as if it would choke her.

"He has joined the rebel army, and 'tis my fault," she thought, in anguish. "If he is killed, his death will be my doing! Oh, why was I so cruel? Naught I could say would have changed his views, but at least he would have gone quietly back to his studies had I not taunted him."

Every nook in the garden seemed haunted by memories of lost happiness, she could not pass the sunny wall to which the apricot trees were fastened, or look towards the stone bench by the briar bush, without seeing in fancy her lover's face; and she knew very well why he had wandered into that special place on the night of the servants' alarm about the soldiers.

The sound of the gardener singing, as he gathered the apples, smote discordantly on her ear, and specially when drawing nearer she caught the doleful words of an old ballad called "The Wife of Usher's Well," in which the ghosts of the three dead sons return to their home, but can only remain for the briefest of visits. The gardener sang with stolid cheerfulness as he filled his basket:

"The cock doth craw, the day doth daw

The channerin' worm doth chide;

Gin we be mist out o' our place,

A sair pain we maun bide.

Fare ye weel, my mother dear!

Fareweel to barn and byre!

And fare ye weel, the bonny lass,

That kindles my mother's fire."

Turning hastily away to escape this dismal ditty she reentered the house, and was glad to encounter her favourite uncle, Dr. William Coke, who, during Gabriel's absence in London, had been appointed to the living of Bosbury, vacant on the death of old Mr. Wall. He had not been among the very few who had been told of Hilary's betrothal, and this fact made her now more at ease with him than with her grandfather or her mother. For a minute she forgot her troubles.

"We have but just returned from Whitbourne, sir," she said, cheerfully. "'Tis indeed good of you to come to us."

"I thought, maybe, your mother would be disturbed at today's news, and rode over to have a chat with her," said Dr. Coke, his genial face clouding a little.

"We have heard no fresh news," said Hilary, eagerly. "What has happened, sir?"

"There has been a great battle in Warwickshire, nigh to Kineton, and though at first all thought the King's troops would be victorious, in the end it proved but a drawn battle, both sides suffering grievously, and naught gained to either. They tell me that thousands lie dead on the field."

His sorrowful face made Hilary realise more than she had yet done what war meant; her head drooped as she remembered her exultation over the fifty Parliament men killed at Powick Bridge, and recalled Gabriel's look of reproach. Very few details had as yet been learnt, and when she had heard all her uncle could tell her she left him to talk with Mrs. Unett, and for the sake of being free and undisturbed sought the cathedral—the only place, save the garden, to which she was allowed to go without an attendant.

Entering by the great north porch, she walked through the quiet, deserted building to the north-east transept, and went to a little retired nook by an arch in the north wall, where lay the effigy of Bishop Swinfield. Here she had often come for quiet during the two years of her betrothal, partly because it was a place where no one was likely to notice her, and partly on account of her recollections of the snow effigy which she and Gabriel had once fashioned after this pattern, in honour of Sir John Eliot. Behind the tomb was a beautifully sculptured bas-relief of the Crucifixion, and Hilary saw, with satisfaction, that it had not been injured at all by the Earl of Stamford's soldiers, who, according to Durdle, had only visited the cathedral on Sunday morning, when they had been somewhat disorderly, and had grumbled that prayers were said for the King, but never a word for the Parliament.

She knelt long in the quiet, and when she once more turned her steps homeward her remorse was less bitter and more practical, and at last, after a hard struggle, she conquered her pride, and knocked at Dr. Harford's door, asking whether she could see Mrs. Harford.

Now Gabriel's mother was one of those women whose affections are strictly limited to their own families. In so far as outsiders were useful to her husband or her son, she liked them; but if they caused her beloved ones the least trouble or pain, she most cordially hated them.

So when Hilary conquered herself sufficiently to pay this visit, Mrs. Harford, unable to see any point of view but her own, received the girl in a most frigid way.

"We have but just returned from Whitbourne," said Hilary, blushing, "and I called to inquire after you, ma'am."

"I am as well as any of us can hope to be in these troubled times," said Mrs. Harford, coldly.

There was an awkward pause, broken at last by an inquiry for Mrs. Unett. Hilary tried desperately to prolong her answer. At the close came another pause.

"We have but just heard from my uncle, Dr. Coke, of the great battle in Warwickshire," she said, falteringly. "Have you had any news, ma'am?"

The mother looked searchingly into the girl's blushing face. "Yes," she replied, "only an hour or two since a messenger brought me a letter from Lady Brilliana Harley, who had heard from her husband. He wrote the day after the battle."

The silence that followed almost maddened Hilary. "Were Sir Robert and Mr. Harley safe?" she asked.

"Quite safe!" said Mrs. Harford, resolved not to spare the girl or help her out in any way. It was some slight satisfaction to her to see this proud maiden suffer.

"And Gabriel?" she faltered. "He was safe, too?"

"Alas, no!" said the mother, with a sigh.

Hilary turned white, but asked no more questions. As if from a great distance she heard the silence at length broken by Mrs. Harford's voice.

"They gave him up for lost that night, but the next morning a young officer, Mr. Joscelyn Heyworth, found him on the field and there was still life in him. They carried him to Kineton, and he lies there grievously wounded."

The girl rallied her failing powers and became obstinately hopeful. "He is young and strong," she said, with forced cheerfulness. "He is sure to recover. My mother will be very sorry to hear your ill news, and—and—if you should again have tidings, she would be glad to hear, I know."

"We cannot hope to hear again," said Mrs. Harford. "It was only by great good fortune that Sir Robert Harley was able to get a letter to Lady Brilliana, and we are little like to hear from Gabriel himself, even if he were well enough to write. This is the hard part of war, the terrible waiting for news." After formally polite farewells Hilary found herself going down the broad oak staircase with dim eyes; but Neptune, Gabriel's favourite spaniel, stood wagging his tail in most friendly fashion in the entrance-hall, and her sore heart was a little comforted when he bounded up to lick her hand as if he recognised the fact that she was still in some subtle way connected with his master.

Unwilling to pass through the street with eyes brimming over with tears, she went back through the garden and by the little wicket gate. But the sight of the sunny south walk did not raise her spirits, and with the terror that even now Gabriel might be lying dead at Kineton, she could hardly endure the sound of the gardener's dismal ditty. He still toiled away at the apple gathering, and still chanted, in lugubrious tones, the gruesome words:

"The cock doth craw, the day doth daw,

The channerin' worm doth chide-"

Hurrying away from this unbearable song and half blinded by tears, she suddenly found herself brought to a pause by Dr. William Coke, who was standing at the door that he might more closely inspect in the sunshine a fossil which they had brought back from Whitbourne.

"Whither away so fast, little niece?" he said in his genial voice. Then catching sight of the wet eyelashes, "Eh, what is amiss, my dear?"

"'Tis only that the stupid gardener will sing gruesome ballads about graves and channerin' worms just on this special day when we have heard how thousands are dead and dying at Kineton," said Hilary.

He sighed as he patted her shoulder, caressingly.

"True, child, it is indeed a dark day for England. May God send us peace! But dwell not on that thought of the grave. Remember rather the words, 'The souls of the righteous are in the hands of God.'"

"But they were not all righteous," said Hilary, in a choked voice.

"True, yet all belong to Him."

"Many were rebels," she said, "and Dr. Rogers thinks that all rebels will burn for ever in hell."

"My dear, though Dr. Rogers is a learned man, he knows no more than the rest of us about the future state. I would even venture to say," and here Dr. Coke's eyes twinkled, "that he knows less than many, for his heart is not dominated by love but by zeal for orthodoxy, a thing which some folk mistake for the following of Christ. And though, as you know, I am loyal to His Majesty, I am bound to own that there has been much in his rule which rightly roused the indignation of free Englishmen, and I see that even in my own parish many of the best and the most God-fearing men have felt it to be their duty to resist the King and to join the Parliamentary forces."

Hilary was comforted by these words, and through that weary autumn, while they vainly hoped for news of Gabriel, she often thought of them, and something of her uncle's wider and nobler way of looking at things began to dispel the bitter and contemptuous spirit which' Dr. Rogers's teaching had fostered in her. Happily for her, he was not just then in residence, and in his absence her heart had some chance of softening and expanding.

At length Christmas came and with it the question whether, for the first time in her life, she should ignore her next-door neighbours. She had not dared to approach Mrs. Harford since the day she had heard that Gabriel was wounded at Edgehill. But she had once or twice encountered the doctor, and he had always paused to greet her kindly and to tell her that, as yet, no further news had reached them. He quietly assumed that she still took some interest in Gabriel, and by his tact and courtesy steered her safely through the difficult renewal of friendly relations.

On Christmas Eve she summoned up her courage and carried to the next-door house a basket full of orange cakes of her own making, which for years she had been in the habit of taking to Dr. Harford for the festival.

She found him in his study, looking less careworn than he had done of late. "So you have not forgotten your old friend?" he said, saluting her with more than his usual kindliness of manner. "Here are holly and mistletoe to remind us of Pagan and Druid rites, now happily at an end, and

'Here's rosemary; that's for remembrance.'

I am right glad that the maiden I have known from cradle days hath a kind remembrance of her old neighbour, who is yet not too old to enjoy orange cakes of her making."

"My mother sends you the season's greeting, sir," said Hilary; "and she would have visited Mrs. Harford, but she keeps the house to-day with a very great cold."

"I am sorry to hear that," said the doctor. "You must have a care of her this winter, Hilary, and let her run no risks. She will, I know, rejoice with us that we have at length heard good news of Gabriel."

He carefully avoided looking at the girl, but was glad to hear the tremor in her voice as she exclaimed, "Oh! have you indeed heard from him? Then there is no need to wish you a happy Christmas, for I am sure you have it."

He turned away and made a pretence of searching for the letter, all the time knowing perfectly well where it was. "Take this with you and read it to Mrs. Unett," he said, still avoiding the girl's eyes. "She will be glad to know that he hath made a good recovery."

Hilary thanked him and made haste to depart. She did not pause to analyse her feelings—life was more simple in those days; but in her glowing face, and even in her quick, eager step as she entered the withdrawing-room, Mrs. Unett read the truth. She had dismissed Gabriel in hot anger, but love for him still lingered in her heart. Would its flickering light kindle once more into lasting warmth and brightness, or would the icy-cold breath of political strife in the end prevail, and finally extinguish it?

She knelt in the ingle nook close to her mother's armchair, and together they read the letter:

"My Dear Sir,—You will doubtless have heard through Sir Robert Harley that I was left at Kineton, with other wounded men, after the fight. Thanks to the rescue of one Mr. Joscelyn Heyworth, and the care of Tibbie Mills, wife of a worthy saddler of Kineton, my wound—a pike wound through the right thigh—healed by the end of November, and learning that my Lord of Essex' army was in the neighbourhood of London, I rode there by easy stages and sought out Sir Robert. I found that Ned, who had been serving under Sir William Waller, hath himself now command of a regiment of foot, and as fresh men were being sent down to Sir William the second week in December, I was ordered to go with them. This left me some days in London, which I spent at Nottinghill; my grandmother gave me a very hearty welcome, and was glad to hear the latest tidings of you and of my mother. Who should I find staying in her house, and painting her portrait, but M. Jean Petitot, the miniature painter? Whereupon she insisted that he should paint my portrait also on enamel, and she intends, when a fit chance arrives, to send it by some trusty bearer to you, for she was right glad, she said, that you had not grudged your only son to the good cause. When you see the miniature, I fear you will quote the scurrilous satire put forth by the Royalists:

This is a very Roundhead in good truth!'

For Tibbie acted the part of Delilah, and shaved off my long hair at Kineton, to the great satisfaction of her husband, Manoah, a very strict Puritan, and to my great comfort as I lay ill. However, she hath left enough to curl over the head and round the nape of the neck, so that I do not take after the fanatic section, who shave their locks in a fashion that shows the very skin of the head, and reduces hair to bristles. There was a man in the Farnham garrison—a vile, sanctimonious hypocrite—who affected this style, and whose ears stuck out most horridly from his close-cropped skull.

"We quitted London the second week in December, and by night march reached Farnham Castle early one morning. You can judge how great my pleasure was to encounter again Mr. Joscelyn Heyworth, now appointed galloper to Sir William Waller. He is a little my senior, and a man that would be after your own heart—strong and vigorous and of a merry humour, though now somewhat downcast on account of family divisions, all his kinsfolk being of the King's party. Spite, however, of their differing views, he remains on very loving terms with some of them, though I learnt from one of Waller's officers that his father, Sir Thomas Heyworth, treated him with great harshness and severity, disinheriting him and disowning him. His friendship is the greatest boon I could have, and the sole thing in which I have found pleasure since the day we heard of the rout of Powick Bridge. We rested for ten hours at Farnham Castle, and then pushed on with the rest of Sir William Waller's force to Winchester, which yielded to us after a very short siege. We are now marching to attack Chichester, and have had a rough time, for the rain has come down in torrents for some days, and to lie in the wet fields o' nights doth not give much rest to such of us as have old wounds much prone to making themselves felt. To-morrow I have an opportunity of sending this to you, as a despatch-bearer is riding to Colonel Massey at Gloucester. I hope it may reach you by Christmas, and carry to you and my mother the season's greetings, and remembrance to any former friends who will receive such greeting from one of Sir William Waller's lieutenants.—I rest, dear sir,

"Your son to serve you,

"Gabriel Harford.

"Written this 17 th day of December, 1642, at Petersfield."

Christmas, with its unfailing call to realise the unity of the one great family, cannot be joyless, however sad its surroundings. Both to Gabriel, marching to besiege Chichester, and to Hilary in the quiet of the old home at Hereford, there came a sense of rest and peace which was not to be marred even by the miseries of a civil war.

But, unfortunately, with Easter came Dr. Rogers's term of residence, and there is no influence so deadly as that of a bitter and unscrupulous priest who, forgetting his ordination vow to maintain and set forwards quietness, peace, and love, among all Christian people, fans the flame of war, or upholds a tyranny that will ultimately ruin his nation.

CHAPTER XII.

"I know I love in vain, strive against hope,

Yet in this captious and intenible sieve,

I still pour in the waters of my love."

—Alls Well That Ends Well.

Gabriel Harford was not a man who made many friends, his great reserve, and a certain fastidious taste gave him an undeserved reputation for pride and exclusiveness. Moreover, all that he had gone through since Hilary's angry dismissal had tended to bring out the sterner and sadder side of his nature. He was respected as an indefatigable worker, but few really appreciated him.

Fortunately, he had found his complement in Joscelyn Hey-worth, a cheerful, buoyant and extremely sociable young officer, whose friendship had done much to save him from falling a prey to the bitterness too apt to overtake those who defend an unpopular truth.

He had also one other firm friend in the regiment—Major Locke, a grey-haired, middle-aged man, who had served in the German wars.

The Major was a character, and anyone looking at him as he sat one cold April evening in the chimney corner of a snug room at Gloucester would have fancied from his melancholy voice and long, grave face that he was a most strait-laced Puritan. Voice and face alike belied him, however, for he was, in truth, the wag of the regiment; and an occasional twinkle in his light grey eyes led a few shrewd people to suspect that he usually had a hand in the practical jokes which now and then relieved the tedium of the campaign. His jokes were always of a good-natured order, and had done much to keep up the men's spirits through that hard winter, with its arduous night marches, its privations and its desultory warfare.

Town after town had yielded to Sir William Waller, but the net result of the war was at present small.

On this evening the officers had dispersed soon after supper, weary with thirty-six hours of difficult manoeuvring, and one or two sharp skirmishes but they had been triumphantly successful in cutting through Prince Maurice's army, owing to Waller's skilful tactics, and all were now inclined to snatch a good night's rest in the comfortable quarters assigned them at Gloucester.

Gabriel, dead beat with sheer hard work, had fallen sound asleep in a high-backed armchair by the fire long before the others had satisfied their hunger; he woke, however, with a start as they rose from the table, responding sleepily to the general "good night," but loth to stir from his nook.

"Come, my boy," said the Major, "why sleep dog-fashion when, for once, you may have a bed like a good Christian?"

"I will wait till Captain Heyworth comes back," said Gabriel stretching himself and yawning in truly canine fashion.

"And that will not be over soon, for he will linger at Mr. Bennett's house, chatting to pretty Mistress Coriton, his promised bride."

"'Tis like enough," said Gabriel, with a sigh, recalling a glimpse he had had of Clemency Coriton's love-lit eyes as her betrothed had marched past the gabled house in the Close that evening. How they contrasted with those dark grey eyes which had flashed with such haughty defiance as Hilary had spoken her last hard words to him—"I will look on your face no more!"

"H'm," said the Major, "here he comes an I mistake not just as I had hit on a first rate trick to play him. No, 'tis one that knocks—see who it is, my boy, we want no visitors at this hour."

Gabriel crossed the room and threw open the door. A tall, handsome man, apparently about thirty, stood without, his long, tawny red hair, his fawn-coloured cloak, lined with scarlet, his rakish-looking hat with its sweeping feathers, together with the scarlet ribbons which were the badge of the Royalists, made him rather a startling apparition in the Puritan city of Gloucester, and especially at Sir William Waller's headquarters.

"Is Major Locke within? they told me I should find him here," he said in a voice which had something peculiarly genial in its mellow tones..

"The Major is here, sir," said Gabriel, ushering him in and wondering much who he could be.

"What, you, Squire Norton!" exclaimed Major Locke in astonishment, as he greeted him civilly, but with marked coldness—"Colonel Norton, at your service," said the visitor, with a short laugh that entirely lacked the pleasantness of his voice in speaking. "You are surprised to see me in the godly city of Gloucester."

"Well, sir, you are certainly the last person I should have desired as a visitor," said the Major, bluntly.

"Major Locke was my most frank and outspoken neighbour," said Norton, turning with one of his flashing smiles to Gabriel. "Next to a good friend commend me to a whole-hearted enemy who hates with a righteous and altogether thorough hatred. But, my worthy Major, you, as one of the godly party, should really obey all Scriptural injunctions. Is it not written, 'If thine enemy thirst, give him drink'?"

"Lieutenant Harford," said the Major, in his most lugubrious voice, "see that this gentleman has all that he requires. And in the meantime, Colonel Norton, I must ask you to explain your presence here."

"I accompanied a friend of mine who was allowed to pass the gates to-night with a letter from Prince Maurice to Sir William Waller. Your General is now writing the answer, and I had leave to seek you out on a private matter."

"I desire no private dealing with you, sir," said the Major, stiffly.

Norton laughed as he replied, "If Lieutenant Harford, who has so courteously heaped coals of fire on my head by filling me this excellent cup of sack, will withdraw, I will explain to you what I mean, Major. I assure you my intentions are wholly honourable."

The Major made an expressive gesture of the shoulders, evidently doubting whether he and his visitor put the same construction on that last word. Gabriel bowed and was about to leave the room when his friend checked him.

"Do not go, Lieutenant," he said, decidedly. "I wish to have you present as long as Colonel Norton remains."

"As you will," said Norton, easily. "I am here entirely in your interest, sir."

The Major drummed impatiently on the table.

"You seem to doubt that I have an eye to your interests," said Norton, laughing.

"Well, sir, I have known you all your life, and I dare swear 'tis the first time you have considered anyone except yourself," said Major Locke, sententiously.

"You have a cursed long memory," said Norton, cheerfully. "But look you, Major, I know for a certainty that, early to-morrow, Prince Maurice will send troops to besiege your house. The Manor is in a position which will serve his purpose, and he intends to have a garrison there. Your property will be ruined, your household turned out, or should they resist, made prisoners, or mayhap, slaughtered. With one word you can save such a disaster."

"And pray what word may that be?" said the Major, frowning.

"Your word of honour that you will give me your daughter Helena in marriage."

The Major flushed angrily.

"Sir," he said, indignantly, "to that request you have already had your answer."

"But the times have changed, Major, and I warn you that your answer had best change with them. Do you not see that I have your whole property in my power? Speak only this word and I will contrive that the Manor shall not be attacked, the Prince will easily be diverted from his plan, and I will get a special letter of protection for your whole household."

"Rather than see my daughter wedded to you," said the Major, sternly, "I would kill her with my own hand."

"I believe you would, my sturdy Virginius," said Norton, with a laugh. "However, I trust you will not come across her. To-morrow, when the Manor yields to Prince Maurice, my first thought shall be to take pretty Mistress Helena under my protection—no need in time of war for parsons or bridal ceremonies."

At that the Major sprang forward white with anger, and struck Norton on the mouth.

"Curse you!" cried the Colonel, drawing his sword. "If you will force a quarrel upon me, let us fight it out at once; but I call the Lieutenant to witness that the provocation——"

"Hold your lying tongue, sir," said the Major, pushing back the table and whipping out his sword, and the next moment the sharp clash of the blades rang through the room.

Gabriel was entirely absorbed in watching the combatants; he did not notice that a stalwart gentleman, with long, light brown hair and a short, pointed beard, had quietly opened the door behind him, and he started violently when Sir William Waller strode across the room, Joscelyn Heyworth closing the door as he followed his chief.

"Gentlemen!" exclaimed the General, striking up their swords. "What is the meaning of this?"

"Sir," said the Major, "I was bound to avenge a gross insult to my daughter."

"You must not fight a duel here," said Sir William, sternly. "Colonel Norton has a free pass, and I am bound to see that he returns in safety to Prince Maurice."

"It is an entirely private matter, sir," said Norton. "It will be a satisfaction to us both to carry the matter through."

"Very possibly," said Waller, giving Norton a keen glance with his blue-grey eyes, and quickly taking the measure of the man. "But private affairs, sir, must ever yield to public duties. Your companion awaits you, with my letter in reply to the Prince. I wish you good night, sir."

Norton, with a shrug of the shoulders sheathed his sword, donned his doublet and cloak, and, with a sweeping bow, waved his hat in farewell.

"Good-night, gentlemen," he said, with easy courtesy. "Major, to our next merry meeting!" and with an ironical smile and a mockingly profound bow to his enemy he strode out of the room.

"I crave your pardon, sir," said Major Locke, "but when that wolf in sheep's clothing shamelessly proclaimed his wicked designs on my child I could not restrain myself."

"Well, Major, we will say no more of the matter," said Waller. "I can well understand that your feelings as a father overpowered all remembrance of your duty as an officer."

"Sir, I implore you to let me ride home at once and place my daughter out of this villain's reach. He tells me that early to-morrow Prince Maurice intends to attack my Manor House, with a view to having a garrison there."

"These outlying garrisons are the curse of the country," said Waller, stroking his moustache meditatively. "Is your house capable of standing a siege if we sent a detachment to help them?"

"No, sir, not at such short notice, though it could be made a formidable place had we time."

"I cannot let you go off on a private errand to-night, Major. You are indispensable to me, and I have given my word to Massey that I will join him at Tewkesbury early tomorrow morning. We must march from here in three hours' time."

The poor Major moved away with a look of such despair that Waller, always a most kindly and considerate man, hastily turned over in his mind two or three schemes for aiding him.

"You say you could place your daughter out of Norton's reach. Where could you place her?"

"Here, sir, in Gloucester, under the care of my trusty friend, Alderman Pury. I know he would shelter her."

"Well, let your servant ride home now and fetch the lady, rejoining you to-morrow evening at Tewkesbury."

"My servant, sir, is the veriest dolt; I could not trust him with so risky a piece of work. Prince Maurice's army is in the near neighbourhood."

"Sir," said Gabriel, coming forward, eagerly, "I beg you to let me serve Major Locke in this matter. I was at school at Gloucester and know the neighbourhood well."

"So ho, young knight-errant!" said Waller, with his genial laugh. "You are in hot haste to rescue this fair lady, and I like you the better for it. But you are somewhat young for so hazardous a venture. We cannot tell what tricks this Colonel Norton may devise."

"If there were two of us, sir," said Joscelyn Heyworth, "we might the better outwit him."

"So you would have me spare my galloper also? Well, tomorrow's march is like to be a straightforward matter, not a difficult bit of manoeuvring like to-day. Rejoin the regiment to-morrow evening at Tewkesbury, and in the interval do what you can for Major Locke."

"We must leave our horses in Gloucester until we return with Mistress Helena," said Gabriel. "They are hackneyed out with all the work they have had."

"True. Latimer was sore spent," said Joscelyn Heyworth. "I will send my man Moirison to hire fresh horses, and by-the-bye, Major, I think we shall do well to take him with us, he is a shrewd fellow, and three horsemen will make a better escort for your daughter."

"Well, gentlemen, I can only accept your help very gratefully," said Major Locke. "To have my little Nell safely sheltered in Gloucester will ease my mind greatly. While you see to the horses, I will write her a letter telling her what I would have her do."

"I would have spared you if I could rightly have done so, Major," said Waller, pausing with his hand on the door. "But a man who has been through the German wars is worth his weight in gold, and I am bound to think first of the public weal."

CHAPTER XIII

"But I am ty'd to very thee

By ev'ry thought I have;

Thy face I only care to see,

Thy heart I only crave."

Sedley.

In an hour's time the preparations were made, and, furnished with a pass from Waller, the two friends, with Morrison, Captain Heyworth's servant, in attendance, rode through the sleeping city and, after a brief delay at the gate, passed out into the open country.

Gabriel forgot his fatigue in the excitement of this unexpected quest. The night was very still, and little fleecy white clouds floated in the moonlit sky; he began keenly to enjoy the prospect of thwarting Colonel Norton, whose brutal words to Major Locke had stirred up in him a resentment which was all the fiercer because he had at first been deceived by the pleasant voice and the buoyant cheerfulness of their visitor. Here was a man who might easily enough betray a young and ignorant girl. He could fancy only too well how Hilary would have been attracted by this light-hearted officer, with his ready smile and his merry-looking eyes; and the thought made him all the more eager to rescue little Helena Locke.

"Has the Major only this one child?" he asked.

"Ay," replied Joscelyn Heyworth, "'tis a case of

'One fair daughter and no more,

The which he loved passing well.'

She inherits the estate, and doubtless Colonel Norton has an eye to that."

They had ridden for some two hours, when Gabriel pointed to a tower darkly outlined against the pale sky. "Yonder lies the church," he said. "We take this turning to the right. What is that ahead? Surely I saw a light through the trees."

"Corpse candles in the churchyard, maybe," said Joscelyn.

"No, 'twas not near the church, but yonder. See, 'tis a light in a cottage; 'tis the gatehouse of the Manor."

"All the better," said Joscelyn, "they will be ready to open to us."

Without replying, Gabriel dismounted and looked closely at the marks on the road near the gate. "A couple of horsemen have just entered, I should say by these hoof-prints," he exclaimed. And picking up a pebble he threw it against the lighted window of the gate-house.

Immediately the door of the lodge was cautiously opened, and an old white-haired man put out his head. "Who goes there?" he cried.

"We have a message from your master, Major Locke, and have ridden in haste from Gloucester," said Gabriel.

The old man, looking much perturbed, took up his lantern and came out to the gate. "Why, that be strange," he said, scratching his head, as he noted the orange scarves with which their buff coats were girt, "you bring a message from master at Gloucester, and but ten minutes since I let in two gentlemen who brought a message from him at Little Dean, where they tell me he lies wounded and a prisoner."

"Was the messenger you admitted Colonel Norton?" asked Joscelyn Heyworth.

"Ay, 'twas young Squire Norton that lives over at Crawleigh Park; known master all his life he has, and was willing to show him a kindness and take Mistress Helena to him ere he die."

"Man," said Gabriel, impatiently, "'tis all a pack of lies. We serve under Major Locke and have left him but now in sound health at Gloucester; he knows that Colonel Norton means to entrap his daughter, and, being unable to come, has sent us to escort her safely to Alderman Pury's house. Here is a letter for her in your master's own hand if you doubt me."

The old man raised the lantern, but his eyes were fixed on Gabriel's face, not on the letter. "I can't read writing," he said, "but the Almighty's given me some skill in reading faces, and yours, sir, has truth in every line. I blame myself for trusting young Squire Norton, but the news that the master was at death's door dithered me, and that's a fact."

"Let us lose no time," said Gabriel, eagerly. "Will Colonel Norton have been long at the house?"

"Nay, sir; for it will take my son, who went with him, a bit of a time to rouse the household. Belike they may be still outside."

"Good; then let us leave the horses without the gate in charge of Morrison," said Joscelyn Heyworth, "and do you guide us to the house."

"We must steal in without noise," said Gabriel, quickly, "and, if possible, convey Mistress Helena away before Colonel Norton sees her. Where does that light come from?"

"It be in the window of the dining-hall," said the gatekeeper, keeping up with the two young officers by means of a shambling trot, which made his words come in a series of jerks and gasps. "But as sure as my name's Amos I don't see how you are to get speech of Mistress Helena now that Squire Norton has the start of you."

"I will see how the land lies," said Gabriel, lowering his voice as they drew near to the house. "Should Colonel Norton be in the hall you can surely convey us upstairs without his knowledge?"

"I'll do my best, sir, but 'twill be a difficult matter," said Amos.

They were walking, not on the carriage road, but over the bowling-green, and Gabriel now hastened noiselessly forward, and, swinging himself up by a sturdy little hawthorn which grew close to the house, he looked anxiously into the hall. It was a great, bare place, wainscotted with black oak, and lighted only by a couple of candles. A flagon of wine stood on the long, narrow table in the centre, and the visitors were refreshing themselves after their long ride. The Prince's messenger had his back to the window, and little was visible of him but his long dark lovelocks. Norton, at the opposite side of the table, lay back in a carved elbow-chair, a silver cup in his shapely hand, and the candle light full on his handsome, reckless face.

Gabriel saw at a glance that the hall was constructed on the usual plan of mediaeval houses, with a minstrels' gallery at the end nearest the outer door of the mansion, and beneath the gallery two open archways leading through the wooden screen to a passage traversing the house from front to back. Across one of the archways hung a thick crimson curtain, but the archway nearest the main door was exposed to view, the curtain having evidently been half drawn back on the arrival of the midnight guests.

He dropped down noiselessly from his post of observation.

"The two of them are in there drinking," he said, in a whisper. "Mistress Helena hath not yet come down. Is there any means of reaching her by the stairs leading to the gallery?"

"Ay, sir, the little stone stair leads up to the gallery, and on beyond to the upper rooms," whispered Amos, his shrewd old face lighting up as he began to hope for a successful issue.

"Good; then let us off with our boots, and steal through to the gallery stairs without a sound."

Amos stepped out of his broad low-heeled shoes easily enough, but the high riding-boots and spurs of the two young knights proved a more difficult matter, and Joscelyn Heyworth waxed so merry over their struggles that they came perilously near to an audible laugh. Their preparations made, the gatekeeper led the way up the steps to the main entrance, softly opened the door and admitted them into a flagged passage; a broad stream of light fell athwart the white stones from the archway on the right leading into the hall; they paused a moment before advancing, and to their relief heard that Norton and his companion were talking—under cover of their voices it would be easier to risk the perilous crossing to the stairs.

"This fair damsel takes a great deal of rousing," said the Prince's messenger. "Doth she intend to make a full toilette before coming down to hear of her father's plight?"

"We won't grudge her time to doff her nightcap," said Norton, "for i' faith, Tom, she hath the prettiest golden locks you ever saw. What shall I tell her of the old Major's wound? Shot through the lungs, eh? Life hangs on a thread? By the Lord Harry! I only wish it did," and he laughed boisterously.

Taking advantage of this noise, Gabriel put his hand on old Amos' arm and walked swiftly past the archway, and on beyond to the spiral staircase which lay concealed behind a door in the wainscot.

"What's that?" exclaimed Norton, "I thought I saw a shadow in the passage."

"Patience, man," said the other. "'Twas doubtless the fellow that let us in. I faith I begin to think your love for this pretty maid is hotter than most of your fancies. She will come all in good time; I drink to the success of your enterprise!"

"And I drink to fair Mistress Nell, the Queen of my heart!" said Norton.

He refilled his silver cup, and the three rescuers stole quietly up the dark staircase. Hardly, however, had they reached the level of the gallery when an exclamation from Norton crushed their hopes.

"And here in good sooth she comes!" he said, as sounds of approaching footsteps made themselves heard, and a flickering light began to play on the dark oak wainscot at the further end of the hall near the entrance to the main staircase.

Gabriel signed to his companions to pause on the spiral steps, and going down on his hands and knees crept cautiously into the gallery, which lay in deep shadow, but commanded an excellent view of the hall between the posts of the massive oak balustrade. He clenched his hands in hot anger when he saw how young and innocent and helpless was Norton's victim.

She came into the hall bearing a silver candlestick, and the flickering light revealed a face of childlike beauty, the cheeks still flushed with the sudden awakening from sound sleep, the blue eyes wide with anxiety and alarm. She had hurriedly thrown on a pink flannel sacque, and her fair hair hung in disorder about her shoulders. Norton stood still for a moment feasting his eyes on her loveliness, then he noticed that close behind her came a certain poor relation who had lived for many years at the Manor, a worthy lady of fifty, known as Cousin Malvina.

"I grieve to be the bearer of ill news," he said, saluting both ladies with great courtesy.

"Oh, sir, tell me all, and tell me quickly. How doth my father?" asked little Mistress Nell, her pretty eyes filling with tears.

"Nay," said Norton, "be not so distressed. He was sorely wounded to-day in a skirmish—you may doubtless have heard that Sir William Waller cut his way right through Prince Maurice's army in the forest; your father is now our prisoner, and lies at the Prince's headquarters at Little Dean. If you will don your riding-gear at once I will have a pillion put on my horse and take you to him."

"Sir," said Cousin Malvina, "it is out of the question that Helena should go with you now. You must wait till morning, then I will bring her in the coach."

"Dear madam, by morning it will be too late; her father lies at death's door, and he himself implored me to bring her to him without delay. Can you not trust an old neighbour?"

"You were a neighbour that my kinsman sorely distrusted," said Cousin Malvina, her grave face bearing an expression of great perplexity.

"But much is changed when we have but a short time to live," said Norton, unblushingly. "Come, madam, let bygones be bygones. You shall ride to Little Dean with us behind my friend."

"Dear Cousin Malvina, pray do not hinder us," said Helena, eagerly. "Perhaps with good nursing we may yet save my father's life. Come, let us go upstairs and dress. Come, please, come!"

The good lady was overpersuaded, and Norton, adjuring them to lose no time, accompanied them to the foot of the great staircase with so many signs of respect and kindly sympathy that Gabriel was fain to own him the cleverest as well as the most audacious villain he had ever encountered.

Creeping noiselessly back to the dim spiral stairs he begged Joscelyn Heyworth to keep a watch on Norton's doings while Amos took him to the other floor to speak to the two ladies. The old gate-keeper, who was trembling with rage and excitement, whispered an assurance that he would return to Captain Heyworth when their plans were formed, and then led Gabriel to Mistress Malvina's room. The ladies had not yet returned, for the main staircase and the corridors made a much wider circuit.

"You wait, sir, and I'll prepare them," said Amos, stealing along the passage, carrying his shoes in one hand, and raising a warning forefinger as little Mistress Nell approached.

"Hush, missie," he said. "Yon wicked young Squire Norton has deceived you; here is a gentleman who hath brought you a letter from my master."

"Did I not tell you, child, that your father ever mistrusted Squire Norton?" said Cousin Malvina, triumphantly.

Helena, looking utterly bewildered, allowed Amos to usher her into the room where Gabriel stood waiting her approach. She lifted up her candle the better to see him, and something in his clear honest eyes brought her instant relief.

"Sir," she exclaimed, "Amos says my father sent you hither."

"Yes, madam," he said, bowing low and handing her the Major's letter. "You will recognise his handwriting, and pray read this quickly, for if we are to save you from Colonel Norton's vile plot we must lose no time."

"Read, child," said Cousin Malvina, "and let us know at once what your father bids you do."

Gabriel took the candle from the girl's trembling hand, and held it for her while she read aloud the Major's brief note.

"Dear Daughter,—This letter is borne to you by Lieutenant Harford, who is accompanied by his friend, Captain Heyworth. I am unable to fetch you myself, but you must ride with them without a minute's delay to Gloucester, where Alderman Pury will shelter you. We have learnt of a probable attack to be made by the Prince's troops on the Manor; do not let the servants attempt a defence, it will be useless. A worse danger threatens you yourself from that vile profligate, Squire Norton. I had thought him safely disposed of during the war, but since he is in your neighbourhood, I dare not leave you at the Manor. Come at once to Gloucester, or I shall not have a moment's peace of mind. I shall be gone to the attack of Tewkesbury when you arrive, but Lieutenant Harford will place you safely under Alderman Pury's care. May God direct you.—Your loving father,

"Christopher Locke.

"Written at Gloucester, this evening, April 11, 1643."

"Is there a third staircase in the house?" asked Gabriel, turning to Amos.

"Ay, sir, there be the kitchen stairs, but they be plaguy steep and apt to creak."

"They are further from the hall," said little Mistress Nell, "and we can slip out of the back door and through the shrubbery to the gate ere Squire Norton thinks us ready. Haste, haste, Cousin Malvina, here is your Lincoln green cloak and hood, do not let us lose a moment."

"Summon Captain Heyworth," said Gabriel to Amos, "and if possible get a couple of pillions, we will meet you by the back entrance. I will guard your door, ladies, while you don your wraps, but pray lose no time."

He stood without in the corridor, each minute seeming agelong in the darkness and silence. Presently a faint sound of stealthy steps at a little distance warned him that Joscelyn and the gatekeeper were moving towards the back staircase, then came silence, broken only by the low tones of Mistress Malvina's agitated voice.

At length, when his patience was well nigh exhausted,

Helena in a long blue cloak and a close Puritan hood, opened the door.

"We are ready, sir," she whispered.

"Can you find your way down in the dark?" he asked.

She nodded, blew out the candle, and with a child's ready confidence slipped her hand into his.

"Take care," she said, beneath her breath, "there are little steps up and down in this corridor, two up here, now one down, now turn to the left and tread softly, there are twenty-six stairs—very steep ones. Don't forget, Cousin Malvina, that the twenty-fourth step creaks."

Silently and with infinite care they went down the long descent, thankful for a gleam of moonlight from the window of the house-keeper's room down below. But, alas! Cousin Malvina, half paralysed with terror as they heard Norton's voice in the hall, lost count of the steps.

The twenty-fourth stair creaked ominously as she trod on it, and the next moment to their horror, Norton's voice grew louder and clearer.

"They are coming at last!" he exclaimed. "I hear steps in the passage. What! no lights? Curse those servants! Why can't they bring a lamp? Hullo! who goes there? a petticoat an I mistake not. Tom, bring one of those candles; here's sport to pass the time of waiting."

Unluckily, as Norton's eyes grew more accustomed to the semi-darkness, he caught sight of three people rapidly crossing a patch of moonlight in the kitchen. He hurried forward, and was just in time to see the little group of dusky figures stealing out of the house. Then the door closed behind them, and though he pulled with all his might at the handle, he could not make it yield, for Joscelyn Heyworth held on to it like grim death.

Meanwhile, Gabriel had hurriedly pulled on his boots, and was half-leading, half-carrying, little Mistress Nell through the dark shrubbery, while Amos panted after him with Mistress Malvina.

When Joscelyn rejoined them, the poor chaperon seemed almost at her last gasp, and the sound of Norton's steps gaining upon them took all the strength from her limbs.

"Take a turn to the right and double back to the house with the lady," said Joscelyn; "you will outwit them thus, and can ride later on to Gloucester."

It was no time to hesitate. Amos blindly obeyed, and dragged Mistress Malvina into the depths of the shrubbery, where she sank on to the ground unable to take another step, but listening in terrible anxiety to hear what would happen.

Joscelyn, running like the wind, overtook his companions, and caught Helena's other hand in his, then, leaving the shrubbery, the fugitives rushed across the bowling-green. The moon shone only too brightly, but they were forced to risk shots from behind, for to drag the girl along the narrow half-overgrown path proved slow work, and their capture would have been certain.

Surely Norton would hesitate to shoot. His feelings as a gentleman would probably be stronger than the savage lust of conquest, and the brute instincts which had prompted him to this night's work.

But they had yet to learn his character; as long as his mind was fully bent on any desire, nothing could baffle him.

A bullet whistled through the air, missing Joscelyn Hey-worth only by a hair's breadth. Little Nell gripped the hands of her rescuers with the intensity of one whose nerves are strained to the utmost, but otherwise she made no sign, and ran bravely on. A second bullet followed, but it glanced aside from Gabriel's corslet. Helena felt the shock of it in the hand which he grasped, and a stifled cry of horror escaped her. Had not her two protectors borne her on more and more swiftly she felt that she must have given up, and have thrown herself on Squire Norton's mercy.

But now at last they were nearing the lodge, and, to their relief, at the sound of their approach, Morrison threw open the gate for them. Gabriel hastily mounted his horse and bade the man lift little Mistress Nell in front of him, for the pillions had been left with Amos in the shrubbery, and he dared not let her ride behind, when at any moment Norton or his companion might again shoot.

"It'll take the gentlemen a few minutes to find their horses," said Morrison, lifting the trembling girl in front of Gabriel. "They'd left them on the other side of the gatehouse, and I've put 'em down by yon pollard willow, and hobbled their hind legs with a bit of rope in a way that will make their riders swear."

He chuckled softly to himself, and glanced at his master, who laughed outright as he mounted.

"You're worth your weight in gold to me," he said. "We shall baffle this villain yet, Gabriel."

And setting spurs to their horses, the little cavalcade started at a sharp trot, which changed as soon as they heard sounds of pursuit, to a gallop. When at length they drew rein for a moment to breathe their panting horses, all was still, and it became clear that Norton and his companion had abandoned the chase.

Joscelyn Heyworth glanced at the little slender figure which clung so closely to his comrade; in the moonlight her girlish face looked pale, but absolutely tranquil, and in her eyes he could read perfect trust in her rescuer. He felt convinced, that ere long such confidence would develop in the girl's heart into the utter devotion of love.

"Now, an' my friend could but rid his heart of old memories, and forget that Mistress Hilary he raved about at Kineton in his fever, here is as winsome and sweet a bride for him as man could desire," thought Joscelyn.

But Gabriel's expression was grave, and his eyes had an absent look in them. He paid very little heed to the Major's daughter when once assured of her safety and comfort, for the clasp of her arms about his neck only made him crave Hilary's presence the more, and he was dreaming his own dream of how one day it might be his happy fortune to rescue her from some deadly peril or save her from the machinations of such a man as Norton.

CHAPTER XIV.

"A mighty pain to love it is,

And 'tis a pain to miss it;

But of all pains, the greatest pain

It is to love, but love in vain."

—Cowley.

The city of Hereford, which had been evacuated by the last remnants of Lord Stamford's army shortly before Christmas, was once more in the hands of the Royalists, and throughout the winter, reprisals had been the order of the day. Price, the Mayor, who had admitted Stamford's troops, was thrown into gaol, his house was plundered, and there was a keen desire to hang him in front of his own door, happily frustrated by the more moderate citizens. Sir Richard Hopton, also, had his house at Canon Frome plundered, while Dr. Harford would probably have suffered imprisonment for his bold advocacy of the Parliamentary cause had not the citizens been loth to lose the services of their first physician.

None needed these services more than Mrs. Unett, who all through the cold weather had been grievously ill, and Hilary could not but feel grateful for his skill and helpfulness, even when the virulent tongue of Prebendary Rogers was kindling the flame of vindictive hatred in her heart, and fanning that fierce resentment of Gabriel's actions which had made such havoc in her life.

On the morning of April the 24th she was roused by Mrs. Durdle's agitated voice, and, opening her drowsy eyes, started up in alarm as she saw the genuine terror in the housekeeper's fat face.

"Is my mother worse?" she asked, anxiously.

"Nay, mistress, she is still sleeping, but I stole up to bid you keep the ill news from her as long as may be."

"What news? What is amiss?" cried Hilary.

"The Parliament soldiers are marching from Ross to attack Hereford," said Durdle. "Hark to the ringing of the common bell! It summons all citizens, my Valentine tells me, to come and help with making earthworks at the gates and by the river."

"Doth Lord Stamford come hither again, then?" asked Hilary.

"Nay, mistress, they do say 'tis Sir William Waller's army—William the Conqueror the folks do call un and they say the city can never hold out."

Hilary's heart began to throb.

"We shall see about that," she said, proudly, her face aflame as she realised that Gabriel served under Waller. "We have gallant Sir Richard Cave to defend us, and only last night the Bishop told me that he had, to protect the city, a hundred of the King's foot guards and many dragoons, beside some three hundred soldiers under Colonel Conyngsby, Colonel Price and Colonel Courtney. Depend upon it, we shall make the rebels fly."

Durdle shook her head despondently, this hopeful view was not shared by many of the citizens; the very sound of Sir William Waller's name made them quake, and Sir Richard Cave found, to his dismay, that they would not respond to the summons to help with the earth-works.

It was impossible to carry out his scheme of defence, and all that he could contrive was to dam up Byster's Gate, while his spirits were much depressed by the arrival that afternoon of a letter from Sir William Russell saying that he could spare no troops from Worcester, and that no help could come from Prince Maurice, who had set out to march towards His Majesty.

Few people slept much in Hereford on that Monday night, and when day dawned on the 25th, Sir Richard Cave, making observations from the Castle, found that Waller's formidable army was within a mile of the city.

The soldiers were at once summoned, and the place resounded with the roll of the drums and with trumpets sounding the alarm. Hilary hastened to her mother's room, no longer able to keep from the invalid the danger in which they stood.

"Child," said Mrs. Unett, in terror, "what does it all mean?"

"Only that Sir William Waller is marching on Hereford, ma'am," said Hilary, "but as the citizens were too panic-stricken yesterday to cast up earth-works near the bridge, as they were ordered to do, we run little risk of bombardment in this house, I fancy."

"Oh!" said Mrs. Unett, with a look of relief. "If it is Sir William Waller's army we shall be safe enough, for Gabriel Harford will, I well know, protect us."

Hilary flushed with anger at these words, and making an excuse to carry the night lamp into the dressing-room, gave a little impatient stamp of the foot the moment she was alone.

"Gabriel, indeed! Rather than be protected by him I would throw myself on the mercy of any other man in England! Dr. Rogers says I did well and loyally in vowing never to see 'my old friend,' as he calls him, again, and if he dares to seek me out, I will make him suffer as he has not suffered yet."

Her eyes flashed as she conjured up a scene pleasing enough to the perverse spirit of pride which at the moment dominated her; but soon all the hardness died out of her face, and she was again her sweet womanly self, for her mother called out to her in alarm as the first sound of firing made itself heard.

"There is naught to fear, ma'am," she said, running into the sick-room and caressing the invalid like a child. "Oh! they must be a great way off, and will not trouble us at all. To my mind"—and she laughed gaily—"'tis not near so terrifying as a thunderstorm."

Nevertheless, though her words were brave the sharp rattle of musketry made her pulses beat uncomfortably. It was not for herself that she feared, but from some dim recess of her heart there awoke a flicker of the love she thought wholly extinguished, and a dumb cry began to ring in her ears, "Gabriel is there in the thick of the fray. That shot, or that, or that, may cause his death-wound."

After a time there came a lull in the firing; then it was renewed, but at a greater distance. While they were both longing to know what had happened Durdle announced Dr. Harford, and the physician, who rarely let a day pass without seeing his patient, entered with his usual quiet, kindly manner and cheering smile.

"I trust all this commotion has not upset you, madam?" he said, "but I think you will not be troubled with any close firing after this. I hear that the main body of Sir William Waller's army is drawn up without Widemarsh Gate, but feints have been made in two or three other quarters, and there has been a sharp little skirmish close by here at the bridge."

"Is it true that your son is with Sir William Waller?" asked Mrs. Unett, revelling, poor lady, in the mere comfort of the good doctor's presence.

"Ay, I have seen him in the distance," said Dr. Harford, his eyes lighting with a look of fatherly pride which could not be hid. "I was standing in the south walk of our garden when he, with a detachment of men in boats, rowed across towards the bridge, and made good their landing hard by, but after a brisk fight Sir Richard Cave's musketeers beat them back to their boats. 'Twas clearly meant only as a feint. You will not probably hear any more near firing and stand in no danger here."

"It must have been strange indeed for you to see your son in that fashion, after a six months' absence," said the invalid, gently. "Hath he greatly altered?"

"Yes; he hath grown from boy to man," said Dr. Harford; and then, happening to catch a glimpse of Hilary's face, he hastily changed the subject, for no one better understood her varying moods, and he saw that directly she was assured of Gabriel's safety her old resentment against him had sprung to life again. Nevertheless, beneath all her faults he could always discern the deeply-loving nature which she, in truth, possessed, and held fast to his conviction that she would conquer the arrogance that at present bid fair to wreck her happiness.

"If the city be taken," he thought to himself as he quitted the sick room, "and that pestilent priest, Dr. Rogers, called to account for the mischief he hath done, then there will be very good hope that the daughter of my old friend may come to take the same calm and just view held by such Royalists as the Bishop and his son."

Meanwhile Gabriel, greatly cheered by the glimpse he had caught of his father, had returned from the skirmish at the Bridge to the neighbourhood of St. Owen's Gate, where, under a sharp fire from the walls, they succeeded in taking St. Owen's Church. This church being within pistol shot of the gate was like to prove of great service to the besiegers, and Captain Grey gave Gabriel orders to take a party of musketeers up the tower.

The terrified verger was at first too much dazed to produce the keys of the tower door, "and the men, annoyed at the delay, were disposed to deal roughly with him.

"Here, you great oaf," cried one, "unfasten the door, or we will hang you to one of your own bell ropes."

"Mercy! mercy!" cried the poor old man, as half-a-dozen stalwart soldiers laid hold of him, hustling him in a fashion which scattered the few wits he still retained.

"Stand back, there," said a firm voice. "Why, Martin! don't you remember me?"

And Gabriel laid a kindly hand on the old man's shoulder. "Oh, Mr. Harford, don't ye let them hang me," said the verger, clutching at the young lieutenant.

"No one shall touch a hair of your head," said Gabriel, "but out with the keys, my friend, for we must lose no time."

Martin obeyed, trembling like a palsied man, and Gabriel, unlocking the door, rushed at full speed up the crumbling and worn steps, then up a crazy and tottering ladder which led to the trap-door in the leads. Springing through this, he emerged on to the top of the tower and had quickly arranged his musketeers on the side from which they could best harass the men on the walls and at St. Owen's Gate. The church stood in the centre of the road which passed round it on the north and south sides, and the musketeers not only carried on a very effective warfare from the tower, but drew the attention of the besieged from the main attack which was made by Massey on Widemarsh Gate.

His onslaught proved so vigorous that the terrified citizens ere long sounded a parley, and, Waller consenting to treat, the rest of the day passed in tedious arrangements about hostages, and proposals as to the terms of surrender.

Gabriel had little fear that the citizens of Hereford would have any just cause of complaint, for Sir William Waller was noted for his forbearance and courtesy, and the people had no reason to fear the looting or plundering too often the sequel to a victory.

The entry was made quietly enough that evening and two of the articles dictated by Sir William Waller were specially pleasing to Gabriel: All ladies and gentlewomen were to have honourable usage; and the Bishop, the Dean and Chapter, and the collegiates were likewise to be free in their persons from violence and in their goods from plunder.

That so ardent a Royalist as Hilary should be sore and angry at the easy way in which the Parliamentary troops had taken possession of the place was natural enough. She was in her hardest mood the next morning when Durdle came up to the sick-room with a beaming face.

"Mr. Gabriel Harford is below, come to inquire after Mistress Unett's health," she exclaimed, her little grey eyes beaming with the pleasure of again seeing the lad she had known so long. "And he craves a word with you, Mistress Hilary. I have shown him into the dining-room."

Amazed at his temerity in calling, Hilary did not pause to think of the long years of friendship that had preceded their betrothal.

"It is just like his audacity to come here now that his side has conquered, and we are in trouble," she reflected. "I will show him how little I care for his rebel comrades and their chief."

And with her coldest manner she turned to the housekeeper.

"Tell Mr. Harford that my mother hath had a disturbed night and that I cannot leave her room."

"My dear!" remonstrated Mrs. Unett, "you had best go down and thank Mr. Harford for his courteous inquiries."

"Pray, ma'am, send your thanks by Durdle," said Hilary, holding her head high. "I prefer not to leave you."

So poor old Durdle had no choice but to go down again to the visitor, and not being blessed with tact she could not even soften his disappointment.

"'Tis sorry I am, sir," she said, smoothing her apron, "but Mistress Hilary will not leave her mother's room."

"Is Mistress Unett worse?" asked Gabriel, anxiously.

"Oh, no, sir. Maybe she did not sleep as well as usual, but she tried hard to persuade Mistress Hilary to see you and thank you for your kind inquiries. But, lor', sir, you must remember well enough that when once she was angered by aught, she was ever an ill-relished maid. Don't you take it to heart, sir," said the good woman, grieved to see the look of pain in his eyes, "maybe some other day she will see you."

He went away in very low spirits; for though it had been hard enough to live through the long months of absence, there was a keener torture in being so near to the woman he loved, yet, alas! so far removed from her heart.

He took the old housekeeper's advice and called to inquire again later in the week, only to meet with a similar rebuff. Nor could he bring himself to speak at home of the purgatory he was passing through. His mother hoped from his silence that he had outgrown his love to Hilary. His father guessed something of the true state of the case, but feared that words, however well meant, might only increase his suffering.

Joscelyn Heyworth, however, rallied him on his depression, not knowing that "the lady named Hilary" was a citizen of Hereford.

"Why are you in the dumps?" he asked, one sunshiny afternoon, as the two walked together down Broad Street. "You should be in high spirits now that you are among your old friends once more, and with your parents as keenly interested in the campaign as you are yourself. I would give something to stand in your shoes." And for a moment his bright face was clouded with bitter memories.

"Many of my old friends look on me as a traitor for whom hanging were too good," said Gabriel. "You forget that Hereford has ever been devoted to the King's cause, and that such of us as fight against his tyranny are here but a small and unpopular minority."

"'Tis to be hoped the army will not long be kept here," said Joscelyn. "The men need to be in active service; already they seem to be waxing unruly," and he glanced at some boisterous soldiers gathered about a fanatical dark-browed man who harangued them from the vantage ground of an inverted barrow, and with bawling voice and vehement gestures was attracting quite a crowd.

"Why!" exclaimed Gabriel, "that is none other than Peter Waghorn, the fellow I saw at Bosbury. What a frenzy the man is working himself into! See how he points to the Cathedral as though he wished to destroy the whole place!"

"Oh, don't linger," said Joscelyn Heyworth. "I loathe these fanatic preachers. What was that he said? The pious work of destruction? Have they been urging on the mob as they did at Winchester? Sir William Waller will be ill pleased if they have done as much damage here. Let us come in and see."

Gabriel told him Waghorn's story as they crossed the green, and approached the beautiful parvise porch at the north-west. They had just entered it when the inner door leading into the cathedral was hastily opened, and the figure of a girl clad in pale puce, with a hat and cloak of tan-coloured velvet, suddenly appeared. Her rich brown curls, her exquisite colouring, but above all, her dark expressive eyes, made Joscelyn look at her a second time; she was evidently in a state of suppressed indignation, and when she caught sight of Gabriel Harford, her wrath flashed into a sudden flame.

He saluted her with great respect, but averting her face she declined to acknowledge him even by the most distant curtsey, and would have passed rapidly through the porch had he not stood in front of her, blocking her way.

Joscelyn saw the look of almost intolerable pain in his face, and instantly knew that this must be Mistress Hilary. But for a moment it seemed that her lover could not speak.

"Sir!" exclaimed the girl, indignantly, "let me pass."

Only too well she knew that old gesture of his, when, with head thrown back, he seemed to wrestle with words which would not be uttered. Only too well she knew, moreover, the low, passion-choked voice, in which at length he spoke.

"You cannot go that way," he said. "There is a noisy crowd of men near the west front."

"Cannot!" she said, contemptuously. "Do you think I care for a few rebels and traitors?"

By this time he had mastered himself, and in his manner there was all the force which is gained by self-repression. "You had better go out by the other door and through the Palace," he said.

"I shall do no such thing," she replied perversely. "I shall go the way I choose, and see what these comrades of yours are like. Let me pass, sir."

"I cannot let you go alone," he said. "If you insist on going through the crowd, I shall attend you to your door."

The quiet determination of his tone almost maddened her.

"And I utterly refuse your escort," she said, with an angry scorn that cut him to the heart. "Rather than walk with you I would have as escort any other man in Hereford."

"Then I will present to you my friend, Captain Heyworth," said Gabriel, steadily, but with an irrepressible note of pain in his voice. "Joscelyn, do me the favour of attending Mistress Hilary Unett to her home."

Joscelyn saluted her gravely. She longed to decline his company, but something in Gabriel's tone made refusal impossible. She gave him one last glance, half from defiance, half from curiosity. What was it that still gave him his power over her? Physically he lacked the height and the fine physique of his friend, mentally she felt that she was more than his match, yet in moral and spiritual force he would always, as she well knew, tower above her. Was it fair that he, a traitor, as she honestly deemed him, both to Church and King, should yet live, as it were, on the heights? The thought stung and irritated her, and so did the unfading picture she carried away with her of that well-known parvise porch, and Gabriel standing just beneath the finely-moulded archway, his hazel eyes full of dumb suffering, his face sad but resolute, and lit up by a radiance which seemed to her, not of this earth at all.

However, her musings were quickly put to flight by the bawling of the fanatic near the west front, whose violent tirade against what he alternately termed, "this House of Dagon," and "this den of thieves crammed with popish idols," made her lip curl scornfully.

"These are your comrades!" she said, with bitter contempt.

"No, madam," replied Joscelyn Heyworth, with a little gleam of amusement in his eyes. "I learn that this is a carpenter from a village in your neighbourhood who was driven half demented by Dr. Laud's cruelty to his father. We come across a good many of these victims up and down the country."

The recollection of a day long ago in the first brief happiness of their betrothal came back overpoweringly to Hilary. Oh! how she longed to be sitting once more with Gabriel on the steps of Bosbury Cross before the parting of the ways!

'Joscelyn saw the more gentle look dawning in her face, and hazarded a word on Gabriel's behalf.

"'Tis a pity, madam," he said, "if you will allow me to speak frankly with you, that you so grievously pained my friend just now."

But at this plain speaking Hilary's pride was at once up in arms.

"'Tis a pity, sir, that you presume to speak on matters about which you know absolutely nothing."

"Pardon me, I know much as to Gabriel Harford's past story," said Joscelyn, not in the least disconcerted by her snub.

"What!" she exclaimed, angrily. "He had the effrontery to tell you, a perfect stranger, that we had been betrothed—when even my own uncle was not admitted to the secret? Oh, it is unbearable! I did well to refuse him a greeting."

"No, madam," said Joscelyn, bluntly. "In my opinion you did a very cruel thing. And you misjudge him now as you evidently have done in the past. He has never breathed your name to me. I found him almost in the last extremity on the battlefield, the morning after Edgehill—only begging to be allowed to die and quit a world that had dealt harshly with him. I bore him back to Kineton, refused to let him give up his life, and all through the next night kept watch over him. There are revelations, madam, that come before the day of judgment, and in the feverish ravings of a wounded soldier lying at death's door, you may learn strange truths. I learnt then the agony of a man who has been jilted by the only woman he has ever loved."

Hilary had grown white to the lips, but pride still held her love in chains. Though this knowledge of what Gabriel had passed through, sent a pang to her inmost heart, her self-love was ruffled and agitated by the fearless, outspoken words which this Parliamentary Captain had dared to speak.

"I thought, sir," she said, with cold arrogance, "that one of the conditions specially guaranteed by your General, was that all gentlewomen should have honourable usage."

"Madam, it is because I honour you and love my friend that I venture to speak as I would fain have any other man speak to my sister were she in like case," said Joscelyn, marvelling at her hardness, but quite failing to understand that she was strenuously keeping back her better nature, which only longed to yield to his arguing.

"She is absolutely heartless, and Gabriel Harford has had a lucky escape," he reflected, too young and impulsive to understand Hilary's character. "If he had any sense he would wed pretty Mistress Nell, as sweet a little maid as heart could wish, and worth a thousand of this haughty, headstrong maiden." Meanwhile the "haughty maiden" was pausing at the door of a grey, gabled house. She lifted her beautiful eyes to his, and swept him a stately curtsey.

"This is my home, sir. I regret that you should have been put to the very unnecessary trouble of escorting me."

"Madam," he said, saluting her with grave respect, "any service I can render to my friend is a pleasure; it was quite apparent to me, that at the very moment you were tying

Sharp-toothed unkindness like a vulture

to his heart, he was seeking to shield you from a momentary discomfiture. I wish you good-day."

"Good-day, sir," said Hilary, stung to the quick by the truth of his words, and by the calm, unsparing severity of his manner. She was well-used to devotion, and flattery, and admiration of every sort, but here was a man undazzled by her beauty, and only repelled by what Dr. Rogers termed her "high-spirited treatment of her old playmate, Dr. Harford's rebel son."

CHAPTER XV.

"The spiritual life is not an elaborate system, but a divine life—not a book of Leviticus, but a Gospel of St. John." —Bishop Walsuam How.

When Gabriel had watched the last glimpse of the pale puco gown as Hilary turned the north-west corner of the cathedral, he went despondently enough into the building itself to see whether any mischief had been done by Waghorn and his adherents.

At first he could see no slightest trace of damage, but in the north-east transept he encountered Major Locke, pacifying one of the vergers who seemed much concerned at the prospect of "such a mort o' clearin' up," as he expressed it.

"It shall be reported to Sir William Waller," said the major; "but in truth 'tis very hard to prevent the men from being stirred up and led into mischief by these fanatic preachers."

"What on earth induced them to attack Bishop Swinfield's monument?" exclaimed Gabriel, genuinely vexed to see that the old Bishop's effigy had been literally hacked to pieces.

"Well, it seems that Waghorn, this crazy carpenter fellow, lured them on with tales of a crucifix, and it proved to be a bas-relief just above this tomb. The men have scarce left a trace of it, but you can see the outline on the wall. Then, quite against the Parliamentary order for respecting the monuments of the dead, they must needs go and hew in pieces this effigy. Hearing that mischief was afoot, I was fortunately in time to order them out of the building before they grew more unruly."

"I see they have hewn off the head without harming it," said Gabriel, stooping to pick it up from the corner into which it had been tossed. "With your permission, sir, I will bear it to the Palace. Bishop Coke will value it, and here it would but be cast away as rubbish."

"Ay, sir, do," said the verger. "The Bishop, God bless'un, he do set great store by all old statutes, and so do his son, Dr. William Coke; and Mistress Hilary Unett she takes after 'm; seems to run in the family like. For my part, I be glad Waghorn set the soldiers on useless stocks and stones and spared the glass windows, for the cathedral do be mortal cold on windy days at service time."

This, then, explained in part Hilary's angry mood. Perhaps had they met under less trying circumstances, she might have been less cruel. Very sore at heart, Gabriel went out again, encountering Joscelyn Heyworth not far from the Palace.

"What plunder are you carrying away, you sacrilegious man?" exclaimed the young Captain, with his genial laugh. "When an honest man turns thief he always betrays himself. What are you hiding under your scarf ends?"

"A bishop's head," said Gabriel, grimly.

"Oh! so this explains some of the lady's wrath."

"Yes, no wonder she was angry. I am taking this to her grandfather—Bishop Coke."

"You would do much better to throw it down on the green, and give up the whole connection. What have you to do now with bishops, either in stone or in the flesh? And as to their granddaughters—may heaven preserve me from ever again escorting home an episcopal lady. Like Benedick, 'I cannot endure my Lady Tongue.'"

"You don't know her," said Gabriel. "To-day she was very naturally incensed."

"Now be a sensible man, Gabriel, and cast that head into the kennel, for I assure you its stony curls are not more stony than the heart of Mistress Hilary."

"Be silent!" said Gabriel, hotly. "I tell you that you do not know her. Tout comprendre c'est tout pardonner, as the proverb hath it."

"Then let us hope the lady will apply that sentiment to the cure of her pride. For truly she knows much more of you than she did before I crossed her path."

"What do you mean?" said Gabriel, aware that Joscelyn was often daringly outspoken and unconventional, and fearing that he might only have angered Hilary the more.

"I told her of the night at Kineton, when, in your delirium the name of Hilary was eternally on your lips."

"So you have known all this time?"

"To be sure; and now she knows one or two eminently wholesome truths."

"I fear you but annoyed her yet more. What did she say?"

"Well, she turned whiter than this old prelate's head, and I could have sworn she was going to soften. But nothing of the sort; she remained as stony as this effigy, and so we parted with freezing politeness and ceremony. Give her up, Gabriel; why let her make your life a misery?"

"You don't understand her," said, Gabriel, in a choked voice. "You have not yet really seen her true self. As to giving her up—why, how should I do that? I have loved her since we were children, and we Harfords do not change."

"So it seems," said Joscelyn, ruefully. "Well, I'm hanged if anybody should trouble my peace who had treated me with the consummate cruelty she showed you to-day."

Gabriel, without reply, turned in at the gateway of the Palace, feeling that even his best friend somehow failed to help him, and quite prepared to be refused an interview with the Bishop.

Strangely enough, however, it was the saintly old man who differed from him on so many points in politics and theology who best understood him at that time. He received him as if nothing had happened since their last meeting, bidding him welcome with the same warmth and the same perfect courtesy he had always shown him.

"They may abolish bishops," thought Gabriel, "yet somehow the best description of Bishop Coke will always be the title, 'Right reverend father in God?'"

The head of Bishop Swinfield, half-concealed by the ends of the broad orange scarf which girded Gabriel's buff coat, quickly attracted the old prelate's attention.

"I had heard of the mischief done just now," he said. "I see you bring me an unharmed fragment; I am glad you rescued that."

"I thought, my lord, you would value it, and perhaps have it in safe hiding till quieter times."

"I will give it to my son, 'twill be safer in his care; and to tell the truth, Mr. Harford, I cannot expect to live till quieter times. These troubles are breaking my heart."

"My lord, indeed 'twas scarce the fault of the soldiers that harm was wrought in the cathedral; they were led on by a poor fanatic fellow whose father was grievously misused by Dr. Laud."

"And therein lies my worst sorrow," said the Bishop, with a long sigh. "Our system seemed to us right and good, yet it hath alienated the people, and wholly failed. Believe me, Mr. Harford, I am not thinking of the misguided zeal of your soldiers, but of my own mistaken zeal in the past. Yet we meant well—God knows we meant well."

Gabriel was silent. Before a humility and sorrow such as this words seemed a profanation.

He glanced round the room, the very one in which he had offered his services to the Parliament during the Earl of Stamford's occupation six months before. Again his eyes turned to the picture of Hilary as a child, and the Bishop, noting this, asked if he had seen her, and by his kindly sympathy gradually drew from him the whole story.

"'Tis no ill cure to set two sad folks to talk with each other," he said, a faint smile playing about his lips. "I am breaking my heart over the direful strife betwixt Christian men, and you are breaking your heart over a difference of opinion with the maiden you love. We must both remember the apostle's words, 'Love never faileth.' It seems to us to have wholly failed now, and for the night of this life it may seem so, but the day will dawn. For you, if God will, it may perchance, after all, dawn here on this earth, though scarce for me."

He crossed the room to a beautifully carved cabinet, and opening one of the inner compartments, took out a miniature of Hilary.

"This," he said, showing it to Gabriel, "was painted for me the autumn you first went to London, and I always intended that at my death it should be yours. I think you were right when that day in the cloisters you said to me that the Harfords do not change, and in these troubled times I shall like to know that you already have it in your keeping, for I have a feeling that we shall not again meet in this world." Gabriel, with tears in his eyes, could only falteringly speak his thanks.

"Nay," said the Bishop, cheerfully. "'Tis a pleasure to me to think it will be some slight comfort to you, my son. And," he added, with a quiet laugh, "you were the first to make a presentation to me of good Bishop Swinfield's head, knowing my special feeling for the past dignitaries of our Church. 'Tis but meet that I should acknowledge your courtesy by the gift of my granddaughter's head—a wilful maid, yet methinks one that will some day ripen into a right noble woman. Believe me, my son, she is worth waiting for."

"I will wait a lifetime, if need be," said Gabriel, looking at the sweet face in the miniature—the Hilary that had been before the war. And then, remembering past times, he made an enquiry as to the treatise on the Epistle to the Colossians. The old Bishop shook his head, sadly.

"The war hath been the ruin of all books," he said, ruefully. "They tell me people will read naught nowadays but the war pamphlets which are poured forth in shoals from the press. Or else they read the news books, which, so far as I can learn, vie with each other in lying, and are crammed with envy, hatred, malice and all uncharitableness. From the curse of such weapons of the evil one, good Lord deliver us!"

The words came with all the more force because spoken by one so habitually gentle, and Gabriel, watching the folded hands and the white head bent in this heartfelt ejaculation, felt more than ever drawn to the Bishop.

Never once had Bishop Coke repulsed him by the illogical arguments about the divine right of the King to govern wrongfully, which were hurled at the heads of the Parliamentarians by most Royalists. He kept altogether on a higher plane where meeting was quite possible, and Gabriel was glad enough to kneel for the old man's blessing when they parted.

The citizens of Hereford had compounded with Sir William Waller for £3,000, and when the fines had been collected in money or plate nothing remained to detain the soldiers in the place.

On the evening of the seventeenth of May, therefore, Waller, hearing that he was needed elsewhere, and unable to spare men to garrison Hereford permanently for the Parliament, gave orders that the troops should be ready to march back to Gloucester early the next morning. By the time Gabriel was free from his duties it was already late, but seeing that lights still burned in Mrs. Unett's house, he ventured to inquire at the door if she were worse.

"In truth, she is very ill, sir," said Durdle, anxiously.

At the head of the stairs, in a nook where she could hear what passed, but could neither see nor be seen, Hilary waited with a beating heart. She was in grievous trouble, and the sound of her lover's voice tempted her sorely to run down and speak to him.

"Give her my kind regards, and I trust she will soon be recovered," said Gabriel. "'Tis late to knock you up, but I leave Hereford at dawn to-morrow."

Hilary's heart sank.

"Shall I tell Mistress Hilary?" inquired Durdle. "Belike she would come down."

The girl waited in an agony of suspense for his reply.

"No, she hath thrice refused to speak with me," he said, with a note of pain in his voice that brought a lump into her throat. "I will trouble her no further; good-bye, Mrs. Durdle."

Like one struggling for life Hilary wrestled with her pride. "Go down and speak to him," urged one voice within her. "I can't before Durdle," retorted another. "Go, go before it is too late!" "Nay, what could I say if I did go?"

And then she learnt that he who hesitates is lost, for the door was closed, and Durdle walked heavily back to the kitchen, and silence reigned again in the house.

Hilary sat down on the top stair, and burying her face in her hands, cried much after the fashion of a naughty child, who is half repentant and altogether weary and miserable. Again and again she had refused to see Gabriel, and had taken pleasure in the process; but now he had declined to see her, and she felt that she was indeed hoist with her own petard.

After this, with the kindest intentions in the world, Joscelyn Heyworth set about the dangerous process of match-making on his friend's behalf. Supremely happy in the love of pretty Mistress Clemency Coriton, he no sooner found himself talking alone with her at Mr. Bennett's house in the Close at Gloucester, than the remembrance of Gabriel Harford's story came to trouble his peace.

"Faith, and I have seen much of little Mistress Helena Locke," said Clemency. "She hath a dull time at Alderman Pury's, and is ever glad to come here and chat about her gallant rescuers."

"She had no liking, then, for Colonel Norton, and did not resent being carried off in that summary fashion?"

"Oh, she feared and detested Squire Norton, and to tell the truth—but be sure you breathe no word of this—I have a fancy that she lost her heart to your friend."

"Ho! that is good hearing," said Joscelyn, with a smile. "There is nothing that would please me more than to see them mated, for in truth he stands in need of just such a sweet-tempered gentle little woman, being over-reserved and apt to grow melancholy over the desperate plight the country is in."

"Let us get my sister to invite the Major and his daughter and you and your friend to supper to-morrow," said Clemency. "Even should the notion fail to come to anything, it can do them no harm to meet."

So it came about that little Mistress Nell donned her prettiest white gown the next evening, arranged her fair curls with anxious care, and, with her blue eyes looking unusually bright, went with her father to the gabled house in the Close.

Her rescuers had already arrived, but Helena had hardly a glance to spare for Joscelyn Heyworth who, for all his six feet and his lion-like mane of golden hair, was, for her, quite eclipsed by a shorter, slighter man, with something in his sunburnt face and liquid hazel eyes which appealed to her.

Gabriel greeted her with the easy cordiality of one whose deeper feelings are not in the least touched.

"You suffered no ill-effects, I hope, from all your fatigues on the ride to Gloucester," he said.

"Oh! no," said Helena, eagerly. "When once we were out of pistol range it was enjoyable enough; but I hope I may never have to run again as we did that night. Had you not both dragged me on I must have given up."

Gabriel laughed.

"We were cruel only to be kind, but I grant you that the feeling of being pursued is unpleasant. I had a longing to stay and fight it out with that dastardly Colonel. But it would have been over great a risk for you, and your safety was the main object. However, I have an instinct that I shall meet the fellow again, and then maybe shall have a chance of fighting him."

At supper, in the panelled room below, Gabriel found himself between Mistress Nell and his hostess, and vis-à-vis with Major Locke, who kept them all merry with his inexhaustible fund of stories.

"Who would think, to hear our laughter, that we were in the midst of a deadly civil war?" said Faith Bennett. "We owe you a debt of gratitude, sir. I have not made so merry for many a day."

"Tell Mistress Bennett the story of the fisher-boy," said Helena. "That mightily tickled my fancy."

"Oh, that is but a simple tale," said the Major. "We were crossing some wild country in Herefordshire, and, the day being foggy, had lost our bearings, so I sent one of the men to ask the way of a lad that was fishing in the Wye. He came back to say that he couldn't understand the boy's language, and knowing something of dialect, I went to him myself and said, 'Which is the nearest way to Horn Lacy?'

"An unintelligible jabber was the response, so that I thought the lad an innocent until I chanced to notice that he was munching a mouthful of something.

"'What have you got in your mouth?' I asked, finding that he made no haste to swallow his meal.

"'Wumsh for bait,' he muttered, trying to indicate by signs the nearest road to Horn Lacy."

There was a general laugh.

"Wasn't it horrible?" said Mistress Nell. "Think of a mouthful of live worms!"

"Is not Horn Lacy one of my Lord Scudamore's estates?" asked Mr. Bennett.

"Ay; he was taken prisoner in Hereford, but allowed to go to London on parole. Horn Lacy was taxed £10 15s. By the bye, Captain Heyworth, is there any truth in this report I hear, that Sir William Waller is sending you to London shortly concerning Lord Scudamore's affairs?"

"Yes, sir," said Joscelyn; "I am to bear a letter for Sir William Waller, who is in some fear that, spite of his assurances, Parliament is not treating Lord Scudamore as well as he deserves. I had private business that needed looking into, and am granted three weeks' leave from Monday se'nnight."

"I wish you would make an inquiry for me while you are in London," said the Major, as the ladies left the room.

"The truth is, though I would not say it before Mistress Bennett, that Gloucester is not an over-safe place in which to leave my little maid, for like enough, they say, the King will lay siege to it. Now, I want to find out whether Helena's godmother is still living. She is a very aged lady named Madam Harford, but 'tis years since we heard of her."

"Why, sir," said Gabriel, laughing, "they say in the regiment that you know well-nigh every family in England—perchance this lady is my grand-dame who lives at Notting hill Manor, some two miles from Tyburn by the Oxford road."

"Upon my soul, that's a strange coincidence," said the Major. "But I had no notion she was of a Herefordshire family. She was a very kind friend to my late wife in London before our marriage, and stood sponsor for Helena. I thought of writing to ask her to advise some safe lodging in the city where my daughter may be sent in charge of Mistress Malvina."

"If you will trust me with your letter, I will bear it to Madam Harford and bring you back her reply, sir," said Joscelyn Heyworth; and he smiled to himself, thinking that fate was about to help his match making.

However, it was not his doing, but the Major's own arrangement which, during the course of the next few days, threw Gabriel and little Mistress Nell into frequent intercourse. The girl lived through a midsummer dream of happiness, but Gabriel, though liking very much to talk to one who was both pretty and winsome, never said a word to her that might not have been proclaimed from the housetops, and never felt his pulses beat the faster when the innocent blue eyes were lifted to his.

Marriage arrangements were most matter-of-fact in those days and the Major, before leaving Gloucester, thought it as well to broach the subject with his daughter.

"Child," he said one evening, when they were alone together in a gloomy little parlour at Alderman Pury's house, "it may be long ere I see you again, for, as you know, we march into the West to-morrow. I have had no proposal for your hand save that from Squire Norton, which I was bound to decline. But if at any time it should chance that I might arrange a marriage for you with Lieutenant Harford, would he meet with your approval?"

"Yes, sir," said little Mistress Nell, blushing.

"He is a man I would very gladly entrust you to" said the Major. "Yet think not over much of it, Nell, for the notion may come to nothing. I merely wished to know that such a plan would not be uncongenial to you."

"Oh, no, sir," faltered Helena, "not uncongenial."

And then she fell awondering whether it must ever be a choice between the fierce passion which terrified her in Squire Norton's eyes, and the easy friendliness which somehow scarcely satisfied her in Gabriel's expression. Was there, perchance, some happy mean betwixt these two, a love which had not yet come her way? If only her gallant rescuer would give her the supreme happiness of requiting in some way his service to her! She half wished herself a man that she might serve under him, and perhaps do for him on the battlefield what Captain Heyworth had done at Edgehill. And so she dreamt her innocent dreams, never knowing of the miniature that hung about Gabriel's neck, or imagining that at Hereford a pair of dark grey eyes were shedding tears more bitter than any that could ever be shed by her.

For in Hilary's home there was great sorrow; the physician's skill could no longer keep at bay the mortal illness which was steadily sapping Mrs. Unett's strength.

"If it were possible to induce Dr. Wright to come to Hereford I should like to consult with him," said Dr. Harford one morning when he felt that Hilary must be prepared for the worst. "He and his wife are still residing at Brampton Bryan for the sake of being some protection to Lady Brilliana Harley, and I scarce know whether he would leave, for they stand in great danger of being besieged in the Castle."

Hilary could not help reflecting that it was strange they should be forced to turn to Parliamentarians in their need, but Dr. Harford and Dr. Wright were by far the most eminent physicians in the neighbourhood, and she found that politics made no sort of difference when one was face to face with a grief and danger like this.

"Lady Brilliana is kindhearted and generous," she said. "I am sure she would spare Dr. Wright, and he need not be away more than four-and-twenty hours."

So the plan was proposed, and the two physicians held a consultation, and for a while Hilary hoped against hope. But at length the day came when she could no longer refuse to recognise the terrible truth—her mother was dying.

There was no great suffering; indeed, Mrs. Unett would have passed away in absolute peace had it not been for the thought of her child left behind in sorrow and loneliness, fortunately Dr. William Coke, her favourite brother, was able to ride over to Hereford on the day this was most troubling her.

"You see, Hilary cannot live on here, as she wishes to do, with no better protection than Mrs. Durdle," sighed the mother. "And though my father would gladly have her at the Palace, she doth not agree with other members of the household, and such an arrangement would never work well. I would that I could have lived to see her married."

"Too late for Mr. Geers of Garnons," said Dr. Coke, with a gleam of merriment in his eyes. "They tell me he is just betrothed to Mistress Eliza Acton. And Hilary, I understand, did refuse his suit with great decision. But do not be troubled as to her future. Why should she not come and cheer her old bachelor uncle? I should most gladly welcome her, and I'll warrant Mrs. Durdle would keep my untidy vicarage in apple-pie order."

"That she would," said Mrs. Unett, with a smile. "You are very good, brother, to suggest such a plan. To leave Hilary in your charge would be the greatest comfort to me."

She longed sorely to tell of the hope she had once cherished of seeing her child wedded to Gabriel Harford, but she had promised secrecy, and felt that matters were now hopeless; moreover, Hilary would probably prefer that her uncle should never know that chapter of her life-story. The silence was the last sacrifice the mother was to make, and it was a very real sacrifice to one who always craved the comfort of a man's opinion.

Even as she lay there musing over the possibilities of the future, Dr. Coke saw a change in her face which alarmed him. He went to the door and spoke in a low voice to his niece.

"You had better send for Dr. Harford, my dear," he said. "I fancy I see a change in your mother."

Hilary would not risk sending, she ran herself without ceremony by the garden way as she would have done in old times, and while the servant went in search of the doctor, waited in the study, looking round with an aching heart at the familiar place.

Very quickly she noted the only new thing in the room. It was the miniature by M. Jean Petitot which Gabriel had mentioned in his Christmas letter, and crossing to the mantelshelf on which it stood, she looked long and earnestly at the portrait of the man who loved her. The strong, clean-souled face appealed to all that was best in her, and the great artist had succeeded in reproducing that quiet spirituality in the eyes which had somehow dominated her in their last unhappy meeting.

An intolerable longing for his presence came over her. Most bitterly she needed him now in this time of her sorrow, and terrible was the shame and misery of realising that her own pride had wrecked his happiness as well as her own.

It was with difficulty that she could control her voice when Dr. Harford entered, and his all-observant eyes at once perceived that the sight of the miniature had been too much for her.

"My mother," she faltered.

"I will come at once," he said, taking her hand much as if she had been a child again.

The action comforted her, and she told him of her uncle's visit, and of how at first the invalid had revived and had seemed better.

But when they reached the sick-room Hilary needed no words to tell her that her mother was at the point of death.

There was a minute's silence while the doctor felt the failing pulse; a courteous word of thanks for his care; a tender farewell to her child, and a grateful glance at her favourite brother as he knelt at the bedside. Then consciousness failed; and after an interval, broken only by the voice of Dr. Coke as he read the commendatory prayer, she passed quietly away.

Hilary, dazed and tearless, let them take her out of the room unresistingly. The whole world seemed a blank to her, and her desolation was the more overwhelming because the one being who could have comforted her was, by her own fault, altogether out of reach. Her mother dead, her lover banished and rejected, and she herself crushingly conscious of her own sins and shortcomings, it seemed to her indeed that the burden of life was more than she could endure.

Dr. Coke went at once to the Palace to break the news to the Bishop, but Dr. Harford returned to the withdrawing room for a minute, feeling ill at ease as to Hilary. He found her restlessly pacing to and fro, trying not to hear Durdle's heavy footsteps as she moved about in the next room, busy with the last offices to the dead.

"My dear," he said, in his fatherly way, "you were up all last night and must rest now. Come," and he himself arranged the cushions for her on the couch and insisted that she should lie down.

"I wonder that you can endure the sight of me," said Hilary, "after all the trouble I have caused you."

He thought that in calmer moments she might regret having spoken so openly, and did not allow himself to refer to Gabriel.

"You forget that your father was my best friend, and that to be of service to you must always be a pleasure to me," he said, kindly. "Try, if possible, to sleep, my dear; your uncle and I will make all needful arrangements."

"What is the use of resting?—all is over; no one needs me," she said, wildly.

"Nay," he said; "be very sure that there will be need of all your strength in a country as full of sorrow as ours is now. So rest, my child, and wait."

And then he bade her good-bye, and went his way to comfort and cure others that were ill in body and sad of soul.

CHAPTER XVI.

Loke who that is most vertuous alway,

Prive and apert, and most entendeth ay

To do the gentil dedes that he can,

And take him for the gretest gentilman.

—Chaucer.

While Hilary was learning at Hereford that in time of sore distress differences of opinion in matters of Church and State lose all hold on the mind, Gabriel was destined to meet in Somersetshire the noblest of the King's Generals—Sir Ralph Hopton.

Waller, while awaiting reinforcements from London, had made his headquarters in Bath, and, though few days passed without skirmishes in the neighbourhood, he had been able to hold in check the combined forces of Hopton, Hertford and Prince Maurice, and to protect not only Bath but Bristol.

The citizens of Bath held him in high esteem, and when on the evening of the 16th June a messenger from the Royalist army was admitted into the city with a letter for the General, he had to run the gauntlet of some pretty sharp criticisms from the onlookers as he drew rein and dismounted at the door of the "Nag's Head" in Northgate Street.

This the young man took in very good part, and Gabriel, who chanced to be leaning against the open door listening to one of Major Locke's stories, felt drawn to him when he saw the imperturbable good humour with which he bore such taunts as:

"Let the barber shave your love-locks!" and, "Here's a curled Court darling!"

"Take the gentleman's horse," said Gabriel, turning to one of the grinning ostlers, and then stepping forward he greeted the newcomer courteously.

"I have a letter from Sir Ralph Hopton, and am to place it in Sir William Waller's own hands," said the young officer. "Is he within?"

Something in his voice and face seemed curiously familiar, and as Gabriel led him to the General's room he could not resist hazarding a question.

"An I mistake not, sir, you must be a kinsman of Captain Heyworth?"

The young officer laughed.

"Truth! I myself am Captain Heyworth—Richard Heyworth of Shortell. Tell me, is my brother Joscelyn here?"

"Unfortunately not. He hath three weeks' leave, and hath gone to London on business."

"A curse on my ill-luck!" said Dick Heyworth. "I made sure I should have seen him here."

He seemed so grievously disappointed that Gabriel felt the more drawn to him and announcing "Captain Heyworth," watched the General's surprise and perplexity as the visitor entered the room. Waller signed to him to remain in attendance, and put one or two rapid questions to Richard Heyworth.

"I sent a letter to Sir Ralph Hopton after the fray at Chewton Mendip by the hands of Mr. Reginald Powell—a prisoner we had taken—did it reach him safely?"

"Ay, sir—a letter proposing an exchange of prisoners. This is the General's reply, and he bade me say he earnestly hoped you would agree to the second proposal he makes."

Waller read the letter thoughtfully.

"I will write a reply," he said at length, "and in the absence of your brother will send it by Lieutenant Harford, who shall accompany you on your return. I see, Sir Ralph writes from Wells; both you and your horse will need rest and refreshment after such a ride. Lieutenant Harford will see that you are well cared for."

"Shall I return for your reply, sir?" asked Gabriel.

"Come for it at sunrise to-morrow," said Waller, glancing again at the letter. Then, looking up at Dick Heyworth, "I would fain comply with Sir Ralph's request could I consult my personal wishes, but I am bound to think only of the Cause. I will wish you good-night, sir."

It only remained for Dick Heyworth to bow and withdraw, but Gabriel noted his look of annoyance as they entered the adjoining room, where the remains of the officers' supper were still on the table.

"'Tis ever 'the Cause, the Cause,' with you Parliament folk," he said, shrugging his shoulders. "Now if our two Generals could have met there might be some hope of making an end of the war."

"Was that your errand?"

"That and the reply as to the exchange of prisoners. You had best not tell it in Gath, however. Sir Ralph Hopton, as you doubtless know, was an old friend of your General's, and they served together in the German wars. He had a great wish to meet him and discuss this accursed civil strife."

"Of what avail would that be," said Gabriel, "when the King will never offer terms that can be accepted, and when Parliament places no confidence in his promises."

"Ay, there's the rub," said Dick.

"Your Cornishmen know how to fight," said Gabriel. "They gave us a smart repulse at Chewton Mendip."

"Yes," said Dick, making great inroads on the plate of beef his companion had set before him. "They are the best soldiers we have, and are men after Sir Ralph's own heart, for they are as little given to plundering as the best of your Puritan troops. Sir Ralph is like to break his heart over Prince Maurice's men, for they plunder right and left."

"It would be little to your General's liking, specially in his own county of Somerset."

"That is what irks him so sorely, for they ruin the property of all his old friends and neighbours. But tell me of my brother, for I have not clapped eyes on him since you took Winchester."

"He hath been several times of late at Gloucester, and was in high spirits at encountering there Mistress Clemency Coriton, his betrothed."

"He was ever a lucky dog," said Dick, laughing.

"He came very near to being shot in the back t'other night, by a treacherous blackguard that serves under Prince Maurice," observed Gabriel.

"Ha! I can guess who that is," said Dick. "Now I understand the dark hints and innuendoes that Colonel Norton has thrown out once or twice of late. Tell me what really passed."

Gabriel, though omitting Helena's name, told the story of her father's duel with Norton and of their subsequent errand.

"That was an affair after Joscelyn's own heart," cried Dick. "Did I not tell you he was a lucky dog? Such chances are for ever coming his way. Never mind, my turn will come."

Just after sunrise the two young officers rode off together to Wells, and by the time they had reached Hopton's quarters, an old house in the Close, they had become fast friends, united by their common affection for Joscelyn. Gabriel was taken into a panelled room, where the Royalist General sat writing at a table in the oriel window. He was a middle-aged man, with threads of grey already showing in his long dark hair, and there was something singularly noble in his clear, open face and dignified bearing. A man of stainless character, he found many of his co-workers very little to his taste, and he seemed grievously disappointed to learn that his old friend Waller had felt unable to agree to the proposed meeting. Gabriel could not help glancing at his expression now and then as he read the letter which he had eagerly opened.

It ran as follows:

"Sir,"—The experience which I have had of your worth and the happiness which I have enjoyed in your friendship, are wounding considerations to me, when I look upon this present distance between us; certainly, sir, my affections to you are so unchangeable, that hostilitie itself cannot violate my friendship to your person; but I must be true to the cause wherein I serve. The old limitation of usque ad aras holdeth still, and where my conscience is interested all other obligations are swallowed up. I should wait on you according to your desire, but that I look on you as engaged in that partie beyond the possibility of retreat, and consequents incapable of being wrought upon by anti-persuasion, and I know the conference could never be so close betwixt us, but that it would take wind and receive a construction to my dishonour. That great God, who is the Searcher of all hearts, knows with what a sad sense I go upon this service, and with what a perfect hate I detest this war without an enemie, but I look upon it as opus domini which is enough to silence all passion in me. The God of Peace send us, in His good time, the blessing of peace, and in the meantime fit us to receive it. We are both on the stage and must act those parts that are assigned to us in this tragedy, but let us do it in the way of honour and without personal animositie; whatsoever the issue of it be, I shall never resign that dear title of

"Your most

"Affectionate Friend

"and Faithful Servant,

"William Waller.

"Bath, June 16, 1643."

Sir Ralph Hopton sighed as he refolded the letter; it had only made him crave more passionately for an end of the war which was dividing England. He glanced a second time at Gabriel, struck by something familiar in his face. "Are you not one of the Herefordshire Harfords?" he asked.

"Yes, sir," replied Gabriel, "son of Dr. Bridstock Harford, of Hereford."

"I met him many years ago at Canon Frome, when he must have been of your age; you are his living image. How is my kinsman, Sir Richard Hopton?"

"He is well, sir, but hath suffered from the plundering of his house at Canon Frome by the Royalists, to revenge his having accompanied my Lord Stamford last year when he took Hereford."

"These plunderings and robberies are hateful to me," said Sir Ralph. "Nothing does so much to embitter the struggle as the wanton destruction of property. By-the-bye, an' I mistake not, you are connected with the Hoptons through a marriage with Madame Martha Harford, so that in somewhat remote fashion you are also akin to me. I could wish you were with us in this contest, but as they tell me Sir William Waller often says, we will part as enemies that may live to be friends." Then bidding Dick Heyworth show all hospitality to Waller's messenger, he dismissed them and began to write his reply to the Parliamentary General.

A few hours later, when Gabriel, with the letter in his wallet, paused at the city gate to take leave of Dick Heyworth, it chanced that Colonel Norton, lounging at his ease at the open window of an alehouse hard by, was roused to sudden interest in the proceedings.

"'Tis the very man!" he exclaimed. "Now I shall get hold of his name, which hath slipped my memory, and will have some sport with the Puritan dog."

He strolled out of the alehouse, carelessly greeted Dick Heyworth, and, with a mockingly profound bow and sarcastic smile, turned to Gabriel.

"Good day, sir!" he exclaimed. "Have you had any more midnight rides with the fair Helena?"

Dick Heyworth, seeing the angry flush which rose in his new friend's face, hastily interposed, hoping to avert a storm.

"To name a lady in such a fashion in the open street, sir,——" he began, but there he was interrupted by Gabriel, who, furious at the insinuation and the insult conveyed in Norton's look and tone, could no longer restrain his tongue.

"In her present abode she is little like to need protection from villainous assaults such as yours, sir," he said, with that sudden fiery vehemence which comes with startling force now and then from the most self-controlled men.

"Ha!" said, Norton, with his short, harsh laugh. "I have no doubt you stowed her away very conveniently in the godly city of Gloucester, where, doubtless, all men are saints. Beggarly hypocrites that you are! But the King will soon triumph now, and I ask nothing better than to have the privilege of hanging you, you Puritan mongrel!"

"The King's cause is ill served, sir, by such words," said Dick, angrily. "You, perhaps, do not understand that Lieutenant Harford bears a letter from Sir Ralph Hopton, and cannot take up a personal quarrel."

Norton burst into loud laughter.

"Bless you, my children!" he exclaimed, his eyes twinkling with genuine merriment. "'Twas precisely the name of this gentleman that I wished to discover—do not let me detain you longer now, Mr. Harford, we shall meet again, for I never allow myself to be baulked."

With a derisive smile he returned to the alehouse, and Dick Heyworth rode on for a little way with his new friend.

"That fellow has a bitter grudge against you and my brother," he said. "You had best beware of him, for he sticks at nothing. 'Tis men of that make who are the ruin of His Majesty's Army."

"But, on the other hand, you have men like my Lord Falkland and Sir Ralph Hopton and Sir Bevil Granville," said Gabriel, his chivalrous nature readily sympathising with what was passing in his companion's mind. "And, as you may guess, we have not a few narrow-minded zealots and fanatics who are ill to work with."

"True, men like that Original Sin Smith that played Joscelyn false at Farnham," said Dick, "Indeed, I think you are right, such a fellow revolts one even more than Colonel Norton, being both villain and hypocrite."

Then, entrusting Gabriel with a letter for his brother, and many last messages, Dick Heyworth returned to Wells, and Gabriel rode back to Waller's headquarters, his mind full of Sir Ralph Hopton's last words, "We will part as enemies that may live to be friends." If only Hilary would have given him as much comfort as that, how hopefully would he have faced the bitterness of this heart-rending strife!

The sun was setting when he rode into Bath, and the Abbey tower outlined against a saffron sky rose in solemn grandeur, which unconsciously soothed his troubled mind, though, like most of his generation, he had very little feeling for the beautiful. What he had was gained almost entirely from the poetry of the Bible—a Book which had been to him and to his father before him the great educator, and to which, in common with all the best of the Puritans, he owed the sterling honesty and the moral courage that characterised him. To the modern world he would have seemed primitive and unsophisticated. But there is a certain kind of simplicity that is very ill compensated by æstheticism, and sturdy Puritan uprightness is sorely needed in these latter days of luxury, lying and greed of gain.

Having delivered the letter from Sir Ralph Hopton, and Dick Heyworth's letter to his brother, into the General's keeping, he went in search of Major Locke, and to his great delight found the rare treat of a letter from home awaiting him. His father gave him the new's of Mrs. Unett's death, and overwhelmed with the sense of what Hilary's desolation would be, he lost no time in writing to her. But it is one thing to write a letter in time of war, and quite another to send it safely to its destination.

The next night the troops were ordered into the Bradford Valley, and a strong position was taken up on Claverton Down, for scouts had brought word that the Royalists meant to attempt Bath from that quarter. Some days passed before Gabriel found any one to whom he could entrust the letter, but at last Major Locke's servant Tobias, who was carrying a packet to Mistress Helena at Gloucester, consented to take charge of it. Tobias, however, though thoroughly honest, was not blessed with brains. Thinking to save himself, he made what he fondly hoped was a short cut across the down, instead of availing himself of the sheltered valley. To his utter dismay, he came across a Royalist officer and a couple of scouts who were reconnoitering to see whether it would be possible after all to capture the city from the Bradford Valley, and while Hopton's men were making a vigorous attack on the position at Claverton, poor Tobias found that his venture was like to cost him his life.

The scouts seized him and one glance at the face of the officer told him that his last hour was at hand.

"You come from Waller's camp," said Colonel Norton, sharply. "Don't deny it, I can read it in your craven face. What strength has he there?"

Tobias told the number of the troops.

"What are you doing here?"

"I was but on an errand," faltered the poor fellow. "I am nought but a servant, sir."

"Whose servant?"

"Major Locke's, sir," said Tobias, sealing his own doom by the words.

Norton chuckled gleefully.

"Ha! that's good hearing. You are carrying his letters no doubt. Here string him up, men, and we'll turn out his pockets afterwards, and save him the discomfort of a struggle. These Puritans have such consciences, he would doubtless scruple to part with his trust."

"Sir, sir," pleaded poor Tobias. "They can be naught to you—they be no despatches—they be but private letters, and both of them only to ladies, sir."

At this, Norton burst into a roar of laughter. The two scouts, hating both the work and the officer in command, took advantage of his convulsions of merriment, to loose the prisoner.

"Chuck the despatches and run," whispered one of them. And Tobias needed no second bidding.

Flinging the letters on the ground, he ran like a hunted hare to the shelter of a little coppice, and though Norton swore at the scouts as they made a feint of rushing in pursuit, and sent more than one shot after the terrified messenger, he was too eager to seize on the letters before the wind whirled them away to trouble much about his victim. Tobias gasping for breath ran madly down the slope, till at length catching his foot on a tree stump he fell violently to the ground, severely spraining his ankle. But a sprained ankle means little to a man who has been at death's door; he lay patiently enough in the wood till next day, and then limped down to Claverton to learn from the villagers that Waller had retired to Bath, and that the Royalists had abandoned the Avon, and were to attempt the capture of Bath from the north.

What with skirmishes and intricate manoeuvring, it was not until the Royalist forces had encamped at Marshfield that Norton had time to open the letters he had seized. But his satisfied chuckle as he read the first, and the malicious merriment in his eyes, showed that the capture had been worth making. The Major's letter was short, and ran as follows:

"Dear Nell,—Captain Joscelyn Heyworth hath returned from London, where, at my request, he visited your godmother, Madam Harford. Strangely enough, she proves to be a kinswoman of Lieutenant Harford, your trusty rescuer. Madam Harford desires that at the earliest opportunity you travel with Cousin Malvina to London, and that you make her house—Notting hill Manor—your home until these calamities be overpast. Mr. Bennett and Alderman Pury will let you know when the journey may be attempted, and will find you a proper escort. I write in great haste; a battle is imminent, Sir W. Waller hoping thereby to save Bath, and to prevent the army of the West from joining the King's forces at Oxford. I am just exchanged into Sir Arthur Hazlerigg's new regiment, known as the 'Lobsters,' and you would smile to see how fine we look, most thoroughly encased in armour, like the knights of old. Truth to tell, I find it mighty cumbersome, but it may serve. God keep you from all ill, and grant us in peaceful times a happy reunion. I could wish to have seen you safely wedded to such an one as Lt. G. H., but have not as yet broached the subject with him.

"Your loving father,

"George Locke.

"To Mrs. Helena Locke,

"at the House of Alderman Pury,

"Gloucester."

Norton refolded this sheet carefully, and thrust it into an inner pocket, reflecting that later on it might suit his purposes to send it to little Mistress Nell. Then, with a smile of malicious enjoyment, he read the address on the second letter.

"To Mistress Hilary Unett,

"care of the Rt. Rev. the Bishop of Hereford."

Unfastening the seal, he read with some surprise, the following words:

"I hesitate to break that silence which you most emphatically enforced when we last met, but the news of your bereavement, which I have just learnt from my father, so stirs my heart that write I must, and should this only offend you more deeply I must pay the penalty. That you are desolate and sad at heart I well know. My beloved, if only I could comfort you I would ask nothing more—but this is the sorest part of our unhappy difference as to the war, that I am cut off from the right of serving you, and am doubtful whether you will even be at the trouble to read these lines. But should you read them, then I pray you read betwixt the lines the love for you which fills my heart—a love that is ill at expressing itself in words, but which will always be longing to serve you while life lasts. It is some consolation to me to know that you are with your grandfather, whose kindness when last he parted with me I cannot forget. I have just had the pleasure of seeing Sir Ralph Hopton, the noblest of all His Majesty's Generals, being sent (in the absence of Captain Joscelyn Heyworth) with a letter from Sir W. Waller. Sir Ralph was kind enough to call cousins with me on account of Mistress Martha Harford, who was afterwards wedded to Mr. Michael Hopton—you will remember smiling over her mistaken epitaph on the monument in Bosbury Church. Was it in some other life that we spent that happy day at Bosbury, when we were betrothed? Would to God we could find ourselves there once more with hearts united! Should you see my father, will you let him know that we are expecting a decisive battle in the neighbourhood of Bath? I will write to him after it is over.

"Dear Hilary, for the sake of old days, I pray you at least to accept my sympathy in your sorrow, and

"Believe that I rest ever

"Your faithful servant,

"Gabriel Harford."

Norton's face, as he read, was a curious study. Anything more unlike his notion of a love-letter it was impossible to conceive. He read it twice, and a new sense of shame began to steal over him. His eyes at length rivetted themselves on the one sentence, "for the sake of old days," but he was looking, in truth, at some scene long ago in his own life—a scene which softened him strangely, and called out the better side of his nature.

"Curse it!" he cried, at length, beginning to pace the room restlessly. "I wish I had never meddled with that boy's love-letter. God! if I could undo the past!"

With a hand that shook, he took up a tankard of ale and hastily drained it.

"Humph! that's better," he muttered. "A pox on such soft-hearted sentiment! It must be as the proverb hath it, 'Every man for himself, and the devil take the hindmost.' I can no more undo my past than I can get this letter back into the messenger's pocket, and there's an end on't."

With that he tore up the sheet and flung the pieces out of the window, watching the rapid way in which the summer wind whirled them into space. Then, drawing out the Major's letter, he once more perused it, and very soon was laughing heartily over the father's matrimonial hopes for his daughter.

"'Twill be hard if I can't contrive to put a spoke in his wheel," he thought. "I'll be revenged on him before long, and on Mr. Gabriel Harford, too. What does the fellow mean by philandering with little Nell, when he is still courting this Hereford lady? I should have had her t'other night if it had not been for his cursed knight-errantry."

And then once more that memory which had no connection at all with little Helena Locke came back to torture him.

With an impatient shrug of the shoulders he drew out his pipe and began to fill it, humming to himself meanwhile a song from The Queen of Corinth:

Weep no more, nor sigh, nor groan;

Sorrow calls no time that's gone;

Violets plucked the sweetest rain

Makes not fresh nor grow again.

The next day one of the most obstinately contested battles of the campaign was fought on the slopes of Lansdown, and Norton, who with all his faults was an excellent soldier, had no time to think of past regrets or of private enmities. Again and again the Parliamentary troops charged down the hill, but Hopton's Cornishmen with their deadly pikes pressed bravely on. The slaughter on both sides was terrible, the Royalists alone leaving fourteen hundred dead and wounded on the field, and Waller's army, forced at length from their position on the brow of the hill by superior numbers, had to retire along the ridge to Bath about midnight.

The city was saved, for Hopton's army was in no condition to attack it, and the noble-hearted Royalist General was full of sadness when, on the return of daylight, he visited the battlefield. He had himself been slightly wounded, but by sunrise he was in the saddle again, giving directions as to the relief of the injured, and by his kindly words bringing comfort to many of the poor fellows who had lain in torture on the hillside all through the night.

While he was thus occupied, Captain Nevill, the officer in attendance on him, drew his attention to a trumpeter from the Parliamentary army, accompanied by one of Waller's officers. As the latter dismounted and came forward, Sir Ralph, scanning his face, saw that it was none other than Gabriel Harford, who, since Captain Heyworth had been left on the battle-field either dead or wounded, was acting as Waller's galloper. He had come with a request from the Parliamentary General for a day's truce in order to succour the wounded and bury the dead.

"'Tis needed indeed by us as well as by you," said Hopton; and his words were spoken to that awful accompaniment of groans and piteous cries for water which Gabriel could so well recall after the battle of Edgehill.

"Sir William Waller bade me also ask if any surgeon from Bath should be sent to the aid of Sir Bevil Granville," he said, watching the General's face with interest.

"The offer does credit to his humanity. Sir Bevil was Carried to Cold Ashton Vicarage," replied Sir Ralph; "but he was dying last night, I think by now he is past surgeon's aid."

The words had hardly left his lips when a tremendous explosion threw both speaker and hearers to the ground. Gabriel and Captain Nevill escaped unhurt, and were soon on their feet again, eagerly bending over the prostrate form of the General, while others rushed to the yet more terribly injured Major Sheldon, and lifted aside the bodies of those who had been actually killed.

"There is life in him yet," said Captain Nevill, with his fingers on the General's pulse.

"Yes," said Gabriel, "but there won't be long, unless we can check this. Quick! off with your scarf, sir, and bind it about his arm while I hold the artery."

"I' faith, sir, you're as good as a leech," said the Royalist Captain, unable even at that moment of anxiety to forbear a glance at the strangely attractive face of Waller's envoy.

"A poor substitute, but the son of a physician," said Gabriel, deftly guiding the rather clumsy efforts of Captain Nevill.

A moan from Hopton brought a look of relief to both his helpers.

"Who is it?" he groaned; "what hath chanced?"

"A powder-waggon accidentally exploded, sir," said Captain Nevill.

"I can't hear a word," moaned Hopton; "it hath deafened and blinded me. Let the troops fall back on Marshfield."

But here the agony becoming unbearable he lost consciousness, and naught remained for his saddened followers but to obey those last words, and carry him from the battle-field.

"I will ride back and send the best surgeon in Bath to wait upon him," said Gabriel, longing to stay and search for his friend Joscelyn Heyworth, who must be lying somewhere on the hillside, though whether dead or wounded he could not tell. But his duty was to ride back to Waller with Hopton's message, and personal wishes had to be stifled.

"Should Sir Ralph recover I shall tell him he owes his life to you, for assuredly he would have bled to death had it not been for your promptitude," said Captain Nevill, warmly. "Doth he know your name?"

"Yes, sir, 'tis Gabriel Harford. Farewell, and may God preserve your leader."

Then, remounting his horse at the too of the hill, he galloped along the Lansdown ridge, making all speed back to Sir William Waller, that help might be sent as soon as possible to those tortured soldiers, whose groans still rang in his ears.

The horrors of the campaign made his heart ache, yet if ever war was unavoidable he honestly believed that it was this war, which had only been undertaken after years of patient endeavour to combat by peaceful means the King's misrule. Again and again, moreover, the disputants had paused during the hostilities and had tried to come to a peaceful settlement, but the fatal bar of the King's insincerity and the repeated discovery of his underhand dealings while negotiations for peace were yet going on had always frustrated the hopes of the distracted country.

Gabriel was ready and willing to lay down his life for the freedom of England and the preservation of the Reformed religion. The recent death of John Hampden the Patriot, had, indeed, filled him with renewed eagerness to sacrifice everything for the cause. And, at the same time, he could not but feel, as his friend Joscelyn Heyworth had felt after the return from Chalgrove Field, a burning desire to call to account the main authors of all this woe. His Majesty and the Archbishop might personally be well-meaning men, but their tyrannical government had filled him with loathing, and he grieved to think of the thousands of homes which their policy had blighted. For Sir Bevil Granville and for the brave Cornishmen who had fallen on the previous day he could only feel admiration, but he would gladly have had in their stead those he deemed the cause of all the misery—the hard and aggressive Dr. Laud and the weak and untrustworthy King.

CHAPTER XVII.

They say it was a shocking sight,

After the field was won;

For many thousand bodies here

Lay rotting in the sun;

But things like that you know must be

After a famous victory.

—Southey.

Never, perhaps, had the hopes of Waller's army been higher than on the morning of the 13th July as they encompassed the town of Devizes, the attack upon which had been fixed for that evening. Throughout the march from Bath they had been able to harass the rear of Hopton's army: they had intercepted a convoy of ammunition coming from Oxford; and though Prince Maurice's convoy had contrived to escape, they held Hopton and all his foot cooped up in Devizes with no match and very little powder.

While still suffering terribly from the effects of the explosion, the brave Royalist General had the wit to devise on his sickbed a plan for supplying match. He ordered the townsfolk to give the ropes which held up the sacking of their beds, and these, when boiled in resin, served very well for the emergency. Still, he was heavy-hearted, for he knew that the unfortified town could not long withstand such an attack as Waller was like to make, and in great suffering of body and anxiety of mind he lay musing over the dire misfortunes which had followed this army of the West.

The hours passed slowly by, and at length early in the afternoon he was roused by the approach of quick footsteps.

"Sir, sir," cried Captain Nevill, eagerly, "we are, I trust, saved. Prince Maurice hath returned from Oxford bringing fresh troops under my Lord Wilmot. They are massed on Roundway Down."

"Massed where?" cried Hopton, still somewhat deaf from his accident.

"A mile off, on Roundway Down," shouted Captain Nevill.

"Then, for the time, Devizes is saved," said Hopton, with a sigh of relief, "for Sir William Waller will assuredly draw off his troops and give the Prince battle at the foot of the down."

Such, indeed was Waller's intention, but his plans were frustrated by the over-eagerness of his friend, Sir Arthur Hazlerigg. Remembering the gallant behaviour of the "Lobsters" at

Lansdown and the terror they had struck into the hearts of the Royalists, he charged gallantly, but rashly, up the slippery and precipitous hill. The Royalists bore down upon them with crushing force, and, to the dismay of Waller and his troops on the plain below, the whole regiment thus sharply repulsed tore frantically down the hill.

It was the most appalling sight Gabriel had ever seen; the maddened horses, forced down perilous heights "where never horse went down or up before," fell by scores, crushing their riders, and, to his horror, he saw his friend Major Locke first wounded in the thigh by a musket ball, and then thrown headlong to the ground with his horse on the top of him.

The sight of this was more than he could endure, for he knew only too well the horrible agony the Major would undergo. Receiving a word of permission from Waller, he set spurs to his horse, and rode in hot haste to the rescue, hoping to bring his friend to shelter. But by the time he had dragged him from beneath the horse and had contrived to lift him on to his own beast, he found, to his utter dismay, that the whole of Waller's cavalry had been put to flight. The terrible sight of the destruction of Hazlerigg's regiment had filled the men with panic, and, seeing that they were hemmed in on the side of Devizes by Hopton's steadily advancing Cornishmen, they broke and fled in the wildest disorder.

To rejoin his routed comrades was for the present impossible; already they were riding pell-mell back to the west, hotly pursued by the Royalists, and all he could do was to try to find some sort of shelter for his wounded friend. Leading his horse cautiously along the side of the down, and supporting the Major as well as he could in the saddle, he gradually drew off from the scene of the disaster. At any moment, as he well knew, they might be seen by the enemy and shot down; but at length, thanks to the general absorption in the pursuit, he succeeded in gaining a little hollow scooped out of the hillside, where, sheltered by a few stunted trees he had the good fortune to find one of the rude huts used by shepherds in the lambing season.

"You shall rest here," he said, helping Major Locke to dismount. "Then, later on, when the coast is clear I will try to get you to less comfortless quarters."

"You have saved my life, lad," said the Major, sinking down on to the mud floor of the hut with a groan. "The plungings of my poor Whitefoot would soon have crushed me to death. Now, an' you love me, help me out of this armour."

"Alas! 'twas the heavy armour that proved the death of many of our comrades," said Gabriel, relieving the Major from his cumbrous burden. "The weight was too much for them to remount quickly if once unhorsed."

Taking the orange scarf from his waist, he succeeded in bandaging the Major's wound; then unrolling the cloak which was fastened on his saddle, he made the injured man fairly comfortable, and having secured his horse to a tree hard by, sat down and tried to form some plan for the future.

"Have you no water?" groaned the Major. "I am half mad with thirst."

"There is not a drop," said Gabriel; "but when dusk comes I will go out and reconnoitre. We must get you out of this filthy hut as soon as may be. I will fetch you water, and make some plan for your removal."

The waiting seemed long, but at length, when all seemed quiet and twilight was coming on, Gabriel stole cautiously forth on his dangerous errand. At a distance he judged to be about a mile from the hollow he saw lights burning in a house, and since it lay in the opposite direction to Devizes, and away from the western quarter in which Waller's flying cavalry had been pursued by the foe, he thought it might be possible to get safe shelter there for the wounded Major. He dared not, however, risk moving him until he had made sure, and hurrying across the open down, through a cornfield, and into a deep lane which led to a main road, he found on approaching nearer that the lights burnt in the windows of a substantial farmhouse.

Should he risk the chance of encountering Royalists, who would instantly make him prisoner? There was nothing whatever to indicate whether the house contained friends or foes. On the other hand, it was impossible to linger, or it would grow too dark to find his way back to Major Locke's hiding-place. He must put a bold face on it and knock.

In response he heard the heavy bolts withdrawn, and the door was slowly opened by an old, grey-haired man, who peered suspiciously at the stranger standing in the gloom of the porch.

"I have come to crave water and, if possible, linen for a sorely wounded man," said Gabriel, his heart sinking a little as he noticed the severity of the old man's face. It was certainly not the face of one who cultivated the virtues of compassion and tender-heartedness.

"As grim an old fellow as I ever clapped eyes on," he reflected, ruefully. "There'll not be much help here."

"Before I say ay or no to that I will hear who thou art for," said the master of the house, sternly.

"Surely you would not refuse a cup of water to a wounded man whether he were friend or foe," said Gabriel.

"Ay, that would I in good sooth, if the wounded man was one of the Amalekites, a foe to the truth," said the veteran, with a gleam of indignant zeal in his hard eyes.

Gabriel gave a sigh of relief; he had not lighted on a fiery Royalist who would hand him over as a prisoner, but upon one of those stern and uncompromising Puritans who literally applied every word of the Old Testament to the troubles of their own day.

"Nay, we are not what you call Amalekites," he replied, biting his lip to keep back a smile; "we were both in Sir William Waller's army. An' you could give shelter to my friend,

Major Locke, you would be doing a good deed, and he will be well able to recompense you."

"I cannot take him in now—the women-folk be all abed and asleep, and we be hard-working folk; but bring him at dawn to-morrow and my wife will tend him before she sets about her business in the dairy."

Gabriel thanked him heartily, and gladly accepted half a loaf of rye bread which the farmer proffered with the flagon of water.

"Now if you could but spare me a bit of linen I should have better hope of bringing my wounded friend here in safety," he said, glancing round the great kitchen to which he had been led.

"The women-folk would ha' known what to give thee, sir," said the farmer, in perplexity, "but beshrew me I can't tell where——"

He broke off with an exclamation of relief, and crossing the room took down a long roller towel on which the household were wont to wipe their hands, apparently without much preliminary washing.

"Here, sir, use this," he said. And Gabriel, treasuring up the story to amuse his father when next they met, but too well-seasoned a warrior after his nine months' campaign to be in the least dainty, accepted the towel with genuine gratitude, and returned to his friend as fast as the fading light and the perplexities of the way would allow.

The Major was so much exhausted by the dressing of his wound that he fell asleep directly he had refreshed himself with the water and the rye bread. Gabriel, not daring to close his eyes lest he should sleep after daybreak, paced to and fro outside the hut, and thought sadly enough over the tragedy he had seen enacted that day. Now and then on the soft summer wind the distant sound of groans reached his ear, for many of the victims still lay as they had fallen on the hill side, and several times the piercing shriek of a wounded horse made him shudder.

He resolved that as soon as he had left the Major in safekeeping at the farmhouse, his best plan would be to rejoin Waller, who, in all probability, would make in the first instance for Bristol, and try to reorganise his shattered army. But as he thought of the desperate condition of the Parliamentary forces, and of the extraordinary conduct of Lord Essex in permitting the reinforcements from Oxford to escape him when, with his whole army, he was lying idle at Reading, his heart was sorely troubled; for it seemed to him that the Cause was being overborne, and that evil was like to triumph.

With a sigh, he stretched himself for a time on the sheep-cropped grass of the steep little hollow, watching the stars and the swaying of the branches in the group of trees hard by. The sight brought to his mind certain long-familiar words about one in olden days who had been troubled by the near approach of an overwhelming army, which threatened to ruin his country—

And his heart was moved, and the heart of his people, as the trees of the wood are moved with the wind.. . . Then said the Lord to Isaiah, "Go forth now to meet Ahaz.... and say unto him, 'Take heed, and be quiet; fear not, neither be faint-hearted.'"

And therewith he fell to thinking of the strange rise and fall of nations, and of the things which make a nation truly great. How transitory was all earthly glory and dominion—how eternal the glory of truth and righteousness, and the joy of struggling to right wrong!

Thus the night wore away; and at daybreak he saddled his horse, and, rousing Major Locke, helped him with great difficulty to mount. Then, slowly and carefully, he guided Harkaway along the slippery down, and, skirting the cornfield, came out into the lane below. The hedges rose high on either side, cutting off all view of the surrounding country; but as they paced slowly round the last turning and came into sight of the main road, a sound of tramping feet made Gabriel pause. Undoubtedly soldiers were approaching, and he cautiously led Harkaway into a shady nook, where they could see but were little likely to be seen.

For a minute his heart beat high with hope, for he was certain that the men wore orange scarves; then, with a pang, he saw that many had been stripped of their buff coats, while, from their dejected bearing, it was only too evident that they were prisoners.

"'Tis Sir William Waller's foot soldiers," whispered the Major, "they are marching them to Oxford."

"Shall we turn back?" questioned Gabriel.

"Nay, lie low here in the shadow, they will never notice us," said the Major.

The words had only just been uttered when, to their consternation, Harkaway, catching sight of the horses ridden by a couple of officers, whinnied loudly.

"The very beast we stand in need of," said one of the officers, with a laugh, "and right willing to come with us, me-thinks."

Setting spurs to their horses the two young fellows swooped down upon the little group in the lane, and Gabriel, seeing that escape was hopeless, stood his ground.

"By your leave, sir," he said, as one that he afterwards learnt to be Captain Tarverfield, snatched at Harkaway's bridle, "I do but carry a sorely injured friend to the farm hard by, and you are welcome to the horse then."

They laughed, boisterously.

"Nay, but you will have to join our merry company yonder, my worthy Roundhead," said the elder of the two. "Short hair and a well-bred accent mark you out as a traitor. 'Tis idle to pretend that you are a Cavalier's serving-man."

"I make no pretence, sir," said Gabriel, angrily. "I do but ask you, out of common humanity, to let a wounded man pass."

"Oh! Lord Harry Dalblane knows naught of humanity," said Captain Tarverfield, laughing.

"So it seems," said Gabriel, with bitterness.

"You must come out of this hole, and see what our Colonel has to say about it," said Lord Harry, gripping Gabriel firmly by the arm and following his companion, who led Harkaway out to the main road. "Here, by good fortune, he comes. Sir, an' it please you to call a halt, we have taken two more prisoners, and a horse that is well worth having."

Gabriel, looking up in the dim light, gave a start of dismay when he perceived that the Colonel was Major Locke's deadly foe.

"Why, Harry! you are worth your weight in gold," exclaimed Norton, with a chuckle of satisfaction. "You have taken the two men I most desired to have."

"'Twas the horse that I desired," said Lord Harry, studying Harkaway's points with the keen eye of one who made the training of horses the chief interest of life. "And this prating Puritan here vows that it must first carry this wounded gentleman to a farm hard by."

"Nay, but Major Locke is coming to Oxford with me," said Norton, with a laugh. "I'll give him excellent safe quarters there in the Castle—surely a better place for you, Squire, than a mere farm."

"I shall scarce reach Oxford," said the Major, faintly.

"Sir," broke in Gabriel, "Major Locke is grievously wounded in the thigh; a thirty-mile ride will be his death."

"Well, an he cannot ride perchance you would prefer that he should walk," said Norton, mockingly. "But rest assured, Mr. Harford, that to Oxford he will have to go. I warned you at Wells that I am a man that was never yet baulked. You robbed me of my ride with the fair Helena, and I shall solace myself with this journey with her father."

There was a gleam of such devilish cruelty in his eyes, as he glanced at Major Locke to see how he was taking this, that Gabriel's wrath could no longer be restrained.

"You have him now at your mercy," he said, "and the tender mercies of the wicked are cruel; but be assured that, in another world, for every brutal deed and word you will have to pay to the uttermost farthing."

Norton laughed till his merriment infected Lord Harry, but Captain Tarverfield looked grave and ill at ease.

"You hear him, gentlemen," said Norton, still chuckling. "Methinks he had best be dubbed Ecclesiastes, or the Preacher. To-night, Lieutenant, you shall have an excellent opportunity for a sermon, but at present I will trouble you to hold your tongue and to tender me your sword."

With great enjoyment he noted the spasm of pain that passed over his captive's face as he reluctantly obeyed. Then, signing to one of his men to come forward, the Colonel gave sharp and peremptory orders:

"Strip the prisoner."

And in a minute the man had robbed Gabriel of helmet and gorget, buff coat and vest.

"Stay," said Captain Tarverfield, who had watched with some compunction the prisoner's keen suffering under this degradation. "Though it is lawful to strip an officer Colonel, you would surely leave the preacher his shirt to serve as surplice." Norton laughed, gaily.

"True. And since he is so devoted a friend to Major Locke we will rope them together, the one mounted and the other afoot. And you had better keep up the pace, Mr. Harford, or your own horse will kick you on."

The prisoner, by a supreme effort, stifled a smart retort, and began to consider how best to spare the Major when they were bound together. By the time the cavalcade moved forward again the rosy glow of sunrise was making the whole countryside beautiful, and in the sore battle that Gabriel was waging with his own nature—in the manly effort to bring his own character and conduct into accord with the high ideal he held, the sight of the rising sun brought him no small comfort. None knew better than a single-hearted Puritan how to wage that strenuous inner warfare which makes men truly great, and the conflict was to Gabriel as real as any visible struggle. As he marched now he fought as he had done on many a battle-field to the well-known battle psalm:

Let God arise, and scattered

Let all His en'mies be;

And let all those that do Him hate

Before His presence flee.

CHAPTER XVIII.

"What thing is love, which nought can countervail?

Nought save itself, e'en such a thing is love.

All worldly wealth in worth as far doth fail,

As lowest earth doth yield to heaven above.

Divine is love, and scorneth worldly pelf,

And can be bought with nothing, but with self."

—From "England's Helicon," 1600.

As they passed the farm in which he had hoped to leave the Major, he saw the master of the house standing at the gate, and, though they could not speak, an understanding glance passed between them, and Gabriel saw the eyes that had looked so hard and stern on the previous night soften in a marvellous fashion. He understood the strong bracing sympathy of the rugged old farmer, and went on his way with renewed courage.

The heat of the July day soon grew intense, and several times the cavalcade was forced to halt and rest. The Major could only just keep in the saddle, and Gabriel watched him anxiously, dreading every minute that he would succumb.

Once when they rested for a short time at West Kennet, Captain Tarverfield approached him, looking with not unkindly curiosity at the young lieutenant—his face burnt ruddy-brown by the sun, and great drops of perspiration falling on his forehead from his rough brown hair. His hazel eyes were extraordinarily clear and bright, and something in his straight, fearless glance attracted the Royalist Captain.

"You have had a hot march," he said.

"I have a good pair of legs, sir," said Gabriel; "but my arm is cramped and numb."

The Captain then noticed that to save his wounded friend he had all these hours had his wrist roped up above his head in a posture that must have long since become torturing.

With a muttered imprecation, the Royalist proceeded to unloose the rope.

"Give me your parole not to escape, and for this hour, at any rate, you can go free," he said.

Gabriel readily gave the promise, thanking the Captain warmly, and between them they then helped the Major from his horse and laid him on the grass by the roadside. The soldiers had contented themselves with stripping the younger prisoner, and had let the wounded man retain his helmet. Gabriel unfastened it now, and carried it down to the bank of the stream close by; then, returning with the water the Major was eagerly longing for, found Captain Tarverfield still in conversation with him.

"Had I known that Colonel Norton had a grudge against you both, I would have let you pass this morning," he said. "For Norton is the very devil when once he has a quarrel with any man. 'Tis of no use to ask him for a surgeon's aid, it would only make him the more brutal. We shall lie this night at Marlborough, however, and I will do what I can for you when Lord Wilmot and my Lord Falkland arrive with the next detachment."

"Did Lord Falkland come with the Oxford contingent?" asked Gabriel, sudden interest lighting up his face. "I owe my life to his kindly help at Edgehill."

And he told the young officer what had passed.

"He is greatly changed since then," said Captain Tarverfield. "They say His Majesty fears and dislikes him, while he is like a fish out of water among the courtiers and fine ladies at Oxford, who spitefully invent evil tales as to his friendship with Mistress Moray. He should never have meddled with statecraft, his conscience is over-tender for the work he is expected to do."

With that he went off to dine at the village inn, and the Major, reviving a little, began to think of the future.

"We may not again have such a chance as this," he said, "and there is a matter I would fain broach with you. I know that I have got my deathblow and am sorely troubled as to Helena. I am leaving her well-nigh alone in the world, and have arranged no marriage for her."

"But Madam Harford will have her in safe keeping, and when once she is in London you may surely rest content," said Gabriel, suddenly becoming conscious of his friend's desire.

"I would fain have had you as Lord of the Manor and husband to my child," said the Major. "The estate hath like enough suffered from Prince Maurice's troops, no details have yet reached me, but Helena's dowry is large, and I would gladly see her wedded to you and safe from Squire Norton."

"Sir," said Gabriel, looking troubled, "I will do all that I can to shield and help your daughter. But I am not free to wed her; for though 'tis true my betrothal was ended by the war, yet my love remains where it was first given."

The Major, accustomed to regard marriage chiefly as a matter of business, scarcely understood such an argument, and having found the very man he could trust—one, moreover, who shared most of his views—was very loth to relinquish hope.

"You will see what time brings forth," he said. "I should rest better in my grave could I think that Nell would be your wife."

But Gabriel, though moved by his friend's eagerness, could not be false to himself.

"I will promise, sir, to be her friend and protector," he said, "when I am out of prison. But to promise more than that would be no true kindness to her."

"The bugle sounds," said the Major. "Come, help me to mount for the last time. Most truly did the Psalmist sing, 'A horse is a vain thing to save a man.' We owe our capture to poor Harkaway's friendly greeting of the enemy's steeds." Gabriel tried to smile at the jest.

"We must take the fortune of war," he replied, cheerfully. But as the weary journey continued in the hot afternoon sun, the Major's strength waned perceptibly, and when at last they reached Marlborough, and were halted in its wide street, he seemed scarcely conscious, though he still kept in the saddle.

A kindly-looking woman came out from one of the houses with a large earthenware mug of home-brewed ale, which she offered to him. He revived a little, thanked her courteously, and made one of his usual little jokes, but with so piteous an effort that Gabriel felt a choking sensation in his throat. He was glad that they were at that moment ordered to march to St. Peter's Church, in which the prisoners were to be sheltered for the night.

The soldiers untied Major Locke and carried him into the building, putting him down on the chancel floor that he might be a little removed from the noise and confusion in the nave, into which the soldiers were driving the weary prisoners roped together in pairs.

Gabriel, relieved to find his right arm available again, dragged down an old moth-eaten cushion from the pulpit and placed it under the Major's head, removed his helmet and chafed his cold, clammy hands. But the lack of all comforts baffled his efforts, and he knew that after the long, hot ride the mere chill of the flagstones was the very worst thing for one in his state. He raised him a little, propping up the grey head on his own shoulder.

"You will send the news to Nell," said the dying man, faintly.

"Yes; but good news I hope," said Gabriel. "Captain Tarverfield will, I think, remember his promise of help, and a surgeon may do much for you. I hear steps drawing near, maybe he hath already sent. No, 'tis but the sentry."

The soldier approached them and looked down silently at the wounded man. He was a tall, powerful Irishman who had come over to England as one of Strafford's grooms, and the Major would have shrunk from him in horror had he known his nationality or guessed him to be a devout Roman Catholic. His face bore an expression which gave Gabriel hope.

"Can you not fetch a surgeon?" he asked. "Surely you may do that much for a prisoner."

"I would do it, sir," replied the man, "but I am on sentry duty, and bound not to leave the church. But sure, then, before dark one of the officers will go the rounds, and it will be him you can be asking."

He moved on, but returned presently with a garment which he had found in the vestry.

"Wrap it about the feet of him, sir," he said. "That's the best chance for him, for sure this place be as cold as any vault."

Gabriel thanked him.

"Was popish vestment ever before of such use?" said the Major, smiling faintly. "Yet, beshrew me! there's something that tickles my fancy not a little in the thought of quitting this world wrapped in a cope!"

"Talk not yet of quitting the world, sir," said Gabriel. "I have seen worse wounded men recover." But he argued against his own fears.

The church was now very quiet, the prisoners, hungry and depressed, were trying to forget their wretchedness in sleep, and only the steps of the sentry could be heard echoing at the west end of the building, until, in response to a peremptory summons, he opened the door and admitted Colonel Norton and Lord Harry Dalblane.

Gabriel at once recognised Norton's voice, and his heart sank.

"Where have you borne the wounded prisoner?" said the Colonel.

"He lies yonder, sir, in the chancel," said the sentry, "and is in sore need of a surgeon."

"Mind your own business," said the Colonel, sharply. "I shall provide him with all that he merits."

"And where is our fiery friend, the lieutenant?" said Lord Harry, staggering a little as he followed Norton up the middle aisle, for he had been drinking heavily. "Where is the little preacher?"

"He is here," said Norton, with his short scoffing laugh; "sitting like an angel on a monument supporting the effigy of a dead saint."

"Sir," said Gabriel, "I beg of you to let a surgeon wait upon Major Locke. If the ball were but removed from his wound I think he would recover."

"Am I to be dictated to first by my own sentry and then by my prisoner?" said Norton, haughtily. "Get up, you vile rebel, or it shall be the worse for you. I see you are not even bound—you need a reminder that you are no free man. Get up, I tell you!"

Gabriel reluctantly obeyed, and laid the Major down as gently as he could on the moth-eaten cushion.

Then he stood silently awaiting his captor's orders, taking meanwhile a rapid, comprehensive glance at the two officers, Norton with his short fawn and red cloak flung carelessly back over one shoulder, his wide hat and long drooping red feather cocked jauntily to the right side, his handsome, but malicious-looking, face lighted by the sunset glow which streamed through the windows; and Lord Harry laughing, foolishly, in semidrunken light-heartedness, at the thought of the amusement he had planned.

"Come, Colonel," he said, "when is the sport to begin? But our preacher is scarce in parson's habit, his knee-breeches and riding-boots are white with dust, and his shirt is like an end of Lent surplice—none of the whitest. I'll e'en go and plunder the vestry for him."

"Don't be a fool, Harry," said Norton, irritably. "Come, lieutenant, I promised you this morning you should have such a chance of preaching a sermon as had never fallen to your lot before. But I see the pulpit will scarce serve my purpose, you shall come here."

And gripping him by the shoulder he dragged him to the first pillar in the south aisle.

"Now for your cords, Harry," he said, with a chuckle. "For this gentleman is of an independent turn, and must be reminded that traitors and prisoners do not roam at large. I must trouble you, Mr. Harford, to stand with your back to the pillar, and to stretch your arms back as far as they will go; hold him steady in that hollowed-out moulding, Harry, while I make these knots fast."

With fiendish delight in giving pain he tied the cords so tightly that they cut into the victim's wrists, then he fastened the ends at the farther side of the pillar, and taking a rope tied it with the same vicious tightness a little above his knees; lastly, to make movement impossible he girdled both the prisoner and the pillar with a leathern bridle.

So far Gabriel had borne all in silence, for his mind was still taken up with the thought of his friend, and of the brutal way in which the Major was being left to die. But he was naturally sensitive to all sarcasm and ridicule, and the gibes and jeers of the half-tipsy Lord Harry, and the more biting cruelties of the tongue to which Norton subjected him, were sharper than swords.

Norton, disappointed at his failure to rouse him, turned presently with a laugh to his companion:

"They say, you know, Harry, that these Puritans will neither swear nor game nor drink. But here you see one who is giving us rare sport, and who would pledge all that he has for a drink—even of water—after the march, and who longs to swear. No, no, my fine fellow, there you stand till to-morrow—we'll have no sentiment over dying traitors. Your friend will soon be safe in hell."

This allusion to the Major at last broke down Gabriel's control.

"'Tis you that are already there!" he exclaimed, the blood boiling in his veins. "Only one led by the devil could thus treat a dying man."

"Preach away, my friend, preach away!" said Norton, with a sneer. "Your fellow prisoners are asleep, and you can't harm anyone. Come! 'tis not every day you can discourse in a church!"

Just then, in an evil moment, Lord Harry noticed that Norton, in dragging his victim from the chancel, had pulled off the top button of his shirt, which had fallen open, giving to view two or three links of a gold chain and the corner of a shagreen case.

He stumbled forward.

"Hullo!" he exclaimed, snatching at the chain and dragging up the miniature attached to it. "Ha, ha! Here's sport! See what the Puritan dog has got hanging from his collar?"

Gabriel, half maddened by feeling the sot's fingers on Hilary's picture, writhed in a frantic effort to free himself. To be forced to stand there helplessly, unable to stir hand or foot, was a torture he had never before felt.

"Oh, fie, Ecclesiastes! we named you well," said Norton, with his scoffing laugh. "You deal, like Solomon, in numbers. Shame on you! the portrait of a fair lady of Hereford on your person all the time you were philandering with pretty Helena!"

"You lie in your throat," said Gabriel, vehemently. "I did but rescue her from your fiendish trap."

"What!" cried Lord Harry, thickly. "Do you give the Colonel the lie direct, you Puritan dog? Take that!"

And he dealt Gabriel a blow on the head which for a minute half stunned him.

Norton drew his friend back.

"Hold your peace, Harry," he said. "You spoil sport. I understand how to bait this traitor."

And going close to the prisoner he lifted the miniature and scrutinised it intently, then began to pour out a flood of ribald comment.

Beside himself with rage and disgust, Gabriel in vain struggled to get free, but he could neither silence his tormentors nor shut his own ears to the foul words which sought to pollute all that he held most sacred.

With cruel delight, Norton, as he held the miniature, could feel the throbbing of his victim's heart, but he was startled when at length Gabriel's voice was heard. It was low and faint, yet there was a vibration in it which rang through the church, and a note of appeal in its tone which arrested the Colonel against his will.

"God!" cried the tortured man, "deliver us from evil."

Lord Harry burst into a roar of semi-drunken laughter. "Ay, preach and pray, my canting Puritan!" he cried.

But Norton let the miniature fall once more on Gabriel's heaving breast, and with an expression of bewildered surprise moved back a pace or two, still, however, keenly watching his victim's face. The fellow had such an extraordinary air of expecting to be delivered; and it suddenly occurred to Norton that it was not deliverance from pain that he looked for, but from something he deemed infinitely worse. For the first time he understood that this man hated evil, that he asked for deliverance from the vile imaginings, the foul suggestions that had been forced upon him. For a minute the sense of shame which had come to the Colonel as he read the letter to Hilary Unett gave him a second twinge of pain; for he recollected that the strange cry for help had not been "Deliver me," but "Deliver us."

It was with a start of superstitious fear that he saw a flickering light moving along through the fast darkening church. Gabriel noticed nothing, for his eyes had closed, his head had dropped forward.

As it drew nearer Norton saw with relief that the light came from the lantern which the Irish sentry had just kindled.

"Did you call me, sir?" said the man, approaching as if in response to a summons.

"No, I did not," said Norton, irritably.

The man saluted and was about to retire, when he caught sight of Gabriel bound to the pillar, his head drooped on his breast, his frame hanging lifeless, supported only by the cords.

The Irishman's eyes widened, he crossed himself rapidly. "The prisoner!" he stammered. "Why—yer honour—sure then he's a dead man!"

"Hold the light nearer!" said Norton sharply, and with an uneasiness he could not have explained he put his ear to the heart that was now strangely still, though but a few minutes ago he had felt it throbbing with passionate indignation.

CHAPTER XIX.

Faith can raise earth to heaven, or draw down

Heaven to earth, make both extremes to meet,

Felicity and misery, can crown

Reproach with honour, season sour with sweet.

Nothing's impossible to Faith: a man

May do all things that he believes he can.

—Christopher Harvey.

He hath but swooned," said the Colonel, after a brief pause "Come, Harry, the game is up and we'll e'en be off to bed. Lord! but this Hereford maid hath thrice the beauty of Nell. I've a mind to woo her myself!"

With a last glance at the miniature he turned haughtily to the sentry. "Bolt the church door after us and then dash some water over this prisoner; he will soon come round. And look that you leave him bound, as he is; none of your cursed Irish sentiment. If you loose him I'll have you flogged within an inch of your life."

He walked rapidly down the aisle, Lord Harry blundering after him and protesting that it had been rare sport, but that he was heavy with sleep and would like to snore the clock round.

When Gabriel came to himself all was very still. The night had closed in, but, by the light of a lantern in the angle of a high pew hard by, he saw the little side chapel and the outline of the windows. His head ached miserably, and the sharp pain caused by the cords which bound him reminded him of all that had passed. Glancing round he gave a sigh of relief on finding his tormentors gone. There was no one but the sentry, and he stood as though watching gravely a rare and unusual spectacle. In his hand he held a chalice full of water, and he now lifted this to the prisoner's lips.

"God save you kindly," he said, with a friendly look in his Irish blue eyes. "I'd be glad to unloose you, sir, if the Colonel hadn't forbidden it."

Gabriel drank thirstily, and thanked his friendly guard.

"Are you a Scot?" he asked, puzzled by the man's accent.

"No, sir. Praised be St. Patrick! I am Irish," said the soldier, with a good-natured smile.

"Irish!" exclaimed Gabriel in amazement. For to his fancy all the Irish were wild, bloodthirsty Papists, whose chief amusement was the wholesale massacre of Protestants. The incident did more to widen his mind than the study even of such a broad-minded book as Lord Brooke's "Treatise on Toleration."

"How is Major Locke?" he asked, anxiously.

"I have given him water, sir," said the man; "but there's death in his face—he'll not last long."

And with that he went on his round, leaving the prisoner to reflect over the events of the day, and to endure as best he could the increasing torture of his position.

Slowly the hours crept on, and when at length the sentry opened the great door and admitted Captain Tarverfield and two others that accompanied him, Gabriel was too much exhausted to take any notice of the sounds which echoed distinctly enough through the quiet church.

"Take the surgeon to Major Locke," said Captain Tarverfield. "Is he still living?"

"Yes, sir," said the Irishman, "he lies in the chancel. And perhaps, sir, you'll do something for Lieutenant Harford up yonder—as for me, yer honour, the Colonel vowed he'd half murther me if I unloosed him."

"If 'tis the Colonel's doing I must ask your help, my Lord," said the Captain, turning to his worn and weary-looking companion.

"Lieutenant Harford is the gentleman you mentioned to me anon?" said Lord Falkland. "He told you I saved his life at Edgehill? Well, let us see what the sentry means."

While the Irishman lighted the surgeon up the middle aisle to the chancel, Tarverfield, carrying his own lantern, led the way up the south aisle, wondering what trick Norton's malice had devised. A sudden ejaculation from Falkland made him pause.

"Look!" said the Secretary of State, his pale, melancholy face transfigured by a glow of wrathful indignation, as he pointed to the pillar and to the slight form of the lieutenant. The Captain, familiar as he was with the horrors of the battle-field, could hardly understand why the sight of this piece of wanton cruelty should anger them both so strangely. Perhaps it was the boyish face of the victim, or some subtle contrast between the nobility and strength of his expression and the cruel helplessness of his attitude.

As they drew nearer, the prisoner, whose head had drooped on his breast, looked up with a gleam of hope in his wide, weary eyes.

"Have you brought help for Major Locke?" he asked, eagerly.

"The surgeon is now with him," said Tarverfield. "What devil's trick have the Colonel and Lord Harry been up to? Have you been bound all these hours?"

Gabriel assented, but his eyes were fixed on Falkland's face; the indignation in it had changed to a look of rare delight, the delight of one who has at last found congenial work.

"Hold the lantern nearer, Captain," cried the Secretary of State, drawing his sword; and going to the farther side of the pillar he severed the cords and the rope, then stepped swiftly back.

"Have a care," he said, as Gabriel, in the first agony of moving his stiffened muscles, gave an involuntary exclamation, and then hastily apologised.

"The rope was pressing all the time on that old wound got at Edgehill the day you rescued me, my lord," he said, colouring. "You have twice made me your debtor."

"'Tis I that would thank you, sir," said Falkland, "for twice giving me an opportunity of doing work in this distracted time without scruple or misgiving. Here comes the surgeon. 'Twere well he should see to your wrists."

"Major Locke?" asked Gabriel, looking anxiously at the surgeon's face.

"'Twas too late," he replied, gravely. "The Major drew his last breath just as we approached."

Gabriel made a step or two forward in the direction of the chancel, then suddenly reeled and would have fallen to the ground had not the surgeon caught him.

"He hath swooned," said Tarverfield; "and no wonder, after the way in which his muscles have been cramped all these hours."

"With your leave he had best be carried to the vestry," said the surgeon, and, lighted by the Irishman, they carried the lieutenant out of the church.

Falkland, with a sigh, picked up the lantern and walked slowly on, glancing now and then into the high pews where lay the wretched prisoners, roped in couples, and most of them sleeping from sheer fatigue, in spite of hunger and discomfort. Reaching the chancel, he paused for some minutes beside the body of the Major. The dead face, with its majestic calm and its strange smile, contrasted curiously with the faces of the sleeping prisoners.

"Happy man!" murmured Falkland. "He is free, and has died for what he deemed his country's good, like my old friend John Hampden." Then, with a deep sigh that was almost a groan, he passed on, breathing the cry that was ever now in his heart, and often on his lips, "Peace! peace!"

When he entered the vestry he found that the leech had dressed the wounds on Gabriel's wrists, but had not yet succeeded in reviving the prisoner.

"'Tis food the poor fellow stands in need of," said Tarver-field. "I can testify that he has had nothing since sunrise yesterday, and doubtless little enough since early the day before, for Waller was too busy preparing to attack Devizes."

"With your permission, my lord, I will fetch him food from my own house," said the surgeon, who, like most of the inhabitants of Marlborough, sympathised with the

Parliament. Indeed, since many of the houses had been burnt and plundered in December by the Royalists, and the town had been constantly harassed on market days by bodies of plundering Cavaliers from Oxford, it was natural enough that the feeling was all in favour of the prisoners and against Prince Maurice's men.

"I will wait here," said Falkland, as the Captain prepared to follow the surgeon, "I wish to speak to the prisoner when he comes to himself."

The Irishman, whose guard had just been relieved, was about to follow Captain Tarverfield, when Falkland detained him, putting a few brief questions as to what he had heard while Lord Harry Dalblane and Captain Norton were with the prisoner. From the replies of the sentry he gathered enough to enable him to judge pretty accurately what had really passed, and when the man had gone he stood beside the unconscious prisoner, watching him intently and with compassion, for he was able to guess at much of his story. Presently he took a small gold pin from his lace cravat, and stooping over the prisoner restored the miniature to its place and pinned together the shirt collar.

Gabriel, opening his eyes, looked in bewilderment at the pale, sad-eyed face bending over him; then recognising it as he regained his faculties, sat up and looked round the dimly-lighted vestry in a dazed way. Some one had laid him down on a long wooden chest, the same which the Irishman had rifled for the cope. On the opposite wall hung an old board on which were painted the ten commandments, and the light from the lantern shone specially upon the words, "Thou shalt do no murder."

He shivered, for that night he had for the first time felt the deadly hatred that is akin to murder, and he knew that he had longed for the chance of taking Norton's life.

"You are cold," said Falkland. "Take this," and he put a short brown cloak he was wearing about the prisoner's shoulders. "Nay," as Gabriel thanked him, but hesitated to accept the loan, "I have no need of it, and it will be of service to you in Oxford Castle, where I fear your quarters will be comfortless enough."

"My lord," said Gabriel, "you have shown me such kindness that I will make bold to ask your help in letting Mistress Helena Locke know of her father's death."

"Where doth the lady live?" asked Falkland.

"She is at Gloucester, at the house of Alderman Pury."

"I will see that the news is sent to her, and I will do what I can, Mr. Harford, to obtain your release, for they have treated you very scurvily, and I shall see that his Majesty hears all the details. Here comes the friendly surgeon with food for you."

"You are fatigued, my lord," said Tarverfield, looking at Falkland's haggard face. "Will you not sleep before the day dawns?"

"Sleep, sir, hath long forsaken me," said Falkland, wearily. "I shall sleep when peace is declared in this unhappy country. Leave me to see Mr. Harford discuss his supper; and do you retire, for doubtless you will be early on the march."

The kindly captain, who was a good soldier, but one who rarely troubled to think of the right or wrong of the cause he defended, gladly enough returned to his quarters at the nearest inn; and the surgeon, having promised to make arrangements for the Major's burial, for which Gabriel advanced the money, walked back to his house, his mind haunted by Falkland's weary, sleepless eyes.

"'Tis not for me to 'minister to a mind diseased,'" he reflected. "As the poet hath it—

'Therein the patient

Nust minister to himself,'

But I fear 'tis over late; the sorrows of this war have broken his heart—he is far gone in melancholy."

His reflections were only too true, yet for a brief time something of the old geniality and charm insensibly returned to the Secretary of State as he watched the hungry young lieutenant forgetting his troubles in the relief of a good meal. In the rare delight of such sympathy as Falkland knew well how to bestow, Gabriel's reserve was broken down, and before the supper was ended he had revealed to his companion the story of his gradual awakening in London, had spoken of Bishop Coke's kindness to him, of one connected with the Bishop to whom he had been betrothed, and of the havoc the war had wrought in his happiness.

Instinctively his hand went to Hilary's miniature as he recalled with a shudder what had passed about it a few hours before; and then finding the way in which his shirt had been fastened, his eyes sought Falkland's with a gratitude that touched the State Secretary. With the incomparable gentleness characteristic of him, he said a few words to the boy, which by their reverent sympathy seemed to blot out the memory of the moral torture he had undergone.

Then, promising to do what he could for the prisoner in the future, he left him to sleep, and slowly paced down the street to his quarters. He had merely joined Lord Wilmot's expedition for the relief of Devizes as a volunteer, and now in his restless mood grudged the delay at Marlborough, and by break of day was riding with a couple of his servants to Oxford, leaving the two troops of cavalry and the long train of prisoners to follow later.

CHAPTER XX.

"One of the greatest clauses in Magna Carta is that which asserts in legal form the legal rights of Englishmen to withstand oppression. If the King broke his promises, he was to be resisted in arms in the name of the powers which Englishmen held to be greater than the King—in the name of God, the law and the great Council."

—History of the English Parliament, Barnett Smith.

On the afternoon of the 15th July, a crowd of courtiers, lounging and chatting in Tom Quad, paused for a moment to glance at the figure of the State Secretary as he passed swiftly through the merry throng on his way to the King's apartments.

Oxford was looking its brightest. On the 14th the Queen had returned, and on the same day despatches announcing the great victory at Roundway Down and the relief of Devizes had been received. The church bells had pealed, and it seemed to most of the Royalists that the King's cause was now certain to triumph throughout the land, and that the Parliamentarians would be utterly crushed. Never had there been more confident boasting, more light-hearted laughter than on that summer afternoon, and the sudden apparition of Falkland, with his pale sorrow-laden face, seemed curiously ill-timed.

"What the plague does my Lord Falkland mean by wearing such dismal looks on this gala day?" said a boisterous young Cavalier, who was about as capable of appreciating the philosopher of Great Tew as of recognising the beauty of a Raphael.

"He volunteered in my Lord Wilmot's troop t'other day," replied his companion. "They say, you know, that he is always thrusting himself into dangers which there is no call on him to face, because he is stung by the report that his efforts for peace spring from cowardice."

"Ha! ha!" laughed the first speaker. "He's found that in this world peacemakers have devilish hard times, and always win the hatred of both sides. I'll warrant you he will have but a chilly reception from His Majesty, who, they tell me, is downright afraid of him, and can't endure his plain speaking, and that inconvenient custom he hath of scrupulous truthfulness."

"He will be ill-pleased that a Council was held last night in his absence, and the siege of Bristol determined on," said the other.

A third courtier strolled up. "Did you see my Lord Falkland's face?" he said, with a sneer. "Is he grieving over the slaughter at Roundway Down, think you? or is it, perchance, that he finds his beloved Mistress Moray is undoubtedly in the last stage of consumption?"

There was a general laugh as the ill-natured gossips made merry over the State Secretary's friendship with this good and high minded lady, and, according to their own foul and depraved nature, judged one of the most spiritual and helpful influences that can be had in an evil world.

Falkland, perfectly well aware of the way in which his private affairs were discussed, and conscious of the hostile atmosphere which surrounded him at the Court, passed gravely on to the King's apartments, to be received by Charles much as the courtiers had prophesied, with very little warmth and no comprehension.

The King in prosperity was never at his best. His arrogance and narrowness were apt then to become apparent, whereas in adversity his courage and a very noble patience were noteworthy. The prospect of speedy triumph, and the unhappy influence always exerted over him by the presence and counsel of the Queen, made him now more than ever antagonistic to his Secretary of State.

He was seated in an elbow chair beside the open window, and on the oaken table beside him was spread a map of the Southern counties, which he had been studying. On the window seat lay a remarkably fine white poodle which Falkland noticed with a feeling of annoyance, knowing that the dog belonged to Prince Rupert, and betokened his near neighbourhood.

"We received yesterday the good news of the victory," said the King. "I trust you bring no worse report of Sir Ralph Hopton, my lord?"

"He remains at Devizes, sire," said Falkland, "and is steadily recovering from his injuries."

The King put several questions as to the doings at Roundway Down, and Falkland having replied to them, was debating how he could suggest that the victory made this a fitting time for the opening of negotiations with Parliament, when the King asked what was being done with the prisoners.

"Some were left at Devizes, sire," replied Falkland, "but a great number are being marched hither, and I am anxious that your Majesty should be in possession of the truth respecting one of Prince Maurice's officers—Colonel Norton—who hath been guilty of very gross cruelty to two of the prisoners, Major Locke, who died last night for lack of a surgeon, and Lieutenant Harford."

"Let me have the particulars," said the King, coldly. "People are over-fond of bringing accusations against my nephew's officers. Scarce a day passes but I have some idle tale of Prince Rupert's men, and he hath but this morning assured me that the men are the best soldiers in our army, and hath told me of his clemency towards the lady of Caldecot Manor."

Falkland's face was a study. Prince Rupert was not without a certain generosity, but in the main he knew only too well that the troops commanded by the two German princes had done much by their burnings and plunderings and wanton devastation of the crops to exasperate the English. The people were not likely soon to forget the cruel burning of the eighty-seven houses in Birmingham which Prince Rupert had ordered in the spring.

"I will tell you, sire, precisely what I saw last night in St. Peter's Church at Marlborough," he said. And, graphically, but without any comment, he described to the King what had taken place.

"Bound to one of the church pillars, you say!" said the King, with a shudder, "and the guard had actually brought him water in the chalice! Horrible profanation! I cannot endure the misuse of the churches in this war, yet they assure me they must at times use them for troops and for prisoners."

Falkland, with something like despair in his heart, marvelled at the extraordinary way in which the King missed the point he had wished to urge, and, in thinking of the church fabric and the communion-plate, failed to realise what cruelty to man really means.

"For my part," he replied, "I am bound to own, your Majesty, that the kindly thought of the guard in fetching the cup of water seemed the one redeeming touch in the whole miserable business. That and the way in which he had wrapped a cope about the feet of the dying Major in the chancel."

"He had actually used a cope for such a purpose?" said the King. "Well, my lord, I regret to hear that any cruelty was shown to the prisoners, but it seems to me you do not the least understand the sin of sacrilege. 'Tis as I ever told you, you care nothing for the Church."

His brow grew dark as he remembered that, little more than two years before, Falkland had made a speech in Parliament in which, report said, he had accused the Bishops of having "brought in superstition and scandal under the titles of reverence and decency, and of labouring to introduce an English, though not a Roman, Popery; not only the outside and dress of it, but, equally absolute, a blind dependence of the people upon the clergy."

The King's reproach had been made before, and Court etiquette forbade Falkland to justify himself to his Sovereign; moreover, he had long ceased to expect his position to be understood. The Laudian practices were hateful to him, but in the narrow dogmatism of the Presbyterians he saw grave danger to intellectual liberty. He stood aloof from both systems, but cherished beneath an outer mask of philosophic calm a passionate yearning for that Church of the future which should be wide enough to embrace all sincere men who took Christ as their ideal, and spiritual enough to dispense with those elaborate outer shows which had so often proved stumbling-blocks.

Stifling a sigh, he caught at the one phrase in the King's remarks of which he might avail himself.

"I well know," he replied, "that any sort of cruelty is repugnant to your Majesty, and therefore make bold to plead the cause of this young prisoner who hath been put to physical and moral torture, and hath claims on your Majesty's clemency, for he was not taken during the battle, but on the following day while endeavouring to save the life of his wounded friend, Major Locke."

Falkland had used no false flattery, but had appealed to the best side of the King's character. Though very limited in his sympathies, and without any genial love for his people, Charles was far from being cruel or merciless; the enormous amount of suffering for which he was responsible sprang partly from his duplicity, partly from his habit of allowing himself to be ruled by unworthy favourites, and drawn into rash courses by his wife. He might often from absorption in other matters fall into cruelty as so many of us do, fatally hurting others because not actively kind to them; but cruelty such as Norton's was abhorrent to him, and he would probably have yielded to the suggestion of his Secretary of State, had not the white poodle suddenly sprung down from the window-seat and, with whines of delight, bounded towards the door.

Falkland knew too well what would follow, and there was bitterness in his heart as he bowed to the handsome young Prince who entered the room.

It was impossible to conceive a greater contrast than that between the fiery Rupert, with his soldierly instincts, his rough, over-bearing manner, his full-blooded, dashing impetuosity, and the grave, far-seeing statesman ten years his senior. Falkland greeted the Prince with the quiet courtesy which was one of his characteristics, but with a disapproval which revealed itself by an indefinable air of strength and resistance not usually apparent in the singularly gentle face.

"So, my lord," said Rupert, gaily, "you have returned from the slaughter of the redoubtable 'Lobsters,' and have made William the Conqueror hide his diminished head! His Majesty will now be able to make short work of Bristol, and when Bristol hath fallen London will soon follow—eh, Boye?" stooping to fondle the poodle's long ears.

The dog licked his master's hand and whined with delight.

"Boye is more eager to crush the Roundheads than is my Lord Falkland," said the Prince, glancing with a smile at his uncle.

"He doth take after his master," said the King, looking with fond admiration at Rupert's soldierly bearing. "You have doubtless heard, my lord, that a Council was held last night and that we have determined that Prince Rupert shall join forces with the victors of Roundway Down and lay siege to Bristol."

"I had heard that it was so determined, sire," said Falkland. "Had I been present at the Council, I would earnestly have begged your Majesty, after having annihilated Sir William Waller's army, to offer to treat with the Parliament. Bloodshed might thus be avoided, and the end of hostilities might well be hoped for."

"My lord, you are no soldier," broke in Rupert, impetuously. "These rebels must be crushed and altogether subjugated before His Majesty can be King indeed."

"You will never crush the national love of liberty, your Highness," said Falkland. "The British nature demands freedom as a right, and the only hope of adjusting our unhappy differences is in recognising those rights which are in accordance with the law."

"Law!" interrupted Rupert, who could never endure remarks contrary to his own views, especially when they came from the Counsellors of civil affairs. "Tush! we will have no law in England henceforward but of the sword!"

"My lord," said Charles, "we are aware that you ever speak on behalf of peace, but those at Westminster do not desire it."

"I do not forget that your Majesty's secret message to Parliament ere hostilities began proved, unhappily, fruitless of good results," said Falkland; "but you will recollect, sire, that since then Parliament hath made many overtures of peace, and that every overture hath been rejected by your Majesty. Might it not be the part of true wisdom to take advantage now of this happy tide in affairs? Surely, sire, this great victory, and the return of Her Majesty after fifteen months' absence, make the present a very fitting time for a gracious offer of terms which the Parliament could accept."

"My lord, our determination is already made," said the King, coldly. "Your suggestions do not seem to us practical, and we are confident that our cause is better served by Prince Rupert."

Falkland bowed gravely. No man could equal him in humility, yet it cost him a pang to be thus set at naught, and to see how the King was dominated by the young German Prince of four-and-twenty, who knew absolutely nothing of the English or of Constitutional law.

Boye, the white poodle, broke the uncomfortable silence which followed, by bounding to the door and barking furiously at the sound of approaching steps. A young courtier entered.

"May it please your Majesty, the two troops in charge of the prisoners from Roundway Down are approaching the city," he announced.

"They will expect you to see the entrance, sire," said Rupert, "as you did when we returned with the prisoners from Cirencester."

"We will not disappoint our brave men," said the King, rising. "And you, my lord, will accompany us," he added, turning graciously to Falkland, as though to make up for the snub he had just given him.

Falkland, sick at heart, followed the King and the Prince, and before long was riding in the royal train to see what he well knew would prove a painful spectacle.

Hundreds of the citizens were flocking out of Oxford to see the return of the victors and Waller's vanquished soldiers. The day was insufferably hot, and the Court party did not care to ride far on the road, but drew rein under a clump of trees by the wayside. As they waited the approach of the troops, the King discussed with Prince Rupert some of the details of the battle which Falkland had mentioned to him, and spoke also of Colonel Norton's conduct at Marlborough.

"I have met the Colonel," said Rupert. "He hath a merry wit and a sharp tongue, and is the very man to enjoy a rough jest at the expense of one who had crossed his path. He is an excellent soldier though. My lord," he said, turning to Falkland, "you must show us this young Lieutenant Harford as the prisoners go past. The fellow must be worth his salt if he has dared to withstand a hectoring officer like Colonel Norton."

By this time the troops were in sight, and loud cheers rose from the spectators as they rode by.

Then in striking contrast came the weary prisoners on foot, escorted by a second troop of cavalry. As the line passed by, tied together in pairs, many of them wounded, and all of them suffering acutely from thirst, they might have inspired pity in the hardest heart. Falkland noted, however, that the courtiers around him looked on, either with utter indifference, or with derisive smiles, as their fellow-countrymen were beaten and driven along the road like dogs.

"Yonder comes the young lieutenant you bade me point out to your Highness," he said to Prince Rupert. "The nearest to us behind the gun, and tied to a man with a bandaged head."

Both the King and the Prince glanced at the prisoner.

"In good sooth the fellow is sunburnt till he is the colour of an Italian!" exclaimed Rupert. "He hath an undaunted air and looks like a man of mettle though."

"Copper metal, your Highness," interjected a shallow-brained fop behind him with a laugh.

The laugh reached Gabriel; he glanced to the left, and catching sight of Falkland saluted him, a look of reverence and gratitude lighting up his tired eyes. His pace had involuntarily slackened a little, and the wounded man tied to his right arm, had throughout the march been a heavy drag upon him; a smart blow across his shoulders from the swynfeather, or spiked pole, of the nearest soldier made his eyes flash, and added a touch of dignity to his bearing. But his salute to the King, though courteous, was merely formal, while the rapid, searching glance that accompanied it had none of that deep reverence with which he had returned Falkland's gaze.

He saw for a moment the well-known handsome features, the cold impassive expression, and remembered how, when he had last looked upon the King, it had been on that memorable January day, at the entrance to Westminster Hall, when Charles had been on his way to arrest the five Members. Now Hampden, the patriot, had been slain; thousands of Englishmen had fought, and bled, and died, and he himself was a prisoner, just when the cause he held at heart most needed service.

Something approaching despair seized him as he marched on, with that vision stamped on his brain—the King in his purple riding suit and white-plumed hat, his attention divided between the remarks of Prince Rupert, and the orange stuffed with cloves, which he smelt as a remedy against infection, as the troops and the long line of weary prisoners made the dust rise. Was the country again to be at the mercy of a ruler who so little understood or loved his people?

"Poor beggar!" said Rupert, following the young lieutenant with his eyes. "I know too well what military captivity will mean to one of his years. Curse me! if I ever pardon the Emperor who kept me mewed up so long! I can see, too, that yonder rebel is a good officer wasted, and with your permission, sire, would fain have the fellow in my troop."

"He shall be pardoned, and set free on consenting to serve under you," said the King. "We depute you, my lord Falkland, to see to the matter."

Falkland bowed low.

"I will convey your Majesty's pleasure to Mr. Harford, but I doubt his acceptance of a post under the Prince, for he is not one of those who entered into this struggle without grave thought," said the Secretary of State, convinced in his own mind that Gabriel would decline pardon bought at the cost of his convictions.

"Then he must pay the penalty of his disloyal obstinacy," said the King, annoyed even by the suggestion that some of his opponents had conscientiously thought out their position before taking arms against him. "He hath brought this misery on himself."

"Look you, my lord," said Rupert, good-naturedly, "make not the offer of release till to-morrow. 'Tis but fair the fellow should know what he chooses if he elects to stay in the clutches of Provost-Marshal Smith. They don't pamper Roundheads at the Castle, I hear."

The talk was interrupted by the huzzas of the spectators as the last contingent of cavalry rode by. Falkland heard one of the courtiers mention the name of Norton, and gave that officer a keen, penetrating glance, perceiving at once that there was a force of character in the Colonel's face which would make him a dangerous enemy, and one likely to pursue the young lieutenant with untiring animosity.

CHAPTER XXI.

"Religious ideas and religious emotions, under the influence of the Puritan habit of mind, seek to realise themselves, not in art, but, without any intervening medium, in character, in conduct, in life. It is thus that the gulf between sense and spirit is bridged; not in marble or in colour is the invisible made visible, but in action public and private—'ye are the temples of the Holy Ghost.'"—Professor E. Dowden.

It was something of a relief to Gabriel to see the well-known spires and towers of Oxford, but he had lived through so much since his undergraduate days that he felt like a returned ghost—aloof from all his past interests, alone in a crowd, remorselessly stared at and criticised by the inhabitants.

At the city gate they were halted while arrangements were made as to their reception. Gabriel was thankful enough for the brief respite; for Norton's treatment at Marlborough had set up keen pain in his old wound, while the thirty miles' march from Devizes, bareheaded under a blazing sun, had given him a racking headache.

The last time he had passed out of Oxford by this gateway, three years before, he had been riding home to Herefordshire with Ned Harley, little dreaming of the future that lay before them. He fell now to wondering whether Ned had recovered from the wound he had got at Lansdown, and whether the letter he had left with him had by this time reached his father at Hereford.

Just then the sound of a mellow voice, with a mocking ring about it which spoilt its pleasantness, roused him from his reverie.

"Well, Mr. Harford!" said Norton. "'Tis warm work, isn't it? You seem exhausted."

Gabriel at once drew himself up with the undaunted look which had taken Prince Rupert's fancy. He glanced at the prisoner with the bandaged head who leant heavily upon him, utterly spent with the march. The poor fellow, Passey by name, was one of his own men, and had been wounded and taken in the pursuit.

"This man is in far worse case," he said. "But I know it is waste of breath to ask mercy of you, sir."

Norton laughed. "You know me better than the day we spoke together at the gate of Wells. I told you I was not one to be baulked, and mark my words, Mr. Harford, the rest of my prophecy will follow in due time. I shall yet have the hanging of you."

"Indeed!" exclaimed Gabriel, stung into a bitter retort, "you seem better fitted to play the part of a hangman, sir, than that of an English gentleman."

"Bravely said, Ecclesiastes! You have clearly studied under the most virulent Puritan preachers of the day," said Norton, regarding his victim with an amused smile.

"Pardon me, sir," said Gabriel, ashamed of his words, "I should have held my tongue, for, truth to tell, on first sight of you at Gloucester, I thought you——"

He broke off, puzzled by that same hint of a better nature which made itself visible in his enemy's face, as if in response to his unspoken idea.

"You thought me as generous and good-hearted a man as ever you had clapped eyes on," said Norton, laughing. "They all do on occasion, but quickly discover their mistake."

He strolled away from the prisoners, and entering the alehouse hard by, called for a cup of claret.

"A second," he said, when he had drained it. "Here, Tarverfield, you are always for pampering these rebels, take this to Mr. Harford, I'll warrant his throat is as dry as a lime-kiln." The Captain was willing enough to undertake the errand, and Norton saw the look of surprise on the prisoner's face when he heard who had sent the claret.

But the next minute an oath burst from the Colonel's lips. "Curse the fellow! doth he fancy himself at the Sacrament? He but tastes it and passes it on to that wounded wretch beside him, and he again to his neighbour."

For the third time a twinge of shame dragged him for a little while out of the slough of brutality which threatened to engulph him, and once more there rose before him the vision of the dead wife he still loved, though his profligacy had broken her heart and brought her to the grave.

The incident drove from Gabriel's mind the despair he had felt since passing the King. He insensibly learnt that in the most unlooked-for ways good would manifest itself in those who seemed most uncongenial, and thus with a brave heart went to meet the troubles that awaited him in Oxford Castle.

Prince Rupert had very truly observed that the prisoners of war were not pampered. The cruelties of Provost-Marshal Smith, the Governor, had been revealed by the Lady Essex, who had been called into the House of Commons some six months before, and had given evidence on her return from Oxford of what the prisoners had to undergo. This had been fully confirmed by Captain Wingate, who after months of imprisonment at Oxford had obtained an exchange.

Still bound to Passey, Gabriel was ordered up to the highest room in one of the towers of the Castle with four other officers and six of the rank and file. The place seemed already full of men, and the exhausted prisoners looked round blankly enough, wondering how they were to find room in these wretched quarters.

The unhappy inmates, however, gave them a warm welcome, and it was pitiful to see the way in which these half-famished men crowded round them, eager to gain some news from the outer world.

"Where do you come from?" demanded a grey-haired prisoner, seizing upon Gabriel.

"We lay at Marlborough last night, sir," he replied, looking with something like awe at the emaciated face of the speaker.

"Marlborough!" cried the prisoner, his eyes lighting up; "I was carried off from Marlborough last winter."

And he poured out question after question in the vain hope of gaining news of his family.

"But may you not receive visitors?" asked Gabriel, knowing that even criminals were not debarred from this privilege.

"We may see no one," said the poor lawyer, for such he proved to be. "Come, you are unbound now, sit here and I will tell you what to expect."

"With your permission, sir, I will first find some place for my companion to lie; he is wounded, and well-nigh spent."

"I should stow him in yonder corner, next to the man with the fever," said the lawyer, bitterly. "The air is so foul there that he'll get a few inches more space."

Gabriel went to reconnoitre the ground, but was fairly beaten back by the pestilent atmosphere.

"Any crowding is better than that," he said. "Here, Passey, stretch yourself by the wall; maybe they will give us food presently."

"Not till to-morrow morning," said the lawyer; "and then the Provost-Marshal will not overfeed you, my friend. For though the King allows sixpence a day for the prisoners—a fair enough sum—this miserable governor of ours keeps for himself all but five farthings a head."

"And what doth that furnish?" asked Gabriel, beginning to understand the lean and hungry looks of his companions.

"A pennyworth of bread, and a little can of a most vile mixture of beer and water," said the lawyer.

Gabriel reflected that by the next morning hunger and thirst would probably be so keen that any diet would be endurable. To him the worst trial at present was the sickening atmosphere of the overcrowded room, which, to one accustomed to sleeping more often than not in the open air, seemed on this hot July night well-nigh insufferable. In a space measuring, perhaps, twenty feet square, some fifty prisoners were pent up night and day.

"'Twas here that Mr. Franklyn, Member of Parliament for Marlborough, died," said the lawyer, in his melancholy voice, "and yonder man with the fever will scarce recover, I think. But hark! there is the curfew ringing, we shall have prayers before settling for the night."

The prisoners all stood, and a short service, led by one of the captive officers, was held. It was this habit which kept the place from becoming the hell on earth which most prisons of the day were apt to become. And that grand simplicity which is the strength of Puritanism made its mighty influence felt, for all present, from the highest to the lowest, held the same religious ideal, and were ready to die for their conviction that each individual soul should have direct communion with God.

Wearied by all that he had undergone in the last few days, Gabriel soon slept with Falkland's cloak wrapped about him, and though stretched on the bare boards of the prison floor, his sleep was more profound and restful than any that for many months had visited the careworn Secretary of State.

It was sheer hunger that at last disturbed him, and feeling stiff and miserable he raised himself, looking in a bewildered way round the room. The moonlight shone in patches on the grim stone walls, and on the strange spectacle of the prisoners lying in rows on the bare floor. The dismal sound of clanking fetters echoed through the place, when some of the men, who for attempted escape were heavily ironed, stirred in their sleep. The man with the fever was muttering and groaning horribly.

A sudden wave of realisation swept over Gabriel. He was in prison, and must starve and pine, and as likely as not die, in this horrible place, no longer a free agent, but wholly at the mercy of tyrants. The bitterness of death seemed already to overwhelm him.

"Let me out! Let me out!" moaned the sick man in his delirium "My house is burning—my children—my wife! How can you do it, you fiends? Let me go home, I say! Let me out!"

Gabriel roused himself from the despair into which he had fallen, and picking his way cautiously across the forms of the sleeping prisoners, sat down beside the man with the fever. There was still a little water left in the earthenware mug near him, and, raising the poor fellow into an easier posture, he held this to his parched lips.

"Where do you come from?" he asked.

"From Marlborough," said the man, speaking rationally for a minute. "I was one of the wealthiest of the burgesses; my name is Rawlyns." Then suddenly relapsing into his fevered ravings, "Let me out! Let me out! They are burning my home."

"I came from Marlborough yesterday, and there was no house burning," said Gabriel soothingly. "Come, be at rest, you'll need all your strength."

His quiet words, and perhaps some subtle magnetism in his hands as he smoothed back the sick man's hair, certainly calmed the poor fellow. The Hereford people always declared that Dr. Harford had what they called "the healing touch," and possibly Gabriel had inherited a similar power. At any rate, the patient fell into a sound sleep, and his sore need had done much to chase despair from the mind of his helper.

Noiselessly he stole back to his former place and once more lay down, and as he mused over past and future there suddenly flashed into his mind the perception that here and now in this distasteful present the wish of his childhood had been granted. He had longed to be like his hero Sir John Eliot, and to give his life for the country's freedom; and now, like Eliot, he was to languish in prison, debarred from air and exercise and all that makes life sweet.

Gazing at the sharp contrasts of shadow and moonlight on the Castle wall, an indescribable sense of strength and consolation came to him; for he grasped the truth that, however the war ended, even if for awhile utter defeat and ruin should overwhelm the cause, in the future Justice was bound to triumph, being Divine, and every sacrifice honestly made in her cause would prove to have been infinitely worth while, and would hearten future generations to resist everything which threatened the liberties so dearly bought.

Musing over Eliot's imprisonment of nearly four years and his lonely death, musing over the eleven years' imprisonment of Valentine and Strode, who still valiantly fought against the despotism of the King, he fell asleep once more, and never woke until the surly gaoler, Aaron, brought the day's rations, when, as he had foreseen, desperate hunger and thirst made the pennyworth of bread and the can of beer-and-water welcome enough.

But the unutterable tedium of the long, hot day in the stifling room seemed to him well-nigh unendurable, and when in the afternoon the gaoler threw open the door and shouted his name, he felt that even if the summons meant death he would hail it as a relief.

Without a word, Aaron fastened a pair of shackles round his ankles, and signed to him to follow up the steps leading to the top of the tower.

"I shall await you below," he said, pushing the prisoner through the small opening on to the leads.

Gabriel drew in a deep breath of the fresh, sweet air. The tower was not battlemented in the ordinary way, but the high wall surrounding it was pierced on the north and south sides by openings. Standing by one of these, he perceived the short and somewhat insignificant-looking Secretary of State, and hurried forward with an eager exclamation of pleasure.

Falkland, who had always been entirely free from the arrogance of manner which characterised his class in those days, greeted the prisoner with his usual simplicity, and with that gentle sweetness of expression which was peculiarly his own.

"You must not hope much from my visit, Mr. Harford," he said. "I have tried my best to plead for you, but I fear you will not see your way to accepting the conditions imposed. Prince Rupert, pleased with your soldierly bearing yesterday, begged to have you in his troop, and His Majesty deputed me to offer you his pardon on your consenting to serve under the Prince."

As he spoke he looked searchingly at the prisoner, and read in his clear, undaunted eyes exactly what he had expected. The offer was not even a temptation to him—to accept it would have been a sheer impossibility.

"My lord," said Gabriel, "for your kindness in remembering me amid all your arduous work I thank you heartily; but for this offer—I feel sure you did not expect me to accept it."

"In truth I did not, and told His Majesty as much with a bluntness he did not altogether like," said Falkland. "Yet I can see that this prison life proves a hard trial to one of your temperament."

"'Tis hard for all of them," said Gabriel. "Some of the poor fellows have already been cooped up in the room for seven months, having been taken at the siege of Marlborough, and they say the winter proved fatal to many, for they were allowed neither light nor firing. Just now the suffocating heat is the worst part of it, for the overcrowding is terrible."

He pulled himself up abruptly, not wishing to trouble his kindly visitor with complaints, but Falkland could well imagine what a purgatory the prison would prove to a man of refined tastes and of great natural reserve.

"Have you written any letters?" he asked. "If so, I will gladly have them sent for you. We must try to get you an exchange."

"Paper and ink and books are all forbidden," said Gabriel.

"There is literally nothing to do the livelong day, except, indeed, to try to slaughter the vermin. One of our officers managed to smuggle in his copy of Cromwell's 'Soldier's Pocket Bible, but it is doubtful if he will be able to keep it, for the gaoler is a very dragon."

"I brought you a couple of books," said Falkland. "You will find them in the pockets of this coat, which you had best don here before the gaoler sees you again. Whether you elected to stay in prison or to fight under Prince Rupert I knew you would stand in need of a garment to replace the one they robbed you of."

"My lord——" faltered Gabriel, touched inexpressibly by the thoughtful kindness which contrasted so sharply with the harshness he had lately encountered, "I wish I could thank you as I would—— He broke off, unable to find the words he wanted, and Falkland, with the smile that since the opening of the war had scarcely been seen, took advantage of the silence.

"Nay, no thanks," he said. "But you shall do this for me, Mr. Harford; you shall tell me something I am eager to know. With your General hopelessly beaten and yourself a prisoner, made to suffer moral and physical torture, how was it that we found you tied up to the pillar in that church bearing the look of a conqueror? Of what were you thinking?"

"One does not think much in pain," said Gabriel. "I believe I thought most of Burton when he had his ears cut off."

"Of Burton!" exclaimed Falkland, in astonishment; for, though he disliked Archbishop Laud's fussiness and disapproved of his system, he held men like Burton, Bastwick and Prynne in yet greater abhorrence. Himself liberal-minded and moderate, both extremes offended his taste. It startled him to find that the prisoner, who was clearly not the type of man to interest himself in dogmatic theology, should speak of the ardent Puritan controversialist in such a way.

"What can have attracted you at such a time to Burton?" he asked.

"The words he used while he suffered," said Gabriel, his colour rising a little.

"What were they?" said Falkland, gently.

"'Seeing I have so noble a Captain that hath gone before me with so undaunted a spirit, shall I be ashamed of a pillory for Christ, who was not ashamed of a cross for me?'" quoted Gabriel, his eyes fixed on the gleaming river down below as it sped on its way to freedom and the sea.

Falkland watched in silence, coming nearer than he had ever done before to a comprehension of the true power of Puritanism, its direct appeal to the individual soul, the force, and simplicity, and strenuousness with which it laid siege not to the intellect and fine taste of the cultivated and learned few, but to the highest and noblest part in the nature of the mass of men.

He sighed heavily, only too conscious of the cruel loneliness that must always be the portion of those in his position during times of strife.

"Think yourself a happy man, Mr. Harford," he said. "You believe in your Cause."

There was something in the sadness and isolation of the speaker that strongly appealed to Gabriel; he knew how bitterly the Parliamentarians condemned Falkland for forsaking his old allies, and he had learnt of late to understand how intolerable to a high-minded and scrupulously honourable man the office of Secretary of State to King Charles must be. It was impossible to be in Falkland's presence without realising that he was, indeed, as commonly reported, "so severe an adorer of truth that he could as easily have given himself leave to steal as to dissemble." The same deep admiration and love which he had learnt to feel for the Bishop of Hereford stirred in his heart now, as he felt the strong but indescribable influence of one who has the power of forming the highest ideals, and the courage to strive for their attainment. There was, moreover, already in Falkland's dark eyes, the pathos which tells of latent disease and an early death. He would strive for peace to the last, but the long and seemingly hopeless struggle had broken his heart.

"My lord," said Gabriel, with some hesitation, "there is a great favour I would ask at your hands."

"If I can in any way serve you," said Falkland, "nothing would please me more. But little enough seems permitted in Oxford Castle. Could you conceal more books? If so, I will gladly bring you more, for books are friends that bite no man's meat or reputation."

"It is that I cannot endure to think that Lord Harry Dalblane should have my favourite horse, Harkaway. If he could be in your hands———"

"A doubtful blessing for the horse," said Falkland, smiling as he noted the eager, boyish face of his petitioner. "For I tell you frankly, Mr. Harford, I ever ride where the danger is the hottest, and am in the case of Job when he cried, 'Wherefore is light given to him that is in misery, and life unto the bitter in soul: which long for death but it cometh not, and dig for it more than for hid treasures.'"

Gabriel was too thoroughly healthy in body and mind to grasp the full import of the words; he thought the speaker only referred to that brief and natural craving for freedom which assails everyone in the extremity of pain, whether mental or physical. He himself had so quickly overcome the craving at Hereford and at Edgehill that it never occurred to him that one so immeasurably his superior could not also overcome it.

But the surgeon at Marlborough had surmised rightly enough; Falkland, handicapped in the race by months of sleeplessness, could only see that his present position was untenable, could only yearn to exchange the prolonged and thankless suffering of one who metaphorically stands between two fires, for a literal and brief riding forth alone between the two armies, welcoming a bullet in the heart from Royalist or Parliamentarian, since with both alike he was out of harmony.

"I shall be sending a messenger to the West to-morrow," he said, after a minute's silence. "If you will give me your father's address I will myself write to him and tell him what has befallen you. Since you are known to Sir Ralph Hopton and Sir William Waller, and since your father and Sir Robert Harley are lifelong friends, it will assuredly be possible in time to get you exchanged. And for your horse, I will speak to Lord Harry about it ere he goes to the siege of Bristol. An you wish it, I will myself ride Harkaway."

So they parted, the prisoner to return to his stifling and noisome quarters, the Secretary of State to the equally uncongenial atmosphere of the Court and the presence of a King whose obstinacy and insincerity made it hard, even for Falkland, who was noted for the sweet graciousness of his manners, to refrain from sharp words and caustic comments.

CHAPTER XXII.

Return him safe; learning would rather choose

Her Bodley or her Vatican to lose,

All things that are but writ or printed there,

In his unbounded breast engraven are.

And this great prince of knowledge is by Fate

Thrust into th' noise and business of a State.

He is too good for war, and ought to be

As far from danger as from fear he's free.

"Lines on Lord Falkland."—Cowley.

Little Helena Locke was made happy one day towards the end of July, by receiving a letter from her father. That it had been long upon the road did not surprise her, for letters naturally led a hazardous existence in war time, and she never knew how nearly she had missed receiving this one; never guessed that for many days it had lain securely in Colonel Norton's pocket, that it had been through the battles of Lansdown and Roundway Down, and had finally been given by Norton, at Marlborough, to the first messenger he came across.

Whether the sight of the Major's dead face had pricked his conscience, or whether he deemed it most to his own interest to have the little heiress safely bestowed at Notting-hill Manor, it would be hard to say. For a minute or two Helena's fate had hung in the balance, but chancing to come across a man who was riding westward, Norton had entrusted him with the letter, and after many vicissitudes it had been delivered.

The very day after she had received it came tidings that Prince Rupert had taken Bristol, and the news so appalled the citizens that Alderman Pury determined to lose no time in sending his charge to London, for it was now almost certain that the Royalists would besiege Gloucester.

Helena, glad of any change, and heartily tired of the somewhat sombre atmosphere of the Pury household, made her preparations in high glee, and was singing a cheerful ditty that evening as she packed up her belongings, when a knock at the door of her bedroom recalled her from dreams of Gabriel Harford to the facts of real existence.

To her surprise, she found pretty Mistress Clemency Coriton standing without.

"How good of you to come and see me; 'tis a sure sign that Captain Heyworth is on the high road to recovery," she said, gaily, "or you would never have quitted him."

"Yes, in truth, he is recovering fast," said Clemency, yet her face remained grave and sad, and something in her tone puzzled Helena.

"Will you not come to the parlour?" she said. "My room, as you see, is all in disorder."

"They gave me leave to seek you out here, because I wanted to see you alone, dear Helena," replied Clemency. "Alderman Pury has received a letter from Lord Falkland, and he tells him that Major Locke was sorely wounded at Roundway Down. You remember

Sir William Waller could give us no news of him when he passed through Gloucester a few days since."

"No, for the whole army was dispersed," said Helena, her face growing white. "But what more does Lord Falkland say, and how came he to know? Oh! I understand! My father is a prisoner."

Clemency put her arms round the girl.

"He is not a prisoner now, dear Nell. He is safe and at rest."

Helena's grief was speechless; she only clung to her friend in the numbing, paralysing shock of a first great sorrow.

"The letter," she said at last. "I want to see it."

And Clemency put it into her hands, knowing that Lord Falkland's delicately worded and thoughtful kindness would be the best means of conveying to her the details of her father's death. She guessed, moreover, that the news of Gabriel Harford's imprisonment at Oxford would rouse her, and fill to some extent the terrible blank that had come in her life.

"I must do what my father bids me, and go at once to London," said Nell, her childlike face looking all at once years older under the strain of this sudden grief and desolation. "Madam Harford may be able to help her grandson, and at least I can tell her of his sore need."

"Yes, you see what Lord Falkland says about trying to effect an exchange," said Clemency, glad that she had turned to this practical thought. "Alderman Pury bid me ask whether you knew who was your father's trustee."

"It is his cousin, Dr. Twisse, the rector of Newbury; he told me so when we parted; and his attorney is Mr. Corbett, here in Gloucester," said Helena.

"I will go and take him word," said Clemency, "for he is anxious that no time should be lost; we are in great danger, they say, now that Bristol hath fallen."

"But what will become of you if Gloucester is besieged?" said Helena. "If you could but come with me to London, you would be far safer."

"My brother-in-law is against it," said Clemency; "and, indeed, I could not bear to be parted just now from Joscelyn. It hath been settled that we shall be married next Saturday." Promising to return, she went down in search of the master of the house, and poor Helena, still with a dazed look of hopeless grief, went on mechanically with her preparations, her mind haunted now by a vision of her father lying dead, now by a vivid picture of Gabriel Harford in Oxford Castle, and again by the thought of Joscelyn Heyworth and Clemency Coriton hurriedly married ere the perils of the siege began.

When the next day she set off on her journey, under the charge of her cousin and an escort which Alderman Pury had provided, she was far more composed than Mistress Malvina, said her farewells without any emotion, and, like one in a dream, quitted Gloucester for the long and dangerous journey to London, caring very little what happened to her.

It had been arranged that they should visit Dr. Twisse, the Puritan rector of Newbury, and her only surviving kinsman, on the way; and Cousin Malvina found some comfort in this plan, for as they journeyed Helena's looks began to alarm her. By day she was silent and pale, at night flushed and feverish, and when at length they reached Newbury, and dismounted at the Rectory, it was quite clear that the girl was very ill.

The rector, however, proved a kindly host, and his wife, though secretly dismayed when the next day the physician plainly told her that weeks must elapse before their guest could travel, was an indefatigable nurse, and never let Helena feel that she was giving trouble.

And so the poor little heiress fought her way through sorrow and suffering, helped on by an illusion, dreaming of Gabriel Harford and of how she could best gain his release, dreaming also—not of the marriage of Captain Heyworth and her friend Clemency—but of that other marriage which her father had twice suggested to her. Had it, she wondered, ever been mentioned to Lieutenant Harford? And if so, had he perhaps thought of her when he so gallantly tried to save her father? And did he now at Oxford call to mind the maid he had so gallantly rescued from Colonel Norton's villainy? Alas! she knew nothing of Gabriel's grave words at West Kennet, and never dreamed that at this very time his red-letter days were the ones when, while others slept, he found a chance of looking at the carefully concealed miniature of a dark-eyed, darkhaired maiden, whose sweet yet wilful lips were the only lips in the world he cared to kiss.

By the time Helena had recovered from her illness, news had reached them that Lord Essex had relieved Gloucester, and was endeavouring to return with his victorious army to London, while the King was concentrating all his efforts on the attempt to block his road. To let two ladies travel while the country was in such a disturbed state seemed out of the question, and though it was now past the middle of September, Dr. Twisse insisted on keeping his visitors. Nor was Helena at all averse to staying, for she was still very far from strong, and shrank from the idea of the tedious journey still before them.

Yet Dr. Twisse half wished he had let them go when on the 18th September it seemed likely that the two armies would encounter each other in the near neighbourhood of Newbury. A sharp skirmish was reported from Aldbourn Chase, and on the 19th the King's forces took possession of Newbury, to the great disgust of the inhabitants, who were strongly in favour of the Parliament. In their breasts bitter memories still lingered which made them little inclined to favour a king who was swayed by his "popish" wife. Some of the old people could well recall the burning of the Newbury martyrs, and all the grown folk had heard from their fathers and mothers details which had sown in their hearts an unconquerable Protestantism, just as past persecutions have firmly established in Ireland an unconquerable Catholicism.

With what feelings Helena watched the entry of the King's forces may easily be imagined, but it was at least some satisfaction to her to learn that Prince Maurice's troop was not in that part of the country, and that she ran no danger of seeing Colonel Norton.

The window of the Rector's study commanded a good view of the street, and she sat looking out at the busy throng below, while Dr. Twisse worked at his Sunday sermon, pausing now and then to ask some question of his sad little kinswoman, more for the sake of breaking the monotony for her than because the movements of the soldiers interested him.

Presently a knock at the front door aroused him.

"Who comes hither, Nell?" he asked. "'Tis late for visitors."

"It is the gentleman you spoke with as we walked to church on Sunday, sir," said Nell.

"What! good Mr. Adam Head, of Cheap-street? I trust he does not want us to lodge any of the King's officers."

"There is an officer with him, sir," said Helena. "A gentleman with lank black hair."

Before more could be said the two visitors were shown into the room, and the good Rector was courteously receiving them with bows, and no apparent lack of hospitality, though in the dim recesses of his mind there lurked a troubled consciousness that the guest rooms were already full.

"I must present you, sir, to my noble guest, Lord Falkland," said Mr. Head.

("After all he does not want to lie here this night," reflected the Rector, his manner becoming still more cordial.)

"My lord, this is Dr. Twisse, who will, I am sure, be ready to serve your lordship."

Falkland's greeting was full of charm. He bowed low to Helena as she was about to glide quietly by them to the door, but the Rector put his hand on her arm and stayed her.

"Wait, Helena," he said, "I am sure my Lord Falkland will spare a moment to let us thank him for the very kind trouble he took in sending you the last details as to your father. This, my lord, is the daughter of Major Locke, whose death at Marlborough you notified to us."

Falkland gave a glance full of kindness and pity at the delicate, fair-haired girl; the colour had risen in her pale face, and her blue eyes were bright with tears. He bent down and kissed her hand, vividly recalling as he did so the face of the dead Parliamentary officer lying in the church at Marlborough.

"It was through Mr. Harford, madam, that I learnt your address; being unable to write to you himself while a prisoner, he begged me to send you word of what had passed."

As he spoke he saw the colour deepen and spread in Helena's pretty face, and knew by the tone of her voice that she was far from indifferent to the young lieutenant. Remembering the miniature of the beautiful dark-haired girl, and Gabriel's own words as to a kinswoman of the Bishop of Hereford, he guessed that there were all the materials for a tragedy in this little maid's romance.

"Is it true, my lord, that the prisoners in Oxford Castle are cruelly treated?" asked Helena. "We have heard such shocking tales of their sufferings."

"I fear the tales are o'er true," said Falkland, sadly. "I did what little was possible for Mr. Harford, and have spoken to those in authority as to his exchange, but at present there is nothing for it but patience, and that he has—the patience of a man who believes in his cause."

"We owe Lieutenant Harford a debt of gratitude, my lord," said the Rector, "not only for rescuing Helena from the vile scheme of Colonel Norton, an ill-conditioned neighbour of her father's, but for all that he did for my dead kinsman. Helena hopes shortly to be in London under the charge of her godmother, Madam Harford, a kinswoman of the lieutenant's, and she will do her utmost to obtain his exchange. But we trouble your lordship too much with our affairs. In what can I serve you, my lord?"

"In truth, sir, I came to ask if you would administer the sacrament to me and to the family of my kindly host, Mr. Head, to-morrow morning, before I go forth to the expected battle," said Falkland.

The Rector gladly consented, and the time having been arranged the two visitors withdrew, Falkland pausing for a few words aside with Helena, regretting that he could tell her so little with regard to her father, since all that he knew had been already put in his letter.

Nevertheless his sympathy was no small comfort to the girl, and did much to take the sting from her grief.

Unable to sleep, partly from excitement, partly from the disturbed state of the town, she rose early and joining the Rector as he was about to go to the church, begged leave to accompany him. The quiet service over, she was waiting at the church door for Dr. Twisse, when Mr. Head and his guest passed out. She looked in astonishment at Lord Falkland's face, for the deep sadness which had struck her so much on the previous night had utterly gone, his dark eyes were radiant, his manner cheerful and buoyant; even in his dress, which had before been somewhat disordered and neglected, she noticed a change. Recognising her, as Mr. Head bowed in passing, he paused, and in his gentlest and most winning manner said, "There is a favour I would ask at your hands, Mistress Locke. By Mr. Harford's express wish I have in my possession his horse Harkaway. I do not propose, however, to ride it this morning, and will give orders that it is to be sent to the Rector's stables. Perhaps you will be good enough to use it on your journey to London, so that it may await its owner on his release."

"But, my lord," said Helena, hesitatingly. "If he wished you to have the horse———?"

"Tell him I have ridden Harkaway ever since quitting Oxford," said Falkland. "And if," he added, gently, "I may venture a word to you in your bereavement, I would bid you not to weep for the dead, but for those who live on in these grievous times. It needs no prophet to foresee much misery to our unhappy country. But I do believe I shall be out of it ere night."

Then, with a kindly and courteous farewell, he walked on with his host, and, mounting at the door of the house in Cheap-street, rode to join Sir John Byron's brigade of horse.

All noticed the cheerfulness of his manner and bearing in, the charge across Wash Common; every hedge in the neighbourhood was lined by the Parliamentary Musketeers, and the guns on the heights in front of them were doing their utmost to decimate the troop. But still in the front rank Falkland rode unscathed; it seemed as if death shrank from taking one whose noble heart and great intellect so far surpassed all others on that fatal field, destined to see the slaughter of well-nigh three thousand Englishmen.

At the end of the Common there came a pause, for it was necessary that Sir John Byron should reconnoitre the enclosed ground. Finding that the Parliamentary foot were drawn up at the further side of a large field, fenced on all sides by high, quickset hedges, and that the only entrance into this field was far too narrow to allow of the safe passage of the cavalry, Sir John gave orders that the gap should be widened, and even as he gave the word it was evident that the whole fire of the foot soldiers would be concentrated on this spot directly any should-pass it, for his horse was shot in the throat. Springing to the ground, he called for another, and in that moment Falkland—ever the first to rush upon danger—spurred his horse forward.

There was a happy light in his face, as was always the case in moments of peril.

Here was the chance he had long looked for! He passed through the gap—one man alone betwixt the two armies; the next instant horse and rider fell riddled with bullets.

The narrow entrance had proved for the heart-broken hero the gate of life.

All through the day the battle raged; the Parliamentary troops under Essex and Lord Roberts, with starvation staring them in the face, knew that they must conquer their foes or die and leave the city unprotected; the Royalists were determined to block the road to London, cost what it might.

At last darkness made further fighting impossible, and it was evident that the Parliamentary army had gained ground; moreover, the men could starve another day, but the King, whose ammunition had failed, was in a worse plight.

At midnight, Helena, lying sleepless in her room at the Rectory, heard the rumbling of gun carriages, and the tramp of armed men, and sprang up to hear what had passed. Dr. Twisse could only learn that the King's troops were falling back on Newbury, and it was not until the next morning that they learnt that the London road was free. Later in the day Mr. Head brought them the news of Lord Falkland's death.

"His body hath but now been recovered from the field," he said; "and is to be borne to Oxford and thence to Great Tew. The peace of which he was a passionate promoter will be long in dawning for England, but it hath dawned for him."

Helena's own grief was too new, however, to endure listening to further details; she stole from the room, and ran for comfort and quiet to the stables, where in Harkaway's stall she could cry unmolested, finding some comfort in leaning her aching head on the neck of the horse which Gabriel had ridden when he had gallantly tried to rescue her father.

It seemed to her that all the great and good were dying; her own father, Hampden the patriot, Lord Brooke and a host of others within the last few months—and now the noble-hearted Falkland, with whom only the day before she had received the sacrament. Who in that generation would rise to fill the terrible gaps which this great struggle betwixt opposing principles had caused?

CHAPTER XXIII.

I cannot mount to Heaven beneath this ban,

Can Christian hope survive so far below

The level of the happiness of man?

Can angels' wings in these dark waters grow?

A spirit voice replied, "From bearing right

Our sorest burthens comes fresh strength to bear!

And so we rise again towards the light,

And quit the sunless depths for upper air!

Meek patience is as diver's breath to all

Who sink in sorrow's sea, and many a ray

Comes gleaming downward from the Source of day,

To guide us reascending from our fall:

The rocks have bruised thee sore, but angels' wings

Grow fast from bruises, hope from anguish springs."

—A. Tennyson Turner.

With incredible slowness the summer months passed by in the stifling atmosphere of the Saxon tower of Oxford Castle. Many times Gabriel cheered himself by a resolute dwelling on the old motto written in Elizabethan handwriting in the great family Bible at Hereford which had belonged to his grandfather, "Hope helpeth heavie hartes, sayeth Henry Harford."

He remembered that the same motto appeared in neat printing characters when the Bible had been handed down to his father, and had become "Bridstock Harford, his Book." Apparently the Harfords had always had troubled times, but had known how to win their way through them, and he tried desperately not to disgrace the family traditions of fortitude and constancy.

It must, however, be owned that his surroundings were enough to discourage the bravest heart. The youngest of about fifty men of various ranks and different callings, but all of them prisoners of war, he found his natural reserve and fastidiousness tried in a hundred galling ways. While the miserably inadequate food and the total deprivation of the exercise to which all his life e had been accustomed, not only affected his health, but made it daily a greater effort to fight against the evil tendencies of his own nature. Solomon, in the days of his wisdom, set it on record that the man who could rule himself was greater than the victorious general who captured a city, but the world still gives the praise and glory to the military conqueror, and reserves sneers and hard words for the man who hates and boldly fights evil—a reflection only too apt to occur to people in moments of temptation.

Gabriel struggled on, however, through July and August and the greater part of September, saved by hope, and always persuading himself that his father would assuredly effect his exchange before another week of this dreary life was ended. He dwelt often, too, on the thought that perhaps his letter to Hilary after her mother's death might reach her heart and awaken his Princess Briar-Rose to love once more. Happily he never dreamt that Norton had waylaid the messenger, and that the fragments of the letter had been trodden down into the mud of Marshfield-street. Like poor little Helena, he was for the time helped by an illusion.

On September the 23rd, while he was poring over the tiny volume of Plato which Falkland had given him, his attention was drawn to a general tolling of bells throughout the city, and when Aaron, the brutal gaoler employed to look after the war prisoners by Provost-Marshal Smith entered with the day's rations, he was beset by eager questions.

"What hath chanced? Hath a battle been fought?" asked the prisoners, for once failing to snatch without delay at the penny loaves dealt out to them from a basket by Sandy, Aaron's half-witted helper.

"A battle," growled Aaron, setting down the buckets from which the cans were refilled with beer and water. "Ay, to be sure, and a victory for the king; but it has cost him my Lord Carnarvon, and my Lord Falkland, and a host of other noblemen beside, all for the trouble of slaying Puritan dogs like yourselves."

Gabriel was well used to the taunt, but at the news of Falkland's death he turned pale.

"Did you say my Lord Falkland was slain?" he asked, hoping against hope that his rescuer might only be wounded.

"Ay, to be sure, don't you hear the bells tolling? He's being borne through Oxford to Great Tew this very moment, though for the matter of that they ought to bury him at night with a stake through his heart at the crossing of the roads, for they say 'twas sheer suicide—he rode out alone betwixt the two armies! just the fool's act one would look for from a bookish coward, always trying to make peace! A pox on all peace-loving cravens say I. Don't stand staring at me like that, you mongrel cur! What was my Lord Falkland to you?" and he emphasized the question with a brutal kick.

All these weeks Gabriel had borne with patience and dignity the galling words and petty cruelties practised by the gaoler, but in the overwhelming shock of these grievous tidings his strength suddenly deserted him. Stung to the quick by the man's coarse attack on the dead hero he turned upon him in fury.

"Don't dare again to take on your foul lips a name you're not worthy to breathe," he cried, with such passionate wrath and a look so threatening that for a moment Aaron quailed.

But anger merely begot anger, and with a fierce laugh the gaoler eyed his victim derisively.

"You will come before the Provost-Marshal for that, you numskull," he exclaimed, and amid a general silence he seized Gabriel by the arm, and grimly escorted him from the room.

To be out of the close, crowded prison was for a minute the most intense relief, and as he went down the steps Gabriel's wrath cooled. Longingly he looked about him with the keen eyes of one whose spare time was chiefly employed in futile plans of escape.

Aaron took him across the courtyard to the Governor's apartments, where they found the redoubtable Smith busy with pen and ink and a huge ledger. He glanced at them as they entered with an expression of annoyance.

"What do you mean by bringing a prisoner into my presence without leave?" he said; "I'll not have them brought straight to my room from that fever-den."

"Beg pardon, sir," said Aaron, saluting, "but it was a bad case of insubordination."

"Sir," said Gabriel, "the only insubordination lay in this, that, forgetting he was my gaoler, I forbade him to speak evil of my Lord Falkland."

"Forbade!" repeated the Provost-Marshal, raising his eyebrows. "You are quite right, Aaron, these rebels must learn their place. You are condemned, Mr. Harford, to thirty days in irons and to be flogged—the number of the strokes not to exceed thirty."

Gabriel bowed in silence; his lips closed in a hard line; a curious look came into his eyes—the same look which had dawned there years ago in the Archdeacon's Court at Hereford, when he had heard his father condemned. As Aaron in brutal triumph escorted him to the whipping-post, he could hear the church-bells tolling drearily, and a sense of blank despair filled his heart as he realised fully what a friend and helper he had lost in Lord Falkland; but beneath that lay the deep, burning sense of wrong—the fierce and bitter resentment of a personal wrong which seemed to change his whole nature.

Many speculations were made by the prisoners as to the punishment that would be meted out to him. He was absent for some time, and when Aaron at length readmitted him the first thing that attracted everyone's attention was the ominous clanking of the irons. He seemed to cross the room with some difficulty, but that was well understood by all who had experienced the weight of the fetters. What no one did understand was the extraordinary change which had come over his face and bearing.

"How long are you condemned to wear irons?" said the lawyer, making room for him on the bench at his side.

"Thirty days," said Gabriel, and his voice had deepened in a strange way. The lawyer looked searchingly into the white, set face, and fierce eyes of the speaker.

"Come, eat," he said, kindly. "You have not yet dined. That brute Aaron haled you away just as he had brought the food."

But Gabriel waved aside the bread, for in truth the thought of eating sickened him.

"You put yourself in the wrong, sir, by seeking to extenuate Lord Falkland's rash act," said one of the officer who was a strait-laced Presbyterian. "Ill fare those who are neither cold nor hot; had his lordship not deserted his old friends and sought Court favour he might now have been a useful and an honoured man. Aaron, though brutal, hath the wit to see how worthless is the man who is true to neither party."

Throughout this pompous speech the lawyer had furtively watched his neighbour, and he was the only man in the room who was not startled when Gabriel suddenly stood up, the colour all at once flushing his pale face, his eyes blazing.

"Sir," he said, angrily, "Lord Falkland never sought Court favour, he loathed the Court, but from a sense of duty tried to save the country by urging moderation on the King. All men know what sort of treatment he received from the vile courtiers. Are we sunk so low that we cannot see the virtues of a great man because in matters of State he opposes us?"

"I repeat," said the Presbyterian, "that you were wrong to espouse the cause of one who had thrown away his life. You should not have sought to gloss over the sinfulness of his suicidal end. Aaron was right—he ought not to have had funeral honours. Lord Falkland was a weak man and sorely misguided, as was natural enough, for his religion was merely an intellectual pursuit, and wholly unorthodox. Hell is now his portion."

"Then I will have no more to do with what you call religion," said Gabriel, passionately. "It is these; accursed systems that are at the root of all our misery—there's not a pin to choose betwixt your bigotry and the bigotry of the Archbishop. England is going to the dogs because Churchmen wrangle over ceremonies and trappings, and Puritans squabble over Holy Writ. You say my Lord Falkland is doomed to hell? Then if so there was never One who called peacemakers blessed, or ordered us to love our enemies and serve them. But he is not doomed. It is a lie! It is this country that is in hell, with its blind bigots and its beasts calling themselves men, and its blood and its boastful tyranny. 'Tis I myself that am in hell, mad with the thirst for vengeance, longing to kill with my own hands the brutes down yonder."

Quite suddenly his voice faltered, he reeled backwards, and would have fallen to the ground had not the room been crowded. As it was, he fell against Passey, who, aghast at the wild words he had uttered, was nevertheless mindful of Gabriel's kindly help in the past, and allowed the head of the unconscious prisoner to rest on his knee.

"A most blasphemous young man," remarked the Presbyterian. "Strange that one who hath hitherto been well reported among us and of modest bearing should suddenly change in this unseemly fashion. He erred in saying he was in hell while the day of grace is yet unspent, and he is permitted to remain in our godly company; but there can be no doubt that he will ultimately go there unless he speedily repents."

There was a silence in the room. A good many of the prisoners felt that there was some truth beneath the fierce words of the lieutenant which was beyond their reach. Others had liked him, and were sorry to see such an extraordinary change in him. It was a relief when the key was turned in the lock and the door cautiously unbarred by Sandy. The half-witted lad, a great, awkward-looking fellow of fifteen, came shambling in guiltily, and locked the door after him.

"Aaron never saw me!" he whispered, grinning from ear to ear. Then, catching sight of Gabriel on the floor, "What, he hath swooned at last? Then belike he'll be crying out a bit when he comes to himself. There was no sport at all for us at the whipping-post, for he never once shrieked for mercy, as some of 'em do. What's the good of sport if you don't hear the prey squeak?"

"Did they dare to flog him for what he said to Aaron?" asked the lawyer, his face darkening.

"Why, yes, gentlemen, to be sure; and as I'm telling you, 'twas poor sport, cursed poor sport. I'd as lief not have seen it. When they unbound him he never spake a word, but just looked as though he could have murdered Aaron, and he never seemed to heed at all when I did what I could to staunch the blood."

"'Tis this that hath changed him," said Rawlyns, the Marlborough burgess; and while the others drew off a little, discussing the matter eagerly, he and Passey did the best they could for Gabriel, Sandy supplying them with certain rough remedies which he had contrived to smuggle up the tower steps during Aaron's absence.

Strangely enough, the half-witted lad had more heart than his brutal chief, and though, as he honestly admitted, he liked "to hear the vermin squeak," he was quick to respond to kindness, and retained a memory of a few pleasant words Gabriel had once spoken to him. So little but curses and blows had come to him throughout his wretched life that he was always hoping to win again some sort of recognition from the young lieutenant, and for the next few days it was pathetic to see the efforts he made to extort something more from Gabriel than the curt thanks which rewarded all his attempts at help. Gabriel did not, indeed, disguise the fact that the mere sight of the idiot's face, the mere touch of his dirty and clumsy hands, repulsed him. Nor did he respond any more graciously to the sympathy of his fellow-prisoners; the brutal punishment had called out all the worst side of his nature, and for days he lay in his corner, ill in body and mind, bereft of all hope for himself and for the country, without faith in God or man, and, as he had very truly said, "in hell."

Every time Aaron entered the room his hatred of the man seemed to increase, and the maddening sense of being wholly at the mercy of this brutal tyrant grew upon him until it seemed to dominate everything else. Even the nightly psalms and prayers of the prisoners became unendurable to him; he turned his face to the wall and tried not to listen, convinced in his mind that they were praying at him, and so wrapped round in himself and his wrongs that it seemed impossible his character should ever recover what it had lost.

At last one October evening, when the Presbyterian was saying a psalm, a few of the familiar words entered his mind with a force and freshness which compelled him, against his will, to turn his thoughts away from his misery.

Through the old tower room there rang the verse: "The earth is the Lord's and the fulness thereof; the world and they that dwell therein."

From his earliest childhood his father had taught him to see God in nature, and the first light that came now to him in the outer darkness was the truth which had really become part of his very being when, as a little fellow, he rode with the doctor through the Herefordshire lanes, learning to observe, and learning to love birds and insects and flowers. God was in His creation and the world was not at the mercy of fate and chance.

Yet it was not until this autumn evening that the breadth of the assertion struck him, or that he in the least grasped the thought that the grand climax, welcoming the entrance of the King of Glory, was the prophecy of the entire ultimate triumph of the Lord strong and mighty—the Conqueror in the battle of love against hate, of righteousness against sin.

Sickened and utterly wearied with the stormy theological disputes of the age, he reached now beyond the clamouring voices, and sought refuge in the living realities wherein alone peace can be found.

Moreover, as he lay that evening in the dark prison room, for spite of the cold and the short days the prisoners were allowed neither fire nor light, there returned to him in helpful fashion the remembrance of the last talk he had had with his friend Joscelyn Heyworth.

They had sat late together in their quarters at the "Nagg's Head" in Bath, and Joscelyn had told him of his visit to his old tutor Whichcote, at North Cadbury, during which the recent death of Hampden had been the chief topic, and in his bitterness of soul the young Captain had found relief in telling an older and wiser man the despair he felt for the country under its grievous loss. A memory returned to Gabriel of some words of Whichcote's as to heaven, which his friend had quoted, and he fell to musing over them. "Heaven is first a temper and then a place; and both heaven and hell have their foundations within us." He knew only too well that the last statement was true, knew it by the brutal thirst for vengeance which was consuming him; by the hatred of his enemies which had changed his whole character, by the harsh judgments he silently passed on the failings and petty weaknesses of his fellow-prisoners. But the tutor had said that heaven also had its foundation within us, and the thought linked itself now to that startling assertion that the world and they that dwell therein are God's, which had first lightened his gloom. Musing over it all, he presently fell into a sounder and more refreshing sleep than any he had of late known.

He was roused at last, not as had been usually the case, by the discomfort of the heavy irons he wore, but by the soft, light brushing of something across his forehead. In the light of the early morning he saw a robin fluttering over him, and only one long shut up in a single room, away from all the interests of outer life, could understand the intense pleasure of the sight. In the sheer happiness of watching the bird he forgot his aching limbs, and the blank despair which for so long had clouded his mind was gone.

What was that quaint legend which he had once heard little Bridstock's Welsh nurse tell in the old nursery at Hereford? The robin had won his red breast because, being the kindest of the birds, it flew every night to hell with a drop of water wherewith to slake the thirst of those tormented in the flame. The bird had been true to its nature when it flew through the narrow unglazed window and came to the desolate prisoner of war in Oxford Castle. And as, perched on one of the old beams, it flooded the place with its blithe song, Gabriel escaped altogether from the dreary prison. Once more he was in the wood in Herefordshire, with the sunshine turning the brake fern into silver and the carpet of russet leaves into gold, once more the sweetest eyes in the world were lifted to his, once more the musical voice told him that all things seemed more beautiful because of love, while the bird of hope sang in the tree overhead.

Spite of all that had intervened, there was gladness in the remembrance, for his love for Hilary was the most divine part of his nature, no fleeting passion to be changed to bitterness by change in her. It was that rare love which war, death or sickness may lay siege to, but which is by its quality eternal.

And thus, through love, he gradually came back to life, and once more the old family motto, "Hope helpeth heavie hartes," strengthened him to endure the sorrows of division and the countless horrors which the war had brought in its train.

The robin did much to cheer all the prisoners. It became the pet and plaything of everyone in the place; to listen to its blithe song, to tame it, and to conceal it safely before the brutal Aaron entered, was a daily occupation, and not a man in the place failed to provide it with crumbs, so that the bird was ere long the one plump and prosperous creature in the tower-room.

With November came a return of the gaol fever, the new fever as it was called, one of the visitations which resulted from the privation and unhealthy overcrowding among the unhappy prisoners. It spread throughout England, sparing neither rich nor poor, and presented such unusual symptoms that no doctor understood how to deal with it.

This, however, made little difference to the Oxford prisoners, for no one troubled to think about doctoring them. It went to Gabriel's heart to see how they suffered, and his whole time was now given to a desperate attempt to relieve the sick. Cure was out of the question, for no medicine was to be had, and all through the month and on into December men were stricken. Those with good constitutions pulled through, the others raved in delirium for a few days, then died. It became quite a usual occurrence to see Aaron and Sandy removing the dead, and at length their numbers were reduced to thirty-nine.

"There's a lot of waste space here," remarked Aaron brutally, as he dragged out the corpse of the Presbyterian who in September had reprimanded Gabriel, but of late had been his best friend. "I shall have to bring you some more prisoners to fill the gaps."

"When once this hateful war is over," thought Gabriel, "I will follow in my father's steps and be a physician. I will fight disease and pain, and bring hope to heavy hearts. For of all terrible things the worst is to watch men dying for want of proper aid."

And then he fell to musing, as he had often done of late, on the strange problem of war. It was easy to account for the extraordinary influence which Falkland had had over him by the largeness of mind and the passionate generosity of the dead hero. And now more and more as he thought of his death, it seemed to him that Falkland was the forerunner of a vast multitude who, in future generations, would band themselves together and resolutely stand for peace, permitting only such force as was needful for the protection of hearth and home, and the maintenance of the just laws of their own country. As he recalled Prince Rupert's favourite saying, "We will have no law in England, save that of the sword," he could not but remember the words of One whom both Royalists and Parliamentarians professed to obey, "They that take the sword shall perish by the sword."

CHAPTER XXIV.

"To say kings are accountable to none but God, is the overturning of all law and government. For if they may refuse to give account, then all covenants made with them at coronation, all oaths are in vain, and mere mockeries; all laws which they swear to keep, made to no purpose. Aristotle, whom we commonly allow for one of the best interpreters of nature and morality writes that 'monarchy unaccountable is the worst sort of tyranny, and least of all to be endured by free-born men.'"—Milton.

Towards Christmas the fever abated, but the sufferings of the prisoners from the intense cold were very great. Gabriel, whose vigorous youth had hitherto withstood better than the rest the rigours of the life in the Castle, began now to show signs of all the long vigils he had kept with the sick and the dying, and Sandy, who was really fond of him, watched him with wistful eyes, feeling sure that he would before long succumb.

It was not until Christmas Eve that Aaron's threat of filling up the gaps was fulfilled. Then, about two o'clock in the afternoon the door was flung open and the gaoler pushed in a young, active-looking man, dressed in mourning attire which had evidently seen hard service.

"Good-day to you, gentlemen," he said, pleasantly. "I am sorry to add to your number, and fear you will scarcely welcome a new-comer."

"On the contrary, sir," said Rawlyns of Marlborough, "though sorry for the evil plight you find yourself in, we are right glad to welcome any visitor who can give us news." Gabriel made room on his bench for the new-comer, looking with a sense of relief at the well-clad figure, and at the refreshing cleanliness of his ruddy face and well-kept light-brown hair.

"You are a prisoner of war, sir?" he inquired, doubtfully.

"'Pon my life! I know not what I am," said the visitor. "Save that I am one Humphrey Neal, burnt out of house and home at Chinnor last summer by the Royalists, and since then a wanderer. To-day, having business to see to in Oxford I rode into the city, and was promptly arrested as a spy."

"Are you for the Parliament?" asked Rawlyns.

"Well, sir, I have never meddled with matters of State, and have thought more of hawking and hunting than of politics; but it is true that since the wanton destruction of my house, the robbery of all my live stock, and the devastation of my crops I bear no good-will to the Royalists."

"I heard of the burning of the village of Chinnor from my friend, Captain Heyworth," said Gabriel. "It was, if I remember right, on the night before Colonel Hampden got his death-wound at Chalgrove Field."

"Oh, you are a friend of Captain Heyworth," said Humphrey Neal. "'Tis a small world, where we are for ever coming across unlooked-for connections. Your friend hath lately wedded a pretty kinswoman of mine, heiress to Sir Robert Neal, of Katterliam Court House."

Gabriel's face lighted up.

"I have heard naught of him since the battle of Lansdown, when we knew that he was grievously wounded. He recovered then?"

"Ay, he not only recovered, but served all through the siege of Gloucester, and as I say, wedded my cousin. I saw her at Katterham but a se'nnight since."

"And met her husband also?"

"No, he had rejoined Sir William Waller, and was at Farnham, and by this time will most like be laying siege to Arundel Castle, which had been seized by my Lord Hopton."

"Sir Ralph Hopton has been raised to the peerage, then?" said Gabriel, remembering vividly his last sight of the Royalist general when he had saved him from bleeding to death after the explosion.

"Ay, the King was anxious, they say, to show him some mark of favour to make up for the scurvy fashion in which Prince Rupert treated him at Bristol."

"We have heard little of the outer world," said Gabriel, "save some account of the fight at Newbury."

"Belike you have not heard, then, of the death of Mr. Pym?"

There was a suppressed exclamation of grief and dismay through the room, for in the death of the great Parliamentary Leader they all knew that the country had sustained an irreparable loss. Great soldiers were left to them, but the greatest statesman of the age had passed away.

"He had been failing throughout the autumn, and died of an internal abscess the eighth night of this month," said Humphrey Neal. "In company with my kinsman, Sir Robert, I was present at his funeral in King Henry VII.'s chapel at Westminster—a great gathering it was, too, the Lords and Commons, the Assembly of Divines, and a host of people besides being there."

"Perchance your presence there was noted by some of the King's spies, and may account for your arrest to-day," said Gabriel. "Your kinsman, Sir Robert Neal, hath all his life opposed the Court party."

"That is true. Years ago he was imprisoned for refusing to pay one of the loans which the King illegally enforced, and hath ever since been a marked man. Doubtless, that explains the matter. What are the chances of escape here?"

"The only hope would be through Sandy, the half-witted lad who helps the gaoler," said Gabriel. "He hath a curious liking for me, which might prove of use. Otherwise, I see no possible way, though I have made many plans to wile away the time."

The advent of this fresh, vigorous, well-fed man seemed to raise the spirits of all the half-starved prisoners, and Christmas Day found them almost cheerful. The friendly robin had never afforded them more amusement, and they were so intent on showing off his many tricks and accomplishments to Humphrey Neal that they never noticed the entrance of Aaron the gaoler. It was too late to conceal the bird, and certain that the brutal fellow would, if possible, kill it, Gabriel deliberately let it fly, and with satisfaction watched it perch on one of the rafters.

"What mischief are you hatching?" said Aaron, angrily.

"We did but watch a bird that hath harboured here," said Gabriel, watching the robin rather apprehensively as it flew about overhead. Aaron made ineffectual efforts to reach it with his rod, growing more surly with each failure.

"Drat the bird," he said. "I can't waste my time over it; but you can spend your Christmas in the sport of taking its life, and I shall expect you to hand it over to me when I next come in."

Gabriel made no reply, but secretly resolved to let the bird out of the window rather than place it in the hands of the gaoler. Aaron turned to vent his ill-humour on Humphrey Neal.

"And as for you, sir, you'd better make the most of this day, for 'tis like to be your last. We give spies short shrift in Oxford."

"I am no spy," said Humphrey, indignantly.

"Men say that the gentleman that journeyed from London t'other day had only come on a matter of business about moneys due to him; but the Governor of Oxford, Sir Arthur Aston, had him racked nathless and hung him the day after," said Aaron, with a chuckle.

Humphrey muttered an imprecation and turned away.

Whereupon Aaron burst into a fit of laughter.

"You'd better have a care, sir, your fellow-prisoners don't allow profane words, and come from the ranks where twelve-pence is the fine for every oath. Oh, yes, I know you well, you dogs. And pray where is now your God, you Roundhead rogues? You prayed to the Lord to deliver you, and you see how He hath delivered you, ye rebels!"

The prisoners maintained a resolute silence, but Gabriel's heart was cheered when, as if in reply to the taunt, the robin overhead burst into a song full of hope and glad confidence.

The daily dole of food having been left, Aaron and Sandy withdrew, and the prisoners spent the greater part of the morning in discussing the possibility of escape for the newcomer, whose life was evidently in danger. About noon Gabriel reluctantly fed the tame robin for the last time, then climbing with Humphrey's aid up to the narrow, deeply splayed window, he let the bird out into the open, and with a sad heart watched it fly away over the snowy country.

"I see the mill stream is frozen," he said, scrambling down again.

"Would the ice bear, think you?"

"Yes, the frost hath held these four days past," said Humphrey. "But we can scarce look for skating," and he laughed forlornly.

"Yet if we could only get hold of Sandy without Aaron, I think we might prevail on him to let you pass—and then to find the Castle ditch frozen might make all the difference to you. There is sure to be feasting among the guard on Christmas Day, and the watch will not be strictly kept."

"Why should you not all make a bold push for freedom?" said Humphrey.

"What, forty of us at one time?" said Gabriel, his breath coming fast. "Oh! if we could but do it! Yet I doubt most of the prisoners are overweak with illness and starvation. And then again all would hinge on Sandy's coming again ere night, and coming alone, which doth not often happen."

Nevertheless the matter was generally discussed, and though some were absolutely hopeless, others thought it might possibly be carried through. The lawyer was not among the sanguine ones, however.

"You are young, you are young," he said to Gabriel. "Mr. Neal merely plans what is the first thought of every prisoner. I made such schemes myself once, but they availed naught Do me the favour, sir, to lend to me one of your books that I may solace myself with reading till the light fails."

Gabriel, somewhat damped by his friend's words, produced the little 12mo copy of the earliest edition of Owen Felltham's "Resolves," which Falkland had given him, then again withdrew to his bench to talk with Humphrey Neal.

In the afternoon, a little before sunset, the door was suddenly yet stealthily opened. Gabriel looked up hopefully, for sure enough Sandy appeared, but the next moment the unwelcome sight of Aaron close at his heels robbed him of all hope. The fellow had evidently been drinking, and was in his most dangerous humour.

"Now then, you rogues, hand over the bird," he said, glancing round the ward and eyeing the lawyer with special suspicion, for he had not failed to note that his hand had hastily sought his pocket. Gabriel stood up.

"The bird is not here it has flown away these two hours or more."

"You lie, you dog. I saw that traitor from Marlborough conceal it as I entered."

"The bird has gone, we all saw it go," maintained the other prisoners unanimously.

Aaron was not, however, to be convinced. He pounced on the lawyer, dragged the coat from his back, and plunging his dirty hands into the pockets drew forth—not, indeed, the bird—but Falkland's little book.

"You dare to conceal books against the Provost-Marshal's rule!" he exclaimed. "You shall be soundly beaten for this, you numskull."

But Gabriel, unable to bear the thought of such a punishment for the haggard and wan invalid who had but lately recovered from the fever, strode forward.

"The book is mine," he said, deliberately taking it from the gaoler and boldly thrusting it into his pocket. This, as he had foreseen, wholly diverted the furious Aaron from the lawyer.

"'Tis yours, is it?" he cried, tearing off Gabriel's doublet, and with one vigorous pull splitting in half his ragged shirt. "You've tried the hangman's whip, you Roundhead rogue, and we will see now if a sound drubbing from my rod will tame you. Ho! Sandy! give me your broad back for a whipping post, and if you don't hold this vile traitor's wrists fast, I'll flog you to a jelly yourself."

Sandy slouched forward whimpering and reluctant, yet not daring to disobey his tyrant. A sob rose in his throat as he felt the prisoner leaning on his shoulders, and gripped the thin wrists fast about his neck as Aaron had bidden him.

Meanwhile Humphrey Neal had stood by intently watching all that passed. The sight of Gabriel's back, however, scarred for life by the flogging he had received that autumn, sent such a storm of rage through him that for a moment he was not calm enough for action. Aaron's rod was raised once, and a violent blow fell on the scarred shoulders. The rod was raised a second time, but Humphrey, knowing now how to intervene, sprang forward, seized it in his strong grasp, and flinging his left arm about the gaoler's throat suddenly tripped him up by an unexpected lunge at the back of his knee. Springing aside he let the half-tipsy fellow fall heavily on to the ground, and a thrill of relief passed through every man in the place when they heard the resounding crash with which this brutal tyrant's head met the floor.

Humphrey Neal bent over him for a moment.

"The fellow is not dead, but I'll warrant him not to stir for the next three hours—he's not the first villain I have tripped up in that fashion."

"Oh! Lord! Oh! Lord! whatever will become of me?" whimpered Sandy. "He'll beat me to a jelly when he comes to himself."

"Look you here, Sandy," said Gabriel, hastily putting on his doublet and cloak. "No one shall harm you if you will but help us to escape. We will take you with us, and you shall never clap eyes on Aaron again. Come, let us down the steps, there's a good fellow."

He put his hand on the lad's shoulder kindly, and Sandy, like a dog that has been caressed by his master, was ready to dare anything in his service.

"They will be feasting and gaming by now, will they not? and the guard will be but slight," suggested Gabriel.

"Ay, sir, but there be a sentry at both the gates," said Sandy, scratching his head.

"Help us, then, on to the Castle wall, the key of the entrance will surely be on this bunch. I know well there is a way from this tower on to the outer wall. Do you seize the keys, and lock Aaron safely into this room while we steal quietly down."

Sandy began to look more hopeful. "You'll be needing ropes," he suggested. "And where be I to find them?"

"I saw a big coil of rope at the top of the tower the day my Lord Falkland came here," said Gabriel. "I will come with you to search for it, and we will leave the rest to follow, bringing the keys with them."

Sandy obeyed blindly, and before long the two had returned with the coil of rope. Never had the old walls of St. George's Tower seen a more extraordinary sight than the escape of the forty prisoners of war in the dusk of that wintry afternoon. The white, haggard faces of the half-starved men bore an indescribable air of grim resolution. Silently as ghosts, they made their way down the tower, and with marvellous self-control crept one by one on to the outer wall.

This was the most dangerous moment, for it seemed only too possible that the guard at the main entrance might see them. From the Osney Gate they were partially screened by St. George's Tower itself, and, crouching as low as was possible, they devoutly hoped that the Christmas feasting would have made the guard more or less drowsy.

Humphrey Neal and Rawlyns of Marlborough were the first to emerge, and they busied themselves with making the rope fast to the battlements; then one ghost-like figure after another glided forth, until, last of all, Sandy and Gabriel appeared, locking the entrance after them and pocketing the bunch of keys.

It was agreed that Humphrey Neal should be the first to test the rope. If it would bear his weight it would certainly bear the lean and fever-worn prisoners.

Breathlessly they watched him slide down and alight safely on the snowy slope beside the millstream.

"Let us not wait for each other," said Gabriel, "but each cross the ice and seek safety beyond in whatever quarter seems to him best."

To this they all agreed, and without risking another word to each other they one by one let themselves over the wall, and crossing the frozen millstream escaped in various directions, mostly going in groups of three or four.

Now and then Gabriel, as he awaited his turn, heard sounds of merriment from within the Castle walls, and as Sandy slid down the rope a distant echo of "The Boar's Head" chorus floated up to him. His hearing seemed to have become preternaturally acute, and he shivered a little when through the frosty air he heard the guard at the main entrance whistling the refrain.

And now at length Sandy stood on the bank below and Gabriel's turn had come. With a heart beating high with hope and excitement he let himself over the wall, and grasping the rope swung in mid air, descending hand over hand, while the distant sound of the singers within floated back to him:

The Boar's head, as I understand,

Is the bravest dish in all the land.

He alighted safely in the snow, and found his arm gripped by Humphrey Neal, then as the chorus of the carol was shouted out they cautiously made their way over the frozen millstream, and were just scrambling up the opposite bank when the sharp barking of a dog startled them into anxious listening once more.

Crouching among the bushes, they heard a discussion being held by the guard, and trembled lest a sentry should pass along to the spot on the walls where their rope was made fast. It was now that Sandy came to their aid, for he knew the dog and coaxed it to his side, fondling it into quiet and good humour.

By this time the other prisoners had safely disappeared in the gathering twilight of the short December day. They resolved to linger no more, but, bidding Sandy follow, began to walk rapidly to the other side of the city, choosing, as far as might be, the back streets and alleys.

Some wandering minstrels on a round of carol-singing before long attracted their notice, and they observed that one of the company lingered far behind the others, rolling about unsteadily as he walked, and tipsily twanging his lute. When by-and-by his companions trooped into an alehouse, he wandered aimlessly along by himself, swearing profusely, yet occasionally chanting a boisterous refrain of "Noel—Noel," in a fashion that made Humphrey laugh heartily.

"In ten minutes the fellow must fall into the kennel," he said, gaily, "and, if so, he may prove of use to us. Ay, to be sure! I knew he couldn't stagger on much longer."

"Don't belabour me like that," groaned the minstrel, apostrophising the stones, "I was keeping the best of time. 'Noel! Noel! Noel! Noel!' my throat's on fire. We'll have a stoup at the 'Pig and Whistle.'"

"As many as you please," said Humphrey, cheerfully. "But, in the meantime, we will do your carolling for you. I'll trouble you for the lute, and—yes, you may as well spare your hat, too!"

Laughing at the placid way in which the minstrel fell asleep on his stony bed, Humphrey tucked the lute under his arm, clapped the felt hat on to Gabriel's bare head and hurried down the street.

"We will pass the guard on Magdalen Bridge as minstrels on our way to perform at Cowley. Do you by chance know any carols?"

"I know one," said Gabriel, beginning to hum the air of the Bosbury Carol.

"That will do. I know the tune, and will catch up the words of the chorus, and, with the lute to twang an accompaniment, we shall make a brave show. Sandy, you will pick up any money that the good Christians throw to us."

"But sir, I see the watchman coming," said Sandy, apprehensively; "for Heaven's sake, let us hide in yon archway."

"Nay; no skulking," said Humphrey, "let us put a bold face on it, and say we have come to sing."

So saying, he turned in at the gateway of Merton, cheerfully twanging his lute.

The porter encountered them with a face of astonishment.

"Now then, you fellows, what are you about? Don't you know that His Majesty the King visits the Queen's apartments?"

"Why, to be sure, master," said Humphrey, assuming the dialect of a countryman. "And we have orders to sing in the quad. You'll not be denying us poor folk our chance of earning a groat in these cruel hard times."

"Well, well," said the porter, good-humouredly, "Christmas is Christmas, and as you say, the times are hard. But see there's no brawling or drinking or unseemly noise."

"Master we be the most mannerley minstrels in the shire," said Humphrey, touching his hat obsequiously as he passed on. "And that be true as the Gospel."

"This will stand us in good stead when we get to the Bridge by-and-by," he added, in a low voice. "Let us cross to yonder window above the archway, the lights are brightest there, and doubtless the Queen holds her Christmas festivities within."

Gabriel, feeling after his long imprisonment in the Castle like one in a dream, fearing every minute lest he should wake and find this strange adventure unreal, crossed the snowy quad, and at a nod from his companion began to sing the Bosbury Carol, Humphrey cleverly putting in an effective accompaniment on the lute. Out into the still frosty air rang the quaint old words, and feverish excitement gave strength to the voice of the half-starved prisoner.

When we were all, through Adam's fall,

Once judged for to die;

And from all mirth brought to the earth,

To dwell in misery;

God pitied then His creature man,

In Scripture as you may see,

And promised that a woman's seed

Should come for to make us free.

Oh! praise the Lord with one accord,

All you that present be;

For Christ, God's Son, has brought pardon,

All for to make us free.

As he sang he noticed the shadows of those within the room moving fantastically on the ceiling, and when Sandy in a startlingly sweet treble caught up the air of the refrain, the figure of a lady approached the window and looked forth. The light gleamed on her bare white shoulders, and on the pearl necklace about her slender throat. Gabriel instantly recognised the Queen, and for a minute scarcely wondered at the thraldom in which she contrived to hold her husband, so radiantly beautiful was her face, so full of charm and vivacity her whole bearing. She turned her head now and imperiously beckoned to some one within.

Gabriel, still with the strangest sense of unreality, sang another verse, half-fancying himself once more in the snowy garden at Hereford, half expecting to catch sight of brave Sir John Eliot's snow effigy.

He thought no scorn for to be born

Of a birth both low and small;

Betwixt ox and ass in a crib He was

Laid poorly in a stall;

To the shepherds in fold the thing was told,

In Luke as you may see,

Who sang glory to the Lord on high

That did come for to make us free.

As once again the chorus rang out, he saw the King join his consort at the window, and, watching the two, could not but reflect how amiable a gentleman His Majesty might have been had he not been fated to fill a position wholly unfitted for him. But then his face grew stern, for back into his mind there came a memory of the long, long list of grievous acts of tyranny and injustice for which the King was responsible; and he thought of Eliot done to death in prison, of Hampden laying down his life in the struggle to free the country, and of Falkland, contemned and misjudged by all, striving in vain to make peace, and dying broken-hearted in the saddest isolation.

Haunted most of all by this memory of Falkland, he stumbled somehow into the final verse of the carol.

And thus in death yielded up His breath,

Saying, consecrated, just,

All this was done by Christ, God's Son,

To bring men's souls to rest.

Therefore you all, both great and small,

That here now present be,

Serve him always, with diligent praise,

The Lord God that made us free.

In the chorus one of the courtiers at a sign from the Queen opened the window and threw down a few coins to the minstrels, after which their Majesties withdrew. Sandy groped in the snow for the money, Humphrey Neal courteously raised his hat, but Gabriel stood motionless, gazing intently up at the brightly-lighted windows.

The weird shadows moving to and fro on the ceiling looked to his fancy like the nodding plumes on a funeral-car, and he shivered as he heard the laughter and merriment of those within, for it sounded to him as hollow and mirthless as the wintry wind which sighed and moaned through the archway below.

Just in that fashion had the wind raged and moaned when His Majesty had entered Westminster Hall nearly two years before on his rash attempt to arrest the five members.

"What are you staring at?" said Humphrey Neal, astonished at the expression on his companion's face. "We had better hasten on."

Gabriel made no reply, but with one lingering look at those strange funereal shadows on the ceiling, he turned away, following his companions across the quiet quad and out into the street.

He had looked his last on the King.

CHAPTER XXV.

"Whatever harmonies of law

The growing world assume,

Thy work is Thine. The single note

From that deep chord which Hampden smote

Will vibrate to the doom."

—Tennyson.

By the time they approached Magdalene Bridge the twilight had faded into darkness, but the stars shone brightly in the frosty atmosphere, and the snowy ground glimmered white through the pervading gloom. Some temporary fortifications, not of a very effective order, had lately been made to protect the bridge, and a strict guard was kept. It was the endeavour to pass through at this late hour of the afternoon which was like to prove their greatest peril.

More than once Humphrey Neal looked with anxiety at his two companions. From Sandy nothing but a dog-like obedience could be expected; and it seemed to him that Gabriel's overbright eyes and feverishly flushed face told their own tale. The lieutenant, whose fortitude and intrepid courage had carried him in a masterly fashion through the escape from the Castle, stood now on the verge of utter collapse. Clearly it rested with him to take the initiative and to pioneer the others through this dangerous attempt to pass the sentries.

"Sing a snatch of some carol as we walk," he suggested.

And Gabriel obeyed, chanting, to a tune he had known all his life, the words:

"The God of love doth give His Son,

The Prince of Peace, to quell

The sin and strife that mar man's life;

With us He deigns to dwell.

On earth be peace,

Bid strife to cease,

To all men show goodwill."

By this time they had reached the first sentry.

"Halt, there!" said the man. "None leaves the city after sunset."

"Good master sentry, let us pass; the sun hath set but an hour, and we be bound to reach Cowley by supper-time," said Humphrey in his countryman's drawl.

The sentry summoned one of the guard.

"Leave the city!" said the burly fellow, with a laugh. "You're too late, my man."

"We should ha' been here sooner, sir," said Humphrey, "but we had to sing in the quad at Merton to Her Majesty. You'll never be denying us when we tell you that we've been carol-singing to the King and Queen."

"Well, well, you seem a harmless fellow, but I don't remember your coming into the city."

"I came in yesterday, sir; and for the love o' heaven let us pass through now to the Cowley road, for it be cruel cold here, and we have but this night to earn a few coins by our minstrelsy."

"Well, go through with you, then," said the guard, carelessly, "and you may thank your stars that it be Christmas night, or I'd not have let you by."

"God bless you, sir, for a good Christian," said Humphrey, touching his hat. "Come, mates, we'll e'en give them a tune as we go."

Then raising the lute he sounded the refrain of the Bosbury carol, and they passed out of Oxford singing the old familiar words which for one of them had so many memories. Once Gabriel glanced back to the bridge, and the dim outline of the towers and spires of the beautiful city, with its lights shining out here and there like glowworms; and most fervently did he hope never again to enter the place where he had suffered such torments.

For some minutes they walked rapidly on, but when at length they were out of earshot the sense of their good fortune in escaping thus far successfully made them forget everything in a rapturous sense of relief. They laughed and shouted like schoolboys released from work, and it was as much as Sandy could do to keep pace with them.

"No more gruesome thoughts of racks and halters!" said Humphrey. "And for you no more months of slow starvation in that fever den. Farewell, a long farewell to Aaron and his rod!"

"I wonder if by now he has recovered his senses," said Gabriel. "'Tis more like that our rope has been discovered by the guard and the escape found out in that fashion—I wish we could have brought it off with us."

"We will press on as fast as may be for fear of pursuit," said Humphrey. "There's a house I know at Cowley where we can get food. 'Tis owned by an old retainer of ours who can be trusted."

They toiled on as fast as might be over the rough road, with its treacherous ruts frozen hard, and all were thankful enough when they saw the outline of St. Bartholomew's leper-house looming into sight, for the frosty air and the exercise had sharpened their appetites.

Old Nicholas, the farmer, gladly gave them food, and they were sitting in his chimney-corner feasting on cakes and hot ale, when to their dismay the tramp of horses and the voices of men without made them fear that already they were pursued.

"Never heed, Master Humphrey," said old Nicholas. "I'll put them on the wrong track, and do you all step up the stairs behind yon door, for maybe they'll be thrusting their heads into the house place."

They obeyed their host, and Humphrey, knowing well that he was a shrewd old man, had faith in his discretion. The others heard in no small trepidation the tramp of feet on the flagged path leading to the door; then came a peremptory knock.

Nicholas opened promptly enough, anxious to keep his questioners in a good temper.

"Have you seen aught of three carol singers here?" asked a voice which clearly reached the fugitives on the staircase.

"Bellringers did you say?" asked Nicholas, feigning deafness. "Up at the inn, sir, supping at the inn."

"Three carol singers," shouted the man.

"Oh! to be sure," nodded Nicholas. "Yes, sir, and one of them had a lute, oh! yes to be sure, I saw them a while ago, and they was singing like archangels."

"Which way did they take?" shouted the pursuer. "Are they like to be at the inn?"

"No, sir, not at the inn," said Nicholas, shaking his head vigorously.

"Which way did they go?"

Nicholas stepped out into the garden and pointed and gesticulated with much energy.

"Where does that lead to?" questioned the officer.

"Where does it lead to?" repeated Nicholas, as though not quite sure that he had heard aright. "It leads to Thame, sir, you'll soon get there; Thame the market town."

"Oh, they have taken the road there, have they. The villains have escaped from Oxford Castle and one of them is a spy. Now then, my boys, set spurs to your horses, we shall soon run the quarry to earth, and the first that comes up with them shall have the hanging of the vile rebels. Keep to the left and press on."

The sound of the horses' hoofs died away in the distance; then Nicholas returned to the house place, and the three hunted men came out of hiding.

"That was a close shave, Nicholas," said Humphrey Neal, shaking the old man's hand gratefully. "Thanks to your ready wit we are safe, but we must press forward without delay or these wolves will be the death of us yet."

"Where do you escape to, sir?" asked Nicholas.

"To London," said Gabriel. "There will be a warm welcome for Mr. Neal at Notting Hill Manor, the home of my grand dame. 'Tis thanks to him I have escaped."

"Thanks to your own courage," said Humphrey. "But we will hasten on, Nicholas, without delay, and at Watlington I will get old Parslow to speed us on our journey."

Nicholas with many good wishes bade them farewell, and, taking the precaution of leaving the road, they went across country, shortening the distance and running less risk of capture.

"I have hunted so often in this part of the country that I know every inch of the ground," said Humphrey, as he pioneered his two companions across the snowy fields and frozen brooks. "'Tis not so pleasant a matter, though, to be hunted oneself, especially on foot. Perhaps at Watlington we can get a mount from Parslow, he is the landlord of the 'Hare and Hounds,' and I've known him all my life."

The bitter wind blew in their faces as they toiled on; and, at length, Sandy began to whimper that he could go no farther. They tried their utmost to cheer the lad.

"We shall soon be at Watlington," said Humphrey, "and I'll get Parslow to give you a berth as stable boy; you shall be as happy as a King, and maybe happier, with plenty to eat and a motherly old cook who'll see you're not bullied. Oh! you'll think yourself in paradise after the life you've led with Aaron."

Sandy grinned placidly, but soon remarked again that he was "cruel footsore."

"This is Chalgrove field, where Colonel Hampden got his death wound," said Humphrey, and Gabriel looked over the snowy ground, gleaming white in the starlight, and tried to think how it had looked on that fatal day when a deadly fight had been fought, and the waving corn had been trampled underfoot and dyed crimson with the blood of the noblest of Englishmen.

By this time the excitement which had carried him on had subsided, and though he said nothing, it was evident to Humphrey that only dogged resolution and an indomitable will enabled him to drag one foot after the other. But he came of a stock that was not easily daunted, and it was not till they reached the "Hare and Hounds" at Watlington that he would admit that he was dead beat.

"Come round to the back entrance," said Humphrey. "I'll get a word with old Mogg the cook."

Softly lifting the latch, he took them into the kitchen of the inn, where an old crone, with a most good-natured face, sat alone by the fire.

"Mogg," said Humphrey, stealing across the room, "a happy Christmas to you, and of your charity take us into hiding, for we stand in peril of our lives."

"Larka mercy, Master Humphrey, how you do startle a body," exclaimed the old woman, beaming with pleasure at the sight of one she had known from babyhood. "What's amiss with yonder gentleman? Methinks he is but ill-fitted for travelling. 'Tis in bed you should be, sir, with a good sack posset and warm blankets."

"In truth, 'tis where I would fain be," said Gabriel, dropping on to the nearest bench. "Yet I would crave leave to have a wash first."

Sandy stared at him, that anyone should actually wish to be clean on this cold winter's night seemed to him the most extraordinary thing he had ever heard.

"Ay, Mogg, the brutes have treated my friend most scurvily," said Humphrey; "do you furnish him with one of your master's shirts and a pair of hose, and look well to him, for he's worn out and half-starved. But first take me to the master's room and let me have speech of him in private, for we will keep our coming quiet if possible."

Parslow, the landlord, who had known Squire Neal, of Chinnor, for many years, gladly undertook to help Humphrey, and Sandy was promised work in the stableyard on the understanding that the two gentlemen he had helped so greatly should start him in life with money for his outfit. By nine o'clock, thanks to Mogg's kindly offices, Gabriel found himself in a state of drowsy cleanliness and comfort in a great four-post bed, and when Parslow ushered his friend into the room and stayed for awhile chatting he was too blissfully sleepy to open his eyes.

"Then, should there be any signs of pursuit, you will let us know," said Humphrey, setting down his candle and pulling off his boots. "Meanwhile we'll sleep."

"'Tis the bed on which Colonel Hampden lay the night before Chalgrove fight," said Parslow. "Well do I remember it."

"And I've good cause to remember it, too, Robin, for 'twas the very night Prince Rupert's men set our house ablaze and brought us to ruin. Well, good-night to you, and many thanks for your aid. We will be up by four, and, as you suggest, go with Jock the carrier to Henley. Once out of Oxfordshire we shall be safe. My friend sleeps already I see. Poor fellow, after lying for months on bare boards, I'll warrant he thinks himself in clover."

They slept soundly for some three hours, then Humphrey was roused by hearing a peremptory knocking without. He started up in bed and listened; someone was going downstairs to the front entrance, and again a thundering knock descended on the door.

Stealing across to the window, he looked cautiously down and descried the dark forms of four or five horsemen—there were sounds of unbolting the door, and then the question he had expected: "Have you seen a party of minstrels from Oxford pass through here?"

"No, sir," said the landlord, with truth.

"Curse the fellows! How can we have missed them? Do you and a couple of men ride on, sergeant, you may yet overtake them on the London-road. Everton, you and I will get some food and a few hours' sleep here."

"I can give you food, gentlemen, but being Christmas night we are fuller than usual," said Parslow.

"Oh, anything will do," said the officer, dismounting. "Everton, see the horses fed and stabled while the landlord makes ready for us, it will be the quickest way in the end." Humphrey whistled softly to himself, dismayed to think of the risk they now ran of being trapped. The notion of being taken in bed and being dragged back to Oxford to be hung was not to be borne. He groped in the dark for his clothes and hastily dressed. His companion still slept, though uneasily, now and again talking and moaning in a way which alarmed Humphrey, who thought it highly probable that the new fever had already attacked him.

Presently there was a soft knock at the door and the latch was lifted by the landlord, who stole in cautiously, candle in hand.

"Sir," said Parslow, "you are not safe here. I've left the King's officers down below supping, and have promised to make a room ready for them. I will put them in here if we can safely manage to take the two of you down to the stableyard. Once there I can hide you among the sacks in the carrier's cart, and will rouse Jock when the officers are abed and bid him drive you with all speed to Henley."

"'Tis our only hope," said Humphrey; "yet I don't know but my friend is too ill to travel. Look at him."

In truth the sleeper's flushed face and burning hands were not reassuring, but they were obliged to rouse him and try to explain matters.

He started up, staring at them in a dazed, bewildered way.

"We are within an ace of being caught," whispered Humphrey. "Don your clothes with all speed and the landlord will help us to escape."

With an effort Gabriel forced himself to attend, though it seemed to him that a couple of sledge-hammers were pounding remorselessly on his brain. He began to dress without a word, but staggered and all but fell when he attempted to cross the room. Humphrey took him by the arm.

"What of Sandy?" he asked. "Let us leave the money for him."

"To be sure," said Humphrey, placing some gold pieces in the landlord's hand. "I know you'll have the poor fellow provided for, Robin, and for your help to us you shall be well recompensed. We'll follow you on tiptoe without more delay."

The landlord had hurriedly re-arranged the bed, and now, candle in hand, crept down the stairs, pausing once or twice to make sure that the officers from Oxford were still chatting over their supper. Humphrey was relieved to see that the sense of danger had for the time restored Gabriel. With admirable selfcontrol he rallied his failing powers, stole softly after the landlord, and left the inn by the back door at which they had made their entrance a few hours earlier. In the stableyard stood a carrier's cart piled up with sacks of corn. Into this the two fugitives climbed, the landlord arranging the sacks round them and covering the whole with a bit of sail-cloth.

"You lie there, gentlemen, and you'll be safe enough," he said, "and when the officers are abed I'll rouse Jock and bid him put in the horses and drive to Henley."

The waiting seemed endless, but at last they heard cautious steps approaching and whispered remarks between Parslow and Jock, and finally there came the grinding of the wheels and a shaking and jarring of the cart which made Gabriel feel as if his last hour was come. He gasped for breath; to move was impossible, for the corn sacks were piled on every side, and on the top of them.

"I can never endure twelve miles of this—we shall be here for hours," he reflected, desperately.

But just then, as the cart rumbled out of the yard and passed into the street, there were sounds of a window being thrust open, and a man's voice shouted out.

"Ho! there! Which way are you going?"

The fugitives held their breath to listen; clearly their pursuers had heard the sounds of departure—were they even at this last moment to fall into the hands of their captors?

"Why, what a fool I was," reflected Gabriel. "I could endure for days in this carrier's cart if needful. Anything—anything rather than to be again a prisoner in Oxford Castle!" Meanwhile Jock was conveniently deaf, and drove placidly along the snowy street.

"Stop, you fellow," roared the officer. "Which way do you go, and what's your errand?"

Jock drew up, swearing vehemently.

"Where be I a-goin?" he shouted, in a surly voice. "To Henley with a load of corn."

And to the horror of the fugitives he got down from his place and began in a leisurely way to alter something in the harness, lugubriously singing meanwhile a snatch of a tune which Gabriel thought would ring in his ears for ever.

The cramp is in my purse full sore,

No money will bide therein—a,

And if I had some salve therefore,

O lightly then would I sing—a.

The officer at the window above burst into a laugh.

"In truth a shrewd fellow!—here's a groat to mend the purse, and if on the road you come upon three soldiers bid them wait on me here as they return, and fail not to tell them if you have clapped eyes on any of these cursed wandering minstrels.-"

The window was closed, and with a cheery word to the horses Jock climbed back to his place. They heard him chuckle to himself as he resumed the reins, and soon the cart had rumbled out of Watlington and was rolling and swaying and grinding its way among the frozen ruts.

"How do you fare?" said Humphrey, anxiously.

"I shall last out," said Gabriel, philosophically. "'Tis better than a halter anyway. Is the driver trustworthy?"

"Yes, an honest old man, he'll stand by us, I know him well. But I thought that fellow at the window smelt a rat and would stop us at the last moment. Heavens! How this road doth churn one up! we shall be knocked black and blue by the time we have got to the end of the journey."

Gabriel was past speaking. He could only lie there in torment, half fancying that he had been sentenced to be pressed to death, so increasingly intolerable grew the weight of the corn-sacks above him. The only relief was from a chink between the sacks which chanced to come just where a rent in the sail-cloth let through a breath of air, and now and then as the cart swayed brought into view a starry patch of the dark blue vault above. He wondered what Hilary would have thought could she know of his dilemma; and then with a rush of hope and a renewed sense of life and strength, he remembered that freedom meant at least the possibility of seeing her again. And spite of his present misery he smiled to himself, and even perceived the humour of Jock's song about the cramp in his purse, with the monotonous chorus of

Ay ho, the cramp—a! ay ho, the cramp—a!

They must have travelled some eight or nine miles when the sound of horsemen in the distance roused him to fresh anxiety. Doubtless the soldiers, finding their errand at

Henley hopeless, were riding back. Now was the time when Jock's fidelity and ready wit would be put to the test. There was a breathless pause; the groaning of the wheels slowly ceased and a harsh voice rang out into the night.

"Stand, in the King's name!" shouted the sergeant, while his men seized the horses. Instinctively Humphrey gripped the hand of his sick comrade. The two lay listening in an agony of suspense to hear what questions would be put.

CHAPTER XXVI.

May heaven ne'er trust my friend with happiness

Till it has taught him how to bear it well

By previous pain.

—Young.

Good Lord, deliver us!" ejaculated Jock. "I'm right glad to see ye wearing red ribbons, for in truth I took ye for highwaymen."

"What are you doing in the King's highway at this hour of the night?" said the sergeant, whose temper had not been improved by the ill-success of his errand.

"Why, sir, as you see, I be a carrier, and be a-drivin' my cart to Henley, same as I've done this many a year."

"What's in the cart?"

"Corn, sir, an't please you," said Jock, with humility.

"Why, yes, it pleases me very well," said the sergeant, grimly. "The corn, I take it, is going by barge to London, eh?"

"Why, that's a fact, sir, it be," said Jock, scratching his head thoughtfully, and sorely perplexed as to what he could do.

"Then you can just turn about, my good man, and drive it to Oxford; our granaries are none too full, and we'll store it in them instead. I annex that corn in the King's name."

The blood ran cold in the fugitives' veins; they listened intently to Jock's pleading voice.

"Oh! sir! for heaven's sake don't do that," he cried. "I'm a ruined man if you take the corn, for I be answerable for it to the owner. And I've other orders for carting back from Henley. Have mercy, sir, on a poor old carrier that's old enough to be your grandsire."

"Curse you, I say we need the corn in Oxford; why should it go to feed those rebel dogs in London?"

"Why, now I think of it," said Jock, "you must be the very man I've a message for. Doth not your officer lie at Watlington?"

"Ay! what of him?"

"Well, sir, he bade me tell you to wait on him at the 'Hare and Hounds' as you returned, and if so be I clapped eyes on some wandering minstrels I was to tell ye."

"Why, yes, to be sure; have you come across them?" said the sergeant eagerly.

"Well, sir, I did hear a man a-singin' as he journeyed along the road a matter O' five miles from here, singin' a ballad, he was, about the cramp in his purse."

"Well, well; and was he alone?"

"Nay, I think there was a couple o' men with him, but I only heard the one a-singin'," said Jock, his honest face boldly confronting his questioner.

"Five miles back! then we shall soon come up with them. Since you have told us this I'll not force you to drive back to Oxford with your load, but my men shall take a couple of sacks before them on their saddles as toll."

Jock grumbled, and the prisoners shuddered, for now, indeed, they feared discovery was certain. But the carrier was equal to the emergency. He folded back a bit of the sailcloth and handed his whip and reins to the sergeant.

"I'll ask you to hold them, sir, for I need both my hands; if the wind once gets hold of this plaguey cloth, there'll be the devil to pay."

With that he cautiously dragged out first one sack and then a second, tucking the cloth carefully round the remainder. As the cold wind blew upon the fugitives a violent shivering fit seized Gabriel; his teeth chattered, and it was all he could do to stifle the cough which threatened to choke him. Nothing but the strong instinct of self-preservation carried him through the agony of the struggle. But at length came the welcome sound of the departure of the soldiers, and Jock, with a cheery word to his horses, drove on.

"That was a narrow escape," muttered Humphrey, "but I shall not feel safe till the barge is under weigh."

Another hour brought them to their destination, and Jock drew up at the wharf, and told them he would seek out the bargee and get him to start with as little delay as possible.

"You are worth your weight in gold, man," said Humphrey, when the carrier returned with a couple of men to unload the cart. "Had it not been for your ready wit, we should now be on our way back to Oxford Castle."

"Eh, Master Humphrey, I'd gladly do more than that for your father's son. But have a care of your friend, sir, for I think he be sore spent."

Glancing at Gabriel by the light of the carrier's lantern on that dark winter morning, Humphrey saw that Jock was right. And all through the long, weary hours on the barge, only sheltered from the piercing wind by the sacks of corn and a load of wood which was already stacked up on board, he watched over his companion, feeling very doubtful whether he would survive to the end of the journey.

It was quite late in the afternoon when the bargee set them down at Chiswick, and after much trouble Humphrey succeeded in getting his friend borne to Notting Hill. Gabriel was by this time quite indifferent to all that passed, and it was only when they actually reached the Manor that he roused himself to speak to the astonished butler who appeared in answer to Humphrey's knock at the front door.

"Is your mistress within? If so, tell her I have made my escape from Oxford and would fain speak with her," he said.

"Let me help you, sir," said the man, shocked to note the change which the war had made in one he had seen a little more than a year ago in full health and vigour. "An' you'll rest in this room for a while I'll go and prepare my mistress. Beg pardon, Mistress Helena, I did not know you were here."

Humphrey, as he helped his friend into the room, saw a little fair-haired maiden whose heavy mourning robe only enhanced the delicate beauty of her face. Her blue eyes lighted up joyously at the sight of Gabriel.

"Oh! Mr. Harford, have you indeed got your exchange at length?" she exclaimed, greeting him with an eagerness and warmth that instantly sent a jealous pang to Humphrey's heart. "We Legan almost to despair of getting you released."

"Don't come too near me," said Gabriel, "for I have the new fever on me, an' I mistake not."

"Then I am well-fitted to nurse you," she said, gaily, "seeing that I myself had it last September. Here comes my godmother to welcome you."

Madam Harford's greeting was almost wordless, but in her smile, and in the clasp of her strong hand, there was a world of expression.

"Thanks to my friend and fellow-prisoner, Mr. Humphrey Neal, we have contrived to escape, madam," said Gabriel. "He will tell you of our adventures, but in truth I am scarce fit to ask your hospitality."

"Nonsense, lad," said Madam Harford, promptly silencing him. "To whom should you come but your grand-dame! Why, you are little more than a skeleton, and in a burning fever! Helena, my child, go and see that the fires are lighted in the blue-room, and in the turret-chamber, and bid Mrs. Malony wait on me at once."

Helena needed no second bidding, but flew off in the best of spirits to prepare all things for the comfort of her knight-errant. But her midsummer dream, nevertheless, came to a sudden end that very night.

Cousin Malvina, an excellent nurse, had been left in charge of the patient while the others supped, but later on Madam Harford and Helena relieved guard. They found that Gabriel already slept, and the old lady, taking Cousin Malvina's chair by the bed, bade Helena in a whisper to set the room in order.

Little Mistress Nell stole gently across to the fireplace, and began to fold the clothes which lay in a heap on the floor; then her eye happened to fall on a belt evidently containing money, which, with a small shagreen case, lay on the mantelshelf. Opening a drawer she stowed these safely away, and only then perceived that under the case lay the miniature of a darkeyed girl, whose radiant beauty filled her with admiration.

For a moment she could think of nothing but the loveliness of the picture. But very soon, with a start, she awoke from her dream to find herself in a cold and lonely world. Her knight-errant had a lady-love of his own, and the marriage her father had hoped for would assuredly never come about.

Taking up the miniature she laid it gently in the drawer beside the belt and the shagreen case, and, turning the key, drew it from the lock and handed it to Madam Harford.

"I have locked up some money and private things of Mr. Harford's," she whispered.

Madam Harford, whose quick eyes instantly detected a change in the girl, sent her on some errand, and then looked to see what the said private things consisted of. Although she had never heard of Hilary's existence, she gave a shrewd little nod as she caught sight of the miniature.

"If the lad loves that maid," she thought to herself, "he'll never do for a husband for my sweet little god-daughter. We must seek a match elsewhere."

But, in truth, for many days it seemed doubtful whether Gabriel would live to wed any one, and the Manor was pervaded by an atmosphere of gloom and of deep anxiety, which did not help poor Helena to rise above her troubles.

Humphrey Neal, who had been pressed to stay by his kindly hostess, watched the girl with much more sympathy and comprehension than she guessed. He listened to her account of the way in which Gabriel and Captain Heyworth had rescued her in the spring; he told all the details of their escape from Oxford, and often succeeded in persuading her to walk in the grounds of the Manor.

One day it happened that they were walking together in the garden when they saw a coach, drawn by two powerful black horses, approaching the house.

"That must be Sir Theodore Mayerne, the great physician," said Helena in an awestruck voice. "Madam Harford wrote begging him to come, but she feared he would not be willing to make the journey, for he seldom goes to any, being very corpulent and unwieldy."

"'If the mountain cannot come to Mahomet, Mahomet must go to the mountain,'" quoted Humphrey with a laugh. "Let us watch the great man dismount. In truth, report was right; he is a very Falstaff, and can scarce pass the door of his own coach."

"But they say he is the greatest physician living," said Helena. "If any one can save Mr. Harford's life he is the man."

"Madam Harford hopes that his own father, a noted physician of Hereford, will be here ere long," said Humphrey. "She sent a messenger for him the very morning after our arrival. They would have done much better, in my opinion, if they had sent for this 'Hilary' he is ever calling for in his delirium—his brother, it may be."

Helena blushed crimson.

"Nay, he hath but one brother—a mere child, named Brid-stock."

"Ah! and now I think of it," resumed Humphrey, "Hilary is a name that may be borne by either sex. Perchance he calls for the lady on whom his heart is set."

"In truth I think he doth," said little Nell, commanding her voice with an effort.

Humphrey walked for some paces in silence. He longed to make love to this little fair-haired maiden, with her pathetic eyes and her dainty air of womanly dignity and reserve, which somehow was scarcely in keeping with her girlish face and tiny figure. But he understood her well enough to hold his tongue for the present, treating her only with deference, and waiting upon her sedulously in a way which she soon learned to like.

They had just returned to the house when the physician's voice was heard on the stairs talking to Madam Harford. Helena hastily retreated into the nearest room, but Humphrey, anxious to hear the latest report of his friend, lingered in the hall, and Madam Harford presented him to Sir Theodore Mayerne.

"This is Mr. Neal, who helped my grandson in his escape from Oxford," she said.

"I wish the escape could have been made a couple of months sooner," said the physician, glancing keenly at Humphrey. "The patient is worn out by want of food and air, and hath no strength left to fight this fever."

"They told me in the prison that he did well enough till the last six weeks," said Humphrey, "and that it was nursing those that fell sick of the fever that were him out. He went by the name of 'doctor' among them, and they told me that he saved several lives."

"Brave fellow! I will do my utmost for him," said the physician. "Let them try, madam, the remedies I have prescribed, and to-morrow I will see him again."

With that he bowed himself out, leaving Madam Harford grateful for such an unusual concession, yet knowing well that it pointed to the gravity of the crisis.

All through the anxious days that followed, while Gabriel hung between life and death, subtle links were slowly forging themselves between the watchers at the Manor House. Instinctively they turned to those of their own generation for solace. Madam Harford found comfort in long confidential talks with Mistress Malvina, and Helena thought the only endurable hours of the day were those in which Humphrey Neal walked with her in the grounds. He was much in the sick room, but when released he invariably sought out little Mistress Nell, and with Lassie the retriever to act as duenna they would take a brisk walk, sometimes going to the village of Paddington, or visiting Kensington gravel pits, or now and then wandering as far as Hyde-park.

During those days Helena heard of the quiet times before the war, when the old house at Chinnor had been one of the happiest homes in England, and Humphrey, the only son of the house, had thought of little but hawking and hunting and fishing. His father, like many another squire, had taken neither side in the great dispute of the day, both parties had seemed to him in the wrong, and, as he truly said, he had not the knowledge to fit him to make choice betwixt them.

Helena heard now with indignation of Prince Rupert's wanton cruelty in burning the entire village of Chinnor, and shed tears over Humphrey's pitiful account of the way in which his parents both of them old and infirm, had been forced to fly from their burning house in the middle of the night. They had never recovered from the shock and from the ruin of the old family home. And Helena understood how much sadness was hidden beneath Humphrey's cheerful manner, and knew that he assumed an air of light-hearted carelessness as a man dons a coat of mail in troubled times.

Another subject on which they liked to talk was of his kinsfolk at Katterham, and their mutual admiration of Sir Robert Neal's granddaughter Clemency, now happily wedded to Captain Heyworth, proved a great bond of union. Humphrey was pleased and yet surprised to hear the girl's warm tribute to Clemency's charms, having the notion common to many men that one woman always tries to detract from another's merits. He therefore set down Nell's glowing words entirely to her credit, and thought they denoted a generosity altogether unique. In fact, day by day, he fell deeper and deeper in love with the god-daughter of his hostess, and Madam Harford watched the process contentedly, and left the two unmolested, hoping that Helena's heart would be caught in the rebound.

But there came a day in January when the struggle to hold death at bay in the sick room absorbed every one's thoughts. Sir Theodore, who took a special interest in the young lieutenant, had been for more than an hour at his bedside, and Helena had gathered that he had not much hope, when, about four o'clock, Madam Harford came downstairs to give some order to one of the servants.

"Yet I know the family constitution better even than this wise physician," said the resolute old lady. "In all things the Harfords show wonderful tenacity, and I do not yet despair."

"There is a horseman galloping up the avenue, ma'am," said Helena, glancing from the window. "Could it be his father?" A gleam of joy and relief lit up the strong face of Madam Alice Harford; she walked firmly to the front door, regardless of custom, and quite ignoring the bitter cold, peered eagerly out into the twilight.

"My son," she cried. "Now, indeed, shall we have good hope. He still lives, Bridstock—I can't say more than that."

"Thank God that I am in time to see him," said the doctor, stooping to greet his mother with tender reverence. "Nay, in truth, ma'am, I fear to see you at the door in this nipping frost; come to the fire and tell me of Gabriel."

"He is at death's door with the new fever, and is terribly weakened by want of food all these months, and the poisonous air of his gaol. Sir Theodore Mayerne would have more hope were it not for his exhaustion; but, indeed, I still trust in his youth and his sound constitution."

"Let me go to him now without delay," said the doctor, and with a heavy heart he was led to the silent room above, where lay the son he had parted from in the spring, so wasted by starvation and suffering that his own father could scarcely recognise him. Gabriel was unconscious, and Dr. Mayerne was administering a strong stimulant, in the hope of fighting off death a little longer. He greeted Dr. Harford with kindly sympathy.

"Try if your voice will rouse him," he said. "But I fear the pulse is failing."

Dr. Harford knelt down by the bed and bent low over the dying man.

"Gabriel," he sard, "I have reached you at last. Look up, my son."

In terrible suspense they watched the eyelids quiver and slowly open; there was amazed recognition in the hazel eyes.

"Father," he whispered, "you here in prison?"

"Here with you at Notting Hill Manor," said the doctor. "Try to swallow this—it will strengthen you."

Gabriel obeyed dreamily, glancing in some surprise at the portly form of Sir Theodore Mayerne, which certainly bore not the remotest likeness to any of the lean inhabitants of Oxford Castle. He began to grasp the idea that his father had journeyed from Hereford, and his lips framed the word, "Hilary!"

"She is well," said Dr. Harford, quietly. "On my way here I saw her at Whitbourne, where she was keeping Christmas with the Bishop. She was grieved to hear of your sufferings, and hopes you will soon recover."

A look of content came into the eager eyes. Gabriel asked no further questions, but lay in a state of dreamy peace. If Hilary hoped for his recovery, why then the worst of his suffering was over. His hold on life grew strong once more, and he fell into a profound sleep.

"I have hopes of him now," whispered Sir Theodore, "tomorrow I will visit him again," and he stole out of the room with a quietness which seemed magical in a man of such bulk.

CHAPTER XXVII.

"When the Established Church of England forsook the spirit of Hooker for that of Laud, it made a false step which could only lead to painful defeat. Presbyterianism, with still less excuse, made a like aggression, and with like result. To a certain extent, therefore, Milton is the spokesman of the bulk of his countrymen. Priest and Presbyter alike he forbade in the name of England to fetter by force her free development, her realisation of her chosen ideals for the time being."—Ernest Myers.

In after days it often seemed to Gabriel that his gradual recovery at Notting Hill was one of the happiest times of his life. The words from Hilary, though few and vague, gave him more reason to hope for a future reconciliation than he had as yet possessed. While the wonderful relief of having his father as his constant companion, after the severe sufferings of body and mind which he had undergone at Oxford, was indescribable.

There were countless things that he longed to hear about after his long deprivation of all news.

"Sir Robert Harley did his utmost to obtain your release," said Dr. Harford, when one day the talk had turned on Gabriel's old friend and schoolfellow, Ned. "But, besides his many duties in Parliament, he hath been himself in grievous trouble. Lady Brilliana, after bravely defending Brampton Castle during a six weeks' siege by the Royalists, fell ill and died last October, not long after the raising of the siege."

"What! was she alone, then?" said Gabriel. "Was not even Ned with her?"

"Neither husband nor son could be there," said the doctor. "And you know how frail her health ever was."

"Yet she had a great spirit, and was the sweetest and gentlest of ladies," said Gabriel. "What hath befallen her children?"

"The six younger ones remain at Brampton, under the care of Dr. Wright and his wife, who were present during the siege and a great comfort to Lady Brilliana. 'Tis a sad household, though, and grievous harm hath been wrought in the village, for the King's troops destroyed the church and parsonage and the mill, besides many dwelling-houses."

"I can't picture the place without its mistress," said Gabriel. "All the noblest and the best seem to perish through this unhappy war. Do you think, sir, we are any nearer hopes of a settlement?"

The doctor shook his head sadly.

"Further than ever," he said, with grave conviction. "Instead of an honourable and high-minded man like Lord Falkland, we have now the rash and unscrupulous Lord Digby as Secretary of State; and Cottington, who is almost openly a papist, has become Lord Treasurer."

"And yet I don't wish Lord Falkland back to the intolerable post he held," said Gabriel. "There were few that shared my love for him among the prisoners at Oxford, but as long as I live I shall be thankful for having known him. I can better bear the degradation of these scars on my back by remembering that they were earned in seeking to shield his name."

"In truth, I must ever hold his memory dear for the help he gave you, my son," said the doctor, with a choking in his throat as he recalled all that Gabriel had borne since their last meeting. "He was a man centuries in advance of his age, and such must ever die broken-hearted."

"Yes; war seemed to him a remedy so brutal that, spite of his natural love of adventure and his fearless and daring spirit, the misery and inhumanity of it drove him into a melancholy," said Gabriel. "I understand him better since living through the hell of last October, and can see now what he meant by the words he let fall at Oxford when he visited me. Father, when my work with Sir William Waller is ended, I would fain follow in your steps and be a physician; for, in truth, the horrors I have seen make me long to save life and to heal as you do."

"I am glad of your choice, lad," said the doctor. "We will tell your good friend and physician, Sir Theodore Mayerne, when next he sees you. Indeed, he seems to have a great regard for you, and has given you more of his time than he usually bestows on the highest in the land. What doth Mr. Neal purpose doing until he regains his property, or so much of it as the war hath left?"

"Indeed, I know not," said Gabriel. "He is much to be pitied—being well-nigh alone in the world."

"Humph!" remarked the Doctor, with a smile, "I'm not so sure that he will long be that. A most promising romance is being enacted down below while you lie here in this quiet room."

"A romance?" said Gabriel.

"Ay, to be sure, there is naught like a mutual friend and a mutual anxiety for drawing hearts together. And then, when the friend recovers, why the two begin to realise that in joy there is need of close sympathy too."

"Can it be that he hath fallen in love with Major Locke's daughter?" asked Gabriel eagerly. "I should be right happy if so good a match could be found for her."

"While your grandmother half wishes that you could have fancied the pretty little heiress yourself."

Gabriel shook his head, with a smile that was more than half sad.

"That was what her own father desired. Ah, poor man! I can see him now lying on the grass on that burning July day with his ghastly wound, and his effort even then to jest with us. I promised him ever to be a friend to Mistress Helena, but told him I was not free to wed her."

"Well, I shall be much surprised if she does not reward the devotion of Mr. Neal, and in truth it diverts me highly to watch his wooing. Now I shall leave you to rest in peace, for you have talked enough, and I purpose making one or two visits in the city. Bishop Coke implored me if possible to bear a letter from him to the Archbishop, and I have leave through Sir Robert Harley to visit him in the Tower. You'll not, I think, grudge me for an hour even to your arch-enemy, Dr. Laud." Gabriel smiled.

"I thought often of him as I lay in Oxford Castle," he said, quietly, "and have lost all my rancorous hatred of him as a man. Now that the days of his tyranny and harsh government are ended I marvel that they do not let him go free."

"I understand that the Parliament would be quite willing that he should escape," said the Doctor thoughtfully. "But I will speak with you again on that point when I return."

Provided with the necessary order, Dr. Harford found no difficulty in gaining access to Archbishop Laud, who, indeed, through the greater part of his imprisonment in the Bloody Tower, was allowed to receive visitors.

Ushered up the winding stairs and into the long, narrow cell, with its deeply-splayed window, the Doctor found himself once again in the presence of the little man who had rated him with such angry violence years before, and he was touched to find how greatly adversity had softened and mellowed the Archbishop. The real goodness of the man, the sincerity of his faith, shone out now like pure gold; his fussiness, his overbearing temper, his misguided zeal, were things of the past—the dross which had sadly marred his career, yet would not in the end triumph over him.

Always an unhealthy man, he was now worn and prematurely aged, seeming, indeed, to have the most precarious hold on life. The physician longed to see him released, for although he was permitted as much air and exercise as he pleased within the grounds of the Tower, and found great solace in the services of the Tower Church, yet the monotony and the inevitable restrictions of prison life were evidently preying on his feeble powers.

"I come as the bearer of this letter to your Grace," said Dr. Harford. "Having occasion to journey from Hereford to London, I visited Bishop Coke at Whitbourne, and he charged me to deliver this into your hands."

The Archbishop thanked him. "Your name seems familiar to me," he said; "yet I think I have never before met you."

"Your Grace would scarcely recall the occasion; it was many years ago in the Archdeacon's Court at Hereford," said Dr. Harford.

A light of remembrance kindled in the Archbishop's face; he recalled the whole scene, the—to him incomprehensible—position sturdily maintained by the physician, and the way in which his little son, with eyes ablaze with indignation, had heard the sentence pronounced. He was as far as ever from understanding the inward and spiritual adoration which avoids everything that may possibly degenerate into mere ceremonialism, and which sees in deep reserve and stillness the truest reverence. But suffering and patient endurance had made him more loving towards humanity, and less engrossed in his favourite religious system.

"I remember your son," he said, "and the love betwixt you. If I recollect right, he used to visit Bishop Coke during his brief imprisonment here; he once came to my aid when I had fallen while pacing Tower-green."

"In truth, your Grace, it was to see my son Gabriel that I journeyed to London. He lay at death's door after undergoing great hardships in Oxford Castle, from which on Christmas Day he, with thirty-nine of his fellow prisoners of war, contrived to escape."

"And he hath recovered his health?" asked Dr. Laud.

"He is out of danger, thank God! Hearing that I was to visit you he told me that often in his imprisonment he had thought of your Grace, and he wished you were set at liberty."

Dr. Laud smiled.

"I am over old to escape," he said; "that is for the young and daring. With your permission, I will read Bishop Coke's letter, and see if any immediate answer is needed."

He read the letter hastily, then carefully destroyed it.

"For the Bishop's sake and for yours, sir," he remarked, "I will take that precaution, lest perchance I receive a visit from Mr. Prynne, who makes free with any papers he can lay hands on."

Dr. Harford had heard that Prynne, whose cruel sufferings at the hands of the Archbishop in the past had aggravated a naturally stern and sour disposition, thirsted to mete out the measure that had been dealt to him, and was full of bitter enmity to Dr. Laud.

"I am sorry you are troubled by visits from Mr. Prynne," he said. "His fierce zeal and the sufferings he hath undergone ill fit him for such an office."

"I could pardon him for taking my papers," said the Archbishop, "but I think he might have spared me the book of private devotions I had compiled, for I sorely miss it."

"He would doubtless find it impossible to understand that written prayers could solace your Grace," said Dr. Harford. "Folk are too apt to think all men are framed on one pattern, and must be fed with the same food; whereas we physicians know well enough that one man's meat is another man's poison."

The Archbishop mused for a minute in silence. Had the system, which had seemed to him flawless, failed just in this particular? With a sigh he reverted to his lost manual of devotion.

"Mr. Prynne knew well enough how greatly I prized the book, for I pleaded hard to keep it. I even"—and he smiled pathetically—"made him a present of a pair of my gloves hoping to propitiate him. He took the gloves, but he took the manual as well."

"That was hard measure," said the physician. "Yet, who knows, some word in the book may perchance shame him for his lack of charity. He will not be the only Puritan who hath found comfort in the prayers of a devout High Churchman. There is my friend, Mr. John Milton, the scholar, whose works on 'Reformation in England' and 'Prelatical Episcopacy' do not keep him from being one of the most sincere admirers of Bishop Andrews—his Latin poem on that dead saint being, as all admit, most noteworthy."

The Archbishop looked interested, and said he would like to see the poem could a copy be procured, an errand which the physician gladly undertook.

"But, your Grace," he said, "something was hinted to me by Bishop Coke, as to the suggestion he had made in his letter, and in obtaining the order to come here I learnt from a Member of Parliament that the plan might very easily be carried out."

"I know it," said the Archbishop, with a long, weary sigh. "My friend, Hugo Grotius, who himself escaped from prison in Holland, would fain have me make a like attempt. I have long observed that my enemies would willingly permit me to fly, for every day a passage is left free in all likelihood for this purpose, that I should take advantage of it. But, sir, I am almost seventy years old, and shall I now go about to prolong a miserable life by the trouble and shame of flying?"

"In truth, your Grace, I see no reason why you should not pleasure your friends by making the attempt," said Dr. Harford.

"Whither should I fly?" * said the Archbishop, sadly. "Should I go to France, or any other Popish country, it would be to give some seeming ground to that charge of Popery they have endeavoured with so much industry, and so little reason, to fasten upon me. If I should get into Holland I should expose myself to the insults of those sectaries there to whom I am odious. No! I am resolved not to think of flight, but continuing where I am, patiently expect and bear what a good and wise Providence has appointed for me, of what kind so ever it be."

 * These are Dr. Laud's own words.

After that it seemed useless to urge the matter further, and indeed the physician was doubtful whether the physical energies of the Archbishop were sufficient to carry him through the toils and perils of an escape. His day had passed, and having in the time of success wielded the greatest power, not merely in the Church, but in secular matters, he had now only the strength left to endure with patience. Whether the past or the present was the time of his truest greatness, was a question upon which men and angels probably held different opinions.

Dr. Harford, being before all things a physician, and one who absorbed himself in trying to relieve suffering of any sort, thought mainly of the old man's needs, suggested one or two remedies for the ailments to which the prisoner was subject, and left him a good deal cheered by the courtesy and consideration of his visitor.

It was late before he returned to Notting Hill Manor, and Gabriel, refreshed by sleep and food, was eager to hear how he had prospered.

"I should have been with you long ere this," explained his father, "but on leaving the Tower I found the city completely blocked by a great concourse of people, proceeding from Mr. Stephen Marshall's sermon to Merchant Taylors' Hall, where the Sheriffs and Aldermen are giving a banquet to the Lords and Commons, the Scots Commissioners and the Assembly of Divines. While you have been lying ill here, a fresh plot of the King's hath been discovered. It seems that the very day after your escape from the Castle a letter was despatched from Oxford which luckily fell into the hands of the Committee of Safety."

"What did it reveal?" asked Gabriel, eagerly.

"It revealed a plot by which Sir Basil Brooke, the well-known papist, was to win over the City to the Royalist cause, and with it was seized a copy of the King's proclamation to those who supported him, to come to what he terms a 'Parliament' at Oxford."

"The plots seem endless," said Gabriel. "Yet the King himself is no papist. Humphrey Neal tells me that at Oxford not long since, he interrupted the Communion Service, and expressly declared himself a protestant."

"Yes, very like," said Dr. Harford; "but he intrigues with men of all persuasions, promises everything, and holds faith with none. His shifty dishonesty will prove his ruin. Truly, I believe that one main cause of his failure to understand the people is that he lacks all national feeling, and 'tis scarce to be wondered at. Himself half Scotch, half Danish, and with a grandmother bred in France by a French mother, why, there is absolutely nothing national about him! The sturdy old English love of honest dealing will, however, in the end baffle his intrigues, I think. Colonel Hutchinson has many fellow countrymen who, rather than betray a trust, would refuse the King's bribe of £10,000 and a peerage. But this is overserious talk for a sick man. I will tell you rather how, by good fortune, I came across an old friend of my youth, Mr. John Milton. He hath returned some three years from his tour in Italy, and as I perforce stood still in Cheapside, where the people were burning a pile of popish trinkets and pictures, I found myself pushed against him by the crowd."

"I remember him," said old Madam Harford, "in the days before your marriage, when he was a boy at St. Paul's School, and truly the most beautiful boy ever seen, I take it."

"He keeps his comely face and long light hair yet," said Dr. Harford, "but hath grown sad and stern through the conduct of his wife; she quitted him when they had but been wedded a few weeks, and doth refuse to return."

"Is it true, as the gossips say, that he wrote that ill-advised pamphlet on divorce, published anonymously, which hath so scandalised all people?"

"Ay, he wrote it in the first flush of his anger at his bride's desertion, and himself told me that he hath now a second edition in the press, which will bear his name on the cover. I have some compassion for the foolish young wife, however, for John Milton doth not understand women. Maybe they will yet make up their quarrel, for 'tis but a matter of lack of understanding—there hath been no great offence on either side."

"Had you much talk with him?"

"Yes, for he would have me go to his house in Aldersgale Street, I having asked him if he yet had the Latin poem he wrote on the death of Bishop Andrews. He hath also let me bring for your perusal two manuscript poems, which seem to me so full of beauty that they should, be published instead of lying unseen in his desk. Here is one, Gabriel, that will delight you, for it hath the very breath of the country about it, and will make you fancy yourself in Herefordshire once more."

"What of the Archbishop, sir?" asked Gabriel.

Dr. Harford told him what had passed.

"I fear," he added, "from what Mr. Milton tells me, that the discovery of Brooke's Plot will make people the more determined to proceed with the Archbishop's impeachment. The plot, will, however, tell favourably for the cause of freedom in this fashion, that it will assuredly alienate many of those who have hitherto supported the King."

And how true this statement was, Gabriel had reason to discover as time passed by, for the so-called "Oxford Parliament" failed utterly, and a steady "stream of converts began to flow from Oxford to London."

Just at present, however, the convalescent was much more inclined to enjoy the exquisite beauty of Milton's "L'Allegro," than to vex his soul over the problems of the day, and as his father read him the poem, he forgot war and strife and theological controversy, and was once more transported to his beloved Herefordshire, and the country life so dear to him.

After that first night of Dr. Harford's arrival, Hilary's name had not once been mentioned between them. Gabriel's rereserve was great; moreover, he was not without an instinctive dread that further questioning might disturb the relief and comparative peace he had gained from those memorable words which had dragged him back from the very door of death. And his father understood the silence, and thought that it would be rash to break it. Only on the very eve of Dr. Harford's departure did they venture to approach the subject which was seldom far from their thoughts.

Gabriel, now so far convalescent that he was able to sit in a great armchair by the hearth, asked if his father would see Bishop Coke on his return.

"Ay, I shall ride to Whitbourne and bear him the Archbishop's message," said Dr. Harford. "Those two will never again meet in this world, for Bishop Coke also grows old and infirm."

"You will see Hilary?" said Gabriel, with an effort.

"Yes, if she is still at Whitbourne," said the Doctor. "She is sometimes there, and sometimes with her uncle, Dr. William Coke."

"I never met him," said Gabriel. "When you see her, sir, tell her that her message had more to do with my cure than the skill of Sir Theodore Mayerne."

Dr. Harford laughed.

"That is all the thanks we poor physicians get," he said, lightly. "In happier times, my son, when you yourself are in the profession, I'll recall that speech to you. Shall I tell Hilary that you wish to forsake the Bar and to tread in my footsteps?"

"I fear that work will not find much more favour in her eyes, than my present work," said Gabriel, ruefully. "She ever held that the Bar was the only profession worthy of a gentleman. I seem fated to displease her."

"I should not trouble much on that score," said the Doctor. "In sorrow or need, or when her heart is really reached, trifles of that sort make no difference to her, as I saw plainly enough at the time of her mother's death. So courage, my son! Wait and see what time will bring forth. It seems likely that for those two young people below, Hymen will shortly appear

In saffron robe, with taper clear,

and I yet hope, when this war is ended, that Whitbourne may be the scene of such

Pomp, and feast, and revelry,

as now you scarce dare think on."

Gabriel did not reply, but a happier light dawned in his eyes, and as he gazed into the glowing depths of the wood fire he saw visions of a future that should make up for all the present suffering and separation.

CHAPTER XXVIII.

"True love's the gift which God has given

To man alone beneath the heaven;

It is not fantasy's hot fire,

Whose wishes, soon as granted, fly.

It liveth not in fierce desire,

With dead desire it doth not die;

It is the secret sympathy,

The silver link, the silken tie,

Which heart to heart, and mind to mind,

In body and in soul can bind."

—Lay of the Last Minstrel.

Meanwhile, in the withdrawing-room, Humphrey Neal was asking Madam Harford to promote his suit with Helena.

"I will do what little I can for you, sir," said the old lady, who liked him and desired to see him wedded to her goddaughter. "But first, I would bid you make sure of the maid's own feeling in the matter. Then, if she approves, you had best seek out her guardian, Dr. Twisse, the Rector of Newbury."

"Oh! is her guardian a parson?" said Humphrey with a groan. "I shall never find favour in his eyes; he'll be asking what view I take of the Divine right of kings to break the law."

"No; you will find him a liberal man, and a kind-hearted kinsman to my god-daughter. Once assured that the marriage is for his niece's happiness, he will not, I think, trouble you with arguings. Why should you not speak to Helena now, and ride to Newbury to-morrow with my son. He could then say a word on your behalf."

Humphrey caught at this idea, and asked where he should be likely to find Helena.

"I left her but now in the south parlour," said Madam Harford. And with a smile she watched the hasty way in which Humphrey at once quitted the room, eager to bring his wooing to a happy close.

"He is a tolerably well-assured lover," thought the old lady. "I do trust Nell will not prove uncertain of her own mind at the last minute."

Humphrey found the south parlour lighted only by the glow from the fire; there was no sound but the soft whirr of the spinning-wheel, and in the dim room the flax on the distaff and little Nell's yellow curls shone out brightly.

"You should keep blindman's holiday," he said, drawing up a stool and seating himself beside her. "Pray idle for a few minutes, and talk with me."

"Why, sir, can I not talk and spin at the same time?" said Helena, gaily.

"No, not when the talk is of a serious matter."

"Is anything wrong? Is Mr. Harford worse?" asked Helena, in alarm.

"Oh, no; he is much better, and already planning when to rejoin Sir William Waller. You think of him, but never trouble your head about me."

His sigh was too theatrical to deceive her. She laughed merrily.

"That reproach comes with an ill grace from your lips," she retorted. "Did I not walk with you, and talk with you, sir, this very afternoon for an hour by the clock?"

"It will be our last walk," said Humphrey, gloomily.

"What do you mean?" she asked, and somehow she dropped her thread and let the wheel stand idle.

"I am going away to-morrow, with Dr. Harford," said Humphrey, intently watching the little girlish face, and hailing with great delight the look of trouble that dawned in it.

"But why?" she faltered.

"It is because I love you that I go," he said, eagerly. "Because I must move heaven and earth to get into favour with your guardian. Helena, tell me, could you ever wed one who, till this war ends, is like to be a half-ruined man? I am ashamed to propose such a marriage, but I love you with my whole heart. We are alike homeless and forlorn. Give me the right to shield and protect you, and I will spend my life in making you happy."

She sat quite silent, with drooped head.

"Can you not trust one that so loves you?" pleaded Humphrey, realising now that this little gentle maid was not, after all, to prove an easy conquest.

She lifted her head for a minute, and looked shyly, yet searchingly into his eyes. There was none of the fierce passion that had terrified her in Norton's gaze, nor was there the quiet friendliness she had often seen in Gabriel's hazel eyes; surely this was the love that would satisfy her! And yet—yet—the pity of it!—could she honestly say she loved him? All at once she hid her face and burst into tears.

"Helena!" he cried, in dismay, kneeling beside her, "what have I done? What have I said to grieve you?"

"Oh, I don't know what to do!" she sobbed. "If my father were but here!"

He drew down one of her hands, and held it in his tenderly. "Tell me about him," he said.

And Helena poured out all her pent-up grief, and did not draw away her hand when now and again he kissed it.

"Tell me," said Humphrey, "had your father still been here, do you think he would have trusted you to me?"

"Yes," said little Nell, with a sob. "Anyone would trust you. It was not you that I doubted."

"What, then, my beloved?"

"It was whether I loved you—enough."

"Suppose," said Humphrey, "I join Sir William Waller's force when Gabriel Harford returns, and then come back in a year and ask you again. By that time you may know your own mind."

But at this suggestion Nell had fresh light thrown on her innermost heart.

"Oh, no," she cried, clinging to his hand. "I could not bear that you should go away for a year. They would kill you, as they killed my father."

"And you would care a little?" said Humphrey, smiling. "Perhaps, after all, you do begin even now to love me."

She did not reply, but she did not resist him when he clasped his arms around her, and drawing the fair little head on to his shoulder covered it with kisses.

"To-morrow," he said, "I will ride to Newbury, and if Dr. Twisse gives his consent, who knows but he may be willing to return with me, and himself tie the knot? For in days like these I am sure Madam Harford will agree with the proverb, 'Happy is the wooing that's not long a-doing.'"

Yet after all it was not till Humphrey Neal and Dr. Harford had made their farewells the next morning, and had left the Manor House to a most dreary quiet—a stillness which might be felt—that Helena became quite sure of herself. The light of her life seemed to have gone out, and she wondered how she had ever endured existence at Notting Hill all through the previous autumn. The next day her spirits sank still lower. What if Dr. Twisse would not consent to the marriage? It was quite possible that he might consider Humphrey Neal's prospects too much injured by the war to make him a desirable husband from the financial point of view.

And, indeed, this consideration was what chiefly filled the wooer himself with anxiety as he journeyed down to Newbury, and Dr. Harford had no little difficulty in cheering him in his depression. So downhearted had he become when they actually reached their destination, that the physician good-naturedly undertook to break the ice for him, and leaving Humphrey at the inn, took the letter from Madam Harford himself to the Rectory. He made a most excellent ambassador, for very few could resist his charm of manner, and his frank, clear way of stating a case. The Rector knew at once that he was a man whose sound judgment could be trusted, and he promised to call on them at the inn in an hour's time to discuss the matter with Mr. Neal.

Fortified by a good supper and by a cheery talk with Dr. Harford, Humphrey underwent the ordeal with composure, and made a good impression on Helena's guardian. He found also, to his amusement, that the mere fact that Dr. Twisse was a parson told after all in his favour. For as the good man informed them, he had only that morning been pondering over the church register, and had found that it furnished sad food for reflection. The burials were many, but the marriages had been few indeed since the war broke out.

"In truth, if the miserable strife goes on much longer, there will be no men left in the country," he said, with a sigh. "There is nothing like a deadly war for the utter destruction of home life and happiness."

"Little Mistress Helena hath already suffered cruelly through the war," said Dr. Harford. "And to see her happily wedded to one able to protect her and to safeguard her property would greatly please my mother."

Then the opinion of Sir Robert Neal was quoted as to the prospect of recovering the Oxfordshire property, and before long Dr. Twisse had consented to the marriage, and had agreed to return to London with Humphrey Neal that he might discuss arrangements with Helena and her godmother.

CHAPTER XXIX.

"He is a friend, who treated as a foe,

Now even more friendly than before doth show;

Who to his brother still remains a shield,

Although a sword for him his brother wield;

Who of the very stones against him cast,

Builds friendship's altar higher and more fast."

—Trench.

Having left this matter happily settled, Dr. Harford rode back to Herefordshire, finding sad evidence on every hand of the truth of the Rector's words, for though during the winter there was not so much fighting, the distress of the country people was even greater owing to the depredations of the soldiers on both sides, and the enforced contributions to maintain them in winter quarters.

It was on a clear, bright day, early in February, that the Doctor, having dined at the house of a friend in Ledbury, rode along the frozen lane which led to Bosbury Vicarage, thinking he would at least inquire whether Hilary had returned from Whitbourne. The pretty village street was deep in snow, and the black and white houses with icicles fringing their dark eaves looked more picturesque than ever. Rime glittered on the trees in the churchyard, and frosted the ivy on the square brown tower of the church, while the steps round the cross, where long ago Gabriel and Hilary had rested, were thickly covered with a white, wintry carpet. By contrast the snug sitting-room in the Vicarage, with its blazing fire of logs, looked all the more warm and comfortable, and the Vicar's hearty welcome left nothing to be desired.

He was busy, as usual, with some of his beloved antiquities, and a sound of girlish laughter arrested the Doctor's attention as he was ushered into the room.

Hilary had returned and had brought with her, for a few days' visit, her friend, Frances Hopton, of Canon Frome. The two girls sitting on an oak settle by the hearth made so fair a picture that Dr. Harford longed to transport Gabriel from his sick-room at the Manor to the Vicarage, while the Vicar, never dreaming that there had been aught but a boy and girl friendship between Gabriel and Hilary, inquired most minutely after his welfare.

"I was right glad to hear of his escape from Oxford, though, as you know, I hold aloof from taking any part in our unhappy divisions. But 'tis grievous to me to think of one little older than Hilary cooped up in so cruel a prison."

"He hardly escaped with his life, sir," replied the Doctor, "for the fever had carried off many of the prisoners, and he was worn out with trying to nurse the sick, and into the bargain was half starved; but, thanks to Sir Theodore Mayerne, he hath been brought back from the very gates of death. Gabriel himself ascribes the cure to your kindly message," he added, glancing at Hilary, "and in truth I think it was the pleasure of hearing your words that recalled him when we thought him sinking fast."

He saw that he was not likely to have any chance of speaking to her alone, and was obliged to risk this allusion.

The girl coloured, but kept her countenance marvellously.

"I am right glad he hath recovered," she said, in an even, carefully-controlled voice. "Hath he rejoined Sir William Waller?"

"Not yet," said the Doctor, admiring her self-command, yet longing to know what her thoughts really were. "He hopes to be strong enough to return next month, and, till then, remains at Notting Hill."

Just then the sound of loud and angry voices in the entrance lobby startled them all, and the next minute the door was opened by Mrs. Durdle, who was installed as housekeeper at the Vicarage.

"Oh, sir," she exclaimed, "here's Zachary the clerk, beside himself, with Peter Waghorn, and I do think, sir, they'll soon come to blows."

"What's amiss?" said the Vicar, setting his college cap straight and hastily rising from his elbow-chair. "I believe, sir, you know this man Waghorn," he added, glancing at the Doctor, who followed him out of the room, thinking that perhaps he might help to pacify the fanatic.

"That hateful Waghorn gives my uncle no peace," said Hilary, indignantly. "Let us come and hear what the dispute is about, Frances."

Now, if there was a man upon earth whom the girl cordially detested it was this village wood-carver, for she had an instinctive consciousness that he was their bitter enemy. Moreover, her earliest dispute with Gabriel after their betrothal had been caused by him, as well as the bitterness of their last interview in the parvise porch at Hereford, an interview which she never recalled without pangs of remorse.

"Hold your peace, Zachary," said the Vicar, "an you rail at the man like that I can understand nothing. What is the dispute betwixt yourself and the clerk, Waghorn?"

"I have no dispute with him," said Waghorn. "I did but cast a stone at the idolatrous painted window in the church, when Zachary fell upon me with railing and abuse and haled me to your presence."

"You have broken the east window!" exclaimed the Vicar, in great distress. "The only bit of old glass we have in the church! Man! how could you do it?"

"The Parliament hath given orders for the destruction of all idolatrous and popish windows," said Waghorn, his stern, square-set face utterly unmoved by the Vicar's distress.

"How can you pretend to see aught popish or idolatrous in a window that represented Michael, the archangel, vanquishing the devil?" said the Vicar, despairingly. "Were Popes of Rome in existence then? And as to idolatry, do you think so ill of your neighbours as to fancy they would bow down to a window?"

"If they don't at Bosbury, they do at Hereford; there's plenty of altar-ducking there, thanks to Archbishop Laud."

"Have I not set my face against all such practices?" said the Vicar. "You know right well that sooner than cause offence to one of Christ's flock I would willingly give up even ceremonies and uses that I personally like. Yet you deliberately destroy a beautiful and inoffensive window that we can never replace; such colours can, alas! no longer be made, the art is lost."

"Thank the Lord for that," said Waghorn, fervently. "Just and holy are all His works."

"Oh!" ejaculated the poor Vicar, intensely exasperated; and, turning aside, he paced the lobby in deep distress.

"In truth, Waghorn," said Dr. Harford, "one can scarce say that your works are just and holy. 'Tis true that Parliament hath very rightly ordered the destruction of some windows wherein blasphemous representations of sacred mysteries gave just offence. But too many folk destroy recklessly; why did you object to the window?"

"'Twas flat against the Second Commandment," said Waghorn, doggedly, "which forbids representation of anything in heaven above or the earth beneath. The archangel's above and the devil's below, and I did well to shatter their unlawful likenesses."

"The Commandment forbids bowing down to things that are seen," said the Doctor. "But, as the Vicar reminds you, no one here thought of doing any such thing. Moreover, Waghorn, there is also an eighth commandment, and I see not why you should break that by the deliberate robbery of a glass window. Next Sunday you will have the villagers complaining of a cold church."

"I'll put in good honest white glass at my own charge," said Waghorn, and at that the Vicar, suddenly perceiving the humour of the words, gave something between a sob and a chuckle.

"But you would be well advised, sir," resumed the wood-carver, "to remove those popish saints out of the chancel, for I do sorely long to dash their pates off with hammer and axe."

"Heaven forefend!" said the Vicar. "Why man, they are no popish saints, but the worthy ancestors of Dr. Bridstock Harford; what possible objection can you have to their monuments?"

"And, moreover, Waghorn," said the Doctor, "Parliament hath ordered that all the monuments of the dead be unmolested and treated with respect."

"I like not such representations," said Waghorn. "But being your ancestors, Doctor, I'll not molest them, for you were once good to my father."

"Ah! it comes back to that," said the Vicar with a sigh. "We do but reap to-day in these frenzied outbreaks of Puritanic zeal the harvest of the far worse cruelties of the past. I mourn over a shattered window, but this poor fellow mourns a father cruelly done to death. I don't forget, Waghorn, how greatly you have suffered in the past, but for God's sake, man, let us try to dwell in peace together."

"There will be no peace in this land till the high places are cast down and the images utterly destroyed," said Waghorn. "How can there be peace while corner-creepers still entice our countrymen to Rome? Yea, the wrath of the Almighty will abide on us until we have brought Canterbury to a just and righteous doom."

"Come, Waghorn," said the physician, laying his hand on the fanatic's shoulder, "I also am a Puritan, but we shall serve the good cause but ill if fierce zeal overpowers Christian love and forgiveness." For a minute a gentler expression dawned in the stern face. Waghorn turned to go.

Nevertheless, he shook his head dubiously over Dr. Harford's words.

"I'll not deny that you're a Christian, sir," he muttered; "but you're half-hearted, one that calls evil good and good evil, a moderate, betwixt-and-between believer, and Scripture tells us the fate of the lukewarm. As for me and my house we will destroy and utterly root out the accursed thing. And to you, sir," turning severely to the Vicar, "with your offers of peace and friendliness, I say in the words of the prophet of old, there is no peace to the wicked. Therefore, prepare yourself for trouble."

With that he stalked out of the house, and the Vicar returned to the hearth meditating sadly over what had passed. Yet there was, in spite of his sadness, a humorous twinkle in his eye as he glanced at the physician.

"Waghorn doesn't mince matters, does he? There is a directness in his attack which, like his stone-throwing, shows great vigour."

"How dare he call you wicked, Uncle!" said Hilary, angrily.

"My dear, we acknowledge ourselves miserable offenders day by day with perfect truth," said the Vicar. "But I confess he seemed to think more of my trespasses than of his own—a snare of the evil one too apt to entrap all of us. I think, sir, if you will excuse me, I will go across and see what the extent of the damage is."

Dr. Harford begged to accompany him, and crossing the garden and the churchyard, they entered the beautiful old church, followed by the two girls.

At that time the east wall was pierced by three Early English windows. The side lights being filled with what Waghorn called "good honest white glass" remained intact, but the central light with its matchless stained glass and rich jewel-like colouring was shivered into a hundred pieces, while the icy wind blew drearily into the building.

The Vicar's eyes grew dim, the loveliness of the old twelfth century church had been one of the joys of his life, but he spoke not a word, only stooped down quietly and began carefully to gather up the broken fragments from the chancel floor.

"You will cut yourself, sir," said Hilary, gently. "And of what use are these broken bits?"

"Nay, I'll gather them up," he said, sturdily, "and in happier times, maybe, someone will piece them together; the picture is lost, but the colours are fadeless."

"Peter Waghorn little understood how much pain his stone-throwing would give," said Dr. Harford. "I think he was blindly feeling after the truth which unites all who side with us, and is the pivot of Puritanism—that the relationship betwixt God and man is direct, and that no human ceremony, no glory of art, must ever stand between as a barrier."

"Yet you do not deem all such things as necessarily barriers?" said the Vicar.

"Not when carefully safeguarded by a true and inward religion," said the Doctor. "Indeed, I have learnt that through nature God doth oft reveal Himself, just as you have found that in His wonderful works of old, and in the beauty of this place, He may teach us of His ways. 'Twas but a few days since that I read words by my friend John Milton the schoolmaster, a noteworthy Puritan pamphleteer, as all will admit. Yet he wrote right lovingly of:

'The high-embowèd roof,

With antique pillars massy proof,

And storied windows richly dight

Casting a dim religious light.'"

"Ay, and now I think of it," said the Vicar, "our good neighbour, Mr. Silas Taylor, a Puritan himself, but one that hath a regard for all that is beautiful or of great antiquity, will sympathise with us as you do, sir. After all, 'tis, in the main, lack of education that drives on such fellows as Waghorn—the man is conscientious, but his conscience is untrained—we must have patience."

"Yet Gabriel would agree with his harsh words about the Archbishop," said Hilary, when for a minute she found herself alone with Dr. Harford, her uncle lingering to lock up the church.

"Nay, there you wrong him," said the Physician, quietly.

"He told me that in prison he had lost all his rancorous hatred towards one who was also a prisoner. More and more we both tend to the Independents, who desire the nearest approach to religious toleration that is at present compatible with the safety of the country."

"I fear you will not tolerate us," said the Vicar, joining them as they re-entered the house.

"The Presbyterians certainly will not; and, indeed, I think that Cromwell himself, who is by far the greatest soul now living, would deem it impracticable to have in power again those ecclesiastics who have truckled slavishly to the Court and laid an unbearable yoke on the consciences of Englishmen. Were all prelates like the Bishop of Hereford, and all parsons like yourself, sir, a reconciliation would be easy enough; but as it is, I fear Waghorn is right in prophesying trouble."

Then he told them of his visit to the Tower, and Hilary's face grew tender and wistful as she learnt of the proposals for the Archbishop's flight.

After all, was not her Puritan lover one who merited deep respect? However much they differed, did she not in her heart of hearts still love him?

"And if I do, I'll never, never admit it," she reflected. "He can go wed some strait-laced, prim, Puritan lady, and I will sing 'God save King Charles,' and die a maid."

As this grey future vision rose before her the haughty brown head drooped a little, and the dark eyes were soft and sad as she made her farewells to the physician.

"I am glad to have seen you," he said, saluting her in his usual fashion. "Perhaps you, with your womanly grace and sympathy, will be able to win Peter Waghorn from his uncharitableness."

Dr. Harford, like the "generous Christian" sung by the poet Quarles, was blest with the necessary "ounce of serpent" to flavour his "pound of dove." The words of appreciation instantly appealed to Hilary, and actually called up for a time those very qualities which were too apt to lie dormant in her heart.

"I will try to feel more kindly to him," she said; "and when you write to Gabriel, pray tell him how glad I am that he hath recovered."

CHAPTER XXX.

"One to destroy is murder by the law,

And gibbets keep the lifted hand in awe;

To murder thousands takes a specious name,

War's glorious art, and gives immortal fame."

—Young.

Hilary found great pleasure throughout the next few months in her friendship with Frances Hopton, and her sympathies gradually widened, not only from constant intercourse with her uncle, but from her frequent visits to Canon Frome Manor. The house was about two miles from Bosbury, one of those fine old moated residences often found in the counties bordering on Wales, strongly built and almost like small fortresses.

The Hoptons, like many another household in those days, were divided on the subject of the war, Sir Richard himself sided with the Parliament, but was too old to take any active part in the strife. He had suffered severely, however, for the action he had taken in marching to Hereford with the Earl of Stamford when the city had first been besieged in the early days of the war, and the Royalists on returning to power had plundered Canon Frome, and carried off or ruthlessly destroyed all the furniture and valuables they could seize. Sir Richard had been cast into prison, but later on, owing to the representations of his son Edward, who had joined the King's army, he was released and allowed to return to his home, which was safe-guarded from further molestation by one of those letters of protection which were granted both by the King and the Parliament under certain circumstances.

So for a time all went well with them, and Hilary learnt to love Dame Elizabeth, who, feeling sorry for the motherless girl, did what she could for her and always gave her the warmest of welcomes at Canon Frome.

One cold March day she had ridden over at noon with her uncle to dine with the Hoptons, and, the meal being over, the ladies of the party were sitting with their needlework in Dame Elizabeth's withdrawing-room, when Sir Richard and Dr. Coke rejoined them with grave faces.

"Hath any news come from the boys?" asked Dame Elizabeth anxiously, for with one son fighting for the King and two fighting for the Parliament, the poor lady knew little ease.

"No, but there is very grievous news of the capture of Mr. Wallop's place—Hopton Castle—by the Royalists," said Sir Richard. "The entire garrison hath been massacred."

The ladies exclaimed in horror, and Dame Elizabeth asked the details.

"In truth they are too shocking to repeat," said Dr. Coke, sighing. "It seems that the place was held for the owner, who was absent, by Governor More, brother to Mr. Richard More, Member of Parliament for Bishop's Castle. They held out gallantly when attacked by Colonel Woodhouse and five hundred men, but were at length obliged to capitulate, being utterly worn out and the castle well-nigh battered to pieces."

"But did not they sue for quarter?" asked Hilary.

"Yes, and were told that they should be referred to Colonel Woodhouse's mercy. Governor More and Major Phillips were taken before him to a house at some little distance, and More wondered after a while why his men did not follow, only then learning that they had been stripped, tied back to back and put to death with circumstances of revolting barbarity. The poor old steward of eighty, being weak and not able to stand, they put him into a chair while they cut his throat."

Hilary felt sick with horror.

"Who is this Colonel Woodhouse?" she asked.

"He is the Governor of Ludlow Castle, and it is only fair to say," remarked Sir Richard, "that when remonstrated with he alleged that he had orders from Oxford."

"His Majesty is surrounded by evil counsellors," said the Vicar. "But if that be indeed true, and sheer butchery was ordered, then it is all over with the King's cause. After that it will never prosper."

This seemed to be the beginning of a much fiercer and more cruel epoch of the struggle. At first both sides had acted with a certain dignity, but the evil passions always kindled by war grew stronger and stronger, and those who, like Hilary, had been inclined to enjoy the excitement of the contest, and to dwell on the "glory" and "romance" of the campaign, began to understand how cruel and devilish was the grim reality.

Hopton Castle was only just over the borders of Herefordshire, and but four miles from Brampton Bryan, and when Hilary heard of the great peril in which the Harleys found themselves her sympathies turned to the orphaned children of Lady Brilliana, and to their friend and guardian, Dr. Wright, who had been kind to her in her own trouble during Mrs. Unett's last illness.

Fresh from the diabolical cruelties perpetrated on the Hopton Castle garrison, Colonel Woodhouse took his men to Brampton Bryan, and the castle underwent a second siege, with no brave-hearted mistress to cheer the unhappy garrison and the luckless children. The tragedy of Hopton Castle would have been enacted once again, for a letter from Prince Rupert was actually on its way to Colonel Woodhouse with such orders; but, after a long and brave resistance, Dr. Wright, desperate at the knowledge of the barbarities so lately committed by these very soldiers, and fearing such a fate for his garrison, sent out to treat, and Colonel Woodhouse, having granted them their lives, they surrendered just before the arrival of the Prince's letter, and were carried away prisoners to Shrewsbury.

"Their lives are happily spared," said Dr. Coke, when he was recounting the story to his niece one evening, "but the splendid castle has been burnt, down by Colonel Woodhouse, and with it one of the finest libraries in the country. 'Tis pitiful to think of the loss, for there were manuscripts there which can never be replaced. For generations the Harleys have been noted for their love of literature."

"I have heard Gabriel Harford speak of the library," said Hilary. "He was a friend and schoolfellow of the eldest son, and will grieve over this sad tale."

"That reminds me," said the Vicar, "that to-day, near Castle Frome, I met Dr. Harford. He told me that they had just heard from his son, who had rejoined Sir William Waller, and had fought in the battle of Cheriton."

Hilary's heart began to throb uncomfortably. She turned away, and made a pretence of rearranging the logs on the hearth.

"He escaped without hurt?" she asked, in a voice that might have betrayed her had the Vicar in the least guessed her story.

"Ay, and hath been promoted to a captaincy. I gathered, however, that he is only longing for the end of hostilities, being now determined to become a physician, like his father, and desiring to heal men rather than to slay."

Hilary was silent, hardly knowing whether she approved this new development or not. With a little shudder, she remembered the flash of indignation in Gabriel's eyes when she had gleefully recounted that fifty of the rebels had been killed at Powick Bridge. Certainly in those early days, before she had in the least realised the horrors of war, it had been possible to speak in a careless fashion that would now have been out of the question.

Indeed, by the end of April the grim shadow of war drew yet closer to Bosbury, for the Parliamentarians under Massey, Governor of Gloucester, began to make inroads and to do their utmost to clear out small garrisons and to raise money for the troops. It was far from pleasant to realise that Massey and his soldiers were quartered at Ledbury, barely four miles off, and Hilary began to picture to herself what would happen if their peaceful village should be invaded.

Musing on this one afternoon, she set off to visit old Farmer Kendrick's wife at the Hill Farm, and to carry her certain remedies for her rheumatism which Mrs. Durdle had made.

"Tell her," said the housekeeper, "that she'd never have had the rheumatics had she taken my advice and carried a potato all winter in her pocket. But folk will be thinking there's no cure without eating or drinking summat, and the worse the taste the better the medicine, they believe. So, my dear, I've flavoured this with camomile, as nasty a herb as grows, and do you tell her to drink it hot first thing in the mornin', she'll have a most powerful belief in that."

Hilary laughed and promised. Crossing the churchyard she encountered Zachary, the parish clerk, who was also the gardener and general factotum at the Vicarage; his ruddy face looked less cheerful than was its wont, and, resting on his mattock, he said, earnestly:

"Don't you be a'goin' far from home, mistress; it be scarce safe for you to be abroad in times like these."

"Why, Zachary," she replied, with a smile, "I do but go to the Hill Farm, and who is like to molest me?"

"They say the Parliament soldiers never misuse women," said Zachary. "But I wish the whole plaguey lot of soldiers were out of Herefordshire, whether they be Cavaliers or Roundheads. There's sore news from Stoke Edith, they tell me."

"What is that?" said Hilary, anxiously. "Have Massey's soldiers molested Dr. Rogers?"

"Well, mistress, they set out for Ledbury with no good will to him, for, as you know, he has ever been severe to the Puritans, and I reckon they thought their turn had come. But, as ill-luck would have it, close by the wall at Stoke Edith they came upon an old parson and, belike, took him for Dr. Rogers."

"Well?" said Hilary, anxiously, as the man hesitated. "Did they harm him?"

"It was old Parson Pralph walking back from Hereford to his Vicarage at Tarrington."

"I remember him, an old man of more than four-score years," said Hilary. "He had white hair and a long white beard."

"That's the man," said Zachary, gloomily. "He'd been Vicar of Tarrington over forty year. Well, one of Massey's soldiers stopped him, saying, 'Who art thou for?' On which he honestly answered, 'For God and the King,' and the soldier without more ado raised his pistol and shot him dead."

Hilary turned pale, the same sick horror that she had felt at Canon Frome on hearing of Colonel Woodhouse's barbarous conduct at Hopton Castle overpowered her again, and as she walked on slowly to the Hill Farm her eyes were dim with tears.

The summer brought them the news of the King's defeat at Marston Moor, but the more distant hostilities really affected them less than the smaller troubles in their own near neighbourhood.

In the autumn of 1644 there was once more grievous trouble at Canon Frome, for, notwithstanding the protection of the King's letter, the Manor was attacked by a party of Royalists, who insisted on converting the house into a garrison.

Sir Richard Hopton resisted this intolerable invasion of his rights, but superior force triumphed, and the poor old knight was seized and cast into prison, while the Manor was at once garrisoned by a force which proved the scourge of the neighbourhood.

As the luckless farmers remarked, "God had sent them good harvests of hay and corn, but what was the use when they had but the labour of mowing and reaping?"

The crops had been safely gathered in, but the Canon Frome garrison plundered the farms, and if any man was bold enough to demand compensation, or to resist the seizure of his goods—well, he found that silent acquiescence would have been more prudent.

The beautiful county, a very Garden of Eden for fertility and loveliness, became a hell upon earth, and the pathetic loyalty of the people to a wholly unworthy monarch was speedily changed to active and determined resistance. The Herefordshire folk cared little for the dispute between King and Parliament, but under the intolerable wrongs they suffered they now began to band themselves together into a neutral party, armed only for the protection of their homes.

Hilary's chief personal loss at this time was the companionship of Frances Hopton, from whom she had not even the poor consolation of a parting visit. A letter received from her soon after the conversion of the Manor into a garrison explained what had passed. It ran as follows:

"My dear Hilary,—You have ere this, I know, heard the ill news of my father's arrest. He lies once more in gaol, and indeed I can well-nigh rejoice in his absence, for he would be heartbroken could he see the havoc the Royalist soldiers are making here. Many of the outhouses are burnt down, and they ruthlessly destroy and waste the property in a fashion that it is piteous to behold. I am bound to say, however, that the Governor is a most pleasant and courteous gentleman, with so genial a manner that one might think all this mischief carried out by his orders was but a pastime amid toys, and not the wicked destruction of an Englishman's house, which we were wont to think his own and free from all assaults by outsiders. The Governor has most considerately urged my mother to retain the rooms in the right wing for our private use, and since she is ailing and unfit to travel she remains here with one of my brothers and three of the servants. But she thinks I am best away, therefore I am to be sent with my sister to Garnons to stay with Mr. and Mrs. Geers, you remember that Mr. Geers wedded recently Mistress Eliza Acton, goddaughter to your Hereford friend, Mrs. Joyce Jefferies. Here came a long pause in my letter, for who should come into the ante-room where I am writing but the Governor. He made many pretty speeches on hearing that I was to leave home. Maybe this is the reason my brother doth not like him so well as we womenfolk do; I often notice that my father and the boys particularly detest these evil, pleasant-spoken gentlemen who know how to turn a neat compliment. I forgot to tell you that the Governor—his name is Colonel Norton—is a remarkably handsome man, very tall, and with bright laughing eyes and auburn love-locks. Pray tell the vicar that I will question Mr. Geers as to the antiquities in the neighbourhood of Garnons, and when these troubles be ended seek to bring him some treasures for his collection.—I rest, your affectionate friend,

"Frances Hopton."

"My youngest brother is now with Governor Massey, and since he is kept so actively at work against various regiments of the Royalists now scattered over the country to seek winter quarters, you may belike see him. Governor Massey doth seem much to affect the neighbourhood of Ledbury, and since his great victory near by at Redmarley last August, he will doubtless hold it in yet more loving remembrance. They tell me that Colonel Edward Harley did there get wounded, and that though he hath now recovered the bullet is yet in him."

Hilary folded the letter sadly.

Everything seemed to be passing away from her, and she began faintly to understand how terrible a condition England was in. Moreover, the closing in of the short autumn days, and the near approach of the hard winter, depressed her. She wondered how she should ever endure the long nights with their dreadful sense of insecurity; she shuddered at the remembrance of the horrible tales she had heard from the village folk of the wickedness and violence of Prince Maurice's troops, and she remembered with horror the fate of the Vicar of Tarrington. If one of Massey's men had shown such brutality to him, what guarantee had she that the Vicar of Bosbury would fare any better?

Sitting by the hearth in the fast-gathering twilight, an unusual stir in the village street suddenly attracted her attention; there was a steady, ominous tramp of many feet, which could not be mistaken, then the hoarse shout of an officer, "Plait!"

She sprang up and ran to the study, where the Vicar sat at a table strewn with fossils, deeply absorbed in the contemplation of an ammonite.

"Sir!" she said, "do you not hear that there are soldiers in the village?"

"Look what a fine specimen Mr. Bartley hath to-day brought me for the collection," said Dr. Coke, looking up at her with a happy light in his eyes. "'Tis the finest I have ever seen."

"Yes, yes," said Hilary, trying to be patient; "but, uncle, there are soldiers halting in the village."

She had at last brought him back from pre-historic times to the seventeenth century. He pushed back his chair and, putting on his college cap, rose to his feet.

"Now I think of it," he said, "I met a couple of scouts when I was out—Massey's men, judging by their ribbons."

"Oh! don't go then; you must not go, sir, if they are Massey's men," she said in terror.

"Why, yes, child, of course I must go," he said, patting her shoulder caressingly. "'Tis my duty to try and keep the peace betwixt the soldiers and the village folk; I only trust they do not mean to stay here long. Let supper be made ready, for whether they be friends or foes we are bound by holy writ to feed them if they hunger. I'll warrant, though, that you'd like to pepper the broth till it choked them!"

And with a laugh he went out, his eyes twinkling with humour at the thought of pretty Hilary with her vehement hatred of Parliamentarians getting ready the best evening meal that the house could provide.

CHAPTER XXXI.

"Nor tasselled silk, nor epaulette,

Nor plume, nor torse;

No splendour gilds, all sternly met,

Our foot and horse.

"In vain your pomp, ye evil powers

Insult the land;

Wrongs, vengeance, and the cause are ours,

And God's right hand!"

—Elliott.

The entry of Massey's men had been watched with eager eyes by one inhabitant of Bosbury. The moment he learnt that the soldiers were at hand, Peter Waghorn laid aside his tools and hasting down the street, eagerly awaited the approach of the officers who brought up the rear.

There was a brief delay of the cavalcade just as the officers rode up to the place where he stood, and Waghorn, with a heartfelt ejaculation of thanks, raised his eyes to heaven. His breast heaved with emotion, though his strong, square-set face betrayed nothing but quiet determination.

"Sir," he said, approaching Massey, "may I crave your help, and entreat that you will spare your men for the pious work of destruction. There stands a cross, sir, in yonder churchyard—a popish cross. Bid your soldiers throw it down."

"My good fellow," said Massey, "I have other work on hand just now, and the men need food and rest."

"It will not take long," pleaded Waghorn. "It stands hard by, and, sir, as you know, Parliament hath expressly ordered the destruction of crosses, because the people do idolatrously bow down to them."

"Yes, 'tis true," said Massey, who, as a matter of fact, cared for none of these things, and was more or less a soldier of fortune. "It shall be done some day, but not now. I am certain to be in the neighbourhood again. Ask me when I have more leisure."

Waghorn drew back, grievously disappointed.

"He is not whole-hearted; my soul hath no pleasure in such. Yet he did help to defend the godly city of Gloucester, and maybe some other day I shall prevail with him. I must bide my time," and, with a deep sigh, he returned to his house, and, falling on his knees, prayed fervently that he might be spared to do the Lord's work, and to cast down every high thing that exalted itself against truth and righteousness.

The man was no hypocrite, his character was absolutely genuine, he hated whatever he deemed likely to lead people astray; but sorrow and loneliness had warped his nature. Since his father's death no spark of love had been kindled in his heart, and incessant brooding over one great grievance had distorted his powers of judgment. His zeal had degenerated into fanaticism, his Christianity had faded into that longing to call down fire from heaven on all who disagreed with him, which has often marred the career of great saints and honest disciples.

Meanwhile, the kindly Vicar—a man who loathed strife and ill-will—made his way out into the village, and with just a comforting remembrance of the splendid ammonite, his newest treasure, to linger in the recesses of his troubled heart with a sort of grateful glow, went from one to another of his parishioners, gathering by degrees the state of affairs. At the door of the "Bell Inn" he saw Massey and two of his officers dismount, and with the quick glance of one who is always studying his surroundings recognised in the stream of bright lamplight coming from the open door, one of Sir Richard Hopton's sons.

"Good evening to you, Mr. Hopton," he said, pleasantly. "I am sorry to learn of the trouble that has befallen Sir Richard."

The young man gave him a cordial greeting; somehow with Dr. Coke everyone's first thought was of the matters they had in common. The Vicar held to his own opinions, and had his likes and his dislikes, but there was nothing combative about him.

"Truth to tell, we are about to march towards Canon Frome," said Sir Richard's son. "We shall not trouble you long in Bosbury, but the men need food and a few hours' sleep. A good many of them can be quartered in the Old Palace. I must go round there and see to the arrangements."

"I will come with you," said the Vicar. "A word to the caretaker may smooth matters. You will find few comforts there, for, as you know, the place was dismantled in the days of good Queen Bess. But here, I see, comes Mr. Silas Taylor, who hath a special love for the old building, and will be able to serve you better than I can. And when you have bestowed your men, come and sup with us at the Vicarage, and bring one of your friends with you; 'tis bitter cold, and you will be glad to sit by a comfortable hearth."

"Good evening to you, Vicar," said Mr. Taylor, joining them. "You and I are, maybe, on the same errand, for though I am all for the Parliament, I should be sorely grieved were any of our much-prized antiquities to be marred by the troops."

"To be sure you would," said the Vicar, with his genial laugh. "I was but saying as much to Mr. Hopton here. For the sake of old times you will, I know, have a care of the Old Palace, and we will seek to quarter as many as can be well stowed there, for it will put the villagers to less trouble."

Sounds of a vehement altercation at a little distance made the Vicar hasten down the street.

"What is amiss now?" said Silas Taylor, straining his eyes to see what was passing.

The purple-grey gloom of the wintry twilight, broken here and there by the glimmer of candles in the windows, or the glare of torches kindled in the road by the newcomers, just revealed the picturesque houses on either side, and the confused mass of weary buff-coated soldiers, girt with orange scarves; while the inhabitants, divided between alarm and curiosity, stood about their doors eager to learn with what intentions these men had come.

"Save us from the dastardly robbers at Canon Frome garrison and we'll give you the best supper we have," cried one good woman, vehemently.

"Ay, down with the vile thieves that pillage every farm around," shouted a man.

"Fool!" roared another burly fellow, "down with both lots, say I; starve 'em both out, and let's keep our homes free from such vermin."

This provoked a perfect babel of retorts of every description, except "the retort courteous."

Happily, at that moment the Vicar pushed his way through the throng, and taking a torch from one of the bystanders, said in his mellow, hearty voice:

"My friends, while we stand here idle our visitors are waiting cold and supperless after a long march; for the honour of Bosbury let us each do what we can to feed the hungry. I have yet to learn that there is anything political in a stomach, and you'll be following the only true Leader if you do as you'd be done by. I'll be bound you fellows feel the pangs of appetite beneath your orange scarves just the same as if they were red—eh?"

His hearty, cheerful manner took the men's fancy; they laughed, the villagers laughed, and, as if by magic, harmony prevailed. Before long not a soldier was to be seen save the sentries, who were bound to keep guard in case of an attack.

Meanwhile, Hilary was hard at work with Mrs. Durdle, preparing something more sustaining than the simple fare that was to have sufficed for their evening meal. To own the truth she would have complied less willingly with her uncle's request had not a wild hope that Gabriel might possibly be with this regiment, begun to stir in her heart. She had no reason to think he would be with Governor Massey, but to youth all desirable things seem possible, and her sadness, and the sense of desolation that had expressed her all the afternoon, made her crave the support of her lover's strength and quiet fortitude.

So she took keen interest in the supper; did not, as the Vicar had naughtily suggested, pepper the broth, but, on the contrary, thickened it with oatmeal in a way which Gabriel specially liked. She robbed the store-room of several eggs, and bade Durdle make a large dish of eggs and bacon; and, finally, herself prepared the bread and cheese from which, at the last moment, the housekeeper was to make that particularly favourite dainty of their childhood—"Welsh rarebit."

Then she flew back to the sitting-room, and piled fresh wood on the dogs in the fireplace, and by the time everything was ready, had become convinced that all would soon be well, and that her lover would really appear.

And now the Vicar's steps were heard without, and his pleasant voice. Hilary's heart throbbed wildly, for surely the courteous reply spoken by his companion was in Gabriel's very tone.

The door was thrown open.

"My dear," said the Vicar, "I have brought in Captain Bayly; this, sir, is my niece, Mistress Unett."

Hilary curtseyed, but she really could not speak, so great was her disappointment.

"We shall be joined in a minute or two by one of Sir Richard Hopton's sons," said the Vicar; "I will speak a word to Durdle. Draw your chair to the hearth, sir, for you look half frozen."

He withdrew to speak to the housekeeper as to arrangements for the two guests, and then lingered for a while in the study with his precious ammonite, so that Hilary was forced to speak civilly to the Parliamentarian, whether she would or no.

"'Tis a frosty night," she remarked, somewhat icily.

"Yes, but 'tis nothing to compare with the severe weather we had after Newbury fight, the other day."

"Were you in the second battle of Newbury then?" asked Hilary, interested in spite of herself.

"Yes, and we lingered on at Newbury for three miserable weeks after, though the men were dying by scores from sickness, want of food, and lack of physicians and surgeons. There was one of Waller's officers that well-nigh threw up his commission then and there, and vowed that he'd turn surgeon, for he saw his best friend maimed for life all for lack of skilled aid when wounded."

"Was he not from Herefordshire?" said Hilary, remembering Dr. Harford's words when he had met the Vicar near Castle Frome.

"I can't tell you, but his name was Captain Harford."

"I thought so," said Hilary, blushing. "His father and my father were old friends, and I heard of his wish to turn physician."

"Cromwell took a great liking to him," said Captain Bayly; "and was himself well-nigh distracted to see the cruel suffering of the men, and angry, too, at the disgraceful mismanagement of those in authority. 'Tis strange how often you find that the bravest soldiers are the most tender-hearted men, and have the greatest loathing of war."

"What did this Cromwell advise Mr. Harford to do?" asked Hilary, trying to disguise her eagerness to learn more about Gabriel.

"He said that no man could judge for another, but it seemed to him that, for the time being, the country was in no condition to spare a man of his calibre, for the training which would be needful ere he could practise the healing art. Harford told me that he could never forget the words he spoke to him, as to avoiding all self-formed plans in life, and seeking at each step the direct guidance of God Himself. All the counsel he would give Captain Harford was to wait until light should come to guide him to a decision as to his next step."

At that moment they were interrupted by the arrival of Frances Hopton's brother, and during supper the talk naturally turned to matters connected with Sir Richard's imprisonment, and Canon Frome Manor. Hilary resigned herself to the inevitable, and felt something of the satisfaction of a hostess mingling with the rueful, yet half humorous reflection that the two young officers evidently appreciated the "Welsh rarebit" as much as Gabriel would have done, and had made a most ravenous assault on the eggs and bacon.

They were thankful after supper to snatch a few hours' sleep, but about midnight Hilary heard the steady tramp of soldiers without, and knew that the Parliamentarians were marching to Canon Frome. The next morning Zachary brought word that an attack had been made on one of the Royalist quarters in that neighbourhood. But Bosbury saw Massey's men no more, and for the present Waghorn had to bide his time.

All went on quietly enough for some days, and Hilary had only too much leisure to feel the loss of Frances Hopton's companionship. One morning Mrs. Durdle, seeing that she looked pale and dispirited, contrived an excuse to make a little variety for her.

"My dear," said the old housekeeper, "I wish you'd be so kind as to save my old bones, and just step over to the Hill Farm to bespeak the Christmas turkey. Zachary, he tells me Mrs. Kendrick has some first-rate birds. But I'll not be trusting to a man's judgment in a matter o' that sort. Men be first-rate judges o' cooking, but for judging a bird uncooked give me a woman."

Hilary laughed.

"I quite allow the superiority of the male palate," she said, "and will do my best to choose a good Christmas dinner. Moreover, to please you, I will take Don with me for protection, for I believe you will never learn to think these quiet country lanes as safe as Hereford streets."

She had not left the village far behind her, when she found that she had been well-advised in taking the dog, for a small party of horsemen, gay with ribbons, encountered her on the Worcester road, and the words of two of them made her face flame; nor did the stern reprimand of one of the officers greatly mend matters, as she passed swiftly on, trying to seem quite unconscious of the insult.

Meanwhile the officer in command, having reproved his soldiers, looked back thoughtfully once or twice, and noticed that the girl turned to the left through a field gate. It was clear that she was on her way to the picturesque gabled house plainly visible through the leafless trees.

On reaching Bosbury, he bade his lieutenant ride on with the men to Canon Frome, saying that he had business in the village; and, having left his horse at the "Bell Inn," he returned leisurely on foot along the Worcester road, and sat down to wait on a sunny bank beside the gate through which Hilary had passed.

"It is the face that has haunted me for more than a year," he reflected. "That exquisite face I saw in the miniature at Marlborough hanging from that rogue's stubborn neck. Would that I had a halter round the throat of him now! What on earth was the name on his precious love-letter? I was a fool to tear it at Marshfield, for 'twas fully directed. Hang it, though, if I can remember a single word save that the lady lived at the Palace, Hereford. Well, I can soon find out all now, for, in spite of her dignity, she is as simple and inexperienced a country maid as little Nell herself. Nell, I understand, hath wedded one Mr. Neal. Never mind! News of the event is not likely to have reached Herefordshire, and she will serve me excellently well in the game I mean to play with Mr. Harford's high-spirited lady-love. There is deadly need of some diversion in this country hole."

Meanwhile Hilary had gone on her way not a little troubled and disconcerted by what had passed. It was not so much that the rude admiration of these soldiers was of any real consequence, as that she knew it would annoy her uncle, and perhaps lead to her walks being restricted entirely to the garden, a prospect that tried her not a little.

She was thankful when she reached the field gate leading to the farm, but in the anxious selection of the Christmas turkey, on which she felt that her reputation for womanly wisdom rested, she speedily forgot the passing annoyance.

Then, after the turkey review was ended and the fateful choice made, she gave the farmer's wife a red ribbon to tie about the leg of the loyal bird, and having had a friendly gossip over Mrs. Kendrick's rheumatism, called Don and ran gaily down the sloping field, racing the dog, and arriving at the gate almost breathless.

She gave a start of dismay when she suddenly discovered at the other side of the hedge a gentleman in a red doublet with a short fawn-coloured cloak thrown back over one shoulder, and an officer's red feather in his fawn-coloured hat.

At sight of her he sprang up from the bank on which he had been resting, and Don growled so savagely at him that she was obliged to call the dog to heel.

"Pardon me, madam," said the stranger in the most musical voice she had ever heard, "I only wish to apologise for the impertinence of my men, who deserve to be thrashed for so rudely troubling you with their ill-bred staring and admiration."

She glanced up at him quickly, and was relieved to find that he was unmistakably the Governor of the new garrison at Canon Frome so graphically described in Frances Hopton's farewell letter.

"It was of no consequence, sir," she said with a stately little bow, which delighted him. "I was chiefly annoyed because it will vex my uncle, and he may forbid me to visit the farm again."

"Let me see him," pleaded Norton, boldly, "and express my regrets at what passed. Doth he live far from here?"

"No, at Bosbury Vicarage," said Hilary. "'Tis not far." Without directly asking to accompany her, Norton moved quietly on, talking as he went, so that it seemed perfectly natural, and, indeed, inevitable that they should walk together. Even Don, after a subdued growl and a disdainful sniff at the officer's riding boots, accepted the situation with philosophical calm.

"I fear you, like most people, have suffered great inconvenience from the war?" said Norton, "but ere long we shall have crushed the rogues and all will be well. Have you many friends and kinsfolk in arms?"

"No kinsfolk," replied Hilary. "We know several gentlemen serving under my Lord Hopton, and in truth almost all our Herefordshire friends are for the King, save two of Sir Richard Hopton's sons and Mr. Hall and Mr. Freeman, near Ledbury, and two or three gentlemen in Hereford who sided with the Parliament."

"One of the most staunch Parliamentarians I ever met hailed from Hereford," said Norton. "I came across him when Waller's army was in Gloucestershire—my own county. However, this young Lieutenant Harford, though as keen on sermons as the rest of his comrades, had, nevertheless, time to carry on a most promising love affair with the pretty daughter of a Puritan squire whose estate adjoins mine."

He avoided looking at his companion, but from the tone of her voice he knew that his arrow had gone home.

"Mr. Harford's sympathies have ever been with the Puritans," she said, haughtily. "'Tis long since he was in Herefordshire, but I learn that he is now a prime favourite with Cromwell."

"He would be a man after his own heart," said Norton. "Prince Rupert dubbed Cromwell 'Ironside' at Marston Moor, and from all accounts there never was a more unyielding, stubborn fighter. They say his power over all whom he comes across is amazing—men are like wax in his hands."

Hilary walked on in a dazed, bewildered way, determined only that she would keep outwardly calm, and hearing all that the stranger said, though as if from a great distance. It seemed to her that the world had suddenly collapsed, and for the first time she fully understood what perfect confidence she had hitherto felt in Gabriel's constancy. Only by a great effort could she keep up the absolutely necessary show of interest in her companion's talk. At length she caught sight of the Vicar coming out of a cottage at a little distance, and awoke to the realisation that she had better overtake him before gaining the village street.

"See, Don!" she cried to the dog, "your master!"

Don bounded on and soon attracted the Vicar's notice. He turned at once, and perceiving Hilary and the stranger, walked rapidly towards them.

"I must ask your pardon, sir," said Norton, bowing low. "I waited to apologise to your niece for the discourtesy of my men, and begged her to let me wait upon you at the Vicarage. I am but newly appointed Governor of the Canon Drome garrison—my name is Lionel Norton."

"Why then, sir, I heard of you many years ago, for I think you wedded the Lady Lucy Powell," said the Vicar, genially.

Hilary, who had not even glanced at Norton since their first encounter at the gate, now looked at him searchingly, and instantly noted the lines of pain about his lips. The pain was genuine—it at once drew her to him.

"My wife died when we had but been wedded a year," he replied, and his musical voice faltered a little.

The Vicar had not heard of this, but his sympathy and his warm praise of Lady Lucy's gentle sweetness of character seemed to touch Norton.

"Will you not come in and dine with us?" he said, in his hospitable way.

For a moment the Colonel hesitated. "I fear I cannot accept your kind invitation," he said at length, with a swift glance at Hilary. "But if you will permit me I will call on you another day."

And at the eastern gate of the churchyard they parted, Norton to call for his horse at the "Bell," the Vicar to see a parishioner who had come home crippled from the war, and Hilary to hasten to her room at the Vicarage, where at last she could permit the tears which had half choked her to over-flow.

All was indeed over—Gabriel's love was a thing of the past!

CHAPTER XXXII.

"Strafford had offered his brain and arm to establish a system which would have been the negation of political liberty. Laud had sought to train up a generation in habits of thought which would have extinguished all desire for political liberty."

S. R. Gardiner.

History of the Great Civil War, Vol. II.

Norton found only one occupant of the snug tap-room of the inn, and this was a severe-looking man, who seemed absorbed in a news journal. His prominent ears, the closely-cropped dark hair, and the austerity of his whole manner tickled the Royalist's sense of humour, and though certain that to draw information from those thin compressed lips would be like drawing water from a dry well, he greeted him pleasantly.

"Good day, Sexton," he said.

Waghorn lifted his piercing eyes and regarded him with grave disapproval.

"I am no sexton, sir, you mistake my calling," he said.

"Your pardon! but, in truth, you look like a sexton, there is an air of graves and mould about you, of skulls and crossbones," replied Norton, laughing. "Perhaps, however, sexton or no, you can tell me the name of the Vicar, for I am a stranger here, and have just spoken with him and his daughter."

"The Vicar is the son of that vile prelate, Bishop Coke, who lives in palaces while the poor starve, one of the hirelings that devour the flock, one of those twelve prelates who sought to break the law of the land, and were justly cast into the Tower. Would that they had remained there," said the Puritan, bitterly.

"And this son of his, your Vicar, doth he share the Bishop's views?"

"I know not," said Waghorn, and an expression of genuine perplexity dawned in his eyes. "He did feed Massey's men t'other day when they were cold and hungry."

"The devil he did?" exclaimed Norton. "Doth he then side with the Parliament?"

"In truth, sir, he is one that hates the war, but whether he thinks one side better than the other I know not. As for the lady, she is no daughter of his, but his niece, Mistress Hilary Unett, and she, I understand, hates all godly Puritans, and favours such godless men as Prince Rupert and Prince Maurice. I speak over-freely, however, for I see you are a King's officer."

"Nay, man, I like the freedom of your speech," said Norton, with a laugh. "Judging by your looks I took you for a man of few words, but, beshrew me! you are as good a talker as I have met in these parts."

"Out of the abundance of the heart the mouth speaketh," said Waghorn. "My thoughts are ever of how to thwart those who are half-hearted in the work of the Lord, those who would keep crosses standing because, forsooth, they are old. Many things are old yet have to be utterly destroyed. The brazen serpent was old, yet, when the people bowed down to it, then it had to be ground to powder. And so shall it be now, in spite of the Vicar. All he cares for is its great antiquity—if a heathen idol were brought across the seas, and if it were curiously wrought, I trow the Vicar would be right proud to place it among his hoards, and he and Mr. Silas Taylor would try to make out its age and its history, as they do with their vain stones, and their bones of those that be dead and gone."

Norton's eyes twinkled, with amusement.

"So the Vicar is an antiquary," he said. "Well, I care not a doit for the churchyard cross, or the church itself for that matter." And with a careless "good-day" he strolled out to the door, where his horse awaited him.

"He cares for little but success," reflected Waghorn, shrewdly. "An ambitious pagan, a carnal man who would ride to his own evil desires through thick and thin. Yet methinks he might serve as a tool in the good cause. I will mark his movements closely, and use him when the time serves."

With a deep sigh he returned to the perusal of the paper. It was an old number of the "Mercurius Aulicus," a most bitter Royalist sheet published at Oxford, and notorious for the lies and the opprobrious language it employed. To read it always stirred the Puritan into a fiery indignation, which would have been excusable had he not afterwards found a secret pleasure in the excitement. He then sought refuge in the denunciatory psalms, and went back to his work breathing threatenings and slaughter against the opponents of all that he deemed right. Waghorn was one of the vast number of well-meaning people who call themselves followers of Christ, but jealously demand an eye for an eye and a tooth for a tooth, and conveniently skip the commandment, "Love your enemies."

Meanwhile a momentary gleam of hope had come to Hilary. She had at first leapt to the conclusion that Norton had seen Gabriel during the campaign of the present year, but now she suddenly remembered that after the siege of Hereford Waller's forces had retired to Gloucester. Was it not possible that he had met him there? If so, it was almost immediately after the cruel rebuff she had given him in the cathedral porch. Could she honestly blame him if after that he had taken her at her word? Was he not perfectly free to fall in love with this Gloucestershire lady?

Then with a sense of relief she recalled Dr. Harford's talk when he had visited them on his return from London. Had he not quoted to her Gabriel's own words—his conviction that her message had brought him back to life? He might perhaps have had a passing admiration for the Puritan maid, but had it amounted to anything more she was certain that he would never have sent her such a message.

With that, however, the cold wave of doubt returned. What if Waller had been this year in Gloucestershire? He was frequently in the West, and what more likely than that long absence, the tedium of the campaign, and possibly the malign influence of the arch-rebel, Cromwell, had gradually wrought a change in Gabriel's character? She remembered how greatly the two years' absence in London had altered him. Was it not only too probable that this apparently endless war had changed him yet more?

"If only I had asked Colonel Norton when he had encountered him," she reflected, miserably, "but in the agony of the moment all I thought of was how to hide everything. He can never have guessed, that is one comfort; and I'll never, never speak of the matter again should he come here. Yet if only I could know for certain when it was! I will, at any rate, see if Uncle Coke knows."

So, after dinner, when the Vicar was filling his pipe, she asked, with well-assumed indifference, "did Captain Bayly give you much news of Gloucester, sir, the other night? Had he been there in the siege?"

"Nay; I gathered that he had only quitted his home at Poole, in Dorsetshire, a short time ago. Governor Massey had persuaded him to come into Herefordshire because he had seen something in Dorset of the movement of the Clubmen, which they say is now spreading to our county."

"What are the Clubmen?" asked Hilary.

"They are those country-folk who are determined to have nothing to do either with Royalists or Parliamentarians, but league themselves together to defend their homes and families."

"In truth, then, sir, I think you yourself are one," said Hilary, smiling. "For you certainly hold aloof from both parties in one sense, and feed the hungry without respect of persons or opinions."

"Child, my first duty is to obey the Prince of Peace," said the Vicar. "I do not understand the violent warlike spirit of most of our clergy, or the bitter words of the Puritan preachers. But it hath never been my fortune to agree well with parsons; the bulk of them seem to me absorbed in the little interests of their parishes, wrapped up in their own narrow opinions and unmindful of greater things."

Hilary was silent; she wondered what it was that made her uncle so unlike such a parson as Prebendary Rogers, of Stoke Edith, and she tried to understand why he was always at his best when with men of other callings. Much as she loved him, and greatly as she had been influenced by his gentle, kindly spirit, and by the quiet humour which had done so much to cheer her sadness, he was still something of an enigma to her. But she had a suspicion that the true key to his life lay in the old saying, "The liberal deviseth liberal things, and by liberal things shall he stand."

But a long digression had been made, and she was determined to bring back the conversation to the question she had at heart before the Vicar lighted his pipe.

"When was Sir William Waller's army last in Gloucestershire?" she asked.

"Well, it must have been just six months ago, I should say," said the Vicar. "Yes, for I remember we were haymaking in the glebe when Mr. Taylor told me how Waller's army had twice well-nigh succeeded in capturing His Majesty, who was chased from one county to another. You must remember hearing of Sudeley Castle being taken, and of how scores of bridges in Worcestershire and Gloucestershire were broken down by the two armies, so that they said it would cost £10,000 to make them good again. That was last June, my dear."

"Colonel Norton said something about it," said Hilary, steadily, and the Vicar was too much engrossed in the difficult operation of lighting his pipe to notice that she had grown white to the lips.

"Ah, a pleasant-spoken man," he remarked, "but I don't like what I hear about the doings of his garrison. Maybe he only carries out his orders, but it is a grievous strain on the people."

Hilary stole quietly away and would gladly have been alone, but Mrs. Durdle besought her so earnestly to come into the kitchen that she could not refuse.

"Come, dearie, and stir the Christmas pudding," said the housekeeper, "just for old times' sake. I'm sadly behindhand this year, but there was no getting the currants from Ledbury with all them soldiers infesting the place. Stir and wish, my dear, stir and wish."

"There's nothing left to wish for," said Hilary, sadly.

"Oh! my dear, how you do talk, and you so young and fair to see."

"I wish, then, that this hateful war was over," said Hilary, stirring the sticky yellow and black compound, which turned so reluctantly in the great basin.

"How I do remember that time when you and Mr. Gabriel was children at Hereford, and both sat on the table a-stirring the pudding," said Durdle. "'Twas the day Sir Robert Harley's dog bit his arm."

"And I wished for a new doll," said Hilary, smiling a little as she moved towards the door.

"And a very sensible wish, too, dearie, seeing that the dog had chewed and spoilt the old one," said Durdle. "Don't you be above takin' on with new friends when the old friends leave you."

"Which means," reflected Hilary, as she sought her own room, "that Durdle has heard of gallant Colonel Norton's appearance this morning, and is already weaving a romance in her foolish old head. No, no, I have done with all that!"

Through the days that followed, Hilary's heart was very sore, but, to some extent, her pride provided an antidote to the pain. She knew that she herself was chiefly to blame for the change in Gabriel, but, nevertheless, his change angered her and wounded her to the quick. Before long she turned resolutely from all thought of him, and resolved to fill her life to the brim with work which should leave no leisure for vain regrets, and, having much' strength of character, she carried out her intentions with more success than might have been expected.

It spoke something for Colonel Norton, that several days passed before he permitted himself to call at Bosbury. His passion for Hilary was no loftier than the rest of his amours. but something in the Vicar's allusion to Lady Lucy had once more touched into life the better side of his nature, nor had he failed to note the womanly insight and sympathy in Hilary's face when she had first heard of his loss. For very shame he could not just yet begin to weave his evil snaring net about her.

But on Christmas Day, when it would hardly do to permit the soldiers to go out on a foraging expedition, he rode over to Bosbury, greatly exciting the congregation by entering the church in the middle of the Te Deum. Sprigs of holly and box were stuck at the end of every seat, and amid the greenery Norton was not long in discovering the face he sought, though only a profile was visible, framed in a dainty black velvet hood, bordered with white swansdown.

He thought it was the most lovely face it had ever been his good fortune to see, and the pride plainly shown in the arched nostril and the poise of the head entranced him. Little Mistress Nell, with her pink-and-white prettiness and her fair hair, was altogether thrown into the shade by this beautiful Herefordshire maiden.

The Vicar, with a considerate care for the anxious housewives and the family dinners, did not preach a long sermon, but said a few practical words as to the possibility of striving, even now, for peace on earth and goodwill to men. Great boughs of fir and festoons of trailing ivy mitigated the ugliness of Waghorn's "good honest white glass" window, and as the familiar Bosbury carol, which had served Gabriel so well the previous year at Oxford, rang out cheerfully, the very spirit of Christmas seemed to pervade the place.

Norton, who, with all his faults, responded quickly to some of the better influences in life, felt touched and softened. When he lingered in the porch to greet the Vicar and his niece, no one could have been more manly and attractive in tone and bearing, so that it was quite inevitable that the hospitable Vicar should press him to stay and dine at the Vicarage.

And thus it fell about that the fateful turkey which had been the cause of that first encounter with Hilary, again appeared upon the scene, and was pronounced by the Governor of Canon Frome to be the finest bird that had ever provided a good Christmas dinner for hungry mortals. In the afternoon Hilary sang to them, and then it conveniently happened that a parishioner wished to say a few words to the Vicar, and Norton to his great satisfaction found himself tête-à-tête with the singer.

"I wonder whether you can guess what a red-letter day this will always be in my life," he said, drawing a little nearer to her. "'Tis years since I had a quiet home Christmas like this, never once since the first Christmas just after our marriage."

She liked him for speaking of his dead wife—it set her wholly at her ease with him; moreover, his manner had been so careful that she had never felt the need of holding him at a distance, as was the case with several of the men she had come across.

They drifted now into a friendly little talk about his Gloucestershire home, about the Lady Lucy, and about the wretchedness of his life at the time of her death. He told her nothing but the truth, for his misery had been intense, and his love for his wife was genuine. But naturally he never allowed her to guess that his wickedness had broken Lady Lucy's heart, and that her death was as truly his doing as if he had actually murdered her.

This interview was the first of quite a series, for it was wonderful how often it chanced that the Governor of Canon Frome was obliged to ride over to Bosbury, and how admirably he timed his visits in order to snatch a talk with Hilary. Sometimes he brought rare curiosities for the Vicar's collection, and would spend hours patiently listening to his remarks on the probable age and possible history of some bit of old oak; and if there was no better excuse he would ride over with a pamphlet or a news book, and linger to discuss the latest tidings.

The death of Archbishop Laud was a perfect Godsend to him, for on no less than three occasions was he able to bring news-books describing from different points of view the last sad scene on Tower Hill.

Hilary shed tears at the thought of the poor feeble old man brought out to die on that cold January day, and forgetting that Gabriel, though disapproving his system, would probably regret his execution, let her heart grow hot with wrath at the thought that he was allied to the party which had carried out the sentence, and hated him with the sort of hatred which can in some natures follow love. Norton's sympathy and his real distress at the sight of her grief drew her much closer to him; she began to reflect that his companionship was the chief pleasure of her life just at present, and to own to herself that a visit from him was a wonderful relief in the grey monotony of that sad winter.

Norton quickly perceived the hold he was gaining on her, and was about to venture on a little very cautious love-making, when to his annoyance the Vicar, for whose return he was nominally waiting, strode into the room. He greeted him gravely, but from his agitated manner the Colonel at once perceived that something serious had occurred.

"Colonel Norton has brought another account of the Archbishop's execution, sir," said Hilary, rising to give him the news-book.

He took it absently and laid it down on the table among his fossils.

"The most horrible scene has just been enacted," he said, in a voice that was tremulous with indignation; "and your soldiers from Canon Frome, sir, were the perpetrators of the outrage."

Norton looked concerned; he had in truth more than once spared the inhabitants of Bosbury because he wished to keep his footing at the Vicarage.

"What hath chanced, sir?" he inquired.

"I walked to an outlying house in my parish," said the Vicar; "Old Mutlow's farm at Swinmore, Hilary, you know the place. To my horror, when I got there it was in flames, the poor old man half frantic, but far too infirm to attempt to save his goods, and your men, sir, protesting that they had the right to burn his home because he had not paid his contribution."

"Well, sir," said Norton, "I confess your tale relieves me. I feared that in my absence the men might have waxed as cruel as General Gerrard's men t'other day in Montgomeryshire, who not only burnt the farm, but the mother and the children inside it. I am glad this old peasant fared better. As you will understand, we must punish those who refuse their aid, and we are bound to get money somehow."

"And how much will your devilish house-burnings put into the King's coffers? How far will they help him to victory?" said the Vicar, in such wrath as Hilary had not imagined him capable of. "I tell you, sir, this cruel and damnable practice will bring down the curse of the Almighty on His Majesty's cause. Leave us for a moment, my child, I have a word or two to say to Colonel Norton in private."

Hilary, with a smile of farewell to Norton, curtseyed and left the room, and a very grave talk between the two men followed. To judge by the expression of the Colonel's face as he rode back to Canon Frome, he had not found it altogether to his mind.

"That old antiquary is a shrewder man of the world than I took him for," he reflected, as he dug his spurs savagely into his horse and galloped over a stretch of unenclosed ground. "I must devise some means for getting him out of the way, or he will be seeing through my little game and suspecting that I am no better than the men he was abusing. He is too plain-spoken by half—actually protested that I was permitting the garrison to become a nursery of lawless vice! Well, I'll avoid Bosbury for a week or two, and then pacify him with some rare old bone. How could I guess that the farm at Swinmore, miles away, was in his parish? He must be mollified with old remains for the present, and when a fitting opportunity arrives, by hook or by crook, I'll have him snugly tucked up in Hereford Gaol. Prince Maurice is soon to be Major-General of the county, and I can do what I please with him. Then, when once the parson is safely clapped up, pretty Hilary will naturally enough be in my power."

He laughed aloud at the prospect of the Vicar's discomfiture, and by the time he had reached Canon Frome Manor was once more in excellent spirits.

CHAPTER XXXIII.

"He seemed

For dignity composed, and high exploit,

But all was false and hollow; though his tongue

Dropt manna, and could make the worse appear

The better reason, to perplex and dash

Maturest counsels: for his thoughts were low—

To vice industrious;—Yet he pleased the ear."

—Milton.

Throughout the winter and the early spring Herefordshire was in a state of misery and unrest. The people, frantic at the ill-treatment they received from the Royalist garrisons at Hereford, Canon Frome and other places, rose in open insurrection. The sturdy men in the Forest of Dean, seeing their country wasted with fire and sword, their sons impressed to serve in the King's army, and their wives and daughters brutally ill-used by the merciless troops of Rupert, and by such well-known tyrants as Lunsford and Langdale, would endure such doings no longer, and the rising of the Clubmen became a new and serious element in the strife.

Massey, the Governor of Gloucester, sought to win them over definitely to the Parliament, and entered into negotiations with the leaders at Ledbury, where some 2,000 of them had gathered; but they would bind themselves to neither party, and in the end were dispersed by Prince Rupert, who, having hanged three of the leading men, withdrew to Hereford.

Hilary's heart had been also in the strangest state of unrest; it was impossible to be in the immediate neighbourhood of all these cruelties and confusions and to remain unmoved. She grieved over the horrible sufferings of the people, and yet now and then the false glamour of war and the halo of romance which invested Norton and the brave and fiery Rupert, resumed its sway over her. Moreover, though no thought of love had entered into her mind, her pride was subtly gratified by the attentions Norton paid her. That a man of his age and standing should hang upon her words, should show her every mark of respect, and even consult her on occasion, was pleasant enough. From open compliments, from praise of her beauty, she would at once have shrunk, but this more delicate flattery ministered to the weakest point in her character—her unconquerable pride.

It was on the morning of the 20th April, nearly two years after her mother's death, that she laid aside her black garments and took from the big oak chest, where it had been all this time laid up in lavender, the grey gown, with its grey and pink hood and cape, which had for her so many memories of the past. She sighed a little as she donned them, but Durdle looked well pleased when she appeared in the kitchen in her spring attire.

"How many eggs do you want this morning?" asked the girl, lightly. "I shall start early and gather primroses on the way."

"Bring me two dozen, dearie, an' Mrs. Kendrick can spare as many," said Durdle. "Ay, but you look as fresh as a daisy—it does my heart good to see you. But to think that here you be unwed at two-and-twenty all through this weary war—it fair breaks my heart."

"It doesn't break mine," said Hilary, laughing and tossing her head as she quitted the Vicarage.

She had passed the last house in the village when, catching sight of a bank by the roadside starred over with primroses, she lingered to gather them. The day was fresh and sunny, the sky intensely blue, the early apple blossom in the orchards exquisite in its colouring; for the sheer joy of being alive in such a lovely world she could not help singing softly to herself. The words of Autolycus' song rose to her lips, while a worse deceiver than that mendacious thief and pedlar quietly pursued her.

"When daffodils begin to peer,

With heigh! the doxy over the dale,

Why, then comes in the sweet o' the year,

For the red blood reigns in the winter's pale."

She started a little when Norton's mellow tones fell on her ear.

"A beautiful song for a beautiful spring day, and chanted by a radiant vision of spring!" he exclaimed, feasting his eyes on her loveliness.

She laughed as she curtseyed in response to his profound bow.

"Sir, you are of a very different opinion to Peter Waghorn, the wood-carver in the tiled house yonder. He frowned on me and my gown, and thought doubtless that grey and pink should be left for the skies at dawn, not worn by a worm of earth, as he deems me. I do detest that talk of earthworms."

"You should never wear any colours save those of the sky," said Norton, gazing into the comely face and dark grey eyes. "May you never again need to wear mourning robes!"

"In truth, when I last donned them," she said, strolling on towards the farm, "I thought I should never be happy again. Yet to-day I am happy once more—I can't help it—the world is so beautiful."

"You who make others happy should be always happy yourself," he said.

"I don't make others happy," she said, drooping her head a little as a memory of her treatment of Gabriel returned unbidden. "I make the people who care for me unhappy."

"Let me be the exception, then," he said, boldly. "I have had sorrow enough in my life; don't give me more."

She glanced at him doubtfully, then turned aside to gather some more primroses.

"Have you seen the Vicar?" she inquired.

"No, but I have a matter to talk over with him," said Norton, "and, with your permission, will return to the Vicarage with you and carry your egg-basket."

"Eggs are fragile things," she said, laughingly. "I am not sure that I can trust you."

"I assure you my hand is as steady a one as you will find, and well practised at tilting at the bucket."

"But mine is more practised at carrying eggs," she said, gaily.

"Ah, but my greatest pleasure is to serve you," said Norton, persuasively, "and you promised never to add to my sorrow."

"Indeed, I never made so rash a promise," she protested. "Still, if carrying the egg basket will satisfy you, I will yield. Have you brought us a newsbook this morning?"

"No, only a legal document just issued by Prince Rupert. I saw him not long since at Hereford."

"How I envy you!" she cried. "I would give the world to see one so brave."

"The Prince hath not a monopoly of courage."

"No, no; all the King's soldiers are brave, of course."

"Yet you will hardly trust this soldier with aught. You hold him eternally at an icy distance."

His tone was that of a dejected lover. Yet even now she was unsuspicious. Her thoughts were of the war, and not in the least of love.

"I think you are very much to be envied," she cried. "Oh! it must be a grand thing to fight for the King, to defend the weak, to make the rebels fly before you."

"Shall I tell you the truth?" said Norton, with a sudden modulation in his musical voice which made her heart stir strangely. "'Tis only when I am in your presence that I know what enjoyment means."

They had passed through the gate and were walking up the grassy slope to the gabled house. At last Hilary could not help understanding in part what he meant. She blushed crimson, and was silent.

"Don't you see that this long campaign means for me privation, tedium, loneliness?" said Norton, with meaning emphasis on the last word. "I can never know happiness without you."

He watched her furtively, but very keenly. Surely she would help him out with some word, some gesture, some glance! He was a well-practised wooer, but never had his advances been met with such baffling silence. It seemed to him that all at once she was far, far away from him, and, in truth, her spirit had flown to the little wood where, nearly five years before, Gabriel had told her of his love. The eager, boyish face, the clear, honest eyes, like wells of light, drew her irresistibly away from the man who walked now beside her. And yet all the time she was aware that over her lower nature Norton's influence was great. His handsome face, his soldierly bearing, his alternations of high spirits and of deep sadness fascinated her; there was something, too, in his audacity and force of character which filled her with admiration.

"If only this thrice-accursed field were a grove I could prevail with her," reflected Norton. "But here!"

And at that moment Don came to the rescue of his mistress by racing with all the ardour of youth among a stately flock of geese, which fled helter-skelter, with much hissing and indignant cackling.

Hilary broke out into a peal of laughter, and, thankful for the interruption, ran after the terrier.

"Don! Don!" she cried. "You wicked dog! Come to heel this moment."

And with a merry glance at the discomfited Norton, she hastened into the garden of the Hill Farm, leaving him to pace up and down savagely among the agitated geese.

Mrs. Kendrick came to the door with a troubled face.

"Good morning, mistress," she said, curtseying. "You find a sad house here. I have two of my poor lads sorely wounded upstairs, and the master be only now getting back his wits. He was that cruelly beaten about the head!"

"Why, when was that?" said Hilary. "Had they joined the Clubmen?"

"Ay, to be sure. They went to Ledbury, and near by Prince Rupert, as you know, made short work of them."

This was the sorry side of war, and Hilary, as she entered the great kitchen and saw the white face and bandaged head of Farmer Kendrick, and the dazed look of suffering in his eyes, felt sad at heart. She crossed the room to the chimney-corner and spoke to him, but he took no heed.

"'Tis no use," said the poor wife. "He's been deaf as a post ever since, and dithered besides. He'll never be fit for work any more, and what's to become of us, God only knows, for the soldiers from Canon Frome have taken all our hay and corn, and every beast on the farm save the old lame horse. We've naught left but the geese and fowls."

"I will tell the Vicar of your trouble," said Hilary. "Why did you not send to him?"

"Well," said Mrs. Kendrick, "we thought it best to hide the men-folk till the country is quieter. And they told me the Governor of Canon Frome was much at the Vicarage. It seems hard when the place has been ours for generations to have strangers making free with all our goods. I do hear folk say that ere long there'll be a battle in these parts, and that Governor Massey be coming from Gloucester again." Hilary went away with a grave face, not thinking so much of the future battle as of the unpleasant fact that Norton's visits to the Vicarage were beginning to be commented on. She was grieved, too, that the poor wounded men had not had the comfort of a visit from her uncle.

Norton at once noticed the change in her expression when she rejoined him.

"You are troubled," he said, gently, taking the basket from her.

"The times are sad," said she, evasively. "I wish this war were ended. I wish we were quite away from ever hearing of it any more."

"I wish," he said, drawing nearer to her, "that I could spirit you right away to a country where all would be peace and sunshine. If I had the right to protect you, all should be as you would have it. Let us build castles in the air of a happy life in sunny France away from all these troubles."

She laughed at such a notion. "Why, I have never been farther than Bristol in all my life," she said, lightly. "And the mere sight of the ships sailing away to foreign parts made me feel a craving to be at home again in Herefordshire."

"But Gloucestershire is a right homelike county," said Norton, "and not far off. Do you understand how I love you, how I long to have you in my home there?"

She shook her head. "I do not want to leave my uncle," she said, feeling round for some excuse.

"Well, well, but he cannot live for ever," said Norton, impatiently. "It is in the natural order of things that you should leave him; and, spite of his white hair, he is but in middle life, and may yet himself marry."

"Then I should go back to Hereford, and try to grow like dear Mrs. Joyce Jefferies, who lives to make others happy."

"You can make others happy now," said Norton, and she was forced to listen to his impassioned appeal the whole way home. Half-frightened and wholly perplexed as to her own mind; she was thankful to gain the village, and avoiding the street, opened the south-east gate of the churchyard that they might cross to the Vicarage garden unobserved. But to her discomfort she found on approaching the old stone cross that Peter Waghorn was standing in the path apparently wrapt in contemplation of the symbol to which he so much objected.

As they passed he turned his gleaming eyes full upon them, and though she gave him a cheerful "Good morning," he made no reply, only touching his hat in a grudging and reluctant fashion.

"A plague on that fellow," said Norton; "he is enough to give any one a fit of the ague only to look on. But, for heaven's sake, take pity on me and give me what I have pleaded for so humbly."

"Indeed, sir," said Hilary, "I do not know what to say, but I think you ask what I cannot give."

They had entered the Vicarage, and she led the way to the sitting-room, hoping to find her uncle there. The room, however, was empty.

"Give me my answer a few days hence," said Norton, setting down the basket, "and to-day I will only ask a few of these flowers as a pledge. Will you fasten them in my doublet?"

She could not well refuse this, and as she slipped the slender pink stalks through the button-hole, Norton suddenly threw his arms around her and kissed her passionately on the lips.

"Let me go!" she cried, indignantly. "How dare you?" And with a half incoherent sentence as to his wishing to see the Vicar, she hurried from the room.

"Now I have frightened her!" reflected Norton. "The one pretty maid in all this dull countryside. Dear innocent little soul! The pursuit grows interesting. I dare swear no man save St. Gabriel ever touched her lips before! Dame Elizabeth Hopton is a she-dragon, but thank the Lord there's no mother here, and that fat housekeeper is a noodle, who will soon be at my beck and call."

As if summoned by his thought of her, Durdle at that moment entered with a tray of cakes and some excellent cider.

"You will take something, sir, after your walk," she said, looking with approval at his long, glossy auburn curls and gay attire.

"Thank you, Mrs. Durdle, there's no better cider in all Herefordshire than yours," he said, with his genial smile. "Everything from this house is good, and 'tis due to your careful management."

Durdle beamed with pleasure at this praise.

"Oh, sir, you flatter me," she protested.

"Not at all, 'tis naught but truth. What are these heartshaped cakes? They should be prophetic."

"They be queen cakes, sir," said Durdle. "Do please to try one, for they be Mistress Hilary's making."

"Ha! then certainly I must have one, for, as no doubt you perceive, Mrs. Durdle, I am playing a well-known game—'I love my love with an H.' Will you keep my secret and lend me your aid, for in these matters a man sadly needs an ally?"

"Why to be sure, sir; to be sure I will!" cried Durdle, with delight. "'Twas but this very morning I was grieving at the thought that so sweet a lady should be unwed. Oh, she'll not be saying no to a King's officer, sir, and I know the very best recipe for bride cakes."

She bustled off to look for the Vicar, leaving Norton with a mocking smile playing al>out his lips.

"Bride cakes, indeed," he muttered. "But she will doubtless prove useful." And with that he tasted the dainty morsel which the housekeeper had handed to him. "Pah! 'tis sweet and insipid. Here, Don!" he said, whistling to the dog, "this heart may be to your liking."

The terrier swallowed it at one gulp, and was still licking his lips when Hilary returned. There was a certain coldness in her manner.

"My uncle is out, sir," she said, "and Zachary tells me he hath gone to visit a dying man at some distance; perhaps you will leave the papers for his signature."

"No, I will come again; let me see, to-morrow will be Tuesday, I will come before noon," said Norton. "Tell Mrs. Durdle the queen cakes are irresistible."

She laughed, but was relieved that he did not attempt to linger, and that he made no further allusion to what had passed on their walk from the farm.

CHAPTER XXXIV.

"Just in so far as we have love which shall survive, though that to which it clings be taken away from us,... in so far as our sorrow has brought us into the wide fellowship of human suffering and anguish, and given us a tenderness that shall endure though years of placid comfort should flow over us—in so far as we have reached a life not subject to change or the workings of Time—so far we have some sense of the eternal realities, so far we may feel that we see God, and may, though with awe-struck humility, ask whether, haply, in some measure, we are seeing as God sees. Infinitesimal as our attainment may be, we shall, nevertheless, know what it is to enjoy, and shall not only strive after, but shall, in some measure, have the life eternal."

—P. H. WICKSTEED.

It was on the Saturday preceding Norton's walk with Hilary that Gabriel Harford rode once more from Gloucester to the scene of his rescue of Major Locke's daughter. His recovery from his severe illness had long ago been complete, and the open-air life had fortunately proved the best cure for the mischief done to his constitution by the long months in Oxford Castle. Though thin and a trifle gaunt-looking after the severe campaign and the insufficient food, the indomitable pluck and manliness which had carried him through so much had stood him in good stead through all the quarrels and discussions and difficulties which had prevailed of late among the Parliamentary generals, to the great discomfort of the whole party.

Sir William Waller had, some time before, perceived, with the sagacity which made him the greatest tactician possessed by either Royalists or Parliamentarians, that an entire reorganisation of the army was needed and that, with the Earl of Essex at the head, nothing but disaster lay before them. The new model army was at length being formed, and, by the self-denying ordinance, Waller retired to his work in the House of Commons and his soldiers were dispersed, some being sent to serve in the new army, others despatched to various garrisons in the South of England.

It was with no little amusement that Gabriel recognised again the scenes of his moonlight adventure two years before, and old Amos, the gatekeeper, gave him a warm greeting.

"Eh, sir!" he exclaimed. "These be better times for the Manor, and 'tis you we have to thank for it all."

"Why, man! you did quite as much to save your mistress," said Gabriel, heartily. "We could never have found our way to her without you for guide. Well! All's well that ends well! Are Mr. and Mrs. Neal within?"

"Yes, sir, and main glad they'll be to see you."

The trim bowling-green, over which Joscelyn Heyworth had helped him to escort Helena in such unceremonious haste, was now in a blaze of sunshine, and on the steps where they had nearly betrayed themselves by laughing, as they drew off their riding-boots, a large tortoiseshell cat lay basking. From within the house came a cheerful sound of voices, and when the servant ushered him into the hall, he found Humphrey Neal and his pretty little wife so absorbed in playing with their baby son and heir on the hearthrug, that they had not noticed the rare arrival of a visitor.

"Captain Harford!" announced the servant, and both host and hostess came eagerly to meet the newcomer with a warmth of welcome which was unmistakable.

"I thought Sir William Waller was in the New Forest!" exclaimed Humphrey. "What good fortune brings you here?"

"We were at Ringwood about Easter, pretty well worn out with long marches and the worst weather of the whole winter, in our journey for the relief of Taunton," said Gabriel. "But now Sir William Waller's army is disbanded, and I was sent for a time to Gloucester with a contingent of the men to serve under Massey in Herefordshire."

"They certainly work you hard and don't overfeed you. Why, you are well-nigh as lean and hollow-cheeked as when I first saw you in that pestilent gaol at Oxford."

"We have in truth been half-starved these many months," said Gabriel. "What else can one expect when the country has been laid waste and plundered for nigh upon three years? And even if provisions were to be had for money, we had naught to pay with, thanks to the mismanagement of the authorities."

Helena, determined that he should at least have all that the Manor would provide in the way of a banquet, hastened off to interview her housekeeper, while Gabriel, with a secret pang, watched the fatherly pride with which Humphrey showed off the perfections of the blue-eyed, curly-locked son and heir, who rolled and kicked in perfect bliss on the hearthrug, quite indifferent to the fact that he was in a most distracted country.

"He is the image of Helena," said Humphrey. "All save his hands; did you ever see such a fist in a brat of his age? You should feel how hard he can grip. Soon we shall have him at work with the dumb bells!"

"You have been reading Mr. John Milton's letter on Education," said Gabriel, with a laugh, "and mean to have him as well skilled in athletics as an ancient Greek. I found my friend, Captain Heyworth, deep in the treatise the other day."

"Oh! you mean the gentleman that married my pretty cousin Clemency. I have heard naught of them since old Sir Robert Neal's death. How do they fare?"

"Sadly enough; you probably didn't hear that he lost his arm at the second battle of Newbury. It came about through sheer lack of surgeons, and through the scandalously inadequate aid for the wounded. Each regiment was supposed to have its surgeon and two mates, but at Newbury the supply had fallen into arrears, and Heyworth's wound gangrened, and many other men lost their lives just from neglect and from the severe privations we had to put up with."

"And you have seen the Heyworths in their home since then?"

"Yes, I was at Katterham about two months ago. It is piteous to see that poor fellow suffering, and like to suffer all his life long, Sir Theodore Mayerne says. We are speaking of my friend, Captain Heyworth," he explained as Helena rejoined them.

She listened to his account with eager sympathy in her gentle eyes.

"I remember him well," she said, "both here and at Gloucester; he was ever cheerful and light-hearted. Doth he keep up his spirits even now?"

"He makes a gallant effort to do so," said Gabriel, "but you can guess what it would be for a man of his active habits to be a helpless invalid at three-and-twenty."

"The crippled soldiers need to be the bravest of all, for the dead have at least due honour accorded to them, and rest in peace, and the victors have praise and glory and success to crown them, but most people forget those who have to drag on a maimed life year after year," said Helena. "How doth his wife fare? She was very good to me when I was in trouble."

"She hath a son of her own, but not such a healthy and fine child as yours, and the anxiety of her husband hath told upon her. Still, brighter times may dawn for them. When I saw him, poor fellow, he was clearly longing to be back again with Sir William Waller. Indeed, he hath been sorely missed, for in February, when the men broke into mutiny, he would have been better able to cope with them than any other officer."

"What made them mutiny?"

"Partly the endlessness of the campaign and the privations, partly that Sir William Waller, though much liked by his officers, fails to tackle his men just in the right way. Then the pay was terribly in arrears, though that was no fault of his."

"Sir Thomas Fairfax is to be Commander-in-Chief of the New Model Army, I hear," said Humphrey Neal.

"Yes, and Skippon Major-General. There is a strong desire that, spite of his remaining in Parliament, Cromwell should be appointed to the vacant post of Lieutenant-General, but I know not how that will be."

There was so much to hear and to tell that the time sped quickly, and when Gabriel was obliged to return to Gloucester he carried with him a very happy picture of his friend and pretty Helena in their home, and felt that Major Locke would have been content to see the daughter whose future had filled his dying moments with anxiety, in the old Manor with husband and child to cheer her.

Partly in the hope of winning over those recently engaged in the affair of the Clubmen, but mainly with the intention of diverting Prince Rupert from his journey northward, Massey set out from Gloucester at dawn on the 20th April, having been reinforced by the contingent from Waller's army, which brought up his strength to about five thousand foot and three hundred and fifty horse.

It was with no little delight that Gabriel found himself marching back once more to his own well-loved county, and his spirits rose when, during the halt at Newent, he heard that his regiment was to remain there for the night, marching early the next day to Bromyard, where Massey had expectation of winning recruits from the dispersed Clubmen.

Bromyard was, he believed, the benefice held by Dr. William Coke, and unless Hilary should happen to be at Whitbourne he might be able to see her. It chanced that, owing to his long and frequent absences from Hereford, he had never heard of the death of old Mr. Wall, at Bosbury, and had no notion that Dr. Coke had been promoted to the vacant living during his two years' probation in London.

His annoyance was therefore unspeakable when, at the last moment, Massey changed his plans, ordering his guards to undertake the expedition to Bromyard, and the rest of the troops to press on to Ledbury. With bitter regret Gabriel had to endure the sight of the blue regiment left behind for the work he so ardently longed to set about, and with the obedience of a soldier to tramp on precisely where he did not wish to go.

The picturesque town of Ledbury was bathed in the glow of the spring sunset as the Parliamentary troops emerged from the narrow cross street into the spacious main thoroughfare with its beautiful black and white timbered houses and, at the further end, the quaint town hall raised on massive black posts, between which on market days the countrywomen set their stalls. Massey and his officers dismounted at the door of the chief inn, a well-managed hostelry known as "The Feathers," and, hungry with their long march, they were chiefly intent on ordering supper when they were checked by a curious-looking man, who, in spite of his short stature, forced his way through them, elbowing a passage without so much as a "by your leave," until he reached Colonel Massey.

Gabriel looked at him intently. Where had he before seen that strong square face with its air of gloomy austerity, its smouldering, resentful eyes?

"Sir," said the man, plucking at Massey's sleeve, "by the mercy of a good Providence I chanced to be in Ledbury this evening; I am sent to remind you of your promised aid."

"Eh!" exclaimed Massey; "who are you, and what aid did I promise?"

"I am one Peter Waghorn, of Bosbury, and last autumn you bade me wait till you came hither again. You broke your word, sir, and never aided us when you were here in March, but this time I beg you to fulfil your promise and cast down the Popish cross which stands in our churchyard."

"To be sure! I remember you now," said Massey, and Gabriel with a sudden flash of recollection instantly recalled both the man and his story. He had last seen him at

Hereford, vehemently addressing the people outside the cathedral. He listened with some interest to Waghorn's words.

"Do not neglect this second call, sir," he said, solemnly; "for as I prayed at noonday, I heard a voice bidding me to rise and haste to Ledbury. Like Abraham, I set forth in faith, and now I well understand why I was sent. Come back with me, sir, I implore you, and cast down the cross."

There was no insincerity about this man, he evidently spoke from his heart and with intense anxiety awaited the officer's answer. Massey, a good-natured soldier of fortune, caring more for the fighting than the cause, regarded him with no little amusement.

"The people desire its destruction?" he said, carelessly.

"It would be for their souls' good," said Waghorn. "Some do idolatrously bow to it."

"Well, well, that's a foolish practice. Moreover, Parliament hath ordered the crosses to be broken down," said Massey. "I will send over some of the soldiers to-morrow morning."

The gloomy face of the fanatic brightened, and without actual thanks, but with the air of one who has gained his heart's desire, he touched his hat and withdrew.

Massey turned to Gabriel Harford.

"I want a word with you in private," he said. "Come to my room while supper is making ready."

Gabriel, wondering what was to happen, followed the Colonel to a room overlooking the High Street, and, at Massey's invitation, took a place in the deep window-seat.

"I think you know Cromwell, do you not?" said the Governor of Gloucester.

"Yes, sir, I was serving under Waller when he acted with him last autumn in the Newbury campaign, and again last month in the Western campaign," said Gabriel.

"There is a very important and secret matter that I must make known to him," said Massey. "I can't entrust the despatch to an ordinary man, but if you will undertake to carry it to him you will be doing him a greater service than I can explain to you. Would you be willing to resign your temporary post in my force and undertake this, even though I can give you no explanation of the signal importance of the work?"

"Yes, sir, I will gladly undertake it," said Gabriel. "Am I to ride at once?"

"Nay, not yet," said Massey, smiling at his ardour. "For I will at the same time send a despatch to the Commander-in-Chief, who, I understand, is still at Windsor organising the New Model with Cromwell's aid. I can't complete that till I have learnt what Prince Rupert is about, and if possible turned him back. But I wanted to know if you were willing to turn despatch-bearer for the nonce."

"There is nothing I should like better than to do a service for Cromwell," said Gabriel, his eyes kindling. "For in truth he seems to me the greatest man I ever met."

"Humph!" said Massey. "There's little doubt that he is an able leader, but he's too religious by half. The man's a mystic, a seventeenth-century Enoch, with the soldierly zeal of a David to boot. By the bye, you may as well take over a detachment of the men from Waller's army to Bosbury to-morrow. I'm as likely as not to forget that fellow's request, and I think you have done that sort of business before, eh?"

"Yes, sir, we hewed down Abingdon Cross," said Gabriel. And when the next day he found that the rest of the forces were to witness the hanging of an unhappy scout of Prince Rupert's, who had shot a sentry in the early morning, he was glad to have had the Bosbury work entrusted to him.

"I would rather hew down fifty crosses than stand by and see a poor wretch hanged," he reflected, as they marched along the rough country lanes. "A fair fight is one thing—every man takes his chance, but hanging is a hateful business."

Then he remembered with deep regret that this despatchbearing that Massey meant to entrust to him would probably rob him of the eagerly-desired glimpse of Hilary, and also of the visit to his home at Hereford. He wondered whether it would not be possible to let his father know of his near neighbourhood, longing sorely to see him and to learn from him more than the few and long-delayed letters he had received could tell. Even if he did not see Hilary he might learn through Dr. Harford how she fared. After all if he did see her, she might possibly refuse to speak to him, as she had done in very cruel fashion at Hereford two years ago. His heart ached even now at the memory of the scene in the Cathedral porch. How was it that although the pain of his wound at Edgehill could never be vividly recalled, the anguish of remembering that last interview remained always so keen? Was it because the body was a mere garment presently to be laid aside, while love, which belonged to the soul and spirit, was eternal and changeless?

But to serve Cromwell in some real, though unknown fashion, was worth suffering for; moreover, he should see Sir Thomas Fairfax, the Commander-in-Chief, and he was naturally eager to learn more about this New Model Army, which was the main hope of his party.

He fell to thinking of the three men who had most influenced his life; his father, Falkland and Cromwell. What was it that had specially attracted him to such opposite types? He tried to think what characteristics they shared, and came to the conclusion that it was a certain breadth of mind and a habit of looking at the inner realities, not the externals, of religion.

He was curiously free from the usual habit of judging men by mere outward appearance, and the fact that both Falkland and Cromwell had been handicapped by nature, and were without form or comeliness had from the first been no hindrance to him. Their largeness of soul had irresistibly drawn him to them; for Falkland, with his wide charity, his philosophic Christianity, had been centuries in advance of his contemporaries; while

Cromwell stood now revealed as the foremost of that band of Independents who most nearly reached the level of toleration for those of other religious views. He was ready to tolerate all sorts and conditions of men, save only the Papists and the rigid Episcopalians; the former because they would fain have handed England over once more to the Pope's jurisdiction, the latter because the recent tyranny of Laud and the servile adulation with which the bulk of the clergy justified the King's misrule had made them for the time a danger to the State.

But his musings were cut short by a sudden glimpse of an orchard by the roadside, and the first sight they had yet had of apple-trees in blossom.

"What an early spring!" he thought to himself. "'Tis but the 21 st of April and here's apple blossom! And there are the poplars at Bosbury already green, and the old tower which Hilary asked me about all those years ago. Well! 'tis a mercy we can't see in life what lies before us. And to point the moral of that reflection here comes Peter Waghorn, like a blot on the fair picture."

"Good-day, sir, good-day!" said the wood-carver, his dark face lighted by a gleam of triumph. "I thank the Lord you have come. My prayers have been heard, and we shall accomplish His work!"

CHAPTER XXXV.

"The real test of a man is not what he knows but what he is in himself, and in his relation to others. For instance, can he battle against his own bad inherited instincts, or brave public opinion in the cause of truth?"

—Tennyson.

On this bright, mild Tuesday morning, Mrs. Durdle was bustling about in the sitting-room at the Vicarage, armed with a goose-wing and a duster, weapons wherewith she waged a daily battle with the dust. Spite of her unwieldy proportions, she was a most active person, but even the energetic are not sorry to pause a little in their work on a balmy spring day, and when Zachary crossed the little lawn and approached the open casement, she willingly went to the window, nominally to shake her duster, but in reality to enjoy a gossip.

"Mornin', Mrs. Durdle!" said Zachary. "A fine growin' day this!"

Zachary was somewhat bent and old, yet his face, though wrinkled, had still a youthful ruddiness, and bore that benevolent expression which comes when the grinders cease because they are few, and the lips take an infantine and gentle smile as a recompense.

"Well, for me, I say, 'tis a day when workin' is none so easy," said Durdle. "Folk talk a deal about the peace and quiet of a country life, but I had a heap more quiet at Hereford before I came to keep house for the Vicar. Look you there!" and she pointed with fine scorn to an untidy table, "he's been and got out them nasty bones again! If they wasn't as dry as an empty cider-press I'd give them all to the dog!"

With laugh Zachary suddenly held up and brandished in the air a long bone which he had hitherto concealed.

Mrs. Dundle gave a horrified exclamation.

"My patience, man! Don't bring that here! Vicar would never take bones from the churchyard. 'Tis animals' bones he's all agog for, and then only when they be as old as Noah's ark."

"I'll put it back in the mould when parson's seen it; but I tell you, Mrs. Durdle, 'tis a marvel. That's a giant's shank bone, and he must ha' stood nine feet high—poor chap, think o' that! I'm glad there's not so much o' me. Think o' nine feet o' rheumatics!"

"Well, rheumatics or no rheumatics, I'm sorry for his wife," said Durdle, laughing. "She must have needed to be a rare good knitter to keep him in hose! If you must leave the thing for the Vicar, let me give it a good dustin' out o' window first. Ah! Zachary, after all, 'tis ill work jesting over bones when England's strewn with the bones o' them as has been killed in this weary war."

"You're right, Mrs. Durdle—you're right. 'Twill be three years come Lammastide since the King set up his standard at Nottingham, and ever since naught but battles and sieges, plunderings and threatenings. And now there's this plaguey garrison hard by at Canon Frome, with a Governor that sticks at nothing."

"What! Colonel Norton?" said the housekeeper, raising her eyebrows. "Why, he be always comin' to see Vicar. But between you and me, Zachary, 'tis Mistress Hilary's pretty face, I take it, that draws him."

"Then, Mrs. Durdle, for pity's sake have a care o' your young lady, for I hear little enough to his credit. But I thought Mistress Hilary had been courted by a young spark at Hereford?"

"Eh, to be sure, so she was. She and young Mr. Gabriel Harford were like lovers since they were no higher than this table. But the war put a stop to that, and from being fast friends they became foes, the more's the pity."

"Well, like master, like man, as the proverb hath it," said the sexton, stooping to root up a plantain from the turf. "Vicar he says, he'll have nought to do with wars and fightings, for he be a man o' peace. And so be I, Mrs. Durdle, so be I. But beware of yon Governor o' Canon Frome, for there's many a wench will have cause to rue the day when he came to Herefordshire."

"For my part, I like the gentleman well enough. He's a fine, handsome officer, and the Vicar always enjoys his visits," said Durdle, pouncing like a bird of prey on the laboriously-woven spider's web which she just then saw in a corner of the window.

"Ah, you women! you women! 'Tis always the same. A handsome spark will ever find you ready to give him a good word," said Zachary, shaking his head.

"And are you so sure, Zachary, that a pretty wench can't turn you round her fingers?" retorted the housekeeper, with a smile.

"Handsome is as handsome does," quoted the sexton, shrewdly. "Give me the woman who knows how to brew good cider; grave-diggin' all among bones and dust is terribly dry work, Mrs. Durdle."

"Well, well, come round to the kitchen, man, though 'tis over early for your noonings," said Durdle, with a laugh, "but, by-the-bye, what was the tale I heard in the village last night about the doings at Drybrook?"

"'Tis o'er true," said Zachary, "though 'twas not the Canon Frome men that plundered there, but a troop of Colonel Lunsford's horse that were serving in Prince Rupert's forces. At Drybrook, when a poor fellow refused to give up a flitch o' bacon to the foraging party, they struck him down and knocked out his eyes."

"Good gracious, Zachary; now don't you be telling that gruesome tale to Mistress Hilary, for she can't abide hearing tell o' such doings, though she do pretend to be so fond o' war and fighting and glory and the rest. There's not much glory in havin' your eyes put out, I'll warrant!"

Zachary lounged off towards the back premises, and Durdle was about to retire to the kitchen, and resume her gossip there, when she heard a knock at the front door.

"Now I do believe that's Colonel Norton's knock," she muttered, bustling out in reply to the summons.

Her surmise was right enough; there he stood, booted and spurred, in all the glory of his gay attire, and with a sparkle in his dark eyes, which instantly banished from Durdle's mind all Zachary's warnings. She ushered him into the room she had just quitted, and though he had only asked for the Vicar his glance had so plainly bade her tell her mistress as well of his arrival, that she promptly sought Hilary, who had just finished making apple pasties in the kitchen.

"I'll clap those in the oven, dearie," said the housekeeper, "and do you doff your apron and tell the Vicar Colonel Norton is waiting to see him."

Hilary departed on the errand, unable to determine whether she wished to see her admirer or not.

"I will leave you to have your chat with the colonel," she said when she had with some difficulty roused the Vicar from a treatise on ancient coins which Mr. Silas Taylor had lent him.

"Nay, nay, child," said the Vicar, retaining her hand in his. "I have scarce clapped eyes on you this morning; come in too, and hear the news."

And to Norton's satisfaction the uncle and niece entered the room together. The Vicar's greeting was always cordial, yet this morning Norton fancied that there was a certain depression about his host which he could not fathom.

"Do you bring us any news, sir?" asked the antiquary wistfully.

"No news, sir, and no treasures for the collection, unluckily," said Norton. "I called mainly on business. You have not been disturbed here, I hope, by Governor Massey? I hear he is hovering about again near Ledbury."

"Nay, we have heard naught of him here," said the Vicar. "I have been up this morning seeing the owner of the Hill Farm. There is sore trouble there, sir, and I wish you would consider the people more than you do. These foraging parties are growing unbearable."

"Believe me, I do what I can, sir," said Norton in his most winning tone. "I dislike the work of plundering as much as you would, but how else are we to keep the army alive?"

The Vicar sighed heavily.

"May God send us the blessing of peace!" he said. "I tell you, sir, it fairly breaks my heart to go about among the people of Bosbury. There is scarce a family but has lost a man in this cruel war, or else hath been well-nigh ruined by marauders."

"Well, Vicar, we must all take the fortune of war. Of course, the rustics grumble when hungry soldiers seize their goods—but how are the officers to check starving men? That is what I was last night urging on old Sir Richard Hopton, who does naught but complain of the Canon Frame garrison. 'Good Sir,' I said to him, 'What would you have me do? If the King gave me money I would pay for what we consume. But we are fighting for the divine right of Kings, and have surely a divine right to feed on something more satisfying than air.'"

"'Tis not alone the taking of gear that I complain of," said the Vicar gravely, "but of cruelties perpetrated by the soldiers—abominable cruelties which did not spare even women and children."

"Such things will happen in time of war, sir," replied

Norton. "What can you expect? Soldiers are but human. 'Tis only the Roundheads that set up for being saints. However, we must not scare Mistress Hilary with talk of cruelties. Believe me," he said, turning to her, "these tales of the village folk never lose in the telling, and we are not so black as we're painted. Prince Rupert——"

"Prince Rupert is one of a thousand!" said Hilary, enthusiastically. "How I should like to see him! Do you think there is a chance that he may come this way?"

"You are of a more martial spirit than the Vicar. That is generally the way. We poor soldiers mostly find favour with the fair sex—'tis one of our few compensations," said Norton, venturing nearer to her and lowering his voice as he noticed that Dr. Coke had moved over to the table and taken up the bone brought in by the sexton. "Yet do not make me jealous of the Prince by dwelling overmuch on his merits. Am I to have my answer to-day?"

She shook her head, and blushed deliciously. Norton had every intention of furtively kissing her hand, when the Vicar suddenly turned round and showed them his latest treasure.

"Most curious! Most interesting! Why, the fellow must have been a giant. Hilary, look here! In life this man must have stood at least eight feet high. Where did it come from?"

"I don't know, Uncle," said Hilary, shuddering. "Ugh! how gruesome it looks! I can't bear skulls and bones!"

Norton with a smile watched the two. "What a contrast," he reflected. "That old bone collector and a maid whose cheeks are like a wild rose! I wonder if the parson will get in the way of my designs?"

He was roused from his reverie by the entrance of Mrs. Durdle and the customary tray of cakes and cider.

The Vicar re-crossed the room with an eager question on his lips.

"Where did this come from, Mrs. Durdle? To whom am I indebted for this very rare bone?"

"Why, sir, 'twas Zachary brought it, and do now let me take it back to him. It gives me the creeps to see churchyard bones lying round loose."

"Well, I suppose if Zachary dug it up we ought to give it Christian burial," said the Vicar regretfully, "but it does seem a pity. A most rare and interesting bone."

"Yes, sir, yes," said the housekeeper, receiving it carefully in her apron, "very interesting, but do now let it be buried decentlike. 'Tis impossible to keep the place tidy—let alone clean—when your antics are littering all over the house."

There was a general laugh as she left the room.

"No more antics for you, Uncle dear, if Mrs. Durdle has her way," said Hilary blithely.

"She is a most orderly person," said the Vicar, with a good-humoured smile, "and to have as master an untidy old antiquary must be a sore trial to her. But pardon me, Colonel, all this time I have been rambling on about my own affairs, and I understand that you had some special matter to talk over with me."

"To tell the truth, sir, I walked over from Canon Frome this morning to ask you to sign your name to the Protestation framed by Prince Rupert. He commands the signatures of the people of this neighbourhood, and I shall be glad to have yours."

He handed a paper to the Vicar, who, with some reluctance, took it, and began to read it to himself.

"Hey! What!" he exclaimed, presently, "the Prince commands? Why, Colonel, he has no right to extort oaths from free Englishmen. He fancies himself back in Germany. Listen to this! 'I do strictly enjoin, without exception, all commanders and soldiers, gentry, citizens, freeholders, and others within the county and city of Hereford to take this Protestation.' I'faith, he goes too far, Colonel, too far! Look at this! I must swear that all the Parliamentarians ought to be brought to condign punishment—I must swear that I will help His Majesty to the utmost of my skill and power and with the hazard of my life and fortune; I must swear not to hold any correspondency or intelligence with Parliamentarians, and to discover all their plans that I may chance to know; and all these particulars I must vow and protest sincerely to observe without equivocation or mental reservation."

"Well, but, Vicar, we all know that you honour the King," said Norton, reassuringly. "No man could dare to call your loyalty in question—why, you are the son of one of the twelve bishops who signed the Remonstrance."

"Very true," said the Vicar "but the signing of that ill-judged and illegal document was, to my mind, my father's great mistake. No, no, Colonel; I try to do my best to honour the King and to love and honour all men; therefore I loathe this unlawful Protestation, and will not say, 'I willingly vow and protest,' as here enjoined."

Norton watched him intently; this was a side of the antiquary's character which had not before been revealed to him.

"But, sir, you scarce realise, I think, what a serious matter this may be," he said. "The Prince has expressly ordered that all who refuse to sign shall be seized without delay and kept in custody. It was enacted, as you see, on the second of this month."

The Vicar again examined the paper, then looked up with an astute expression. "So it seems, sir, but you will also note that this Protestation is ordered to be tendered to all by the High Sheriff and Commissioners of the county, assisted by a Divine."

Norton veiled his annoyance by a laugh.

"Of course if you want to keep to the letter of the law, we must bring over the whole posse from Hereford, but I thought as we were friends——"

The Vicar smiled genially, and held out his hand.

"We are friends, certainly—very good friends. But as to keeping to the letter of the law—I don't acknowledge this document to be law at all, 'tis grossly illegal. You see, sir," he added reverently, "I must try to remember that at Ordination I vowed to maintain and set forwards quietness, peace and love among Christian people."

As though the words had cost him something to utter in what he knew would be a hostile atmosphere, he turned away and stood for a minute by the window, looking out at the church he loved so well, and the strong tower of refuge and the quiet graveyard.

Norton stroked his moustache to conceal a scornful smile, then bent low over Hilary's hand and kissed it, conveying to her by look and touch much more than the customary salute.

"I am not without hope, Mistress Hilary, that where I have failed you will succeed," he said gently. "Try if you can to persuade your uncle, for his refusal places him in some danger. I know well how much influence your sweet words have over men, and trust you will permit me to wait on you before long to learn of your success."

With one of his sweeping bows he turned to take leave of the Vicar, who accompanied him to the door and bade him farewell very cordially, but being pre-occupied with the thought of the Protestation, forgot to give him the usual invitation to stay to dinner.

Hilary, with a restlessness which she had never before felt, paced up and down the room unhappily. Did this man indeed love her as he professed to do? And did she in truth care for him? That he was handsome, clever and fascinating was beyond dispute—she thought she did care for him—certainly she was far from being indifferent to him—and yet? Yet it was not like that day years ago when Gabriel had spoken to her in the wood, and a whole new world had opened to them.

"Nothing can be like first love, of course," she said to herself dreamily, and then bitterness overwhelming her, "but my first love was all a miserable mistake! Gabriel cared more for this phantom of parliamentary government—loved that better than he loved me."

She impatiently dashed from her eyes the tears that had started at this thought, and with sudden energy caught up her lute and began vigorously to tune it.

"I won't be a fool!" she thought, resolutely forcing back the old memories that tried to rise. "I will wed this loyal Colonel Norton. He said my words had power over men, and I see they have over him. They had none over Gabriel!"

At that moment the Vicar returned to the sitting-room.

"Well, my child," he said, stroking her hair, "yonder is a pleasant-spoken man, but I can never sign that paper he brought. We will talk no more of it, the very thought of it chafes me. Sing me one of your songs, dear, let us have 'Come, sweet love, let sorrow cease!'"

Hilary winced, for the plaintive sweetness of "Bara Fostus Dream" was for ever associated with the summer days when Gabriel had wooed her; but she could not refuse her uncle's request, and sang the song in a more subdued frame of mind.

She had just begun the last verse—

"Then, sweet love, disperse this cloud—"

when sounds of confusion in the village street and an uproar of voices brought her to a sudden pause. Running to the window, she called eagerly to the Vicar.

"See, Uncle, the people are thronging this way. What can have happened?"

And as the Vicar joined her and looked forth, Durdle and Zachary rushed without ceremony into the room, breathless with haste, but each eager to give the news.

"Oh, sir, come out and stop it, for pity's sake," panted Durdle.

"Yes, sir, do'ee now. Mayhap they'll hearken to you," said Zachary.

"What is wrong?" asked the Vicar, looking from one to the other.

"The soldiers, sir—they've marched from Ledbury!"

"Parliament soldiers, sir," panted Zachary. "Fetched by Waghorn a-purpose to pull down the cross."

"And they're a-goin' to do it, too," put in Durdle, determined to have the last word.

The Vicar's indignant amaze almost choked him.

"What!" he cried. "Pull down Bosbury Cross! Why, Hilary, 'tis one of the oldest in all England—one of our most valued antiquities. God grant I may be able to save it."

He hastily crossed the room towards the door.

"Ay, sir," said Zachary, "you speak to the captain, he be a pleasant-looking young officer. But as for Waghorn, I do think he be gone stark mad."

"Don't come into the crowd, Hilary," said the Vicar, excitedly, as he hurried from the house. "Wait in the garden and leave me to plead for this treasure of the past."

CHAPTER XXXVI.

"Could we forbear dispute, and practise love,

We should agree as angels do above."

—Edmund Waller.

The churchyard, which during Norton's visit had looked so peaceful, had become, before the Colonel had ridden halfway back to Canon Frome, the scene of an extraordinary gathering. With bewildered astonishment the Vicar saw the villagers hurrying in from all directions—men in their smock frocks, women fresh from their household work in cap and apron, and eager children pressing to the front that they might the better see the soldiers in their glittering steel helmets and corslets, their buff coats and orange scarves. A cornet carried the blue banner of the Parliament, with its motto, "God with us," and the Captain brought up the rear. The Vicar, glancing at him, saw that he was young, slight and alert-looking; but his attention was quickly drawn away to Waghorn, who, springing up on the steps of the cross, turned with a vehement gesture towards the leader of the detachment.

"There it stands, Captain, just as I told you!" he cried. "There is the accursed Popish idol! Down with it! Down with it! even to the ground! So may all Thy enemies perish!"

Anything more violent and frenzied than his manner it was impossible to conceive; his dark eyes blazed, his sombre face was transformed.

But the ludicrous inappropriateness of his quotation tickled Gabriel's sense of humour, and under the violence of the attack he grew restive.

"Your text seems to me ill-chosen," he said. "But if this be indeed an idol, then by all means let it come down. An idol is a visible object which men bow down to or worship. Do any of you people of Bosbury bow down to this cross?"

There was a quiet force in his tone which instantly arrested the villagers' full attention.

"No, sir," they cried, unanimously.

And at that the Vicar hastened forward, courteously greeting the young Parliamentarian, and exclaiming eagerly, "Sir, the answer of the people of Bosbury is true. None of my people are so foolish as to bow to sticks or stones. I humbly hope that they have learnt better than that."

"'Tis a lie!" shouted Waghorn. "A lie! How about old Jock? How about Billy Blunt?"

"Old Jock," explained the Vicar to the Captain, "had been brought up a Papist, and I admit that he did superstitiously nod his head when he passed the cross; he is now bedridden. As for Billy, he, poor lad, is an idiot, and 'tis impossible to reason with him."

But explanations could not satisfy Waghorn.

"Down with all idolatrous symbols!" he shouted. "Down with the cross!"

And his vehemence and excitement proved infectious, for now the soldiers and a few of the spectators caught up the cry, and the churchyard rang with shouts of "Ay! down with it! down with it!" while the villagers began to press forward in an uncertain way, scarcely knowing what to think.

The Vicar rushed between the cross and the soldiers as though to guard it from attack, and turned with outstretched arms to his parishioners.

"I tell you, good people," he said, in his ringing, manly voice, "that this cross was set up by early Christians. Beneath it there lies buried the ancient stone which was worshipped in heathen times. This is no idol, but a witness to the truth."

"Don't heed the Vicar! Obey the word of God!" shouted Waghorn. "Break it in pieces like a potter's vessel!"

Again the contagion of the fanatic's excitement spread, and elicited yet fiercer shouts of "Ay! Pull it down! Break it in pieces! Remember Smithfield!"

Gabriel saw that a serious riot would ensue unless action were quickly taken.

Shouting an order for silence, which was promptly obeyed by the soldiers, he said to the Vicar, "Sir, 'tis true enough that Parliament hath ordered the destruction of images and crosses. In many places the people truly did bow down to them. We wish that God alone should be glorified, and we dread homage to symbols. I fear that it will be my duty to carry out the Parliamentary order."

"In truth, sir," pleaded the Vicar, "I assure you that I dislike acts of homage to the cross as much as you do. I merely plead with you for our right to keep the ensign of our faith. What is that blue banner yonder officer holds?"

"'Tis the banner of the Parliament, sir," said Gabriel.

"Well, sir, you do not worship your flag, but you would not lightly part with it. That cross, sir, is my flag, and, unless your looks belie you, I think you will refuse to destroy the witness of our common faith."

Gabriel had listened with respect and deep attention to this earnest appeal. The long years of controversy and strife had accentuated every religious difference. Hard words had been remorselessly hurled on both sides; but here was a man who boldly appealed to "our common faith."

In a sudden flash he seemed to realise how overwhelmingly great was this faith they shared. All lesser differences were dwarfed. He no longer saw the stone cross, the buff-coated men-at-arms and the villagers—he saw instead a jeering rabble, and Roman soldiers and the Eternal Revelation of God's great love to the world. All that he had known from childhood, and honestly striven to carry into practice, was flooded by one of those inspiring gleams which make us understand how much nearer is the Unseen than the Seen; so that for the time there seemed to him nothing in the whole universe save that perfect Revelation of Love.

He was recalled from his Mount of Transfiguration by the urgent need of help down below. Like a false note in a symphony, Waghorn's voice broke the silence which, to his violent zeal, had seemed unendurable.

"Don't heed him, Captain! Don't heed him! Down with the accursed idol! So let all Thine enemies perish, O Lord!"

Gabriel strode towards him.

"Silence!" he cried, sternly. "The devil, as we all know, can quote Scripture. Sir," he continued, turning to the Vicar, with a look that told of genuine respect, "your words stir my heart strangely. If you will promise to have graven on the cross these words

Honour not the cross,

But honour God for Christ,

no man shall touch what you rightly call the witness of our common faith."

The Vicar grasped his hand with grateful warmth.

"I thank you from my heart, sir, and I promise right willingly. Zachary! Go fetch Tim the mason, and bid him carve the words without delay. And, good people," he added, as the villagers crowded round him, two little children plucking at his sleeve till he put his kindly hands caressingly on their shoulders, "let us never allow the emblem of Divine Love to become the target for bitterness and division. Above all the unhappy strife of to-day, there is one thing which may yet unite us—it is love, the bond of peace."

All this time Hilary had obediently waited in the garden, but the garden was separated from the churchyard only by a low hedge of clipped yews, and in one place the trees had been allowed to grow higher and had been cut into a sheltered arbour. Here, quite hidden from view, she had seen and heard all that passed.

For a minute or two she had not recognised Gabriel, for his face had been turned from her and she had only once before seen him with short hair and in uniform. But when he stepped forward and spoke to the people her heart gave such a bound of joy that in reality all her perplexed musings as to the answer she should make to Colonel Norton were solved.

When she heard the word of command given to the soldiers to march from the churchyard, and saw the crowd beginning to disperse, she hastened from the arbour, and was just approaching the little gate in the hedge when she saw the Vicar drawing near, and heard him warmly pressing the Parliamentary Captain to dine with them.

"Uncle!" she said, opening the gate, "you do not know our old friend, Mr. Gabriel Harford."

Gabriel looked in amazement at the dear familiar face in the grey and pink hood, at the trim erect figure in the old grey gown, outlined against the arch of dark yew. Surely that white hand holding open the gate was an emblem of hope? Surely he could read signs of love in the bright eyes and in the glowing cheeks?

"Hilary!" he cried, with a choking sensation in his throat. "Are you here?"

He bent down and kissed her hand, and they were both relieved when the Vicar came to the rescue.

"Captain Harford! Why, this is excellent hearing. I had no notion, sir, what your name was, but if aught could make my rejoicing greater, it would be the knowledge that this kindly deed was done by one well known to my dear sister now at rest, this child's mother," and he took Hilary's hand caressingly in his.

"I will see if dinner is ready," she said, nervously.

"No, child, I must myself go in, and will speak to Durdle. Do you entertain Captain Harford. You were children together and will have many a matter to talk over, I'll warrant."

He went into the house, and Gabriel drew a little nearer to Hilary.

"Your uncle does not know, then, that we were ever more to one another than just playmates?" he said; and as for an instant she glanced at him, she saw how much he must have gone through since their last parting.

"No," she replied, shyly. "He never heard about it. So much has passed since then. You had tidings of my dear mother's death, Gabriel?"

"Yes, I heard of it at Bath, before the fight at Lansdown. My thoughts have always been with you, but you never replied to my letter."

"No letter ever reached me," she said.

"This miserable war too often makes writing useless," said Gabriel, with a sigh. "For nigh upon two years I have been hoping against hope for an answer. Ah! here comes Mrs. Durdle."

"Dinner is served, mistress," said Durdle. "I hope I see you well, sir," she added, curtseying and beaming as her eyes fell on Gabriel.

"Why! Mrs. Durdle," he said, laughing, as he shook her by the hand. "I could fancy myself at home once more now that I see you again."

"And it's glad I am to welcome you to Bosbury, sir," said the housekeeper, blithely. "Begun your work you did by guarding me and that silly wench Maria when the Parliament soldiers first came to Hereford; and now here you be to guard Bosbury Cross from that crazy-pated Waghorn."

They entered the house and were soon dining together. Hilary, far too much excited to eat, keeping up a gallant show with a mere fragment of meat and a large helping of salad, but Gabriel making satisfactory inroads on the cold stalled ox, which usually made the household dinner on Sunday, Monday and Tuesday.

"I only hope that in the excitement of that scene in the churchyard, Durdle hasn't let my apple pasties burn to cinders in the oven," said Hilary, smiling. "You always used to have a liking for hot apple pasties when we were children," she said, glancing at him.

"And 'tis many a day since I had a chance of tasting one," he said, laughing. "Soldiers are supposed to keep alive and well on the strangest fare."

"Ah! sir, you have done a grand work to-day," said the Vicar, with such relief and happiness in his tone that Hilary found tears starting to her eyes. "You have shown a generous forbearance which coming generations will have cause to remember with gratitude."

"In truth, sir," said Gabriel, "'tis I that am indebted to you for words that will often cheer me in these harsh times. Our rasping differences are ever confronting us and shutting out all thought of what we share."

The talk turned on Dr. Harford's visit more than a year before, and of Waghorn's attack on the East window. Gabriel had heard nothing about it, for letters from Hereford had more than once failed to reach him. Indeed, as he explained, he had imagined that Dr. Coke was still at Bromyard.

Just then the Vicar was called away to speak to some one, and as Gabriel could not be induced to eat a third pasty, Hilary proposed that they should return to the garden.

"It was from this little arbour that I saw and heard all that passed just now," she said, as they sat down in the cosy little retreat. "I hope you appreciated Durdle's words of praise."

"Durdle was kinder to me at Hereford than you were," he said, reproachfully.

"She urged me to see you, and so in truth did my mother," said Hilary, drooping her head.

"And you always refused. I wonder if you knew how cruelly you hurt me," he said, with that note of pain in his voice which always disturbed her.

"What would have been the use of inviting you to come in?" she replied. "You know that it was worse than useless when we met in the cathedral porch. We parted because of our great differences. Naught had changed."

"Yet," pleaded Gabriel, "the Vicar told us but now that there was one thing which must always unite us."

She drew up her head with all her old pride and hardness.

"I could never love a rebel," she said, perversely.

Gabriel, bitterly disappointed, remained absolutely silent. A bee flew humming loudly into the arbour, then roamed forth once more to the apple blossom on a tree hard by. There was a faint stirring, too, in the shrubs just behind them in the churchyard as Peter Waghorn, who had followed the movements of the Parliamentary Captain with stealthy malevolence, crouched down that he might hear what treason was being plotted betwixt this half-hearted officer and the Vicar's Royalist niece. The two noticed nothing, for they were absorbed in their own thoughts.

"Why are you a rebel, Gabriel?" said Hilary, more quietly, as she lifted her face to his pleadingly. "Oh, think better of it! 'Tis not too late. Many men have changed sides. Think how good our King is!"

Her appeal moved him painfully, a look of keen distress dawned in his eyes.

"A good man, but an untrustworthy King," he said, controlling his agitation with difficulty. "Nay, we won't argue. You well know that I fight for the ancient rights and liberties of Englishmen, and even for love of you, Hilary, I can't turn back! I can't turn back! And yet, oh! my God! how hard it is!"

"I did not mean to pain you," said Hilary, remorsefully. "Nay, I longed to tell you how it pleased me to hear all that you said when Waghorn would have pulled down the cross. Are you still in Sir William Waller's army?"

"No, at present I am serving under Colonel Massey, but I hope ere long to be sent to Sir Thomas Fairfax at Windsor, where he is forming the New Model Army."

"You will serve under him?"

"My great wish is to follow in my father's steps, but just now I am to act as the bearer of important despatches. Enough, however, of my affairs. Do tell me of yourself. If only you guessed how I had hungered for news of you!"

"'Twere far better that you forgot me," she said, beginning to play with the little housewife that hung from her girdle.

"I can never forget," he said, vehemently. "Surely you understand that my love for you is unchanged."

Suddenly there darted into her mind the remembrance of Norton's words about the pretty daughter of the Gloucestershire squire. When spoken they had seemed to turn her love to hatred, yet in the sudden rapture of Gabriel's return she had absolutely forgotten all about them. He could not understand the change that now came over her whole manner and bearing.

"Don't speak of your love," she said, indignantly. "All that is at an end—at best we can now be only friendly foes. More is impossible."

"Why impossible?" he pleaded.

Then terror seizing him, he exclaimed, "Do you mean that someone else loves you?"

"Why do you ask?" she said, with some embarrassment.

"Oh! have pity on me, Hilary," he cried. "At least tell me one way or the other. Is there some other lover?"

"Yes," she owned. "There is one that loves me, and a right loyal gentleman he is—the Governor of Canon Frome."

He turned pale. The silence and the suffering in his face angered Hilary.

"What right have you to be concerned?" she said, indignantly. "You have not really been constant to me; I well know that you have been making love to the heiress of a Gloucestershire squire."

"Who told you so base a lie?" said Gabriel, starting to his feet.

"One whose word I trust," she replied, quietly, "the loyal Governor of Canon Frome."

"His name?" asked Gabriel, eagerly.

"His name is Colonel Norton," she said, triumphantly.

"Norton!" he cried, in horror. "He is the man you trust? The man who has dared to speak of love to you?"

"Yes; why not? Is he not a brave soldier and active in the King's service?"

"Brave, no doubt. He is an Englishman. But surely you have heard that even his own party are aghast at his doings?"

"I have heard naught against him," said Hilary, indignantly. "You are jealous, and if there is one thing on earth I despise 'tis jealousy."

"The fellow is not worthy to touch the hem of your garment," said Gabriel, sternly. "Listen to me. You shall hear the plain truth. 'Tis well known that he is a Cavalier of the type of my Lord Goring. I would sooner see you dead than in his power."

"It would be unfair of me to heed your attack on the absent," said Hilary, coldly. "You are jealous, and ready to believe evil of Colonel Norton."

"You torture me!" cried Gabriel, desperately.

"Oh, you pretend that you are unchanged," said Hilary, with scorn. "But there is no smoke without fire, and the Gloucestershire heiress——"

"Hush!" he said, sitting down beside her once more, and his quietness of manner and restrained force dominated her.

"Now I am resolved that you shall hear precisely what passed, for it is due to Mistress Neal as well as to you and to myself."

Very briefly he told of Norton's interview with Major Locke at Gloucester, of the interrupted duel, of the way in which he and Joscelyn Heyworth had rescued Helena from the cruel trap that had been set for her. In spite of herself Hilary's sympathies were enlisted on the side of the poor little maid, and perhaps she inclined to her all the more when she heard that she was now happily married to Mr. Humphrey Neal.

"And her father?" she inquired. "What has become of him?"

"He died at Marlborough, mainly, I do believe, because Colonel Norton forced him to travel when he was desperately wounded and refused him the aid of a surgeon," said Gabriel.

There was a silence. He would not speak of the way in which Norton had treated him in the church.

"After all," said Hilary, with a mutinous little toss of the head, "I have but your word for this. You tell me one tale and Colonel Norton another. Why should I trust a rebel and distrust a Royalist?"

A sigh of despair broke from Gabriel at her perversity.

"I can only repeat," he said, "that I love you with all my heart and soul, but if it were to save you from wedding this vile profligate I could rejoice to see you the wife of any honourable man."

"You leap to conclusions," she said, relenting a little, "I am in no haste to wed. There is not even a promise given yet. I merely said he loved me. But enough! Let us come into the church and you shall see what havoc Waghorn wrought there."

CHAPTER XXXVII.

"We must admit nothing which turns our worship from inward to outward, which tends to set the transitory in place of the eternal. Nothing external, however splendid and impressive, can bring us nearer to the Divine; but external things may engross and exhaust our powers of devotion. Veils of sense, no less than veils of intellect, may come between us and the spiritual, in which alone we can rest. To rest in forms is idolatry. Earth may hold us still under the guise of heaven."

—Christian Aspects of Life.—Bishop Westcott.

When the two had passed through the little gate in the churchyard, and had disappeared inside the building, Peter Waghorn crept cautiously from his hiding place among the shrubs. Shaking his fist at the cross which was so obnoxious to him, he slowly made his way to his own house, his mind full of what he had overheard.

The long-delayed scheme for the destruction of the cross, upon which he had set his heart, had been frustrated at the very last moment by this young captain. Doubtless, Waghorn thought, he had been secretly persuaded beforehand by the soft blandishments of the Vicar's niece. She had discreetly kept in the background throughout the scene, but, of course, it was all really her doing.

"Well, well," he muttered grimly, as he sat down in his lonely room, "I have him in my power now, and can revenge myself on him! He baulked me as to the cross, and as good as called me a devil. The man's a traitor! He's one of the ungodly. I'll unmask him even if for the nonce I have to play into Colonel Norton's hands. I'll take word to Canon Frome as to the despatches he is to bear to Windsor. Eh, eh! Captain Harford. I shall have you laid by the heels, and you shall bitterly rue the day when you set your hand to the plough and then turned back."

With bitter vindictiveness he drew an inkhorn and pen towards him, and laboriously began to write the following words:

"I have a carpentering job in the ante-room at Canon Frome Manor this day, and shall be there at three of the clocke. If Colonel Norton wishes to gett tydings of a dangerous ryvall, who is moreover a rebel, he cann obtayne it on certaine con-dishuns."

He had just sanded this document, and was about to fold and seal it, when the sound of the Old 113th in the village street made him pause. He stepped out into the road in front of the house, and saw that the Puritan soldiers were ready to march back to Ledbury, and, evidently at the Vicar's request, were first joining the villagers in a Psalm. As the words floated towards him a look of wonder and hesitation crossed the stern face of the wood carver. It was as if he caught a momentary glimpse of a unity as yet far beyond his reach.

O children which do serve the Lord,

Praise ye His name with one accord,

Yea, blessed always be His name;

Who from the rising of the sun

Till it return where it begun,

Is to be praised with great fame,

The Lord all people doth surmount,

As for His glory we may count

Above the heavens high to be.

With God the Lord who may compare,

Whose dwellings in the heavens are;

Of such great power and force is He.

But the bitter memory of his father's death returned to him, and when another psalm was started he closed his door and hardened his heart; as soon as the soldiers had left the village he resolved to set out for Canon Frome.

Meanwhile Gabriel and Hilary were viewing Waghorn's work in the church.

"It was such a grief to my uncle," said Hilary. "Often in former times I have seen him sitting here about sunset quietly enjoying the beauty of the place and the jewel-like colouring of the window."

"I am sorry Waghorn destroyed it," said Gabriel. "Yet it would be dishonest of me to let you think that I am wholly without the usual Puritan feeling. To paint an imaginary picture of the Christ seems to me taking an unwarrantable liberty, which we should not allow a painter to take with any other friend or kinsman."

"Don't you mind spoiling a beautiful thing?" she said, wonderingly.

"I never saw anything to complain of in the Bosbury window," he replied, "but some representing the Trinity I gladly saw destroyed. At Abingdon, when Sir William Waller had the market cross hewn down, I helped to break in pieces the images of the saints surrounding it, for some folk still knelt to them. And though at Winchester we regretted the irreverence shown to the tombs of the dead, and did our utmost to check it, we found it well-nigh impossible to control the people, for they connect all pictures and sculpture with the hated tyranny of Popish times."

"I don't understand how you can endure such sights," said Hilary.

"Perhaps you hardly understand that a soldier has to endure sights so much more dreadful. Human beings crushed, battered, mangled—homes destroyed, and families destitute and starving—all the horrors of war. When once you have learnt to love people, you can't think so much of mere things."

"I don't think you ever really cared for what was beautiful," she said, reproachfully.

He winced. For was not her radiant loveliness tugging at his heart—torturing him with an intolerable longing to have her for his own to all eternity?

Norton would skilfully have taken advantage of such an opening and used it for his selfish ends, but Gabriel's voice only sounded a little constrained, as he replied:

"You are right in deeming me no artist."

Into his mind there came a sudden recollection of the comfort that Hilary's miniature had been to him through these years of pain and separation; and then a horrible memory of what had passed about it in the church at Marlborough, and the sickening thought that Norton was even now seeking to ensnare her.

What was he to do? How could he best serve her? Their differences in religion and politics seemed to loom up larger than ever, and hopelessly to part them.

The sound of the soldiers and the villagers joining in the thanksgiving psalm broke in upon his sad thoughts. When the verse ended, he turned to Hilary and there was again a look of hope in his eyes. He was standing beneath the beautifully carved old rood screen and she was strangely moved by the pathos of his expression.

"After all," he said, cheerfully, "we may find a parable in this Bosbury window which will show us how small are our differences. You and the Vicar love to see through a coloured picture; we Puritans should, as a rule, prefer the clearest glass, but we are both looking through the same outlet to the same sunlight."

The thought appealed to her; she smiled with something of her old comprehending sweetness.

"I am very glad you spared the cross," she said, gently, as they paused for a minute in the south porch. "If—if I pained you just now, I am sorry, Gabriel."

"Promise me that you will at least take counsel before you again speak to Colonel Norton," he pleaded.

"What right have you to demand promises of me?" she asked proudly.

"No right," he said, his voice faltering, "but by the memory of your mother I implore you, Hilary."

"I will think of it," she said. "What! are you going?"

"I distrust that fanatic Waghorn, he may stir up the soldiers once more," he replied. Then, with an irrepressible sigh, "'Tis like enough, Hilary, that you and I may never meet again; will you not give me that one word of comfort?"

The sudden stab of pain at the thought that this might indeed be their last meeting, broke down her pride.

"Well—I promise," she said, gently. Then, as he bent down and kissed her hand, the familiar notes of "In trouble and adversity," fell upon her ear. "Do you hear what they are singing?" she cried. "'Tis our psalm that we sang years ago in the Cathedral, that day when——" she broke off in confusion.

"You still remember?" he said, tenderly, his eyes full of happiness as they met hers.

At that moment, to his bitter regret, they heard steps on the path, and looking up, saw a burly sergeant approaching. Gabriel went to give him his orders, then returned to the porch.

"We must march as soon as they have ended the psalm," he said, stooping once more to press a passionate kiss on her hand. "I am glad you remember that day, Hilary. Remember always! Remember always!"

She heard his voice tremble, yet could not speak; she watched him walk rapidly down the path to the lych-gate, and then as the hearty voices of the soldiers and the villagers rose in the final verse, she sank down on one of the benches in the porch, and, hiding her face in her hands, burst into tears.

About three o'clock that afternoon Norton, waking from an after-dinner nap, sauntered out into one of the corridors at Canon Frome Manor.

"There is a carpenter-fellow, sir, at work in the house, and he bade me give this into your hands," said his servant, approaching him.

Norton carelessly broke the seal and glanced at the laboriously-written lines. A smile began to flicker about his lips, and with some curiosity he made his way to the ante-room which led to Dame Elizabeth's apartments. Here he found Waghorn busily engaged in mending a spinning-wheel.

"Good-day, Colonel," said the fanatic, gloomily. "Hath my missive been delivered?"

"So this is from you!" said Norton, with a sarcastic smile. "You are the fellow I met once at Bosbury. Have you thought better of it, and are you going to change sides?"

"Nay, nay, I trow not," replied Waghorn, his eyes gleaming. "But I would fain be used as the instrument of vengeance on the ungodly, even though for the time I do serve thee and thy cause."

Norton gave one of his short scoffing laughs.

"I faith I scarce know if I could be served by one of such a vinegar aspect!"

"Dost thou love Mistress Hilary Unett?" asked the wood-carver, sternly.

The Colonel started.

"What is that to you, scarecrow?"

"I had heard gossip in the village as to thy wooing of her, and I thought mayhap a knowledge of the doings of her old lover, Captain Harford, might be worth something to thee."

"Harford!" cried the Colonel, in surprise. "What do you know of him?"

Waghorn carefully adjusted a screw in the spinning-wheel, then looked up shrewdly.

"What would the knowledge be worth to thee?"

"Oh! You want money! Here! I'm as poor as a rook, but for the whole truth about this cursed lover I'll give you a crown piece."

He took a coin from his pocket and flung it on the floor. Waghorn, with an angry frown, pushed it from him.

"Thy money perish with thee! I want none of it. Nay, 'tis something more than money that I must have for the tidings. Promise to use me as the instrument of vengeance on this traitor."

"Dost take me for a murderer hiring assassins?" said the Colonel, scornfully.

"I speak not of murder, but of bringing the ungodly and the traitorous to just punishment."

"Well, I will use you if I can, but you must tell me more. Where is this Mr. Harford?"

"This very morning he yielded to the entreaty of the Vicar of Bosbury and spared the Popish cross in the churchyard. I vowed in my heart that he should suffer for that treachery, and, concealing myself, I heard all that passed later betwixt him and Mistress Hilary."

"What did the fair lady say to him?"

"Why, she was just a second Eve, leading him on, and then the next minute sorely paining him; but methinks she hath a liking for him all the same, and left him some hope."

"Hope of winning her?"

"That, doubtless, would follow: but what he urged on her was to walk warily with respect to you, sir."

"What! Did my name pass betwixt them?"

Waghorn smiled grimly. "Ay, verily; and he plainly told her what you are, sir."

"The devil he did! Pray, where can I find him?"

"He'll be back at Ledbury by now, and I heard him say that he was to be sent off with important despatches to Sir Thomas Fairfax at Windsor."

"You heard that?" cried Norton. "By the Lord Harry! we have him then! Waghorn, you are worth your weight in gold. Dog this fellow's steps for me, have him waylaid with the despatches on him, and you may ask what you will of me. Ha, ha! We'll have some sport with this outspoken young fool! He plainly told Mistress Hilary what I am, did he? I'll be revenged on him for that, the prating, Puritanical marplot!"

"Only give me your orders, sir, and trust me he shall not escape. The ungodly shall be trapped in the work of his own hands!" said Waghorn, rubbing his hands with satisfaction.

Norton laughed. "Take care you don't get trapped, Waghorn; you are not exactly what I should call a godly man yourself! A good deal of the old Adam in your thirst for vengeance, isn't there?"

"Sir, Captain Harford hath treacherously spared a Popish idol, and he hath baulked me, although it was through my zeal and love for the truth that the Parliament soldiers were marched out from Ledbury for the pious work of destruction."

"'Tis not pleasant to be baulked, I grant you," said Norton, his eyes still twinkling. "But avenge yourself, and you'll avenge me. How soon can you be in Ledbury?"

"As soon as this job is done, sir, and that will not be long."

"Good! Let me know how you prosper, and see—you may be put to some charge in the town; so take this crown piece, and the devil send you luck!"

In high good humour at the prospect of getting Gabriel Harford into his power, the Colonel left the room, and Waghorn, having completed his work, packed up his tools and returned to Bosbury.

On the road he encountered the Vicar and his niece, for Hilary, ill at ease after her talk with Gabriel, had determined to seek advice from the motherly Dame Elizabeth, while the Vicar was anxious to see Sir Richard Hopton, and to congratulate him on his recent release from prison.

Fortune favoured the girl, for they encountered not only Sir Richard in the courtyard, but Mr. Geers, who had ridden over from Garnons to bring tidings of Frances and her sister, and to learn how Sir Richard fared. The gentlemen remained without, chatting together, and Hilary was ushered into the house, where, in the ante-room which Waghorn had just quitted, she found Dame Elizabeth, a stately, white-haired old lady, with kind far-seeing eyes.

Greeting her visitor warmly, she made her sit on a stool beside her, lamenting that Frances was still absent.

"In truth, dear madam, though it sounds unfriendly, I am glad she is not here," said Hilary; "for I greatly want your help and counsel."

"Now that is always a pleasant thing to hear," said Dame Elizabeth, smiling. "There are many drawbacks to growing old, but the best part is that the maidens and the young matrons come to us with their joys and their sorrows."

"They do well to come to you, dear madam, for you always understand so well. How the Queen can lay bare her heart to a priest is to me passing strange. But in sore need one might come to a mother-confessor."

"What is your trouble, dear child?" said Dame Elizabeth, kindly. "How can I help you?"

"It all comes from this sad war," said Hilary, with a sigh.

"In truth it hath brought sorrow to every home," said Dame Elizabeth. "Think what it means for us to have one son fighting for the King and two for the Parliament! I love them alike, and there is never a moment's ease or relief."

"But you can rightly love all your sons, madam. My case is different. I—I am half ashamed to tell you how it is with me," faltered Hilary, drooping her head.

"Perchance I can guess," said Dame Elizabeth, caressing her. "Methinks, child, you do not know your own heart."

"That is the very truth," said Hilary, blushing, and lowering her voice. "This morning I thought—I fancied—that a loyal King's officer had the chief place there; and now—now—I am half afraid that all the time my heart has been harbouring a rebel."

"Try to forget their opinions, and think of them only as men. Believe me, child, love has naught to do with matters of State."

"That is what Gabriel Harford always said—we were betrothed before the war began."

"And then, I suppose, you quarrelled."

"Yes—we—parted. I vowed I would never wed a man who was not loyal, and he protested that loyalty meant faithfulness to law."

"'Tis what my sons said, too. The King had unlawfully imprisoned, unlawfully taxed and unlawfully governed without a Parliament for eleven years, and they said they must defend the ancient liberties of England. Tell me of this other lover, child."

"Gabriel thinks him unfit to speak to me, and says that the Royalists themselves blame his way of life."

"Have you known him long?"

"Not very long. But to Uncle Coke and to me he hath been all that is kind. I wish you would tell me the truth about him, dear madam."

"Surely it is not possible that you mean Colonel Norton? Hath he dared to force himself upon you?"

"Why, he hath shown great attention to my uncle, and is ever bringing him rare antiquities that greatly please him, and many and many a time I have talked with him."

"Oh, child! you are too inexperienced. I know Colonel Norton, for the officers of the Canon Frome garrison live here at free quarters. Have no more to do with him, Hilary, for, believe me, he is cruel and dissolute. At this very time, Sir Richard is writing to beg for the appointment of some other governor, and I am writing of our grievances to our kinsman, Lord Hopton, the noblest of all the King's generals."

"Were we, then, so deceived in Colonel Norton? I know that I am ignorant enough, but Uncle Coke——"

"My dear, the Vicar of Bosbury is the most genial and kind-hearted gentleman, and very slow to suspect that all men are not of a like disposition. You must warn him—you can tell him of our talk."

"He ought to know, but, oh, dear madam! I cannot tell him," said Hilary, blushing to the roots of her hair. "Why, only this morning I fancied—oh!" she cried, springing to her feet in a burst of indignation, "how dared that man trifle with me!—how dared he!"

"The best plan will be for me to say a word to Mr. Geers, he is your uncle's friend, and he knows more of Colonel Norton than Sir Richard doth. Do not grieve your heart any more, my child," said Dame Elizabeth, embracing her. "Stay to supper, and I will arrange matters for you. And as for Mr. Harford, remember this, 'tis not a man's opinions that make him a good husband, but his life and character."

With great tact, the hostess contrived in a few words to tell Mr. Geers the state of affairs, and the good-natured owner of Garnons undertook, in his cordial, friendly way, to talk matters over with the Vicar.

"It seems that I am predestined to plead the cause of my rival, the grapegulper," he reflected, with a smile. "But I can do it this time with even more zeal than when I talked years ago with the Bishop, being myself an excellent example of the happy married man. Both for the sake of Mrs. Jefferies' godson and of the pretty maid that rejected my suit, I will do my best to open the eyes of my friend the antiquary."

CHAPTER XXXVIII.

We wait beneath the furnace-blast

The pangs of transformation,

Not painlessly doth God re-cast

And mould anew the nation.

Hot burns the fire

Where wrongs expire;

Nor spares the hand

That from the land

Uproots the ancient evil.

—Whittier.

On returning to Ledbury, Gabriel seized the opportunity of writing to his father, begging that, if possible, he might see him before he left the neighbourhood; and by the time he had found a messenger to despatch to Hereford, Massey had returned from reconnoitring the surrounding country. The Governor of Gloucester was in excellent spirits, for he had reason to believe that Prince Rupert, having learnt of his arrival at Ledbury, had halted in his march to join the King, and would probably return and give him battle.

"I only wish it were possible to fortify this town," he remarked as he and his officers supped at the 'Feathers,' "but it is out of the question."

"Do you think we shall have a night attack, sir?" asked Gabriel.

"'Tis possible, for Prince Rupert ever loves that device. Yet he could scarce be here to-night. Some of the men had best, however, bivouac in the High Street: your detachment has had light work to-day, Captain Harford, and shall be told off for this under Captain Bayly; I may need you anon for the work of which we spoke."

"In truth the men have had lighter work than we thought for, sir," said Gabriel, "for the desire to pull down Bosbury Cross seemed to be only on the part of that fanatic Waghorn, and the Vicar pleaded for it with such excellent good arguments that, under certain conditions, I gave leave that it should be spared. I think, had you been there you would have done the same, sir, and I trust you don't disapprove of what I did."

Massey laughed good-humouredly. "If you choose to incur the wrath of that mad fellow 'tis no affair of mine," he said. "And now I think of it, the Vicar of Bosbury was a sensible and kindly man."

"Ay, and hospitable," said Captain Bayly. "He gave us a good supper when we halted last winter at Bosbury. There was a pretty niece, too, I remember."

This remark brought upon Gabriel much laughter and raillery, which he took in good part.

"Were you not there with one of the Hoptons?" he asked.

"Ay, to be sure, the younger one, that tried to defend Castle, Ditch near Eastnor. He was worsted, and thrown into gaol at Hereford, but managed to escape by leaping a wall, and rejoined us at Gloucester. I don't know where he is serving now."

Supper being ended Massey retired to finish his despatches, and Gabriel had orders to supervise the barricading of the streets with carts, which kept the men hard at work throughout the evening.

The moon had risen, and the picturesque High Street with its gabled black and white houses would have looked like a place in fairyland had it not been for the grim preparations for defence and for the busy soldiers moving to and fro, some carrying torches which threw a fitful glare over the scene and made the bright helmets and gorgets glitter. Everyone was far too hard at work to notice the silent spectator who, wrapped in a long cloak and a hood of the sort much worn by aged men, noiselessly shadowed Captain Harford wherever he went.

Waghorn's hatred only increased when he saw how remarkably active in the cause Gabriel could be, how swiftly the orders he shouted were carried out, and what an excellent officer he made. It was impossible to conceive one more in touch with his men, and the fanatic gnashed his teeth when he reflected that one authoritative word from this young fellow of two or three and twenty would have been sufficient to level the cross with the ground.

By the time all was in readiness it was growing late, and Gabriel and his successor, Captain Bayly, walked down the High Street to the "Feathers," at the door of which Massey lounged smoking his pipe.

"Bid them sound the bugle for the evening psalm," he said, as the two officers joined him. "The men had best sleep while they may."

As the bugle rang through the little town and the men assembled in front of the market-house, Waghorn, stepping forward like a bent and aged man, stealthily approached Gabriel.

"Now will this sparer of crosses join in a psalm with the godly," he reflected, wrathfully. "Let his days be few! Even in the midst of his sin shall he be stricken!"

Little dreaming that one of his worst foes stood close behind him, Gabriel joined with rather a heavy heart in the psalm which seemed to haunt him at every crisis in his life. Standing now in the street at Ledbury with the manly voices of the soldiers ringing out into the night, he remembered how the same words

In trouble and adversity

The Lord God hear thee still

had strengthened him as he stood waiting for the first attack at Edgehill; how in the Cathedral long ago with his eyes on Hilary's pale face, the same words had fallen on his ears, and how in the porch at Bosbury the psalm had on this very day been to them a bond of union. No thought of personal danger came to him now, though Waghorn's cloak brushed his sleeve. It was of Hilary he thought, and of the peril that threatened her.

At the close of the psalm the bugle sounded the "Last post," and such of the men as had quarters marched off; those who were to bivouac in the street scattering into groups about the market-house, and a detachment moving torch in hand to the upper end of the town where four ways met.

Massey invited Gabriel and Captain Bayly to have a cup of mulled claret with him at the "Feathers."

"Well, sir, if you will pardon me," said Gabriel, who longed to be alone, "I will ask to be excused. Truth to tell, I am dog-tired, and would fain sleep."

Massey slapped him on the shoulder with a laugh.

"Art sick, or in love? Eh? Beshrew me, but I believe you did leave your heart at Bosbury to-day. I'll be with you anon, Bayly."

Then, drawing Gabriel aside, he moved with him to the further end of the market-house just at the corner of the narrow alley which led steeply up to the church. Against the pale moonlit sky they could see the dark outline of the spire betwixt the gables of the houses.

"I have written both despatches," he said, in a low voice, "and as we can't tell what the next four-and-twenty hours will bring forth I will give them now into your keeping, yet do not start until you can bear tidings of Prince Rupert's doings."

"I may take part in the battle, sir?" asked Gabriel.

"Yes, if you are minded to volunteer. I will give you word when you had best go. And remember this: a despatch-bearer needs something more than mere courage. He needs dexterity, diplomacy and caution. If I cannot get speech with you, and the fighting goes against us, lose no time in escaping and make whatever circuit you deem best to reach Windsor in safety. I' faith, I think we have no eyes upon us now in the dark alley, and at the 'Feathers' we are over-tightly packed for privacy. Stow these safely away, and give the Commander-in-Chief all the details I am unable to set down. But at all costs see that both despatches are delivered. More hangs on it than you wot of."

Under the shelter of their military cloaks the transfer of the despatches was easily effected, and Gabriel thrust them into the inner pocket of his coat.

"I will guard them with my life, sir," he said, in a low voice. "And I thank you for trusting me with the work."

Massey laughed.

"Small matter for thanks! 'Tis ever a risky and troublesome business. Well, good-night to you, Captain. May your affair of love prosper!"

"Good-night, sir," said Gabriel, forcing a laugh, as he paced slowly up the narrow alley.

Alas! was it not a very one-sided affair of love? he thought to himself, with a sigh. If for a moment he ventured to hope that Hilary still cared for him, the next he remembered with a pang the way in which she had permitted Norton to dangle about her. He wondered, uneasily, what the Vicar could be dreaming of to allow it. Dr. Coke had seemed a shrewd as well as a generous man, yet had evidently no notion that the Governor of Canon Frome was playing the mischief in his very household. And then he remembered how plausible and fascinating Norton could be, recollected, too, that strange glimpse of a noble nature which he had now and then seen in him, and realised that very probably the Vicar and Hilary only knew the Colonel at his very best.

A storm of despair swept over him as more and more plainly he saw the great danger which threatened her.

"'Tis enough to madden a man!" he said to himself, writhing at the sense of his powerlessness to help. "It may be months or years ere I see her again, while all the time Norton can prowl round in his devilish fashion! Yet, if I rave like this, I shall lose all control over myself. After all, she gave me her promise to speak—I know she will keep her promise."

The thought calmed him, and, pausing at the head of the alley, he stood for a minute praying silently in his usual brief, formless, but thoroughly heartfelt way, "God of Justice! grant her Thy help and guidance, and keep us from all evil this night."

The wind blew softly down the narrow alley, the dark spire pointed silently towards heaven, and in the stillness the soul of the Puritan grew once more strong and undaunted.

As he paced back again to the High street he did not notice the dark figure standing in the shade of a doorway, but in the manner of one well used to bivouacking for the night he laid his sword on the ground, put his helmet and gorget in place of a pillow, and, with his military cloak wrapped about him, was soon sleeping soundly in one of the shallow recesses betwixt the wooden posts on which the market-house was raised.

At some little distance a sentry paced to and fro; Waghorn, watching his movements with a keen and wary eye, waited patiently in his sheltered nook until he was assured that all the soldiers slept. Then seizing his opportunity as the sentry marched back to the farthest point of his beat, he glided noiselessly out of the shadow, heartening himself with fierce inward ejaculations.

"Let destruction come upon him at unawares! I dread that sentinel. But courage! I will remember Jael, the wife of Heber, the Kenite, and my part is not to slay, merely to filch!"

Crouching down beside Gabriel he saw that he slept profoundly. In the cold clear moonlight it was easy to trace marks of care and suffering in the face, and, as the fanatic stealthily unbuttoned the coat, he reflected with grim satisfaction that worse would be in store for the sleeper when he woke.

Just then, to his dismay, he heard the footsteps of the sentry drawing steadily nearer, and hastily stretching himself out beside his victim he lay motionless until the danger was past and the footsteps were once more retreating.

Then in trembling haste he partly raised himself, thrust his hand with the control and caution that he had acquired in his wood-carving within the pocket of the buff coat, and had actually got hold of the despatches when the barking of a dog in a neighbouring house roused Gabriel.

"Hullo!" he cried, sitting up and gripping Waghorn by the arm. "What are you about, fellow?"

Waghorn in vain tried to escape; he was held as in a vice. Fortunately for him his face was in shadow, and he was completely disguised by his cloak and hood. With ready tact he began to whimper and moan like one half-witted.

"'Tis naught but daft Lubin, sir; naught but daft Lubin," he pleaded.

"Daft Lubin, indeed!" said Gabriel, impatiently. "I should think you were daft to wake up a tired man in the dead of night. Ho! sentry! call the guard and let this crazy fellow be taken up, or he'll be disturbing the men again."

Waghorn whimpering, struggling and protesting all the way up the street that he was "naught but daft Lubin," was remorselessly hurried away by the guard.

Yawning and shivering with the discomfort of one roused in his first sleep, Gabriel stretched his stiff limbs.

"What was the row?" muttered Captain Bayly, drowsily.

"Naught but an old half-witted beggar," said Gabriel. Then suddenly noticing that his coat was unbuttoned, he felt in consternation for the packet, and gave an ejaculation of relief on finding the despatches safe.

"The night grows cold," said the other, wrapping his cloak more closely about him.

"'Tis naught to some of the nights we had in Waller's time," said Gabriel. "He took no heed of frost or damp, though now and again he was sorry for the horses."

With another prolonged yawn he stretched himself out face downwards, and was soon once more wrapped in profound sleep.

Towards morning he had a curiously vivid dream. He thought he was swimming across a blood-red lake, and he knew that he bore despatches which should warn Cromwell of a dastardly attempt about to be made on his life. He had nearly gained the shore when the dark hull of a boat loomed into sight, and Norton leaned over the bows with a mocking smile on his lips and dealt him a blow which sent him down—gaspingly down—through the red depths. Yet he rose again to the surface, and flung the despatches with a last dying effort to the shore; and when for the second time he rose, the packet was being lifted from the ground by his father. Then he finally sank and was vainly fighting for breath when a bugle sounded "To arms!"

He sprang up instantly on the alert; the red light heralding the sunrise suffused Ledbury, drums beat the alarm, the guard shouted, "To arms! to arms!" and Massey's soldiers came pouring out of their night quarters in every direction. In two minutes Gabriel was in the stable saddling Harkaway with his own hands, and learning with a thrill of excitement that Prince Rupert, by a forced march through the night, was now close to the town, and was resolved to give them battle.

Colonel Massey, in excellent spirits, came riding out of the courtyard of the "Feathers," and rapidly gave directions to his officers. To Captain Bayly fell the work of defending the market-house and the entrance to Church-alley, and soon from the upper end of the town came sounds of incessant firing, and the hoarse cry of the contending watchwords, "St. George!" and "Queen Mary!" from the Royalists, and "God with us!" from the Parliament soldiers. The chief barricade higher up the street kept the Prince's troops at bay for some time, but in the meanwhile an attempt was made by a detachment of the Royalists to enter the town by Church-alley at right angles with the High Street, and some sharp skirmishing took place there, in which Gabriel bore a part.

Scarcely had they beaten back the attack from this quarter when shouts and uproar warned them that the main barricade had been broken down after a resistance of about half-an-hour. This opened the High Street for the Prince's horse to charge, and though Massey made a gallant counter-charge and his men fought bravely, they were borne down. Rallying for a time by the market-house, he endeavoured to protect the retreat of his foot, and signing to Gabriel to approach, spoke a few hurried words to him.

"Seize your chance now," he said, "and ride off. With a circuit you should be able to bear them safely. We shall charge again and fall back in good order on Gloucester."

Without further delay he urged his men forward against the approaching Royalists. And Gabriel obediently, but with not unnatural reluctance, turned Harkaway's head in the opposite direction, and was about to ride from the town when a loud outcry made him glance to the right.

Down Church-alley rode once more a detachment of Prince Rupert's men, and he saw the figure of "daft Lubin" wildly accosting the leader, and heard him shout the words: "Fire on yon officer! He bears despatches! Fire in the King's name!"

Urging on Harkaway, Gabriel rode like the wind. A sudden crash and a numbness which made the reins fall from his left hand and his arm drop powerless at his side warned him that a ball had struck him; for a moment his eyesight threatened to fail him, but with an effort he recovered himself, gathered up the reins in his right hand and set spurs to his horse.

Waghorn at the corner of the alley stood staring after him in blank astonishment.

"Curse him! how can he ride after that?" he exclaimed. "Ha! he reels in the saddle! Fire again, men! fire again! Now he clings to the horse's neck—he must fall—he is ours! he is ours! Evil shall hunt the wicked person to overthrow him!"

At that instant one of the Prince's troopers, finding his way blocked by the fanatic, pushed roughly past.

"Out of the way, you prating Puritan!" he cried, "or I'll dash your brains out!" And with that he dealt Waghorn a blow on the head which left him groaning on the ground.

CHAPTER XXXIX.

One loving howre

For many years of sorrow can dispence;

A dram of sweete is worth a pound of sowre.

. . . true is, that true love hath no powre,

To looken backe; his eyes be fixt before.

—Spenser.

Meanwhile Massey, with great coolness and ability, retreated in good order with the remainder of his men to Gloucester, but many had been made prisoners, and about a hundred and twenty had been killed in the street and in the hot pursuit.

Had it not been for Waghorn's words to the Royalists, Gabriel might have made his escape as easily as the Governor of Gloucester had anticipated. But, learning that important despatches were so nearly within their reach, some four or five troopers gave chase to him with a heat and determination that only increased with each mile traversed. Bullets whistled about his ears, but on he sped, every nerve strained in the wild excitement of the ride, all pain for the time overcome by the intense desire to carry out his task.

A second ball struck the already injured arm, making a ghastly flesh wound. Still he galloped on, but, alas! with the horrible consciousness that his pursuers were gaining on him.

His strength was fast failing when the sound of church bells fell on his ear; surely they were the bells of Bosbury? Hardly conscious of the direction he had taken, only galloping madly across country to baffle his pursuers, he had indeed approached within a short distance of the village, which lay in the valley below embosomed in trees.

For the time being he was out of sight of the Royalist troopers, and, with a word to Harkaway, he put the horse at a hedge which seemed a little off the course he had ridden.

The horse did his part gallantly, and alighted in a field which sloped steeply down to a tiny brook, but the agony of the leap was too much for the rider. With a stifled groan he fell to the ground, and Harkaway, not understanding his grievous plight, but thankful to find the desperate gallop at an end, unconsciously served his master by going quietly down to drink at the brook.

The pursuers were puzzled at suddenly losing all trace of the despatch-bearer. They paused to listen, but no sound of distant horse-hoofs fell upon their ear, only somewhat further on they could hear children's voices. Riding forward, they came into sight of an orchard in which two little girls with their skipping-ropes were playing on the daisy-flecked grass. As they skipped they sang an old May-pole song, their childish voices rising high and clear in the country quiet:

Come, ye young men, come along,

With your music, dance and song;

Bring your lasses in your hands,

For 'tis that which love commands.

Then to the May-pole haste away,

For 'tis now a holiday.

It is the choice time of the year,

For the violets now appear;

Now the rose receives its birth,

And pretty primrose decks the earth.

Then to the May-pole haste away,

For 'tis now a holiday.

Suddenly they broke off, and the elder child cried out: "Look! Look, Meg. There be soldiers yonder."

"Three, four, five of them!" said the little one, counting with keen interest.

"And two of them have left their horses and be coming this way," said Nan. "See their red ribbons; they be King's soldiers."

"Oh, Nan, I'm frightened! They said they would hang the boys and drown the girls!" cried Meg, clinging to her sister.

"That was because the children of Broxash sang

If you offer to plunder, or take our cattle,

Be assured we will bid you battle.'"

said Nan, reassuringly. "We were only singing the May-pole song."

Nevertheless her eyes grew large with fright as the soldier approached.

"Here, you brats!" he shouted. "Have you seen a Puritan officer gallop by this way?"

"No, we have been skipping," she replied, sturdily.

"A wounded man on a bay horse."

"We have not seen him—he hath not been here," said Nan.

"Curse him! What a dance he hath led us! How a man that's been twice hit can ride across country that fashion, beats me. The devil must be in him. Come, mate, we must to horse again, and push on—the plaguey fellow shan't give us the slip."

They hastened back to rejoin their comrades, and Nan looked wistfully after them.

"I hope they won't find him," she said, shivering. "If they do they'll kill him."

"I'm glad we're not men," said Meg, picking up her skipping-rope. "We shall never have to kill folk."

By this time Gabriel had recovered his senses, and the sight of the Malvern Hills roused him to the remembrance that he was near Bosbury; with a vague idea of getting Hilary to bind up his wounds for him, and then of somehow reaching his father, he staggered to his feet, hoping to find Harkaway at no great distance. The horse, however, was nowhere to be seen, and, with faltering steps, he made his way with great difficulty across the field to a gap which he saw in the hedge. The children's voices reached him, and helped him to persevere.

"Here each bachelor may choose

One that will not faith abuse,

Nor repay with coy disdain

Love that should be loved again."

It was the same maypole song that he had listened to years ago at Bosbury just after their betrothal.

Utterly spent with pain and loss of blood, the effort of making his way through the gap in the hedge proved more than flesh could bear.

"'Tis no use—no use!" he thought, despairingly as he entered the orchard. "I can't go another step! My God! Must I be so near to Hilary, and yet die like a dog in a ditch?" He reeled back, and, with a groan, fell senseless to the ground, to the horror and dismay of the children, who dropped their skipping-ropes and fled in terror.

"The Puritan!" they screamed; "he has fallen down dead!" But before very long curiosity conquered terror; they stole back hand-in-hand, and gazed at him with awe-struck faces.

"He looks as if he were asleep," said little Meg.

"That's how folks do look," explained Nan, "just asleep, you know. But all the time they're really awake up in the sky."

"Wondering, perhaps, why we don't understand," said Meg, dreamily.

"Oh, see!" cried Nan, in great excitement, "he's down here still, he's not dead. His hand is moving!"

Gabriel tried to get up, but fell back again.

"Oh! what hellish pain!" he moaned.

"What can we do for you, sir?" said Nan.

"Who is it?" he asked, looking up in a dazed way. "Where?"

"We be Farmer Chadd's children, sir, and this is our orchard nigh to Bosbury," replied the little girl.

"How far from Bosbury?"

"'Tis but a little way across the hop-yards, sir."

"If I could see Hilary before I die!" he muttered. "I will see her! I will see her! What became of Harkaway? Children, do you see a riderless horse near?"

They ran off and soon returned with beaming faces.

"There be a strange horse down by the brook," said Nan. "A bay with two white feet."

"He is gentle enough; could you bring him here for me? I am sorely hurt."

They gladly promised and ran down the sloping field, leaving Gabriel in a curious borderland of semi-consciousness.

"I shall remember it all if I try," he reflected. "My head is getting clearer. There was something I had to do! What on earth was it? Massey trusted me with something. If the Prince overpowered him I was to go—where? This agony makes all else a blank! I shall be no better than that daft vagabond who woke me last night. Ha! the despatches! I remember all now!"

With intense anxiety he felt for them. They were bloodstained but safe, and exhausted with the effort of concealing them once more, he sank back in a dead faint.

Now it chanced that on this Wednesday morning the Litany being ended, Dr. Coke and Hilary left the church and went to see Farmer Chadd, who was in great distress because his horses had been seized by the Canon Frome garrison. They were talking to him in the farmyard when his two little daughters came running up to beg his help.

"There's a horse, father, down by the brook," they explained breathlessly, "and the wounded Puritan officer in the orchard asked us to fetch it, but it won't let us come near."

"A Puritan officer? One of the fugitives from Ledbury, I reckon," said Farmer Chadd.

"He is wounded, do you say, child?" asked the Vicar.

"Ay, sir," said Nan, dropping a curtsey. "Wounded and well-nigh dead."

"I wish you would stable the horse and say naught about it in the village, Chadd, as likely as not the poor fellow will be haled to prison if the Canon Frome folk hear of this," said Dr. Coke.

"I'd do aught that would go against them" said the farmer, thinking wrathfully of the looting and plundering he had had to endure.

"I will give help to the officer, then, and you will put up the horse," said the Vicar. "Come, children, show us where this poor Puritan lies."

Hilary, with a horrible presentiment of coming sorrow, hastened across the orchard, and, with a low cry, knelt down on the grass beside the wounded man.

"Uncle," she said, looking up with wild eyes, "see who it is!"

"Poor boy! poor boy!" said the Vicar, with deep concern. "What a change since yesterday, when he stood bold and strong at the head of his soldiers. He has swooned. Help me, dear, to remove his armour."

Hilary obeyed, and, giving the helmet to Nan and Meg, asked them to fetch water from the brook. The Vicar, who had some little knowledge of surgery, managed, for the time, to staunch the wounds, and, presently, feeling a woman's soft fingers at his throat unfastening his gorget, Gabriel regained consciousness, and lay watching the sweet, grave face which bent over him.

"Hilary!" he said, faintly. "Thank God! Now I can die in peace!"

"No, no," she said, smoothing back the hair from his forehead. "You must live, Gabriel, I—we—cannot spare you. Uncle Coke is half a leech, he will bind up your wounds."

The Vicar gave a rueful smile. "I may be half a leech, but I'm not a whole conjuror, and can't make a couple of handkerchiefs into bandages that will serve. No, Hilary, you must get me some linen from Mrs. Chadd. Here come the children with the water; take them with you."

The Vicar went to rescue the helmet full of water which Nan in her haste was spilling by the way, and Hilary bent over her lover.

"I will be back again very soon, Gabriel; promise not to move rashly. I wish I need not leave you—I can't bear to go."

He raised her hand to his lips. "What a nightmare these years of war have been! If we could but wake and forget them!" he said, with a tired sigh.

But before anything further could be said the Vicar interposed, cheerfully, "Come, my dear, the children will help to carry the things, and not even Prince Rupert's Protestation forbids me to obey the commandment and give a thirsty enemy a cup of water to drink."

While Hilary and the children ran to the farm he held the helmet to the wounded man's lips.

Gabriel drank thirstily. "If you have signed the Protestation, sir, the less you have to do with me the better," he said, reviving a little.

"I have not signed it," said the Vicar, sturdily, "and I have every intention of taking you to my house that you may be properly tended."

"Sir, indeed I dare not let you run such a risk; if aught should befall you what would become of Hilary?" said Gabriel, his eyes full of anxiety.

"You are right to think of her; you two were old friends at Hereford."

"More than friends—we were betrothed before this war divided us."

"Yet, did we not agree yesterday when you spared Bosbury Cross that, spite of the war, there was one bond which still united us?"

"You would not object to my suit?" said Gabriel, eagerly.

"On the contrary, I should welcome it. The friendship betwixt the Harfords and the Unetts is a two generation friendship, and truth to tell, I have just learnt that my niece is in some danger from the attentions of Colonel Norton—a man in whom I have been much deceived."

Gabriel lay musing for a minute, then asked abruptly—"How soon could I be fit to ride, sir?"

"It will be a matter of a month at least," said the Vicar.

"Surely, I could ride as far as Hereford—to my father?"

"Nay, 'tis out of the question. Oh, we will hide you safely somehow. Hilary hath a ready wit and will doubtless hit on some device."

"If I could but have speech with my father," said Gabriel, restlessly.

"Well, I could myself ride over for him, and he could dress your wounds," suggested the Vicar.

With an effort Gabriel rallied his failing powers.

"I will be true with you," he said, firmly. "'Tis not for that I would see him, but I bear despatches to Fairfax and Cromwell, and am in honour bound to see them in safe hands."

"Despatches!" exclaimed the Vicar with a troubled look. "This is a grave matter. Yet 'twas honest of you to tell me. I think I might at least bring your father to-night to see you."

"And should I die ere he comes—promise to give them to him," said Gabriel, pleadingly. "Dying folk must often have asked your aid, Vicar. I ask that—nothing but that?"

"Now, may God forgive me if I do amiss," muttered the Vicar. Then, turning to meet the eager hazel eyes which watched him so intently, "I promise you, my poor boy. Be at rest."

After this Gabriel lay with closed eyes until he heard Hilary's voice.

"I fear we have seemed long," she said, "and you are suffering so much."

He smiled. "Not now," he replied, reviving for a while from sheer happiness in the change that had come over her.

"You little folk run over and play under the apple trees," said the Vicar to Nan and Meg, "while I tend my patient."

And with Hilary's help he rapidly bound up the wounds in a somewhat rough and ready fashion, and put the arm in a sling.

"Captain Harford has told me much, my dear, while you have been gone," he remarked. "Do you feel disposed to take on you the duties of nurse?"

Hilary blushed and glanced shyly at her lover. "Yes," she replied. "Where can we best shelter Gabriel?"

"He thinks that his presence at the Vicarage could not be hid from the villagers. We must not risk awakening Colonel Norton's suspicions."

"Uncle! Why should we not use the room in the Church tower? The bell-ringers never go up the steps. No one but Zachary ever goes, and Zachary must be taken into the secret."

"'Tis well thought of, child; Captain Harford would be safe enough there if we can once carry him up unseen."

"Why should you not give out that you mean to use the tower room for your antiquities?"

"You can truthfully say that you are making a study of bones," said Gabriel, smiling in the midst of his pain.

"The notion is not amiss, but yet it will be hard to take him there in broad daylight," said the Vicar, securing the last bandage.

Hilary's face lighted up. "Why," she cried, eagerly, "you and Zachary might carry him in a hop-pocket? If you go by way of the hop-yards you would scarce be likely to meet a soul, and if you did, 'tis easily explained that you are carrying something you have just discovered. The villagers will only think 'tis what Mrs. Durdle calls one of Parson's 'antics.'"

The Vicar turned with a smile to Gabriel. "Did I not tell you she would hit on some device? But before I go I will help you to move to the other side of the hedge, for there is a right of way through this orchard to Ledbury, and you had best not risk being seen."

"The pursuit was hot, but I think it must be over by now," said Gabriel, allowing himself to be helped to a place where he was sheltered from the orchard by an elm tree and a low hedge.

"There! now don't stir till I return," said the Vicar. "I will go home and bid Mrs. Durdle prepare the room, and bring Zachary back with me, as soon as may be. And you little people, let Mistress Hilary know if anyone comes in sight."

"Ay, sir," said the children, curtseying.

"You are like two good little watchmen," he added, smiling and patting their heads. "See that you don't fall asleep at your posts, for the sun is hot. Now,"—he thought to himself with a humorous gleam in his eyes—"if Hilary and her lover do not patch up their ancient quarrel I shall wish I had sent her on this errand instead of going myself."

CHAPTER XL.

"Duelling, in this country at least, is no longer legal, and we believe that war, which has been aptly styled international duelling, is alike doomed.. . . It is certain that the time must assuredly come (for is not this the darkness before the dawn?), and it will be probably sooner than we can conceive, when there will be a tremendous upheaval and revulsion of feeling with regard to it." —J. J. Green.

For some little time Gabriel lay back in perfect silence against the grassy bank, and, spite of the acute pain he was in, he nevertheless felt ready to echo the children's chorus which floated to them from beneath the apple trees—For it is now a holiday.

Hilary sat on the grass beside him, and from time to time he opened his eyes to watch the tender womanly hand as it ministered to his needs, or to look into the sweet face, as it bent over him. He realised, too, with a happy sense of homecoming, that he was indeed in his native county every time he caught sight of the lovely Malvern Hills which, in the morning light, seemed to take all the hues to be seen on a pigeon's neck, and formed a fitting background for Hilary's rare beauty.

"Ought I to let you do all this for a 'friendly foe'?" he said, looking up at her with a hint of the old mirth in his eyes.

"Forget what I said yesterday, Gabriel. I did not mean half of it," she said, blushing.

"I knew you meant to keep your promise—that was my sole comfort last night at Ledbury," he replied, with a sigh.

Hilary continued nervously, but yet with no little force: "I went that very afternoon to see Dame Elizabeth, and you were right, it was just as you said. Oh! I hope I may never again see the false face that deceived me."

"God grant you never may!" said Gabriel. And then a silence fell between them, and the merry talk of the children could be heard.

Hilary mused sadly over her shortcomings, but presently, noticing a change in her lover's face, gave an exclamation of dismay.

"Gabriel! how white your lips are growing! Is the pain so great?"

"'Tis very bearable while you are near," he said, his eyes resting on her with indescribable tenderness. "I was thinking how love can lift one out of all that is worst in the world."

She instantly responded to his thought as in the first days of their betrothal. "'Tis stronger than war, or differing views," she said, gently.

"Ay, or death," he replied.

"Don't talk of death!" she cried, shuddering. "Oh! when we heard of the battle this morning, and I remembered the cruel words I had spoken to you, I thought my heart would break."

"My beloved," he said. And in the strong emphasis of the word there seemed to lurk all the pent-up passion of the long years of separation.

For the first time since that September morning when they had talked in the garden at Hereford, before hearing of Powick fight, their lips met in a kiss that was like a sacrament, and each knew that nothing could ever again part them.

But their happiness was short-lived, for the children ran through the gap in the hedge, and Little Meg said, breathlessly, "Mistress Hilary! there be someone coming into the orchard."

"It looks like one of the officers from Canon Frome," said Nan, uneasily, her mind dwelling on cattle-lifting and plundering.

"What if it should be Norton!" said Gabriel, trying to get up.

"You must not show yourself," said Hilary, earnestly.

"All will be ruined if you are seen. Dear love, promise me, and then I shall have no fear."

"'Tis true I should be worse than no defence," said Gabriel, reluctantly.

Hilary hastily placed her cloak so as to screen him a little better from view, and made the children sit in the gap to block the way.

"Nan and Meg, you will not betray him, I know," she said.

"Sit there and weave daisy chains."

Glancing at the approaching figure, she saw that it was indeed Norton, and, anxious to prevent him from drawing too near to the hedge, she went forward to meet him. She wondered now how she could ever have been deceived by him, and hated herself for having allowed him for a moment to make her distrust Gabriel's love.

Norton's greeting was eager and full of charm.

"This is clearly a red-letter day in my calendar, Mistress Hilary. First, I have news of Prince Rupert's success at Ledbury, and then I have the crowning happiness of meeting you."

"'Tis indeed a fair morning," said Hilary. "You are doubtless going by the field-path to Ledbury to gain further tidings. I will not detain you. Good day, sir," and she curtseyed, hoping to dismiss him.

"Oh! I am in no haste; my horse has cast a shoe, and I have sent it on to Diggory, the smith. Prince Rupert is sure to pursue Massey most of the way to Gloucester, 'tis ever his failing to press the chase too far. I will rest awhile in this pleasant orchard."

Poor Hilary, only longing for him to go, felt that she was indeed being punished for having allowed him in former times to be too much with her.

"I wonder whether you have thought over what I said to you the day before yesterday," observed Norton, eagerly watching her.

"The day before yesterday," she said, with a puzzled look. "What happened then?"

"You are not complimentary," he replied, laughing. "Perhaps you have forgotten all about it. But I remember very well that I had the happiness of walking with you from the Hill Farm to the Vicarage, and of offering you——"

"Was that only the day before yesterday? To me it seems half a lifetime ago," said Hilary.

"You were not altogether kind to me; in fact, when we got to the Vicarage you followed Colonel Massey's example, and beat a hasty retreat."

She made a brave effort to divert him from the subject, observing with a smile: "And I am going to beg you, sir, not to follow the example of Prince Rupert; pray do not push the pursuit any further."

"Pardon me," said Norton more gravely, "but I have every intention of carrying it to a successful end. Don't you understand that I love you?"

"Sir, it is of no use," she replied. "I cannot listen to your suit. Pray, pray leave me."

"I will not leave you," he said, fiercely, "till I clearly understand why you are thus cold and indifferent."

"Sir, I have no love to give you," she said, with quiet dignity.

"Never mind that, my love is hot enough to serve for both."

"I do not want your love," she said, emphatically.

His eyes gleamed with an anger that made him look devilish.

"The meaning of which is, that you love another. Rumour spoke truly, and the young Parliamentary captain who spared Bosbury Cross—:—"

Hilary started, and a wave of colour suffused her face.

"You see I know all about it."

She remained quite silent, with drooped head.

"Do you love this Captain Harford? Speak—for I will know the truth!" he said, savagely.

Hilary raised her head. There was such suffering and pathos in her face that any man not the thrall of passion would have been touched. "Sir, all our lives we have loved each other. Oh! if you understood, you would be generous," she said.

"Why did you not tell me the truth on Monday?"

"Our betrothal had ended at the beginning of the war. I vowed I would not love a rebel. But yesterday, when we met again, I found that war was weaker than love, that it could not really part us."

"So you became disloyal to your King?"

"No, no; I shall always honour His Majesty; but in truth I can think of only one man in all the world, and that"—her face lighted up—"that is Gabriel Harford, for he is all the world to me. I have told you the whole truth, sir, and now, by your honour as a gentleman, I ask you to leave me."

"Shall I tell you what you have done?" said Norton, speaking low and rapidly. "You have made me all the more in love with you—all the more determined to win you. What is this Captain Harford? A mere boy, your old playmate, perchance a pleasant comrade, but wholly unfit to be your lord and master."

"Sir," she said, with a new dignity in her manner, "he is the man I love."

Norton muttered an impatient oath.

"Had he been of our party I might have left you to him with a good grace. But nothing shall make me yield to a miserable Roundhead, a strait-laced Puritan, who glories in self-control, and keeps a conscience on his premises. Much good may his conscience do him! I have him like a rat in a trap!"

The words almost paralysed her with terror. What did he know? What did he mean? Had he caught sight of Gabriel?

"And you!" cried Norton, passionately. "You are in my power. Do you understand that?"

Beside himself with wrath, Gabriel dragged himself up on to his knees and drew his sword from the scabbard. Meg and Nan glanced round at him uneasily; and Hilary, conscious of the movement though her back was turned to the hedge, grew desperate in her anxiety.

"No, no!" she panted. "You are too brave a man to take so base an advantage."

"Pshaw!" said Norton, sneeringly. "The man's a fool who neglects to use his advantages. You think only of the dear Puritan. You only fear what I may do to him. Well, I will confide in you. I have sent a trusty ambassador to Ledbury, and he is sure to make Captain Harford prisoner. Then, when he is in my power—well, there are many ways of exterminating rats—and rebels."

Hilary choked back a sob, and moved a few steps from the hedge.

"I am told," said Norton with a cruel smile, "that Sir Francis Doddington hung fourteen rebels at Andover t'other day. And elsewhere twelve of them were strung up to one apple-tree. We might hang Captain Harford from one of those apple-trees yonder; it would be a fitting death for a Herefordshire man."

With a wild hope of getting him out of the orchard she moved as though to go, trusting that he might follow. But Norton was too quick for her.

"Come! cheer up and don't be so silent," he said, throwing his arm round her waist. "We'll talk no more of the Puritan. Let us kiss and be friends."

"Don't touch me!" she cried, indignantly, wrenching herself from his embrace. "You are worse than a murderer."

Norton laughed mockingly.

"Now that was a foolish speech, for as I warned you, the game is in my hands."

"Thank God! there is someone coming," cried Hilary, catching sight of a man slowly approaching by the path from Ledbury, and running swiftly towards him. "Why, Waghorn! is it you?" she exclaimed, recognising the well-known face of the wood-carver beneath a bandage tied about his forehead. "You have little liking for us, but I know you will help me now."

"Mistress!" said Waghorn grimly, "I have a word to speak with yonder Governor of Canon Frome, and I cannot serve you."

Norton strode angrily towards him.

"A word to speak, indeed! What have you been about? Where is your prisoner?"

Hilary in great astonishment stood by, glancing from one to the other. Waghorn, then, had been the Colonel's ambassador! Had he suddenly turned Royalist, or was it merely to revenge himself on Gabriel that he had become a spy?

"Sir," said Waghorn, "I did all that you told me. Last night, having changed my outward man, I followed Captain Harford wherever he went in Ledbury. As the shadow followeth the wayfaring man when the sun shineth, so did I follow him. I saw Colonel Massey give him the despatches."

"Well! Well! did you take them?" asked Norton, impatiently.

Not heeding the interruption, Waghorn stolidly resumed his tale.

"He hid them in his buff coat and lay down to sleep by the market-house. I well-nigh took the packet from him, but a cur barked and he roused up, gripped me by the arm and called the guard."

"Idiot! I might have known that you would bungle the business. How was it you did not get him disabled in the skirmish instead of being knocked on the head yourself?"

"I adjured Prince Rupert's men to fire on him," said Waghorn, with solemn vindictiveness, "and the ball of the avenger entered into his arm; but he still galloped on, clinging to the neck of his steed. Then one of the ungodly clouted me on the head and I saw him no more."

His slow speech, and the failure of the enterprise irritated Norton past endurance.

Seizing him by the coat-collar, he gave him a sound shaking.

"You prating, pig-headed, sour-faced lunatic! I wish I had managed the matter myself. Did you not ask which way he rode? Was there no pursuit by the Prince's troopers?"

Waghorn groaned. "Mercy! Mercy! Oh, my head! My head! Remember I've a sore head."

"You've no head at all, you gaping fool, or you wouldn't have made such a cursed mess of this matter. Did you not ask, I say? Could no man give you news of him?"

Freeing himself and groaning as he adjusted his bandages, the wood-carver replied, sullenly, "I have news of him. When you will leave me time to speak, I will tell you all."

"Speak then," said Norton, impatiently.

"I am a righteous avenger," said Waghorn, with an air of offended dignity, "and, though thrice baulked, I will yet lay hands on the ungodly man that dallies with malignants, and doth not destroy graven images. 'Let his days be few, and let another take his office!'"

"Go to! You are not preaching on a tub, you fool, but speaking to a King's officer," said Norton, with an angry frown.

Waghorn continued deliberately. "When I could think of aught but my clouted head, I sought to pursue Captain Harford, asking from one and another if they had seen a wounded Parliament officer on a bay horse. At length I fell in with some troopers who vowed they had pursued him in this direction, but had lost all trace of him and were returning to Prince Rupert."

"They had seen him this way?" said Norton, musingly.

Waghorn turned his piercing eyes on Hilary and looked at her fixedly. She tried bravely to keep an unmoved face.

"Doubtless he had his reasons for riding towards Bosbury," said the spy, with scornful emphasis.

"A good notion," cried Norton. "After all, you have a head on your shoulders, Waghorn. Methinks the lady's face hath an anxious look."

"Sir," said Hilary, drawing herself up, "no maiden could listen to such words as you have forced me to hear to-day without showing some sign of anxiety."

Waghorn watched her with the eyes of a hawk, and his solemn voice broke the brief silence which had fallen upon them.

"I adjure you, Mistress, by all you hold most sacred, to speak the truth. Have you seen Captain Gabriel Harford?"

The girl breathed hard, but kept silence, gazing like one transfixed into Waghorn's keen eyes.

"Speak, Mistress," he repeated. "Have you seen Captain Gabriel Harford?"

"I saw him—yesterday," gasped Hilary.

"We know that. Have you seen him this morning?"

There was a minute's pause, while in agony she tried to see some way out of the dilemma. But way there was none.

"You have seen him?" urged Waghorn, merciless as any Inquisitor.

"Yes," she replied, a sob rising in her throat.

Norton, with fury in his eyes, stepped nearer to her.

"You dare to protect this rebel, and yet you knew that he carried despatches to the rebel army?"

Hilary bowed her head in assent, then turned away.

"When did you see him?" urged Norton, wrathfully.

She looked up, and her terrible distress was evident.

"I saw him—anon," she said, in a broken voice.

"How long ago?"

"A little while before you came," she faltered.

"Which way did he ride?" cried Norton, maddened at the thought that this girl was thwarting them and making them lose precious time. "Tell me at once."

Utter despair seized her.

"Oh!" she sobbed, "have pity on me!"

"Pity!" said Norton, savagely. "Have you pitied me? Tell me which way he went, or I'll——"

At this, Gabriel, driven desperate, struggled to his feet, but, turning faint, was forced for a while to lean against one of the hedge-row elms. The children, terrified by his movement and by the dispute in the orchard, dropped their daisy-chains and ran at full speed down the field, while the Colonel, becoming aware of a stir behind him, glanced round.

That was too much for Hilary. She sprang forward and diverted Norton's attention by pointing to the hills. Her voice was the voice of one goaded beyond all endurance.

"He rode yonder!" she cried, "to Malvern!"

Norton turned to the wood-carver. "Haste, Waghorn! Take word to my servant at the blacksmith's, and do you ride with him in pursuit. I have a word to say to this lady."

Waghorn was only too ready to undertake such congenial work, and the moment he was gone Norton seized Hilary roughly by the wrists.

"By your tears and your pretences," he said, with fierce scorn, "you have done your best to hinder me; but I would have you know, Mistress, that I am not one to be baffled. You are wholly at my mercy now."

In wild terror, she felt the pitiless brute force of the man.

"Let me go!" she panted, struggling to free herself.

"No, by Heaven! you shall not," said Norton, passionately. "Waghorn can settle matters with your lover, and I will make sure of you."

In the agony of her resistance she forgot everything else, and was as much startled as Norton when suddenly an indignant voice rang out close to them.

"Coward!" cried Gabriel, and his tone made the Colonel wince as he released Hilary, and stood staring at the wounded man, who, apparently almost at his last gasp, nevertheless confronted him with drawn sword.

His left arm was bandaged and in a sling, the sleeve of his buff coat had been ripped from wrist to shoulder, and hung down soaked in blood; his face was ghastly pale, with eyes like a flaming fire. Norton felt that he could not fight one in such extremity.

"What, the Puritan here, after all!" he cried. "I'faith, this is excellent. I arrest you, sir, in the King's name."

Gabriel's breath came in gasps, but with a gesture he urged Hilary to stand back under the trees, and, with flashing eyes, turned upon her assailant.

"Defend yourself!" he cried.

"Nay, an' you will fight," said Norton, drawing his sword. "Your blood be on your own head."

Hilary, with hands clasped on her breast, stood by frozen with horror, every shade of colour gone from her lovely face. In awful contrast to the peaceful orchard with its grass and daisies, its pink-and-white apple blossom, its glimpses of the Malvern hills, was the unequal fight in the foreground, the deadly thrust of the flashing swords, the clash of the steel, the gasping, sobbing breath of her lover.

Everything seemed against Gabriel; not only was he exhausted by pain and loss of blood, but he was a shorter, slighter man than the Colonel, and a less practised swordsman. He had nothing in his favour but a good cause, and a dauntless courage, and these will not ensure success.

Although he made a brave fight it was before long only too evident that he was failing; twice he staggered and almost fell, and though each time recovering himself, Norton was convinced that in another minute he must succumb. And now the better side of the Colonel's nature once more asserted itself; he felt a certain admiration for his foe, an uneasy consciousness that there had been truth in that indignant cry of "Coward!" The thought disturbed him, so did the panting, agonising gasps of the Puritan, and an uncomfortable chill went to his heart when, in the heat of the combat, he felt a ring which he specially valued slip from his left hand.

Suddenly he was taken off his guard; with a desperate thrust Gabriel ran him through the body, and in the same instant both duellists fell to the ground, the one severely wounded, the other wholly exhausted by the rescue of the woman whom he loved, and in the defence of whose honour he had spent the last remnants of his failing strength.

CHAPTER XLI.

"Yet since that loving Lord

Commanded us to love them for His sake,

Even for His sake, and for his sacred Word,

Which in His last bequest He to us spake,

We should them love, and with their needs partake;

Knowing that, whatsoe'er to them we give,

We give to Him by Whom we all doe live."

—Spenser.

There was no more skipping that day for Nan and Meg; frightened out of their senses, they made their way home, and were just crossing the stable-yard when their father caught sight of them.

"I have stabled that bay horse as Vicar said," he remarked, "and do you two little maids keep a still tongue in your heads or we may get into trouble. Why, what's amiss with you both?"

"Oh, father," said Nan, sobbing, "our wounded Puritan is going to fight the officer from Canon Frome, who is in the orchard threatening Mistress Hilary."

"I'll teach un to mind his manners in my orchard!" said Farmer Chadd, hastily picking up a stout cudgel. "Threatening did you say? and the lady there with no better protection than a wounded soldier! Good Lord! but these evil living Cavaliers will be the ruin o' the land! Run in to your mother, my maids, and say I'll be back soon for dinner."

Just as he reached the orchard by one entrance the Vicar and Zachary entered at the opposite side, and all three men gazed in horror at the sight before them. The Governor of Canon Frome was stretched out on the grass, bleeding and unconscious, and Gabriel Harford, to all appearance lifeless, lay with his head on Hilary's lap.

The Vicar bent over him and felt his heart.

"He still lives! but how can he possibly have fought Colonel Norton when in such a plight?"

"It was to save me, sir," said Hilary. "Oh! let us take him quickly to shelter before it is too late."

"There's life in this plaguey Governor o' Canon Frome, sir," said Farmer Chadd, "What be we to do with un?"

"If you and your wife could bind up his wound; the best way would be to take word to his men, and get them to bear him hence on a litter. Could you do that, Chadd, and say naught as to Captain Harford? He is the son of Dr. Bridstock Harford, of Hereford."

"Then I'll do anything in the world for un, for Dr. Harford saved my good woman's life," said Farmer Chadd. "You shelter the young gentleman, sir, and me and the missus will see to this here plaguey Colonel."

With Zachary's help the Vicar lifted Gabriel on to the bier which they had brought from the church, and carefully covering him with sacking they bore him down through the hopyards to Bosbury. Fortunately, it was the dinner-hour, and they did not encounter a single person, but were able to cress the churchyard and to carry their burden up the step-ladder to the first floor of the tower. Here they found Mrs. Durdle hard at work; she had already laid a mattress on the floor, and was bustling about with a broom in despair at the dust and the cobwebs which had accumulated.

"I do wish I had time to scrub the place down, sir," she lamented. "It bean't fit for a dog to lay in, let alone a Christian."

"Never mind," said the Vicar, "I'll warrant 'tis cleaner than Oxford Castle, and the main thing is to hide him and save his life. Zachary, can you fix boards in three of the windows, or at night the villagers may see our light?"

Leaving the wounded man to the kindly offices of Mrs. Durdle and Hilary, both of them well skilled in sick-nursing, the Vicar hastened back to his house, returning before long with a box full of pre-historic bones under one arm and a flagon of Hollands under the other.

"If anyone chances to ask you why we come to and fro to this tower, Zachary," he remarked, toiling up the ladder and setting down his burden, "you can tell them I am keeping my antiquities here, and can say you've seen them. What! hath Captain Harford not yet regained his senses? Try to get a little of this down his throat, Hilary. That's better; he will soon revive, and I will then set off for Hereford."

The last word seemed to reach Gabriel. He opened his eyes for a moment and caught a misty glimpse of Dr. Coke and Hilary with a rough stone tower wall and a deeply splayed narrow window in the background. Was he once more a prisoner in St. George's Tower at Oxford? The horror of the thought roused him. Then he noticed that he was lying in a bed on the floor, and that they had removed his buff coat, a perception which vaguely troubled him. ..

"My coat?" he said, anxiously, yet still not knowing why he wanted it.

"Are you cold," said Hilary, spreading another blanket over him. But the Vicar understood, and fetched the buff coat from the corner where Durdle had thrown it.

"The inner pocket is here," he said, placing it within reach of Gabriel's right hand. And then, with a look of relief, the wounded man drew out the despatches.

"Will you give them to my father?" he said, pleadingly,

"Yes," replied the Vicar; "but I shall beg him to come here first and dress your wounds. Will you give them to him yourself?"

"He may not come in time," said Gabriel, faintly.

And the Vicar, seeing that he longed to have the anxiety off his mind thrust the despatches into his black doublet, and bidding them keep the tower door locked, set off with Zachary to the stable, where the old servant saddled the cob for him, and, promising to be about the premises ready to give Mrs. Durdle help should she need him, watched his master ride off in the direction of Hereford.

Dr. Coke was not a man to shirk anything which he had promised, but he could not help feeling that in this despatchbearing he had undertaken work which he would have preferred to leave alone. To stand quite aloof from the strife and never to forget that he was before all things pledged to the service of the Prince of Peace had been his aim throughout the Civil War; but to refuse the request of one who lay apparently at the point of death, seemed to him impossible, while Gabriel's gallant rescue of Hilary increased the desire he felt to give him whatever ease of mind was possible.

On reaching Hereford he rode straight to the physician's house and, learnt from the servant that her master was about to ride out into the country. However, he was shown into the study.

"I will not detain you many minutes, sir," he said, after the greetings had passed. "I know how precious time is to such a busy man."

"Nay, 'tis not on an urgent matter of life and death that I am riding out this afternoon," said Dr. Harford. "I had last night a letter from my son, who, it seems, is at Ledbury, and I hope to meet him."

"Alas!" said the Vicar, "I bring you bad news of him. There was a sharp fight this morning at Ledbury, and your son is sorely wounded. We have hidden him from his pursuers in the tower at Bosbury, and he begged me to give you these despatches which he was bearing from Massey to Fairfax and Cromwell."

Dr. Harford took the blood-stained packet, but for a minute could not speak. At length he asked further particulars as to Gabriel's wounds, and when he, heard of the desperate ride across country and the duel with Colonel Norton, hope died out of his face. But, as usual, he was full of consideration for his visitor.

"I am inclined to think, sir," he said, "that you have been hurrying to and fro in aid of my son and have not yet dined. I will bid them prepare a meal, and then, when your horse is rested and my arrangements for leaving home made, we might, an' you will, ride together to Bosbury."

The Vicar, being in truth extremely hungry after his arduous work, did not decline the offer of food, and was soon discussing a fat capon in the dining-room, while the doctor saw his wife and his assistant, made hasty arrangements for a week's absence, and put into his bag such things as he thought likely to prove needful for Gabriel's case.

His wife, only longing to go herself to Bosbury, watched the preparations with tearful eyes.

"I cannot bear to feel that the headstrong girl who is to blame for it all should have the nursing of him," she sighed.

"Well, my dear, had you seen his face at Notting Hill when he was at death's door, and I merely gave him her message, you would understand that Hilary Unett is the only woman in the world who has a chance of nursing him back to life. 'Tis hard, dear wife, but there comes a time when a man is bound to leave even his father and mother and cling to his——"

"Well," said the poor mother, wiping her eyes, "she is not his wife yet, and if he dies, I for one shall account her his murderess."

The physician stooped and kissed her tenderly.

"Keep up your heart," he said, with assumed cheerfulness. "And I know that the kindly Vicar will bring you word how he fares, and if need arises fetch you to him. But if possible we must avoid that, since he cannot be safe when once his hiding-place hath been discovered. The Canon Frome garrison will know that he is not far off, and we may be sure will seek to lay hands on him."

They were interrupted by little Bridstock, who came running into the room to show them a toy sword which the groom had made for him.

"At any rate, you shall never be a soldier," said the mother, catching him up in her arms and kissing him. "And you can't marry that headstrong maid!"

"I shall marry little Betty Brydges," said the child, with decision, "and be Member of Parliament like Sir Robert Harley."

The sublime confidence of his tone made the parents laugh.

"'Tis a great thing to know one's own mind," said the doctor, patting the child's curly head. "We have had our troubles, but at any rate our two sons will not vex our souls by weak and unstable characters. There is grit in both of them."

"I would we had the choosing of their wives," said Mrs. Harford, ruefully.

"Yet you didn't think that the best plan years ago," replied Dr. Harford, with a mirthful glance.

And recalling their own extremely early and rash marriage, his wife could but smile and own that he was right.

Her heart relented a little towards Hilary, and when Dr. Coke told her from what peril Gabriel had that day rescued her, and spoke words of warm gratitude and praise as to her son's courage and sterling character, her face brightened, and she watched the two riders mount their horses with a more hopeful spirit than might have been expected.

Yet could Dr. Harford have looked at that moment into the tower room where his son lay, he would certainly have taken his wife with him.

CHAPTER XLII.

"Ruined love, when it is built anew,

Grows fairer than at first, more strong, far greater."

—Romeo and Juliet, Act I., Scene I.

As Hilary kept guard over her lover through those long hours of waiting, seeing the pain which she could do nothing to relieve, fearing, as she watched his failing strength, that the end was indeed drawing near, it seemed to her that the punishment of all her pride and perversity was falling on her with overwhelming force.

When conscious, he lay absolutely still, too much exhausted to speak, and when drifting back into a semi-conscious state his moans tore her heart, and filled her, moreover, with terror lest some villager crossing the churchyard should possibly hear the sound.

At last, when it was growing dusk, she heard horsemen on the road, and, after an interval, when doubtless the travellers were leaving their horses with Zachary in the stable-yard, came the welcome summons from below which had been agreed upon. Durdle clambered down the step-ladder and unbolted the door, and in another minute the Vicar and Dr. Harford made their way into the dim tower room.

Looking up into the physician's strong, calm face, Hilary felt as if a load of care had been suddenly lifted from her shoulders. He greeted her with more than his usual cordiality, understanding well enough how sore her heart must be. Then he knelt down beside the mattress and looked with keen anxiety at his son.

"Will there be any risk in having a light?" he asked.

The Vicar thought not, and, producing a tinder-box, began to strike a flint and steel and to kindle the lantern that had been brought from the house.

Then when the light fell on the white face drawn with pain, the doctor regretted that he had not brought Gabriel's mother, for not even at Notting Hill had he seemed so near death.

Hilary saw the change in his manner and her heart sank. Yet it comforted her a little when Dr. Harford proceeded to examine the shattered arm, for surely, she argued to herself, had there been no hope he would have left his son's last moments undisturbed.

"I did the best I could for him in the orchard," said the Vicar; "but fear it was but rough-and-ready treatment."

"The duel would have been enough to defeat the most skilful surgery," said the Doctor; "and clearly the bone must have been broken as he fell. But he hath great rallying power, and I don't despair of him yet."

On those words Hilary stayed her failing heart all through that terrible night, while Gabriel passed from one fainting fit to another, and it seemed as if the angel of death hovered above him ready at any moment to bear him away from her.

At length towards daybreak he slept for a time, and woke with a look of renewed life in his face which cheered them.

"The despatches?" he asked, looking from his father to the Vicar.

"Dr. Coke has given them to me," said the physician.

"And you will bear them without delay?" said Gabriel, anxiously.

Dr. Harford's face clouded.

"To leave you now may mean your death," he replied. "I do not think I can leave you."

"But I promised to guard them with my life, and they are urgent," pleaded Gabriel. "Let me still serve."

Hilary's eyes grew dim, but she spoke in a low, steady voice.

"I will do all that you bid me, sir," she said. "Surely good nursing may save him."

"Well, my dear," said the physician, "if anyone can keep him in life, I verily believe 'tis you; and if he urges me to go, I cannot say him nay."

"You will see them both yourself," said Gabriel.

"Ay, the despatches shall be placed in their own hands."

"And tell General Cromwell," said Gabriel, "that if I recover, I more than ever desire to serve the wounded."

With many last directions, the physician at length tore himself away, well knowing that it was doubtful whether he should ever again look on his son.

The Vicar went to see him mount, glad that he should leave Bosbury before the village was astir, and as they quitted the tower Gabriel turned to Hilary with a look that made her heart bound.

"Now do you repay a hundredfold all the suffering of these years," he said. "Living or dying, I am content."

She bent down and kissed him tenderly. And long before the Vicar rejoined them he had sunk into a dreamless sleep.

Cheering himself with the old family motto, Dr. Harford rode with all speed to Windsor, where he was able to deliver the despatches to Sir Thomas Fairfax and to give him an account of Prince Rupert's doings in Herefordshire. He found, however, that Cromwell had quitted Windsor, and, after taking Blechington House, was sweeping round Oxford, taking possession of all the draught horses in the neighbourhood, and thus disorganising the King's plan of campaign by preventing Prince Maurice from removing the heavy guns from Oxford. It was not until the night of the 28th April that the physician was able to overtake him near Farringdon, as he was on his way to rejoin Fairfax, after defeating Sir Henry Vaughan at Bampton.

The troops had halted for a couple of hours beside the Lambourn, and the physician on asking to be taken to Cromwell, was conducted by a burly corporal to a pollard willow beside the stream. Here, with his armour removed, and a little gilt-edged volume in his hand, rested the tired leader, his back against the tree trunk, the expression of his face more that of a prophet than a soldier. Clearly what Massey would have termed the "Enoch" side of his character was now uppermost, and the "David" side no longer visible.

As the corporal mentioned the name of the physician, he promptly slipped the little volume into his pocket, and with a brief and not particularly ceremonious greeting, received from Dr. Harford's hands the blood-stained despatches.

"Pray be seated, sir," he said, resuming his place under the tree, with the fatigued air of one who has for many days known scant rest. Then without comment he broke the seal and hastily read Massey's communication.

"You have done me a greater service than you know by bearing this," he said, glancing up from the closely-written sheet.

"Sir, I am but my son's ambassador," said the physician. "He would have delivered the despatch himself, but was attacked and grievously wounded as he rode from Ledbury."

Cromwell glanced at the blood-stained letter, which told its own tale.

"I remember Captain Harford well," he said. "He did excellent work at Newbury, and again, two months ago, when we were in Wiltshire."

"'Twas only through his great wish to serve you that I have consented to leave him in a risky hiding-place, and in grave peril of death from his wounds," said the physician.

"Poor lad!" said Cromwell, his stern face softened to such tenderness as amazed Dr. Harford. "The moral courage of his nature is a thousandfold more needed in England than mere animal bravery. There is one of my troopers, Passey by name, who was his fellow prisoner in Oxford Castle, and he hath told me how no skilled physician could have shown a more tender care for the fever-stricken inmates."

"Should he recover, he more than ever longs to serve the sick and wounded," said Dr. Harford.

"Then in God's name bid him do it," cried Cromwell. "I urged him at Newbury to wait for clearer guidance, bidding him beware of men and to look up to the Lord, letting Him be free to speak and command in his heart, and without consulting flesh and blood to do valiantly for God and His people. And here, doubtless, in this pain he hath passed through, his guidance hath come."

"Should I find him living on my return, I will repeat your words to him," said Dr. Harford.

"God grant that he may be spared to you, sir," said Cromwell. "I know too well what the loss of a first-born son means to the heart of a father. Look you, an' it should chance that Parliament still desires to retain my services in the Army, let your son act as one of the mates to the surgeon of my troop, thus would he gain knowledge whilst still serving the Cause."

Dr. Harford welcomed the suggestion, and anxious to lose no time on his return journey, took leave of the great leader, understanding better than he had done before what it was that gave this man his extraordinary power. He had the insight to perceive what the greatest of modern historians has called Cromwell's "all-embracing hospitality of soul," and to understand that this, combined with a rare sagacity in seeing what was practically possible and a matchless faith and courage, marked him out as the true steersman in those troubled times.

During these days Peter Waghorn had in deep depression brooded over the utter defeat of his schemes. His fruitless search for Gabriel in Malvern had not improved his temper, and on going next day to Canon Frome Manor to interview Norton he learnt to his dismay that the Governor had been carried home from Bosbury desperately wounded and was raving in delirium. Nobody knew how he had met with his wound, but Farmer Chadd had found him lying unconscious in his orchard, and it was conjectured that the mishap must have occurred while he was seeking to arrest some of Massey's men in their flight.

Waghorn kept his thoughts to himself and trudged back to Bosbury, guessing shrewdly that Captain Harford had all the time been within earshot, and, in spite of his wound, had managed to fight his rival. Had he encountered Hilary he would probably have asked her some direct question, but the villagers reported that she was ill and obliged to keep the house, a rumour which was confirmed by her non-appearance at church on the following Sunday.

On the Thursday a soldier rode up to the wood-carver's house, and Waghorn, in some trepidation, went out to him.

"The Governor bids you come with all speed to him at Canon Frome Manor to report on some work undertaken for him," said the messenger, looking with some curiosity at the austere Puritan.

"Good; I will come anon," said Waghorn. "Doth the Colonel recover him of his wound?"

"Ay, 'tis healing, and his head is clear, but I counsel you to come with all speed, for he's in a devilish ill-humour, and to be kept waiting is what he can't abide."

Waghorn laid aside his work, and in very low spirits tramped over to Canon Frome. To do him justice, he was ill at ease, and detested his alliance with an officer of Norton's type. It might be permissible to use the ungodly as tools, but as he recalled Hilary's appeal to him in the orchard, and reflected that he had left her wholly at the mercy of the Colonel, his conscience pricked him. He had, as a matter of fact, forgotten everything in the burning desire to prevent Gabriel Harford's escape.

Evidently the soldier had drawn a truthful picture of Norton's state, for, as the wood-carver was ushered into his room, he peremptorily ordered his servant to quit him, and beckoning Waghorn to come near to the bed, looked up at him with an angry scowl.

"Well, scarecrow! What news do you bring?"

"No news, sir," said Waghorn, gloomily.

"You great bungling idiot! Of course, I know you didn't find Captain Harford in Malvern; he was lying within a stone's throw of us behind the hedge."

"And challenged you in order to save Mistress Hilary?—I guessed as much," said the wood-carver. "I like your doings very ill, sir, and you well deserve what you got."

"You vile hypocrite! Do you sit in judgment on me?" said Norton. "You! a turncoat—a spy! Why, you can't even carry out the dirty work you undertake. Prate no more, but tell me what they did with Captain Harford. We fell at the same moment, and he, as I well remember, had death in his face as he ran me through."

"I know not where they bore him, sir, and had there been a burial at Bosbury I must surely have known of it."

"Maybe, then, he still lives, and they have hidden him away somewhere. Doubtless the Vicar hath sheltered him; he is one of those soft-hearted fools who seek to overcome evil with good, and models his life after the Sermon on the Mount, not in your fashion, on the cursing Psalms."

There was enough truth in this remark to cause Waghorn another twinge of conscience.

"I may have been ill-advised to leave you in the orchard with Mistress Hilary," he admitted. "But the flesh is weak, and I remembered only the duty of securing that half-hearted sparer of crosses. The lady told a most shameless lie, and if her lover was slain in the duel his blood will be on her head."

"That may be a very soothing reflection for you," said Norton, with a grim smile, "but it doth not better my case. Now, look you here, I will do anything in reason for you if you discover this man's whereabouts. You think, had he died, you would have heard of it.

Well, by hook or by crook, you can surely find out where they have stowed him away. Have you seen aught of Mistress Hilary?"

"Nay; she keeps the house, I hear, and is ill."

"A blind! A mere trick!" cried Norton, angrily. "Depend upon it, she keeps the house to nurse that accursed lover of hers. Oh! if I had but the strength to mount my horse, I would soon track him down."

"I could keep watch on the house, sir," said Waghorn, "and let you know who comes and goes."

"Well, do that, it may serve," said Norton; "for I will not live to be thwarted by that Puritan Captain. And, look you, Waghorn, you might do me a service by worrying the Vicar. Go and seize the Prayer-book in the church, and bid him obey the Parliamentary order and use this blessed Directory they have concocted. 'S life! what wouldn't I give to see his face when you confront him with it."

And he broke into a laugh, which was cut short by a paroxysm of pain.

"I could do that," said Waghorn, sternly, a gleam of satisfaction kindling in his eyes. "I reckon he would take it even more to heart than the breaking of his painted window. Ay, I could do that."

"Do it then," said Norton, mockingly, "and serve the Cause that you are for ever prating about. I care not a jot, for it will serve me."

With that he dismissed the wood-carver, and Waghorn walked straight to Ledbury, where he had the good fortune to find a trusty waggoner who was willing to carry a letter for him to Gloucester and bear back the reply. He then adjourned to a small alehouse, where he laboriously wrote an order to one of his Puritan friends for a copy of the Directory, which was already in use in Gloucester, but had not yet been enforced in Herefordshire.

Having accomplished this work to his entire satisfaction, he tramped back in the dusk of the evening to Bosbury, but had only gone about half the distance when the sound of a horseman following him made him look round. He saw with a start of surprise that it was none other than Dr. Bridstock Harford.

"Good e'en to you, sir," he said, touching his hat.

"Good evening," said the doctor, as he galloped past.

"Now what should that bode?" muttered Waghorn. "Where hath he been? And whither doth he ride now? I'll light my lantern when I reach home, and see if the hoof-prints stop at the Vicarage."

CHAPTER XLIII.

"But true religion, sprung from God above,

Is like her fountain, full of charity,

Embracing all things with a tender love!

Full of goodwill and meek expectancy;

Full of true justice and sure verity,

In heart and voice free, large, even infinite;

Not wedged in strict particularity,

But grasping all in her vast active spright;

Bright lamp of God! that men would joy in thy

pure light."

—Henry More, 1642.

There was something indescribably desolate in the blank silence of the tiled house when Waghorn unlocked the door, and fumbled in the dusk for the tinder-box. No human being shared his dreary home, no animal kept him company or enlivened his solitary hours. It was undoubtedly owing to his loneliness that his tendency to gloomy fanaticism had, since his father's death, so greatly increased. The one joy left him appeared to be this morbid and exaggerated desire to root out all that he deemed wrong, and to punish all those who withstood his fiery zeal.

Without pausing to eat or drink, he kindled his lantern and stole quickly out into the street. Early hours were kept in those days, and all seemed still in the village; stepping cautiously, he soon descried in the dust the prints of horse-hoofs, and was eagerly following them up to see whether they turned in at the Vicarage, when Zachary suddenly emerged from the gate.

"Good e'en to you, Waghorn," said the clerk, in a more friendly tone than he usually employed towards the wood-carver. "Ha' ye lost summat, that ye go groping like the woman that dropped her tenth bit o' silver?"

"Ay," said Waghorn, "that's just what I have done, but I shall find what I seek yet, never fear."

Zachary with apparent good nature swept his broad foot energetically to and fro among the dust, effectually wiping out all trace of the hoof-prints.

"Better search by daylight," he suggested. "And come now to the 'Bell' and have a pint o' home brewed."

Waghorn deemed it prudent to accept the invitation, for he desired to get into Zachary's confidence, and hoped that some day he might gather from the garrulous old man the information he eagerly sought. But on this particular night the clerk was on his guard, and the fanatic gained nothing by his plot.

Meanwhile, in the tower room, Dr. Harford, to his great joy, found his son in far better case than he had dared to expect. Hilary's good nursing and the patient's healthy life and sound constitution had triumphed over all the other drawbacks, and although some weeks must pass before he really recovered, all danger to his life was practically over.

The Vicar and Hilary listened with intense relief to the doctor's verdict.

"The question now is, whether we shall try to remove him," said his father. "It seems unfair to let you any longer run the risk of sheltering a rebel. Yet I scarce know where we could take him; we should never get him to Hereford without his being made prisoner."

"Sir, don't think of moving him. 'Tis hard, indeed, if the church tower may not afford him sanctuary," said the Vicar. "If, indeed, there be any risk in the matter, I gladly take it."

"And how about his nurse? What hath she to say?" asked the physician, looking into the girl's beautiful face.

"Sir," said Hilary, blushing vividly, "I am his betrothed wife, and only this very day we were saying that we wished the Vicar would wed us."

Gabriel took her hand in his, and looked with eager hope at the kindly antiquary who had done so much for him.

"In the orchard as I lay in even worse plight, sir, you made no objection to my suit, and if, indeed, you will make us man and wife before I go, I should be for ever your debtor."

The Vicar and the physician glanced at each other.

"This comes, sir, an' I mistake not," said Dr. Harford, "from your words in the churchyard when Waghorn would have had the cross pulled down. I have heard that those who hearkened to you could never forget your plea for love, which is the bond of peace."

"In truth, sir," said the Vicar with a twinkle in his eye, "I trow it comes from the quiet days in this tower of refuge, when my niece had in your absence to nurse the wounded. Very gladly will I wed you, my children, and some fine morning we will steal across to the church before the villagers are astir. In the meanwhile I can read your banns in here each Sunday, with Durdle and Zachary for congregation."

Then Dr. Harford told of his interview with Cromwell, and of the suggestion for Gabriel's future.

"An you could spare your niece, sir, it would perchance be no bad plan for our bride and bridegroom to journey to London, for possibly the Governor of Canon Frome may yet give some trouble. Hath anyone heard whether he recovers?"

"Farmer Chadd heard that, though still kept to his bed, he mends apace," said the Vicar. "Your plan seems an excellent one, sir, and though I shall sorely miss Hilary, it would take a load off my mind to know that she was in safety."

"Then by the earliest opportunity I will write to my mother at Notting Hill Manor," said the physician. "I well know that her house will be at your disposal, and that you, sir, would be an honoured guest there."

The Vicar gave a courteous little bow, then turned with a mischievous glance to the invalid.

"Nothing will please me more than to meet Madam Harford, yet don't make yourself uneasy, Gabriel, I shall not ride with you on the wedding journey, but shall visit you later on, when you are settled down into the prose of everyday life."

There was a general laugh, and before long, the Vicar suggested that they had better return for the night to the Vicarage, leaving Dr. Harford to talk matters over with his son.

Far into the small hours the two discussed future plans, and it was arranged that the Doctor should not again risk drawing attention to the hiding-place by a visit, unless actually sent for. Early in June, when the arm was likely to be quite sound again, he proposed to ride over at night, bringing Gabriel's mother with him, that she might be present at the private marriage, and see her son before he left the west. In the meantime he impressed on the wounded man the need of the greatest caution and secrecy, and then, stifling the anxiety he could not but feel, bade him farewell just as dawn was breaking, and saddling his horse, rode quietly back to Hereford before anyone else in Bosbury was stirring.

Waghorn, with a grim smile on his sleeping face, dreamt of the bonfire he would make of the great Prayer-book in the church. The Vicar wandered in a happy valley where wonderful remains of pre-historic times delighted his astonished eyes. Hilary had visions of standing beside Gabriel in the porch, where in those days weddings were celebrated, and softly breathing the "I will," which should make her indeed his wife. And Gabriel, in wakeful happiness, lay watching the light as it stole softly through the narrow window of his hiding-place, musing over the words the Vicar had daily used when he visited him:

O Lord, save Thy servant; which putteth his trust in Thee.

Send him help from Thy holy place: and evermore mightily defend him.

Let the enemy have no advantage of him; nor the wicked approach to hurt him.

Be unto him, O Lord, a strong tower; from the face of his enemy.

Such a strong tower, such a helper and defender, must be, in his degree, prove to his promised wife; and he looked the future in the face far more soberly than in the first days of their betrothal long ago, but with a calm manliness which augured well for their new life.

The Vicar's anxieties, though lessened by Dr. Harford's reassuring report as to Gabriel's health, were by no means over. He went about continually with the uneasy consciousness that Waghorn was not only a dangerous fanatic, but actually a spy, and, as Hilary had discovered in the orchard, a spy who had not scrupled to aid such a man as Colonel Norton.

One evening, when as usual he had repaired to the tower at dusk, taking with him the food Gabriel would need during the night, he found himself a prey to the most unwonted nervousness. He unlocked the door and summoned Hilary from her day's watching in the tower room, waiting with restless impatience while she bade her lover good-night and crept down the ladder.

But the sight of the girl's happy face cheered him, and he greeted her with a smile.

"I believe you revel in these ghostly crossings of the churchyard," he said, wrapping her long cloak more closely about her. "I will be with you anon when I have had a word with Gabriel."

He watched her till she had disappeared in the Vicarage garden, then paid a visit to the invalid, who was far from sharing Hilary's enjoyment of her risky journeys to and fro, and always liked to hear that she had gained the Vicarage in safety.

"When I think of all that you are doing for me, and of the danger of discovery, it makes me eager to be gone," he said, watching his kindly host as he placed within reach all that he could need.

"Nay, I'm in no haste to get rid of you," said the Vicar, with a smile. "You forget that I shall be left a lonely old bachelor when you and Hilary fare forth on your wedding journey."

"It seems unfair, sir, that I should rob your home of its brightness," said Gabriel.

"Ay, and not only that, but rouse in me a certain dissatisfaction with my lot," said the Vicar, his eyes twinkling. "I have serious thoughts of entering upon the holy estate of matrimony myself, an I can prevail on Sir Richard Hopton to accept my proposal for the hand of his daughter."

"Hilary's friend, Mistress Frances?" said Gabriel, with keen interest.

"Ay, but say naught about it till I learn my fate," said the Vicar. "The lady, for aught I know, may refuse me as decidedly as Hilary refused Squire Geers, of Garnons."

The recollection of this made them both laugh, and in much better spirits the Vicar quitted the tower, locking the door and putting the key in his pocket as he groped his way across the graveyard to the garden gate.

It was now dark, save for the stars which just revealed here and there a white gravestone or the dim outline of bush or tree. Suddenly the Vicar became conscious of the presence of some living creature; though as yet he could see nothing he felt that he was not alone, and, pausing to listen intently, he distinctly heard the sound of breathing.

"Who goes there?" he said, in a hearty voice which belied his real anxiety.

"'Tis I, sir, Peter Waghorn," said the fanatic, gloomily.

"What, man! still longing to cast down the cross?" said the Vicar. "I had hoped you had come to see that we look on it with no superstition. But I know well 'tis a hard matter for all of us to see with each other's eyes. I should make a rare bungle did I try my hand at wood-carving, and you would make nothing at all of the pre-historic tooth which I am carrying from my museum room in the tower to show to Mistress Hilary."

It was too dark for him to see the expression on Waghorn's face, and he remained in ignorance of the man's intentions. Did he suspect that they used the tower to shelter Gabriel? Or did he merely keep a watchful eye on the Vicarage? Either surmise was disquieting. Dr. Coke fell back on his usual kindly sympathy, hoping to reach the heart of this strange and complex character.

"Come in and see me some night," he said, genially, "for I have some rare old oak which you would be interested in. I've a great mind to get you to carve me a corner cupboard for my study, an you think the wood will serve."

"I will come, sir," said Waghorn. "But before you order the cupboard belike you had best be sure in your own mind that you'll be staying on at the Vicarage. Good-night to you, sir."

With this vague and most discomforting speech the wood-carver quitted the churchyard, while the Vicar made his way home to ponder over the dark saying with growing uneasiness.

On the following Saturday morning he was busy with his sermon when a knock at the door and the furious voice of the parish clerk recalled him from the study of St. Paul's words about charity to the difficulties of the present.

"Sir!" cried Zachary, crimson with anger, his face making the most strange contrast to Waghorn's grim pallor. "Look what this pestilent fellow hath done now! 'Tis the Prayer-book, sir, from the church—he's slashed and torn it to bits!"

The Vicar looked with indignation at the ruthlessly-torn pages, and hastily rising, paced the room, wrestling with a burning desire to kick the fanatic out of the house. When he had conquered himself, he returned once more to the writing-table.

"By what right do you destroy the parish property?" he said, gravely.

"I am a parishioner, and do intend to see the law of the land obeyed," replied Waghorn.

"I have yet to learn that the law of the land orders the tearing up of books," said the Vicar.

"It orders the disuse of the Book of Common Prayer, and that's the same thing," retorted Waghorn.

"Not at all," said the Vicar. "If Parliament ordered you to cease from carving wood, it would not be lawful for me to come and burn your tools. Leave us, Zachary; I must discuss this matter alone with Waghorn."

With keen anxiety he recalled his encounter in the dark with the spy, and wondered how much he really knew.

"I warned you, sir," said the wood-carver, "that you might not be staying on at the Vicarage."

"Hath Parliament, then, abolished me, as well as the Prayer-book?" inquired the Vicar, with a humorous gleam in his grey eyes.

"It will turn you out unless you use the Directory as the law orders," said Waghorn, grimly, handing him a copy of the document. "There be those at Gloucester that will see it is enforced; you must not look again to have a half-hearted officer, like Captain Harford, sent."

Dr. Coke glanced with a sigh at the mangled prayer-book, wondering why it had become hateful to so many men.

"It must be that they identify it with the harsh dealings of Archbishop Laud and Bishop Wren, and others who tried to enforce a system rather than to follow Christ," he thought to himself; and then he carefully read through the Directions which had been issued as to public worship. If he refused to obey he must leave his people as sheep without a shepherd just at a time when their distress was greatest, owing to the war and the constant harassing of the Canon Frome garrison. He must also imperil Gabriel's life by moving him from his present place of refuge.

Dearly as he loved the liturgy he could not hesitate as to the right course of action. The thought of having to pray in public without a book was a nightmare to him, but with a moral courage that gave a curious new dignity to his manner and bearing, he said, quietly:

"I shall give my father all the facts of the case, and for the present shall endeavour to follow the directions here given. Chapters shall be read from each Testament. Prayer, and especially the Lord's Prayer, shall be used. There shall be thanksgiving and singing of psalms. The Communion shall be frequently celebrated, and children shall be baptized only in church. Here are all the essentials of Christian worship, and though I sorely grieve to lose for a time the book that is far dearer to me than you guess, I see that for the present distress it is the only way."

"And the surplice—that rag of popery—it must go also," said Waghorn.

"Oh! Is it a rag of popery?" said the Vicar with a smile. "I had a notion that it was meant to represent the fine linen which is the righteousness of the saints. But though to my thinking 'tis a seemly garb, and I like things done as St. Paul advised, 'decently and in order,' yet doubtless I can minister as well in my black doublet and hose."

"Much better," said Waghorn, emphatically.

The Vicar sighed.

"Maybe 'tis a more appropriate garb," he reflected, "for a man that well-nigh flew into a towering passion at sight of a torn Prayer-book.".

"We will discuss the matter no more," he said, presently, "but to-morrow in church let us try to meet in all sincerity as fellow-worshippers. Now I will show you the piece of oak we spoke of, and you shall take the measurements for the corner cupboard."

There was no sleep that night for Dr. Coke, but, as Durdle often remarked, he was one of those whose looks did not pity them, and no one seeing the ruddy face and the long white hair had a notion what the man was undergoing when he took his place in the reading-desk on Sunday morning.

"Dearly beloved brethren," he began, "owing to the present troubles in Church and State, it is not to-day in my power to use the Book of Common Prayer. I would remind you, however, that greatly as many of us love our liturgy, and helpful as we find it, God may be worshipped by us all in spirit and in truth, though our prayers be but halting and imperfect. I ask you, therefore, to kneel and to make after me, sentence by sentence, supplication to our Heavenly Father."

The startled people knelt, and very earnestly repeated the brief petitions for a more perfect faith, for a wider hope, for a more self-sacrificing love. They prayed for peace and for the needs of soul and body, and then with a gasp of relief the Vicar began the Lord's Prayer.

The ordeal was over, and with a most thankful heart he gave out the Hundredth Psalm, which was valiantly played by flute and fiddle and heartily sung by all the congregation.

After which, with the reading of che lessons, more psalm-singing and a sermon, the service came to an end.

"Well," remarked Farmer Chadd, "Vicar may not ha' spoken with the tongue o' angels as the text said, but he certainly did make folk see what charity means."

"Ay," said Farmer Mutlow, "and though I'm with him in preferrin' the Prayer-book, yet I will say it cheered my heart wonderful to pray for a good apple year, and above all to ask straight out for a blessin' on the hops. Parson he knows well enough what plaguey uncertain things they be, and though the liturgy lumps 'em all in with 'fruits o' the earth that in due time we may enjoy them,' yet I always did hold with prayer for each child by name, and if for children why not for crops?"

"Quite right, neighbour, quite right," said Farmer Chadd. "We'll ask him to say a word for the hops every Sunday."

CHAPTER XLIV.

"Trouthe is the heighest thing that men may kepe."

—Chaucer.

"Truth is God's child, and the fortunes of truth are God's care as well as ours."

—Bishop Phillips Brooks.

The little room in the church tower had become curiously dear to Gabriel. Its bare walls, its bell ropes, its dusty rafters and the narrow window half veiled by ivy, were associated with those happy days when life and health gradually returned, and Hilary, with all her old winsomeness, and with that new and half-wistful humility which changed her from a self-willed child to a noble woman, grew hourly more precious to him.

One day, however, nearly six weeks after the Battle of. Ledbury, he noticed how thin her hands were growing, and, looking more searchingly into her face, thought less of its beauty and more of the dark shadows round her eyes.

"You are pale and weary, dear heart," he said, caressing the hand that had done so much for him. "These long weeks have overtaxed you."

"No, no; I shall be well enough when you are quite safe," said Hilary, her voice faltering. "But—don't laugh at me, Gabriel!—I feel as if you would be called on to suffer for my sin."

"Your sin?" he questioned.

"'Tis no idle superstition," she said, her eyes filling, "'tis an instinct that my punishment will come that way."

"But what sin? That of playing good Samaritan to a rebel?" said Gabriel, smiling.

"I mean the lie that I told in the orchard," she said, drooping her head.

"That was as much my fault as yours," said Gabriel, tenderly. "I moved, and that affrighted you; but to listen to that villain was more than I could endure."

"Oh, you'll never know what it was to feel when you were carried here that, but for my cowardice, the duel need never have been fought," said Hilary. "Had I only kept silence, Waghorn would have been present, and would at least have saved me from Colonel Norton."

"You were not cowardly!" he protested.

"Yes; to lie is cowardly," she said. "And it is the one thing I thought I never could do."

"Dearest," he said, drawing her nearer to him, "you are not the first who in a moment of peril has lost faith. Though silence would have been best, who would dare to judge you?"

"And yet silence might often betray—might seem to give consent," she said, musingly.

"God has charge of consequences," he said, quietly. "And I suppose we always do amiss when we take into human hands the guidance that belongs to Him alone."

"You mean that at all costs we must be true?"

"Yes, dear heart. But a truce to disputations."

"You and I have done with disputes," she said, tenderley. "Love and danger and the shadow of death have lifted us above our old arguings."

"We are somewhat nearer than the day you suggested that we might be friendly foes," said Gabriel, putting his arm round her.

She laughed softly.

"The day when Mistress Helena roused my jealousy! No; you shall be a friendly foe to every honourable Royalist, but to me you are—all the world!"

"Dearest, then must I share your troubles, but I fear you are keeping them back from me. Zachary tells me the Vicarage hath been searched!"

"Yes, the Governor of Canon Frome sent to search for you, but that was no great matter. He did not dare to come himself."

"There is something else, then, that makes you anxious. What is it?"

"Only that on Saturday an order came from the High Sheriff for my uncle to go to-day to Hereford and sign Prince Rupert's Protestation. Of course he refuses to go, but I fear it may lead to trouble."

"I trust not," said Gabriel, gravely. "We seem so nearly through our difficulties. To-morrow night my father and mother coming, and on Wednesday our marriage and escape. By-the-bye, what of Waghorn?"

"He has been quite quiet since the Directory was adopted. My uncle cannot make him out."

Even as they spoke of him, Peter Waghorn, in the tiled cottage by the churchyard, was musing over the Vicar's words the last time he had heard him preach. Against his will the man had been impressed by the way in which Dr. Coke had behaved during the past few weeks under great provocation; and now as he sat carving the delicate pattern of vine leaves on the cupboard door, he remembered how on the previous day the Vicar had made his carving into a parable, and had shown in the sermon that just as no two branches, and even no two leaves were precisely alike, yet all grew from the parent vine, so it was with Christians.

This was an astonishing notion to Waghorn; he doubted whether it was sound doctrine, yet it haunted him curiously. As he sat brooding over it that Monday afternoon, there came a peremptory knock, and his door was flung open by no less a person than the Governor of Canon Frome.

Norton was now quite recovered, and evidently in a very bad humour; the wood-carver noticed that the lines of cruelty about his mouth were much more clearly marked.

"Well, scarecrow," he observed, flinging himself into a chair. "You have news, I hope, at last of Captain Harford."

"No news, sir," said Waghorn. "I have watched the Vicarage and have made close inquiry in the village, but can learn naught."

"Yet I am certain he can't be far," said Norton. "And find him I will. If only you'd a head on your shoulders you would have trapped him long ago."

"I have done my best, sir," said Waghorn.

"I greatly doubt it," sneered the Colonel. "But I have every intention of spurring you on to the work. Find out Captain Harford's whereabouts, and you may ask what you will of me. Fail, and some fine night you mustn't be surprised to find your house too hot to hold you. These little accidents will happen in war time."

And with a mocking laugh he quitted the cottage, leaving Waghorn to uneasy thoughts.

The threat about the house had touched him to the quick, for if there was one thing on earth that he prized, it was this old home in which his father had died.

"I must bestir myself," he reflected. "That malapert young captain shall not escape. Maybe Zachary can help me. I will ply him with cider this evening and worm out his secrets."

Now, through all those weeks the old sexton had been most discreet, but unfortunately he was one of those who as success draws nigh grow less cautious. Having baffled Colonel Norton and Waghorn for nearly six weeks, it seemed unlikely that failure should now overwhelm him.

He, therefore, accepted the wood carver's invitation to drink at the "Bell," and Waghorn plied him with cider so lavishly that he became most cheerful and communicative.

"There's no drink in the world like cider," he maintained, smiling benevolently. "You can't take it too late nor begin it too early. Did I ever tell you the riddle that the painter gave me—him as did Mistress Hilary's portrait? 'What's the difference,' says he, 'betwixt a tankard o' morning cider and a pig's tail?' Give it up?"

Waghorn nodded.

"The pig's tail's twirly, and the morning cider ain't too early," said the sexton, laughing boisterously.

"Talking of Mistress Hilary," said Waghorn, "I understand that she's betrothed to Captain Harford. When is the marriage to be?"

"Are you looking to be bidden as a wedding guest?" chuckled Zachary. "I thought you bore neither o' them any goodwill."

"Truth to tell I thought the Captain was dead," observed Waghorn.

Zachary emptied his tankard and laughed foolishly.

"I've not had the digging of his grave, and yet he ain't far from the grave," he said, with the air of one who could say more if he would.

"Zachary!" called the landlord. "You're wanted at the Vicarage, there's the housekeeper looking for you."

"These women! these women! they never can let a man have a minute's peace," growled the sexton. "Well, goodnight to you, Peter, good-night. We've had a rare pleasant chat together."

Waghorn smiled grimly.

"It has served my turn," he muttered, and fell into deep thought.

Zachary meanwhile was despatched to the tower with Gabriel's supper and the next day's breakfast, and was still talking in the dusk with the two lovers when Dr. Coke's summons was heard below. The sexton admitted him, and was surprised to find that Mrs. Durdle stole in on tiptoe after her master.

"Gabriel," said the Vicar in an agitated voice, "I greatly fear your hiding-place is known, and I have come to urge you to escape."

"How hath it chanced, sir?" said Gabriel, starting to his feet in dismay.

"All the fault, sir, o' that fool Zachary with his long tongue," said Durdle, indignantly.

"Why, Zachary is a kindly old soul, he would never betray me," said Gabriel, incredulously.

At that moment the sexton came up the ladder, and with an angry exclamation Mrs. Durdle flew at him and dragged him forward.

"Here, you zany! Come and tell the Vicar what you said just now at the inn, you silly old man to go mag, mag, mag, over your cider, bringing trouble on us all."

"Gracious goodness, Mrs. Durdle! and what have I been about to fluster you like a turkey cock in a tearing temper?" protested the sexton.

"Gently, gently!" said the Vicar, "remember that walls may have ears. The truth is, Zachary, I learn from Bettington, of the 'Bell,' that you and Waghorn were drinking together, and that he heard you let fall words as to Captain Harford being above ground still, but not far from the grave."

Zachary scratched his head. "I do mind me now that we jested about graves, and that 'twas mighty pleasant to think how little he knew, for all he looked so wise."

"I fear, Zachary, the man was too wily for you, he plied you with cider till you all but told him where Captain Harford lay. You should drink less, man, you should drink less."

"The fall o' man came from that same plaguey apple-tree that's been my undoing!" said the sexton, ruefully.

"Nay, Zachary," said the Vicar, with a smile, "both falls came from lack of self-control. Don't blame the apple-tree. But we must not waste time. I think, Gabriel, I had best not wait for the arrival of your father and mother, but wed you at daybreak, and speed you on your journey before Bosbury is astir."

"Can you be ready, dear heart?" said Gabriel, glancing at Hilary.

She did not reply, her eyes were fixed on the narrow window, and a look of horror was on her face.

"What is it, child?" said the Vicar, puzzled by her expression.

"We are watched," she faltered. "I saw eyes peering betwixt the ivy leaves."

"I see naught," said Gabriel. "But, maybe 'twas the white owl that lives among the bells, it flies past often enough."

"It was Waghorn," she said, shivering.

"I'll catch the villain, then, and pound his cropped head for him," said Zachary, scrambling down the ladder. "Spiteful, scheming gossip that he is! I'll teach him what comes of playing tricks on the parish clerk."

"We must surely have heard him had he climbed up by the ivy," said Gabriel.

But Hilary was not to be comforted.

"I know it was Waghorn! He will betray us," she said, tears gathering in her eyes.

"There be no sign of him, mistress," said Zachary, climbing the stairs once more. "You need have no fear, 'twas naught but the hoolet. What about your horse, sir?"

"Why, that's at Farmer Chadd's, and had best be fetched, I suppose," said Gabriel.

"Yes, fetch it, Zachary," said the Vicar, "when the villagers are asleep, and do you keep watch here to-night in the tower. I shall not breathe comfortably till we have you both safely started for London. Come, Hilary, my child, you have all your preparations to make, and we must not linger."

Zachary and Durdle went down the ladder arguing about the pillion and the saddle-bags, while the Vicar endeavoured to quiet them, pointing out the need of special caution.

And Hilary clung to her lover, bidding him a last goodnight, and vainly striving to imitate the brave cheerfulness of his manner.

The only comfort was in the feeling of his strong arms around her, and the happy consciousness that, having made a perfect recovery, he was fit to travel.

CHAPTER XLV.

Revenge, at first though sweet,

Bitter ere long back on itself recoils.

But mercy, first and last, shall brightest shine.

—Milton.

Zachary was the only member of the household who slept that night. Hilary and Mrs. Durdle were too busy preparing what would be needed for the journey; the Vicar, full of anxiety, looked at his watch every quarter of an hour, and failed to find comfort even in ammonites or elephants' teeth, while Gabriel, in the tower room, lay listening to the soft hooting of the white owl, and the unearthly stamping and knocking made down below by Harkaway. At the first glimmer of light he hastily put on the plum-coloured costume which had been laid by at Hereford since the early days of the war, and brought over by Dr. Coke for his journey. Then he filled his saddle-bags, and with a last look round the place which had made him so secure a refuge, stole down the ladder to feed and fondle his horse and saddle it in readiness for the journey. Zachary, with his head on the pillion, snored serenely, and Gabriel let him remain in peace till the first sparrow began to chirp, then cruelly roused him, unable to endure another minute's delay.

"Lord! Lord! I'd but just closed my eyes," groaned the old man. "You can't be married in the dark, sir."

"'Tis morning, Zachary. Come, fix on the pillion; we shall have the Vicar here in a minute."

Yawning and stretching, the sexton struggled to his feet, and by the time the pillion had been strapped on, steps were indeed heard without, and on opening the door Gabriel was greeted by Mrs. Durdle in the choicest of white neckerchiefs, and her best Lincoln green hood.

"Good day to you and good luck to you, sir," she said. "Vicar and Mistress Hilary be crossing the churchyard."

His face was aglow.

"We have seen no more of Waghorn," he said, blithely, breathing the delicious morning air with rapture after his long imprisonment. "But the owl hath hooted most dolefully. I have not slept a wink."

Then catching sight of the Vicar in his college cap and black doublet and hose leading Hilary in the grey and pink gown he had specially begged her to wear, he hastened forward to greet them, and together they walked to the south porch, where, according to the old custom, the actual marriage was to take place.

Suddenly an ominous sound—the tramp of many feet close by made them pause and listen anxiously.

"Oh, sir, what is it?" cried Durdle, in great terror.

"Be still; let us hearken," said Dr. Coke, holding up his hand.

Hilary, with widening eyes, clung to Gabriel.

"Don't be afraid, dearest," he said, reassuringly; "soldiers often pass through the village. They are not like to molest us here."

The Vicar went forward a few paces, and, catching sight of the uniform worn by the men of the Canon Frome garrison, realised the peril they were in.

"Shelter in the church!" he cried. "'Tis you they seek."

But even as he spoke he saw that it was too late. Another file of soldiers rushed round from the west of the church, where they had lain in ambush till the rest of the men arrived, and Norton, with a contemptuous smile on his face, shouted his orders: "Seize the Vicar! Arrest the rebel!"

Amid a scene of wild confusion Hilary was torn from her lover, while, with unnecessary roughness, which turned her faint and sick, the soldiers bound Gabriel's arms. He saw that resistance was useless, and in the sudden revulsion from happiness to despair anguish overwhelmed him. Like one turned to stone, Hilary stood watching while the Vicar was also bound; and, roused by Durdle's screams and the unusual confusion of voices in the churchyard, men, women, and children came hurrying from the neighbouring houses to see what was amiss.

As for Waghorn, in the excitement all his worst characteristics had started into view again, and like a maniac he stood shouting on the steps of the cross: "Now am I avenged on mine enemy! They that dally with malignants shall rot in dungeons! No longer shall they hinder the work of the godly!"

The Vicar turned indignantly to the Governor of Canon Frome. "What is the meaning of this outrage, Colonel Norton? You are interfering with me in the discharge of my duty!"

"Your duty, sir, was to sign Prince Rupert's Protestation, and to refrain from aiding the King's enemies," said Norton, with a sneer.

"Sir, you are wrong," replied the Vicar, firmly. "I hold the King in all due reverence, but my first duty was to tend the wounded and shelter the homeless. And my next duty was to shield my niece from your wicked schemes."

"I' faith, you are a bold and outspoken man," said Norton, chuckling. "But I can bide my time, Vicar."

He turned to watch Waghorn, who, in wild excitement, had sprung down from the cross and was shaking his fist derisively in Gabriel's face.

"Ha! young bridegroom! I'll warrant you wish now that you'd pulled down Bosbury Cross!"

The taunt had the effect of restoring Gabriel to a quiet dignity of manner which impressed the soldiers. He made no reply whatever, but looked Waghorn in the face till, with an uneasy sense of guilt, the man withdrew a little. But the fanatic's place was quickly taken by Norton, and there was something in the malevolence of his smile which made the blood boil in Gabriel's veins. He remembered what this man had made him endure at Marlborough.

"I am sorry, sir," said the Colonel, with a sneer, "to spoil your highly virtuous device of holy matrimony, but as the proverb hath it, 'Marriages are made in heaven,' and we intend to send you there. Sergeant! the halter!"

A murmur of surprise and horror ran through the crowd. Gabriel felt as if a grisly hand had suddenly clutched his heart. He glanced anxiously at Hilary. Her face was marble white, she seemed scarcely conscious.

"Nay, sir, will you proceed so far?" cried Waghorn, with a troubled look. "This can be no hanging matter."

"What is it to you, fellow?" said Norton, haughtily. And with satisfaction he saw the sergeant slip a rope about Gabriel's neck, and noted that a spasm of pain passed over the prisoner's face. He was too young and healthy to be without a most ardent love of life.

"Sir, sir," cried the Vicar, with passionate indignation, "you cannot take so cruel a revenge! Captain Harford may lawfully be a prisoner of war, but——"

"He is a rebel, and I know for a certainty that he bore about him traitorous despatches. Is it not so?" said Norton, sharply turning towards the parliamentarian.

"If you know, why ask?" said Gabriel.

"Answer me!" cried the Colonel, angrily. "Did you not bear despatches?"

"Your own spy hath already answered you. And for the despatches," said Gabriel, triumphantly, "you'll not get them. They are long ere now delivered."

"Away with him, sergeant! String him up to yonder tree," said Norton.

But with a wild cry of despair Hilary rushed forward "Oh! no! no!" and she threw her arms round Gabriel. "You shall not take him! You shall not!"

The soldiers were touched by her anguish, the villagers made indignant murmurings, some of the women began to sob. As for Waghorn, he turned away, muttering: "Alack, poor lady! But nay, let me not falter! No weakness, Peter Waghorn! No weakness!"

Gabriel kissed the weeping girl with passionate tenderness; then, unable to endure the sight of her grief, began to crave only for an end of this torture.

"Go, my dearest!" he said, his voice faltering. "I pray you—go!"

But the Vicar stepped towards Norton.

"Sir," he said, "I appeal to your better nature. As prisoner of war you have it in your power to send Captain Harford to gaol, but——"

"Why, that would be to make him your companion, dear sir," said Norton, lightly. "No, no; I have quite other plans. You go to prison, he goes to Paradise. Come, you, as a parson, must own that I am giving him promotion."

Waghorn meanwhile paced to and fro wrestling with himself, and muttering like a madman through his teeth: "Nay, nay; I will not relent. The enemies of truth must be punished. Let their habitation be desolate, and let none dwell in their tents! Add iniquity unto their iniquity."

He was suddenly jostled aside by old Zachary, who, in deep distress, approached the Colonel.

"For pity's sake, sir, hang me instead," he pleaded, "'twas my silly old tongue betrayed him—that and the fourth tankard of cider—hang me instead, for I deserve it."

Norton laughed noisily.

"Not at all—you have been a most useful tool. Come, get you gone! There will be work for you yet. You shall dig the grave, and Waghorn shall preach the funeral sermon. Why do you tarry, sergeant?"

They tarried because it was no easy thing for Englishmen forcibly to part the sobbing girl from her lover.

"Dearest," said Gabriel, controlling his voice with an effort, "you must go. Let some of the women take you to the Vicarage."

But as she raised her head and saw the rope about his throat, a new strength of resistance awoke within her. He should not die! She ran to Waghorn, and caught his hand in hers in eager entreaty.

"Waghorn! you are not wicked like that man—you mean well—I know you mean well—help us now! Show mercy!"

For a moment the wood-carver wavered. Then a grim expression settled down upon his features.

"Nay, nay," he said, "Captain Harford hath but met with his deserts. What saith the Psalmist, 'Let there be none to extend mercy unto him! Let the iniquity of his fathers be remembered!'"

"Oh, that was said by them of old time! But now we are bidden to be kind to one another—and tender-hearted," pleaded Hilary.

But Waghorn, with a scornful look, exclaimed indignantly: "Do not teach me, Mistress! I well know that you are of a carnal mind. Did you not deceive us in the orchard? You are a liar!"

The villagers made angry protests at this plain speaking. Hilary, however, with a look that would have melted the hardest heart, continued her eager appeal.

"Yes, yes, I did speak falsely that day. But, oh—have you never sinned?"

The Puritan started back as if she had struck him. "I?" He hung his head, and in a flash it seemed as though his life with its bitter unforgiving lovelessness rose before him—a hideous vision. He crossed over to the Colonel, and put a hand on his sleeve.

"How now, scarecrow? What is it?" said Norton.

"You promised me that if I secured the despatches and Captain Harford, I might ask what I would of you."

"Well, what do you want?"

"I ask for the life of yonder Captain."

Norton stared at him. "Are you sure you don't mean his head in a charger? That, I think, is more in your line."

"I ask you to spare his life," said Waghorn, sturdily, while all the people waited breathlessly for the reply.

Norton gave a short scoffing laugh.

"Well, well, you may ask what you will, but I shall not grant such a request. You shall be reasonably paid for your services, and must content yourself with that."

Then the Puritan's wrath burst forth. "Shame on thee for a promise-breaker! Dost think I served thee in this matter for filthy lucre? Nay, but to avenge the cause of truth, to save the land from the curse of those that break not down the high places, that destroy not the graven images!"

He walked a few paces from the group and stood silently watching Hilary, who had again forced her way to her lover. Clinging to Gabriel, she sobbed, pitifully, while he whispered in her ear words of love and comfort.

"Hearken, Mistress Hilary," said Norton, striding across towards them, "with one word you can save Captain Harford's life."

"What must I do?" sobbed Hilary.

"Only promise to be mine," he said, his eager eyes scanning her intently.

"I cannot!" she replied, clinging closer to Gabriel.

"Very well," said Norton, with a shrug of the shoulders. "Sergeant, proceed!"

Hilary looked round at him in terrible agitation—then turned again to Gabriel, "What am I to do?" she cried, wildly.

"Dear heart!" he said, quietly, "remember what we agreed. Cost what it may—be true!"

"But—your life—oh, my dearest!—your life!"

"It will not be ended by the hangman," he replied, with a strange vibration in his voice, "it will go on elsewhere. We have but to wait."

Norton stamped his foot impatiently.

"Well, is your choice made?" he asked.

"Go, my beloved!" said Gabriel, tenderly, but with a firmness which steadied her failing powers. Then he gave her a long, lingering kiss, and she slowly took her arms from about his neck and staggered towards the Vicar, hiding her face on his shoulder.

Gabriel watched her in heart-broken silence, understanding for the first time what the bitterness of death meant. An awful stillness reigned in the churchyard. He turned towards Norton.

"Sir, I am ready," he said, in a low, firm voice.

Norton watched him with mingled feelings. It was impossible not to admire his courage and dignity, yet never had he hated the man more.

"Fool! You would die in your youth?" he said, sneeringly.

Then into Gabriel's eyes there suddenly came a light that was Divine.

"Why," he cried, "I would live in hellish torments to save her from such as you—and shall I fear death? You think that when I am hung and the Vicar cast into gaol, you will be free to carry out your vile schemes—but I tell you, in spite of all, evil will not triumph. There is a God who hates tyranny, who loves mercy and justice!"

His whole face was transfigured. It was Norton whose cheek paled and who looked like the man about to die.

"String him up, sergeant. I loathe this cant," he said. "Be quick, you fools—hang the rebel and have done with it!"

The soldiers threw the end of the rope over a branch of the tree under which they stood; the sergeant adjusted the noose more carefully round the prisoner's neck, and Gabriel gave one last glance at the familiar scene—the tower of refuge clearly outlined against the roseate sky, the green churchyard, the old cross so curiously linked with his fate, the gabled houses in the village street, and the Vicar's white head bent down over Hilary's brown curls. Then the rope tightened about his throat, he closed his eyes and prayed, while through his brain there floated the old Psalm which he had last heard in Ledbury High Street

"In trouble and adversity,

The Lord God hear thee still.

The Majesty of Jacob's God

Defend thee from all ill."

Suddenly an exclamation and a sound of tramping feet made him open his eyes again. He saw that another detachment of Royalist soldiers was marching through the lych gate, but close at hand, having evidently approached quietly from another quarter, stood an officer whom he at once recognised as Lord Hopton.

"Hold, in the King's name!" shouted the new-comer, and the sickening pressure about the prisoner's neck was relaxed.

Hilary rushed forward and threw herself at the General's feet.

"Oh, my lord," she pleaded, "help us! Do not let them take his life."

"Madam," he said, raising her courteously, "be of good cheer. I heard your lover's brave words. I also heard your words, Colonel Norton," and he glanced sternly at the Governor of Canon Frome.

"Sir, if you had heard the whole case against Captain Harford——" stammered Norton.

"What! 'tis Captain Harford?" cried Lord Hopton. "Ay, to be sure I recognise you now, sir, and remember that 'tis to your kindly offices when I lay wounded at Lansdown that I owe my life. Sergeant, remove that halter and unbind Captain Harford."

Hilary, radiant with joy, ran to her lover, and—his bonds removed—he clasped her in his arms with a rapture which made them utterly oblivious of the thronged churchyard. They only felt that life laid down had been wonderfully renewed, and that every heartbeat was a wordless thanksgiving.

Lord Hopton meanwhile had turned to the other prisoner.

"What! you also bound, sir?" he exclaimed, indignantly.

"What is the meaning of this, Colonel Norton?"

"The Vicar of Bosbury," said Norton, sullenly, "hath for weeks, sir, sheltered this rebel, and he is but a lukewarm supporter of His Majesty."

"His Majesty would fare better were all parsons such kindly peacemakers," said Lord Hopton, himself cutting the cords which bound the Vicar's arms. "'Tis men like you, Colonel, who are the ruin of the King's cause. Oh, I have heard of your cruelties, and I know how the whole country-side has cause to hate you."

"If you give ear, sir, to the complaints of an aged gentlewoman like Dame Elizabeth Hopton, and the murmurs of a pack of peasants, you will hear strange tales."

Lord Hopton frowned.

"I intend to examine into matters later on, and you can then make your defence. Meanwhile I hold a letter from the King depriving you of your Governorship, and appointing Colonel Barnold. And I shall be obliged to you now, Colonel Barnold, if you and a detachment of the soldiers from the garrison will escort the ex-Governor to Canon Frome. I shall be with you anon."

"You pardon a rebel despatch-bearer, sir, and overlook the persistent way in which Dr. Coke hath refused to sign Prince Rupert's Protestation," said Norton bitterly, "but give me scant justice."

"I hope to show you not only justice but clemency," said Lord Hopton. "What of your despatches, Captain Harford?"

"Massey entrusted me with letters, my lord, to Fairfax and Cromwell," said Gabriel, "but as I was sorely wounded they were borne to Windsor by another hand some weeks ago."

A shade of relief was visible about the General's lips.

"That matter is ended, then," he said, "and with regard to what you say against Dr. Coke, I hold, sir, that he was bound to set the safety and honour of his niece before any matters of State, and that as a Christian he had a perfect right to shelter and tend a wounded man, whatever his political views."

Norton was led away, and the Vicar eagerly thanked Lord Hopton for all that he had done for them. Then, seeing the expectation in the faces of the villagers, he added, "Betwixt Hilary and Captain Harford, my lord, there was an attachment of long standing, and this very morning I was to have wedded them."

The women in the crowd smiled and nodded at each other, and Lord Hopton, catching sight of the radiant faces of the lovers, smiled too.

"Now what a happy thing it was," he said, "that I chose to make a night march, and reached Canon Frome at dawn! Finding the Governor absent, I was minded to see for myself what pranks he was after, and arrived in the nick of time."

"You were in time to save a life, my lord," said the Vicar, "and now, an you will, may witness a wedding; we keep to the old custom here and wed at the church door."

"I'll not only witness it, but will give away the bride if that is agreeable to you, sir," he said, glancing at Gabriel.

"My lord, the memory of your kindly dealing will long outlast the bitterness I have just passed through," said Gabriel.

His face aglow with happiness, and still shining with that spiritual light which had arrested even Norton's notice, touched the Royalist general.

"I very well know," he said, laying a kindly hand on his shoulder, "that you were the first to show considerateness in the matter of Bosbury Cross, and till people of widely differing views act with the good sense and moderation shown by you and the Vicar, we shall never have true peace in England."

He turned to offer his arm to Hilary, when she suddenly perceived Waghorn gravely watching them from a little distance. Running towards him, she took his hand gratefully in hers.

"I shall never forget, Waghorn, that you tried to save Captain Harford," she said, warmly.

"Mistress," said Waghorn, earnestly, and with a quiet manliness wholly unlike his former manner, "he was right. In spite of all, evil did not triumph."

And now the psalm which had rung in Gabriel's ears as he awaited death, sounded indeed through the churchyard as Hilary walked towards the porch between Lord Hopton and her lover.

The villagers drew together in a group close by them, but little Nan and Meg being on the outskirts chanced to look back, and saw Waghorn standing afar off as though he had no part or lot in the service. With a kindly impulse they ran towards him.

"Don't stand there so all alone," said Nan, coaxingly, "come nearer!"

"Yes," echoed Meg, "come nearer!"

Waghorn's stern face relaxed. He sighed, but let them take him by the hand and draw him in with the rest.

EPILOGUE.

"I pray God our zeal in these times may be so kindled with pure fire from God's altar that it may rather warm than burn, enliven rather than inflame, and that the spirits of good men may truly be qualified with Gospel principles, true fruits of the Divine Spirit. And truly I believe that the members of the Church, if not the leaders—notwithstanding all the perfections of times before us, so much pictured or applauded—have very much yet to learn. For I am persuaded that Christian love and affection is a point of such importance that it is not to be prejudiced by supposals of difference in points of religion in any ways disputable, though thought weighty as determined by the parties on either side; or by particular determinations beyond Scripture, which, as some have observed, have enlarged divinity, but have lessened charity and multiplied divisions. For the maintenance of truth is rather God's charge, and the continuance of charity ours."—Letters of Benjamin Whichcote, 1651.

"And were they married here in this very porch where we're sitting, grandfather?" said little Bobbie Coke, looking up into the Vicar's kindly face, which the forty-five years had made only somewhat thinner and paler.

"Here in this very porch, Bobbie," he replied, his arm about the lad, while on his knee sat little Mollie Harford, the orphan daughter of Gabriel's brother, Bridstock, who had died seven years before.

"Never was there such a happy wedding before or since, for it is not often that the bridegroom is rescued at the last moment from the jaws of death. The villagers were ready to cry for joy, and the soldiers—brave fellows!—why, they were only too glad to be let off the horrid piece of work their Colonel had set them to do."

"And when did my grandfather come?" asked Mollie.

"He came that evening, and Mrs. Harford with him, and they all stayed at the Vicarage a couple of days, rejoicing. Then the bride and bridegroom went to say farewell to the Bishop at Whitbourne, and thence to London, where Madam Harford gave them a right loving welcome, and took good care of Hilary, while her husband joined Cromwell, and began his career as mate to the surgeon of his regiment. It was in that fashion that he again saw Colonel Norton. For after the great battle at Naseby, when he was going about the field succouring the wounded, he came upon the Colonel lying there half dead, and was able to bind up his wounds, and bring him the water he cried out for. When the Colonel had drunk it, he looked up with startled eyes at his helper.

"'Why, God bless my soul! Is it you?' he cried. 'What are you doing?'

"'Helping the sick and wounded,' said Gabriel.

"'Confounded queer work for a gentleman,' said Norton.

"'It was good enough for Christ,' said the other.

"Then up came the surgeon, said 'twas no use spending time over one that couldn't live an hour, and bade his mate come and rest. But Gabriel, saying that he knew the wounded officer, asked to remain with him.

"'Why should I lie shivering here for an hour?' said Norton, in his devil-may-care tone. 'It will be quicker work if I die on my feet, and I'll be bound you think I shall be hot enough in the next world.'

"'Lie still,' said Gabriel. 'Here's the cloak Lord Falkland gave me at Marlborough. We'll wrap it about you.'

"Now at the word Marlborough, the face of the dying man changed, and he fell a-thinking.

"'Say the words you said that night,' he gasped.

"Gabriel, unable to think what he meant, said the first words that came to his mind:

"'Forgive us our trespasses as we forgive them that trespass against us, and lead us not into temptation, but deliver us from evil, for thine is the kingdom, and the power and the glory, for ever.'

"And after that the dying man lay in his arms fighting hard for breath, but never speaking, only once he gripped Gabriel's hand and looked in his eyes, as though he would have thanked him. Then, as darkness fell on the blood-stained field, he passed away."

"And what happened to my uncle Gabriel?" asked Mollie.

"The war ended not long after that, and he went to London, and studied for two years under Sir Theodore Mayerne, and then for two years more at Paris. In 1650 he settled finally in London, and there became a celebrated physician, and all went well with him. He had twenty years of happy wedded life, marred only by some trouble at the time of the Restoration for the part he had played in the Civil War. However, that was no very serious matter, and there were few happier homes in the country till the year of the Great Plague.

"Knowing that his duty lay with the poor sick folk in London, he parted from his wife and four children, sending them, as he hoped, out of all risk to Katterham, a country place some eighteen miles off. But it fell about that, as they halted at Croydon to bait the horses, some that were also flying from the plague, sat with them at the common table in the inn, and even as they dined one of these fellow-travellers was seized with illness. Spite of all precautions, my dear niece herself sickened the next day, and ere twenty-four hours had passed she and her children were dead.

"An old comrade, Sir Joscelyn Heyworth, travelled to London to break the news to his friend, who seemed for the time wholly crushed. But as they sat together talking very sadly, there came in Sir William Denham, who for many years had known them both.

"'Doctor,' he said. 'I scarce like to break in upon your sorrow, but my friend Judge Wharncliffe and his wife have just died of the plague, and their two sons are at death's door, with no one but an old man-servant to care for them, and the doctor who had attended them hath now died in the very house.'

"At that Gabriel put aside his own trouble, and went forth to see what he could do. He found the elder lad, a fine fellow of one and twenty, beginning to rally, but the younger, a tiny, delicate child of but two or three years, lay at the point of death. He fought for its life, and never left it till it had passed the crisis, and by that time, as he afterwards told me, life had again become bearable to him, and he found what the joy of battle meant; it was not the brutal love of bloodshed, it was the God-like desire to overcome evil with good, disease with health, and death with life."

"And did the little boy get quite strong?" asked Mollie, eagerly.

"Ay, to be sure, he's alive to this day, and has lived a right noble life. Few men have suffered with a better courage than Hugo Wharncliffe, and one day I'll tell you his story."

"And now tell me the rest about Uncle Gabriel," said Mollie. "Did he live much longer?"

"Only five years more, but they were five years full of good Work. It was in 1670, I remember, that he wrote to say he was advised to take a few weeks' rest and hoped to pay us a visit at Bosbury on his way home to his father. Now Dr. Harford was attending some sick folk at the Grange, and chanced to be here the very day he arrived. As we all dined together Gabriel told us with much interest of certain people called Quakers that he had lately come to know. Their way of thought had great attraction for him, especially the effort they made to obey literally the teaching of Christ as to using no oath, and avoiding all war and violence."

"'Seeing the quiet way in which they laid down their lives for their peace principles,' he said, 'set me wondering whether Christ must not be grieved to find the war spirit so strong still among His followers, and that 1670 years after his birth the bulk of us still demand an eye for an eye and a tooth for a tooth.'

"We found that in addition to all his usual work he had been visiting many of these Quakers, who, under the persecuting laws of those times, were imprisoned in Newgate, Bishopsgate Gaol and the New Prison. It was in this fashion that he had taken a fever, for gaol fever raged among these prisoners for conscience' sake; but he said he grudged not having taken the infection from them, for he hoped that he had caught from them, also, some of their noble and true thoughts. He spoke, too, of Lord Falkland's craving for peace, and thought that, like him, the Quakers were in advance of the times, and were to lead the nation to truer and nobler ways of thought, particularly on this point about peace, which one day all men would see to be the only true Christ-following.

"We were still talking of the Society of Friends when Dr Harford said he must go out again to visit two more patients. I remember we all three stood for a minute at the garden-gate, and can almost hear your uncle's voice still as he said, 'When they spoke of the duty of Christians to take no part in war, I used to feel as on the day when Waghorn would have pulled down the cross, and you spoke of love which is the bond of peace, and then coming hither we found Hilary standing beneath the yew tree holding open the gate for us.'

"His eyes grew wistful, and I noticed that his hand rested for a minute on the gate, as though anything she had touched was sacred to him. Then, his cheerfulness returning, he said he must pay a visit to the Tower of Refuge, and so we parted, for I knew that the place was full of memories to him and that he would fain be alone.

"In about an hour your grandfather returned, and we went across the churchyard to find your uncle, talking as we went of the way in which the fever and the overwork had changed him.

"'He will need a long rest,' said Dr. Harford. 'He hath worn himself out with the woes of others and with the noisome air of those pestilent gaols.'

"I said it was after all natural enough, for he had ever had a special feeling for prisoners since his time in Oxford Castle, and Herefordshire was the very best place he could have come to for a rest and change.

"Well, by that we had drawn near to the porch, and saw that he was sitting on this western bench and must have fallen asleep, for he had taken off the long curled wig that all gentlemen wore then much as they do now, and with his short hair he looked curiously like the Captain Harford who had saved Bosbury Cross.

"But something in his perfect stillness struck Dr. Harford with sudden anxiety. We bent close down to him—he had ceased to breathe, and from his face death had smoothed away all the lines of sorrow, so that he looked once more young. I wish I could describe to you the wonderful serene dignity of his expression—but that is not to be put into words. Here in this porch where five-and-twenty years before I had wedded him to my dear niece, God had once more united the husband and wife."

"It is such a pity people have to die," said Bobbie, kicking the flagstones with energy, because he saw tears in Mollie's eyes and wished to keep them from his own.

"You think so?" said his grandfather, with a smile. "And quite right too at your age. But when like me you are an old man of four-score years and ten, there'll be so many waiting for you on the other side of the river that you'll be glad when you are told to cross over. I hear your grandfather's step on the path, Mollie, and when we two old friends chat over old times together, 'tis hard for you young ones to get in a word, so you had best go in and see the Harford monuments, and Bishop Swinfield's head which was rescued from Hereford Cathedral."

"There's no monument to Uncle Gabriel," said Mollie, wiping away her tears.

"My child, his body lies in the chancel, but Bosbury Cross is his monument, and he could not have a better," said the Vicar.

As the two children entered the church he took from the pocket of his doublet a small note-book, and added a line to an epitaph he had been trying to write, smiling to himself over Bobbie's notion that it was a pity anybody died.

I lay me down at expectation's door;

Weary and worn with age I crave no more. But

Christus Jesus meus est omnia.

—Will. Coke, 1690.

As he finished the verse, Dr. Harford, marvellously erect and active for his eighty-five years, crossed the churchyard and sat down beside him in the porch.

"I have come across a curious link with the past," he said. "Chancing to be at Farmer Chadd's just now where Meg is laid up, as you know, she gave me this ring which her husband had found yesterday when digging in the orchard. I fancy it must have dropped from Colonel Norton's finger on the day of the duel, and have lain there unnoticed these five-and-forty years. The initials as you see are L. and N."

"Ay," said the antiquary, putting up his glass and scrutinising the letters carefully; "two L's for Lionel and Lucy. It must have been his wife's wedding-ring. And here is the posy

'Till death us departe—

Nay not so deare harte—

Death shall us more truly unite.'"

"Poor Norton!" said the Vicar. "He was a man who might have lived such a different life! Well, who knows but that on Naseby Field God's grace may, indeed, have delivered him from evil?"

"I am always glad to think that he was one of Gabriel's first patients," said Dr. Harford, "and that those poor imprisoned Quakers, suffering so bravely in the cause of peace, were his last. We may say truly that in helping them he gave up his own life."

"And God be thanked that since our peaceful Revolution there are no more persecutions for opinion," observed the Vicar. "We have passed through rough waters, doctor, yet have each of us been blessed with a loving wife, and have lived to see our children and our children's children blessed in their career. But to my mind the noblest race was run by your son, Gabriel, who, indeed, died a hero of peace."

THE END.

AUTHOR'S NOTE.

To the kindness of Mr. Joseph J. Green, of Tunbridge Wells, the Quaker antiquary and genealogist, and a collateral descendant of the Harfords, I am indebted for some of the particulars relating to my hero's family. Dr. Bridstock Harford is also mentioned by the historian, Webb, and in Duncomb's "History of the County of Hereford," as one of the few residents in Hereford who sided with the Parliament, and there is a reference to him in the interesting old account-book of Mrs. Joyce Jefferies, of Widemarsh Street. The celebrated physician lived until 1695, surviving both his sons; the elder one is buried at Bosbury; the second son, Bridstock, was M.P. for Hereford in the reign of Charles II., and died in 1683. Dr. Bridstock Harford is buried in Hereford Cathedral, and a long Latin epitaph speaks of the ancient and honourable family from which he was descended, and of the way in which the city grieved for the loss of its greatest physician, whose skill had rescued so many from death, and who had never taken fees from the poor.

Particulars as to Sir Robert Harley and his household have been gathered from the "Letters of Lady Brilliana Harley" (Camden Society). The Archbishop's visitation at Hereford is mentioned in Baine's "Life of Laud," and details of the fines and penalties, described in Chapters II. and V., are given in Dr. S. R. Gardiner's "History of England from the Accession of James I. to the Outbreak of the Civil War," Vols. VII.-X., and in Brook's "Lives of the Puritans." The words as to the proposed escape from the Tower of London in Chapter XXVI. were really spoken by Laud to his friend Pococke.

For the sketch of Lord Falkland's character the books consulted were Gardiner's "History of the Great Civil War," Tulloch's "Rational Theology in the Seventeenth Century," "History of the Falklands" (Longmans), Falkland's "Discourse on Infallibility," with a memoir by Dr. Triplet, Whitelocke's "Memorials," and Clarendon.

With regard to Bishop Coke, "Even Prynne could find nothing to say against the Bishop of Hereford save that he had a hand in the canons." He is described by a contemporary as "A serene and quiet man above the storm" (see Webb's "Memorials of the Civil War in Herefordshire," Vol. I., p. 51). Of his son, William Coke, Vicar of Bosbury, tradition says that Bosbury Cross owes its preservation to the considerateness of a Parliamentary Captain who yielded to his entreaty to spare it, the condition being made that the words "Honour not the cross, but honour God for Christ," should be graven on it. These words may still be read on the cross. The fact that William Coke held the living of Bosbury continuously from 1641 to 1690 speaks for itself as to his tact and his tolerant spirit. His epitaph, partly effaced, is as follows:

I lay me down at expect.. . .

I crave no more. But

Christus Jesus meus est omn.

Will: Coke, 1690.

The sufferings of the prisoners of war at Oxford under Provost-Marshal Smith are mentioned by many contemporary writers, and an account of their hardships will be found in Nehemiah Wallington's "Memoirs," also details of the way in which prisoners were treated on the march, and of the use of churches as prisons. The escape of forty of the prisoners at one time from Oxford Castle really happened. Sir William Waller's letter to Sir Ralph Hopton is taken from Webb's "Memorials," Vol. I., p. 261. See also Dr. S. R. Gardiner's "History of the Great Civil War," Vol. I., p. 197, footnote. Webb also mentions Prince Rupert's saying, "We will have no law in England henceforward but of the sword."

A letter from Sir Richard Hopton, of Canon Frome, has been preserved, in which he complains of the misdoings of the garrison and the harsh treatment and great loss of property he had been forced to endure at the hands of the Governor. Norton appears to have been succeeded by Colonel Barnold as Governor of Canon Frome, but of his personal character nothing is known. With regard to the siege of Hereford in 1643, and many other local matters, I am indebted to the kind help of Prebendary Michael Hopton, of Canon Frome, and of Miss Hopton, of Clehonger. The clemency of Lord Hopton, in Chapter XLV., though in accord with his character, is not historic. But some time after writing this scene I came, across a very similar incident in Nehemiah Wallington's "Memoirs"—a Royalist officer named Tarverfield intervening in much the same way.

The latter part of this novel was first written by me in the form of a play, which was produced by the Ben Greet Company under the direction of Mr. A. S. Homewood, at Eastbourne, on January 4th, 1900, and was subsequently given at Cambridge and at the Comedy Theatre, London.

Edna Lyall.

Printed in Great Britain
by Amazon